CHICAGO

Also by Alaa Al Aswany

The Yacoubian Building

CHICAGO

A Novel

Alaa Al Aswany

Translated by Farouk Abdel Wahab

HARPER

An Imprint of HarperCollins*Publishers*

www.harpercollins.com

HarperCollins books may be purchased for educational, business, or sales promotional use. For information, please write: Special Markets Department, HarperCollins Publishers, 10 East 53rd Street, New York, NY 10022.

First published in Arabic in 2007 as *Shikagu* by Dar El Shorouk. English translation first published in Egypt in 2007 by The American University in Cairo Press.

FIRST U.S. EDITION

Designed by Emily Cavett Taff

Library of Congress Cataloging-in-Publication Data is available upon request.

ISBN: 978-0-06-145256-7

08 09 10 11 12   OV/RRD   10 9 8 7 6 5 4 3 2 1

To my mother and my father,
hoping I haven't disappointed them

TRANSLATOR'S ACKNOWLEDGMENTS

I WOULD LIKE TO THANK the following friends and colleagues for help with various aspects of the translation: Robert (Bob) Wiley and Kelly Zaug, and from the American University in Cairo Press, Neil Hewison and Nadia Naqib, and from HarperCollins Publishers, Jeanette Perez.

CHICAGO

CHAPTER

 Many do not know that *chicago* is not an English word but rather Algonquian, one of several languages that Native Americans spoke. In that language *chicago* meant "strong smell." The reason for that designation was that the place occupied by the city today was originally vast fields where the Native Americans grew onions, the strong smell of which gave the place its name.

Native Americans lived for scores of years in Chicago, on the shores of Lake Michigan, growing onions and herding cattle. They lived peacefully until the year 1673, when a traveler and mapmaker by the name of Louis Joliet, accompanied by a French Jesuit monk named Jacques Marquette, "discovered" Chicago. Soon thousands of colonists descended upon it just like ants on a pot of honey. During the hundred ensuing years the white colonists waged horrific genocidal wars, in the course of which they killed anywhere from five to twelve million Native Americans throughout North America. Anyone reading American history must pause at this paradox: the white colonists who killed millions of Indians and stole their land and other possessions were, at the same time, extremely religious Christians. But this paradox is resolved once we learn about the prevalent views in that era. Many white colonists believed that "American Indians," even though they were, somehow, God's creatures, were not created in the spirit of Christ but rather in another imperfect and evil spirit. Others confidently asserted that they were like animals, creatures without a soul or conscience, hence they did not have the same value as white men. Thanks to those convenient theories, the colonists were able to kill as many Native Americans as they liked without any shadow of regret or feelings of guilt. No matter how horrific were the massacres they conducted all day long, it did not detract from the purity of their bedtime prayers every evening. The genocidal wars ended with a crushing victory for the founding fathers. Chicago was incorporated as an American city in the year 1837 and in fewer than ten years had swelled to sixteen times its original size. Adding to its importance was its location on Lake Michigan and its vast pastures. Then the railroads made Chicago the indisputable queen of the American West.

The history of cities, like the lives of humans, however, suffers vicissitudes of happiness and pain. Chicago's black day came on Sunday, October 8, 1871. In the west of the city lived Mrs. Catherine O'Leary with her husband, children, one horse, and five cows. That evening Mrs. O'Leary's animals were grazing quietly in the backyard of the house. At around nine o'clock, one of the cows was suddenly bored, so it decided to leave the backyard and go to the back barn, where its curiosity was aroused by a kerosene lamp. It circled around the lamp for a while and stretched its neck to sniff at it, then suddenly it responded to a mysterious desire to give it a strong kick, whereupon the lamp overturned and the kerosene spilled and the floor caught on fire. There was a pile of hay nearby that was ignited, and soon the house burned down, then the neighboring houses also burned down. The wind was strong (as is usual in Chicago), so the fire spread everywhere. Within an hour the whole city was engulfed in flames.

The catastrophe was made even worse by the fact that the firemen were exhausted from staying up the whole previous night putting out another fire that had damaged much of their equipment, which was primitive to begin with. The flames soared in the sky and began to devour the houses of Chicago, which were mostly made of wood.

People's loud, anguished cries mixed with the sound of the raging fire as it gutted the city, producing a frightful din, as if it were snarling a curse. The scene was frightening and mythical, like the description of hell in holy scriptures. The fire raged mercilessly for almost two full days until it was finally extinguished at dawn on Tuesday. The damages were tallied: more than three hundred people killed, a hundred thousand (about one-third of the total population) left homeless. As for monetary damages, they exceeded two hundred million dollars in nineteenth-century monetary values. The catastrophe did not stop there: fire and destruction brought forth total anarchy. Roving gangs of miscreants and criminals, thieves, murderers, addicts, and rapists spread like maggots coming from all over to wreak havoc in the unfortunate city. They began to loot contents of burnt-out houses, stores, banks, and liquor stores. They guzzled liquor on the street and killed whoever crossed their paths. They abducted women to gang-rape them publicly. In the midst of the catastrophe the churches in Chicago organized special masses and prayers to lift the pain and suffering, and all the clergy spoke in a sincere penitent tone about the catastrophe as just punishment from the Lord for the spread of heresy and adultery among the citizens of Chicago. The destruction was so rampant that whoever saw Chicago at that time was certain it was irrevocably lost.

But what happened was contrary to expectations. The enormity of the catastrophe was such that it motivated Chicagoans and gave them courage. A merchant by the name of John Wright, who throughout his life understood only the language of numbers and deals, and who was never known for literary inclinations to eloquence, found himself standing in the midst of dozens of shocked and bereaved citizens milling about after having lost all they had to the fire. Suddenly a mysterious, poetic energy burst forth from him and he improvised a speech that was to become memorable in the history of the city. John Wright held out his arms in front of him and his features hardened in what looked like pain (he was a little drunk), then shouted in a loud, cracked voice, "Courage, men! Chicago did not burn; it entered the fire to get rid of its bad elements and will come out stronger and more beautiful than it has been."

Thus the latent instinct for survival was sparked and the natural solidarity that unites people at dangerous moments erupted. The survivors started working tirelessly—armed volunteers ready to die for their city joined forces and began to chase and fight the gangs, killing them or forcing them to flee. Dozens of nongovernmental shelters were opened and donations poured in to provide food, clothing, and medical care for thousands of homeless families. Tens of thousands of dollars were pumped into Chicago from all over America for reconstruction and investment in its commercial projects. Reconstruction, however, caused new problems; the city council passed an ordinance prohibiting the building of wooden buildings because they had caused the fire to spread. This ordinance resulted in higher rents, which meant that most inhabitants of the city remained on the street because they couldn't afford the rent in new buildings, especially since labor had become so cheap as thousands of non-Chicagoans poured into the labor market. The economic crisis worsened to the point that hordes of poor and hungry people staged violent demonstrations, raising signs with the clear-cut three-word slogan: BREAD OR DEATH. But the American capitalist system was able, as usual, to present a temporary solution to the crisis—one never mentioned in the history books. Investments created several new millionaires while the majority of the population remained in abject poverty. Despite that, John Wright's prophecy came true. In a few years Chicago was more beautiful and stronger than it had been and was crowned, for many years to come, as the most important city in the West, as well as being the third largest American city and a major center of commerce, industry, and culture in America and the world. A popular song at the time claimed that "Chicago is queen of the West once more." And just as parents pamper their children more after the latter survive deadly diseases, many endearing nicknames were used to refer to Chicago. It was called "Queen of the West" because of its importance and beauty; the "Windy City" because of its strong winds throughout the year; "City of the Century" because of its amazing expansion in a short time; the "City of the Big Shoulders" in reference to its extremely tall high-rises and the abundance of workers among its citizens. It was also called the city of "I will," in reference to the ambition that impels Americans to converge on it in search of a better future; and the "City of Neighborhoods," in reference to seventy-seven neighborhoods throughout the city where different ethnic groups lived: black, Irish, Italian, German, etc. At the time, each neighborhood preserved the culture and customs of its inhabitants.

More than 130 years have passed since the Great Fire, but its memory lived on like a scar on a beautiful face, recalled by Chicagoans from time to time sorrowfully and emotionally. The word *fire* acquired a different meaning for them. If anyone anywhere in the world uttered the word, it wouldn't have quite the same impact as it would in Chicago. Fear of fire has led to the city's development of the best firefighting system in the world. A firefighting academy was established on the site of Mrs. O'Leary's house where the Great Fire started. Thus the citizens of the city did their utmost so that the tragedy might not be repeated. Officials in the city, half jokingly, but proudly, have come to repeat a famous saying: "The firefighting system in Chicago is so efficient that it warns you of a fire even before it starts."

HOW WOULD SHAYMAA MUHAMMADI KNOW all this history, having spent all her life in the Egyptian city Tanta, which she rarely left other than to attend a relative's wedding or to go to Alexandria and spend the summer with her family as a young girl? Shaymaa came from Tanta to Chicago, in one fell swoop, without preparation or preliminaries, like one who, not knowing how to swim, jumped into the sea fully dressed. Anyone who saw her roaming the hallways of the medical school at the University of Illinois (in her loose, shari'a-dictated garb, the veil covering her chest, her low-heeled shoes and wide, straightforward strides, her rustic face unadorned by any makeup, turning red for the slightest reason, and her faltering, heavily accented English, which made communicating by gestures easier than speaking) must have wondered: what brought this girl to America?

There are numerous reasons:

First, Shaymaa Muhammadi is one of the most accomplished and highest ranked graduates in the Tanta College of Medicine. She is extraordinarily intelligent and has a legendary capacity for work, which makes her devote long, continuous hours to studying without sleeping or getting up except to perform her prayers, eat, or go to the bathroom. She studies in a calm manner and with deep concentration, without haste or impatience. She spreads the books and notes on the bed, crosses her legs, and tilts her head a little to the right, letting her soft hair cascade down the side of her head. Then she bends, and in her beautiful, fine handwriting she writes down the main points of the lesson and proceeds to memorize them. She savors that, as though indulging in a favorite hobby or weaving a garment for a faraway lover. Her unmatched distinction in her studies easily earned her an official Egyptian government scholarship.

Second, Shaymaa is the eldest daughter of Ustaz Muhammadi Hamid, principal of Tanta Boys' Secondary School for many years, during which dozens of students graduated and assumed prominent posts. Five years after his death people throughout the governorate of Gharbiya still remember him with love and appreciation and sincerely pray for mercy on his soul as a rare model, almost extinct, of a true educator: in his dedication and integrity, his firmness and kindness toward his students. However, Ustaz Muhammadi's life, like that of all others, was not without setbacks, as providence chose to deprive him of male offspring, giving him three daughters one after the other. After the third one he stopped trying, much to his grave chagrin. But he soon overcame his sorrow by channeling his unbounded love to his daughters and raising them just like his students at school to be straightforward, studious, and confident. The result was dazzling: Shaymaa and Aliya were instructors in medicine, and Nada, the youngest, an instructor in the department of communications in the College of Engineering. Thus the education and upbringing that Shaymaa received played a role in her accepting the challenge and the scholarship in America.

The third and most important reason: Shaymaa is over thirty, still unmarried because her position as instructor in the College of Medicine has greatly reduced her chances, since Eastern men usually prefer that their wives be less educated than they. Besides, Shaymaa lacks the instant qualifications for marriage: her loose garb totally hides her body, and her face is not strikingly beautiful. The most that her plain features leave a man with is that she looks familiar, and that, of course, is not a sufficient incentive for him to marry her. She is not rich; she lives with her sisters and mother on their salaries and the pension of her father, who refused throughout his life to work in the prosperous Arab Gulf countries or to give private lessons. In addition, and despite her academic excellence, she is totally ignorant of methods of seduction—methods that most women are good at and which they use skillfully, either directly by preening and using perfumes and wearing tight and revealing clothes, or indirectly by using titillating modesty, enticing coyness, or awkwardness fraught with meaning and a captivating, voluptuous stammer coupled with meticulously using the weapon of the distant gaze enveloped in sadness and mystery. Nature has provided women all these real techniques for the preservation of the species but, for one reason or another, decided to deprive Shaymaa Muhammadi of them.

This does not mean at all that she suffers a deficiency in femininity. On the contrary, her femininity is overpowering and would suffice for several women to lead a natural life; but she's never learned how to express it. Her feminine desires persist so much that they cause her pain and make her irritable, capricious, and prone to weeping fits. Nothing relieves her tension except her forbidden dreams of the famous Iraqi crooner, Kadhim al-Sahir, and her stealthy bouts of delight in her naked body (after which she repents every time and performs two prayer prostrations in sincere penitence before God; but she soon does it again). The psychological pressures that she's suffered because of her failure to get married thus far were a direct reason for her traveling to the States, as if she were running away from her situation or postponing facing reality. For many months Shaymaa exerted strenuous efforts to complete the requirements for the scholarship: she had to fill out applications and forms and go on endless trips from her college to the university's administration and vice versa. Then there were those violent and complicated negotiations with her mother, who as soon as she learned of her desire to travel, erupted angrily and yelled at her, "Your problem, Shaymaa, is that you're obstinate, like your father. You'll regret it. You don't know what it means to be away from home. You want to travel to America where they persecute Muslims and while you are veiled? Why don't you get your doctorate here and protect your dignity in the midst of your family? Remember that by traveling you lose any chance of getting married. What good would a PhD from America do when you are a forty-year-old spinster?"

The idea that a girl might travel alone to America for four or five years was alien to the family, acquaintances, and perhaps the whole of Tanta. But Shaymaa's diligence and persistence and her resorting to violent quarrels sometimes—and to begging and crying at other times—forced her mother finally to acquiesce to her desire. Shaymaa's enthusiasm kept increasing as the appointed time drew near. Even in the last days she had no fear or anxiety. And when it was time she was not affected by the tears of her mother and sisters. As soon as the plane took off and she felt that little tightness in her belly, she felt quite refreshed and optimistic. She thought to herself that only at that moment was she turning over a new leaf and leaving behind the thirty-three years she'd lived in Tanta.

Her first days in Chicago, however, were contrary to what she'd expected: headaches and exhaustion due to jet lag, insomnia, and interrupted sleep and harrowing nightmares. Worse than that was a feeling of dejection that never left her after she landed at O'Hare Airport. The security officer was suspicious of her and made her wait out of the line, then fingerprinted and began to interrogate her, fixing her with an untrusting gaze. But the scholarship papers she carried, her extremely pale face, and her voice that grew softer then totally disappeared from sheer fright all dispelled his suspicions, and he dismissed her with a wave of his hand. Shaymaa stood on the moving walkway with her large suitcase (her full name and address written in India ink on it, the Egyptian peasant way). The hostile reception made her somewhat dejected. She soon discovered that the walkway on which she stood was moving inside a giant tube intersecting with hundreds of neon tubes, making O'Hare seem like a children's toy that had been magnified thousands of times.

As soon as she left the airport, she was dazzled. She saw streets so wide she could not imagine they existed anywhere and gigantic skyscrapers that spread as far as the eye could see, giving the city an enchanted mythical look like those in comic books. She saw waves upon waves of Americans, men and women, streaming forth from all directions like giant lines of ants moving fast and earnestly, as if rushing to catch a train about to leave the station. At that moment she felt like a stranger, lonely and lost, as if she were a straw tossed about by a tumultuous ocean. She was overcome with a fear that soon turned into a bellyache pinching her guts, as if she were a child lost from her mother in the crowds of al-Sayyid al-Badawi's *mulid*. Despite her strenuous attempts, two long weeks had passed, and she hadn't yet got used to her new life. At night, when she lay in her room enveloped in a thick darkness penetrated only by the yellow streetlights through the window, Shaymaa remembered sadly that she'd sleep in that desolate place for several years. It was then that she would be overcome with an overpowering longing for her warm room, her sisters, her mother, and all those she loved in Tanta.

The previous night worries had assailed her and she was unable to sleep. For a whole hour she tossed and turned and felt miserable. She cried in the dark and wet her pillow. Then she got up, turned on the light and said to herself that she couldn't possibly bear such a hard life for four full years. What would happen if she were to write a request to withdraw from the scholarship? She would suffer for some time from the gloating and sarcastic taunts of some of her colleagues in Tanta, but her two sisters would welcome her with open arms, and her mother would never gloat at her misfortune. The desire to withdraw from the scholarship took hold of her and she started wondering how to carry it out. Suddenly another idea occurred to her: she performed her ablution, opened the holy Qur'an, and recited the chapter of Yasin, then performed the prayer for guidance and followed it with supplications. As soon as she lay her head on the pillow she was fast asleep. In her sleep she saw her father, Ustaz Muhammadi, wearing his fancy blue wool suit that he wore on important occasions (such as visits to or by the minister or graduation parties at the school). Her father stood in the garden in front of the main door of the histology department where she studied. His face was clean-shaven and without wrinkles, his lucent eyes gleamed, and his hair was thick jet-black without a single gray hair, which made him appear twenty years younger. He kept smiling at Shaymaa and whispering to her in his affectionate voice, "Don't be afraid. I'll stay with you. I won't leave you, ever. Come." Then he held her by the hand and pulled her gently until she entered through the department door with him.

Shaymaa woke up in the morning at peace with herself, her misgivings totally gone. She said to herself, "This is a true vision from God Almighty to give me strength in my difficult task." She believed that the dead lived with us but that we didn't see them. Her father had visited her in her sleep to encourage her to continue her studies, and she wasn't going to let him down; she would forget her sorrows and cope with her new life. She felt profound relief now that she had made up her mind. So, she decided to celebrate. She had certain rituals she was used to performing with her two sisters on happy occasions. She began by making the well-known paste of sugar and lemon juice on the stove, and then she went into the bathroom and sat, naked, on the edge of the bathtub and began to remove unwanted hair from her body. She enjoyed that repeated, fleeting, delightful pain caused by plucking the hair from the skin. She followed that by a long, warm bath during which she gave every part of her body a rubbing that refreshed and liberated her.

A few minutes later, Shaymaa stood in the kitchen enacting a purely Egyptian scene: she put on a flannel gallabiya with a pattern of little flowers and a pair of *khadduga* slippers with a wide face and four intersecting straps, which were her favorite because they were easy on her toes and gave them freedom of movement. She let her long, soft wet hair cascade down her shoulders and decided to enjoy everything she loved to do. She put in the cassette player Kadhim al-Sahir's song "Do You Have Any Doubt?" of which she was so fond that she recorded it three times on the same cassette tape so she wouldn't have to rewind it. Kadhim's voice boomed out and Shaymaa began to dance to the tunes and, at the same time, slide bell peppers, one by one, into a frying pan of boiling oil to make her favorite dish, Alexandria-style moussaka. Little by little she became completely absorbed in the act and began to roam all over the kitchen, dancing and singing with Kadhim as if performing on stage, then going back to the stove to slide in a new pepper. When Kadhim sang "My Murderess Is Dancing Barefoot," Shaymaa extended her feet and threw off her *khadduga* slippers into the corner of the kitchen. When Kadhim asked his beloved, "Where'd you come from? How did you come here? And how did you storm my heart?" she became so ecstatic that it occurred to her to perform a dance move that used to earn great admiration from her girlfriends in Tanta. She suddenly got down on her knees, raised her arms, and began to rise slowly, shaking her waist and jiggling her breasts. This time she slid in two peppers at once, and when they hit the boiling oil the impact produced a great bang and released thick plumes of smoke. For a moment she imagined hearing something like an alarm. But she dismissed at that moment anything that might spoil her good mood and began another dance move: she extended her arms, as if getting ready to embrace someone, then began to move her breasts forward and backward while standing in place. When she picked up another pepper to drop it into the oil, at that very moment, she experienced a horrifying nightmare. She heard a loud bang, after which the door of her apartment was forcibly opened. Some huge men surrounded her, shouting in English things that she did not understand. One of the men jumped toward her and hugged her hard, as if he wanted to carry her off the ground. She didn't resist because she was too shocked until she felt his strong hands clasping at her back and she smelled a putrid smell after her face got caught in his black leather coat. It was only then that she realized the enormity of what was happening and she channeled all her strength to her hands to push off that stranger and began to let loose a stream of very loud, piercing screams that reverberated throughout the building.

 The University of Illinois is one of the largest schools in the United States. It is divided into several campuses: the Medical Center on the west side comprises the medical colleges. The nonmedical colleges are in other parts of the city. The Medical Center started in the 1850s with modest means then developed and expanded, like everything in Chicago, at a very fast rate, until it became a huge self-contained town on thirty acres, occupying more than a hundred buildings that constitute the medical school, pharmacology school, school of dentistry, nursing, library branches, and the administration. In addition there are movie theaters, theaters, athletic facilities, giant stores, and a free local transit system working around the clock.

The University of Illinois Medical School is one of the largest in the world and has one of the oldest histology departments, housed in a modern five-story building surrounded by a large garden, in the middle of which is a bronze bust of a man in his fifties who seems to stare into space with big, tired, dreamy eyes. On the pedestal the following words are inscribed in large letters: "The great Italian scientist, Marcello Malpighi (1628–1694), founder of histology. He started it and we are here to finish the job." This fighting tone epitomizes the spirit of the department. As soon as you enter through the glass door, you feel you've left the world with its preoccupations and noise and found yourself in the sanctum of science. The place is very quiet with soft, light music coming from the internal public address system. The lighting is uniform, designed to be comfortable for the eyes, not distracting and not tied to time outside. Dozens of scientists and students are in constant motion.

The word *histology* has its origins in a Latin word meaning "the science of tissues," the science that uses the microscope to study living tissues. It constitutes the basis for medicine because discovering a cure for any disease always starts with the study of the normal, healthy tissues. Despite histology's extreme importance, it is neither popular nor lucrative. A histologist is most likely a physician who chooses to forgo specializations that bring fortune and glory (like surgery or gynecology) to spend his life in a cold, closed lab, bent over a microscope for long hours, his utmost hope to discover an unknown element of a microscopic cell about which no one will ever hear. Histologists are unknown soldiers who sacrifice fame and fortune for science and, with time, acquire the characteristics of craftsmen (like carpenters, sculptors, and palm leaf weavers): a comfortable, staid sitting style, heft in the lower body, few words, the power of observation, and a scrutinizing gaze. They are also distinguished by patience, calm, clarity of thinking, and a great ability to concentrate and reflect. The department is comprised of five professors ranging in age from fifty to seventy. Each of them attained his post after years of constant, arduous work. Their days are very tight and their calendars busy for weeks, and because they have so much research to do, they have to spend all their time in the lab. Other than on weekends, they rarely have the chance to talk. In the weekly departmental meetings they usually make their decisions quickly to save time. Hence what happened last Tuesday is considered out of the ordinary.

The departmental meeting came to order and the professors sat in their usual seats: Dr. Bill Friedman, the chairman, at the head of the table with his mostly bald head, white complexion, and meek features that make him look more like an honest, hardworking paterfamilias. To his right sat the two Egyptian-American professors, Ra'fat Thabit and

Muhammad Salah, then the statistics professor John Graham, with his heavy build, light white beard, gray, always disheveled hair, and small round glasses behind which gleam intelligent, skeptical eyes. He has a faint, sarcastic smile and a long pipe that never leaves his mouth, even though it was not lit because smoking was not permitted at the meeting. Graham bears a considerable resemblance to the American writer Ernest Hemingway, which always elicits humorous comments from his colleagues. On the other side of the table sat George Roberts, whom they call "the Yankee" because everything about him is stereotypically American: blue eyes, shoulder-length blond hair, casual attire, a broad, strong, athletic body, and sculpted muscles indicating strict regular exercise, a habit of putting his feet up on the table in the face of people he is talking to, licking his fingers while eating, and a soda can always in his hand, from which he takes a small sip then shrugs his shoulders and speaks in a twang harking back to Texas, where he grew up before coming to Chicago. There remained the oldest and most prolific professor, Dennis Baker, silent, wearing simple, clean clothes that are always slightly wrinkled, perhaps because he couldn't find the time to iron them properly. He is tall, and his old body is taut and firm. He is completely bald, his big eyes sometimes radiating with a piercing glance, gleaming so much as to display a mysterious authority. Dennis Baker's colleagues tease him by saying that he uses speech just like a driver uses a car horn: only when absolutely necessary.

The meeting went on the usual way, and before it adjourned, the chairman, Bill Friedman, asked his colleagues to stay. He blushed as he usually did when he had something to say; then he looked at the papers in front of him and said in a calm voice, "I'd like to consult you about something. You know that the Egyptian Educational Bureau has an agreement with the department to send Egyptian students to study for the PhD in histology. We now have three students: Tariq Haseeb, Shaymaa Muhammadi, and Ahmad Danana. This week the bureau sent the papers of a new student, whose name is"—he stopped and read the name with difficulty—"Nagi Abd al-Samad. This student is different from the others: first, because he wants to get an MS and not a PhD, and second, because he does not work at a university. I was surprised at the beginning—I couldn't understand why he wants to get an MS in histology if he doesn't work in scientific research or teaching. This morning I contacted the head of the bureau in Washington, D.C., and she told me that that student was denied a job at Cairo University for political reasons, and that his obtaining an MS would strengthen his position in his lawsuit against Cairo University. I looked at the student's file and found it to be quite promising: he has high scores both in English and overall. And as you know, the bureau will cover his study expenses. I'd like to know what you think. Should we admit this student? Graduate study slots here are limited, as you know. I will listen to you, and if you don't all agree I'll put it to a vote."

Friedman looked around. George Roberts, "the Yankee," was the first to ask to speak. He took a sip from his can of Pepsi and said, "I don't object to admitting Egyptian students. But I'd only like to remind you that this is one of the most important histology departments in the world. An opportunity to study here is rare and precious. We shouldn't squander it just because a student from Africa would like to win a lawsuit against his government. I believe education here has a higher purpose. The spot that this Egyptian would get is needed by a genuine researcher to learn and discover new things in science. I refuse to admit this student."

"Okay. This is your opinion, Dr. Roberts. How about the rest of you?" the chairman asked, smiling. Ra'fat Thabit raised his hand then started speaking like someone telling an anecdote. "Having been an Egyptian at one time, I know very well how Egyptians think. They don't learn for the sake of learning. They get MSs and PhDs, not for the sake of scientific research, but to get a promotion or a lucrative contract in the Arab Gulf countries. This student will hang his diploma in his clinic in Cairo to convince the patients that he can cure them."

Friedman looked at him in astonishment and said, "How do they allow that in Egypt? Histology is an academic subject that has nothing whatsoever to do with treating people."

Ra'fat laughed sarcastically and said, "You don't know Egypt, Bill. Everything there is permitted, and people don't know what the word *histology* means to begin with."

"Are you exaggerating a little, Ra'fat?" asked Friedman in a soft voice.

Muhammad Salah intervened, "Of course he's exaggerating."

Ra'fat Thabit turned to him and said sharply, "You, in particular, know I am not exaggerating."

Friedman sighed and said, "Anyway, this is not what we're discussing. We now have two opinions, from Dr. Roberts and Dr. Thabit, against admitting the Egyptian student. What do you say, Dr. Graham?"

John Graham took the unlit pipe from his mouth and said vexedly, "Gentlemen! You're talking more like secret police detectives than university professors!"

There were some noises of objection but Graham continued loudly, "The right thing to do is quite obvious. Anyone who fulfills the requirements of the department is entitled to enroll. It's none of our business what he'll do with his diploma or what country he's come from."

"This kind of talk gave America September 11," said George Roberts.

Graham rolled his eyes and said sarcastically, "What led to September 11 is that most decision makers in the White House thought like you. They supported despotic regimes in the Middle East to multiply the profits of oil and arms companies, and armed violence escalated and reached our shores. Remember, this student will leave his country and his family and travel to the end of the world for the sake of learning. Don't you find this to be an honorable endeavor deserving respect? Isn't it our duty to help him? Remember, Dr. Roberts, you've often objected to admitting any non-American students, haven't you?

As for you, Ra'fat, do you think your speech is culpable under the anti-racial-discrimination statutes?"

"I didn't say anything racist, Comrade Graham!" said Ra'fat with some irritation.

Graham turned toward him, ran his fingers through his beard, and said, "If you call me 'comrade' in jest, I take that as a compliment and I can assure you that what you say is racist. Racism is the belief that a difference in race leads to a difference in behavior and human abilities. This applies to what you said about Egyptians. The amazing thing is, you yourself are Egyptian!"

"I used to be Egyptian some time ago, but I've quit. And, comrade, when will you recognize the American passport I carry?"

Chairman Friedman made a gesture with his hand, saying, "Control your tempers. We've got off the subject at hand. Dr. Graham, you agree to admit the student. How about you, Dr. Salah?"

"I agree to admit the student," said Salah calmly. The chairman's smile widened and he said, "Two in favor and two against. I'll keep my opinion until the end. We'd like to hear from Dennis. I don't know if today is one of the days Dr. Baker can talk, or do we have to wait a few days?"

Everyone laughed and some of the tensions caused by the discussion dissipated. Baker smiled and remained silent for a moment, then his eyes grew wider and he said in his gruff voice, "I'd rather we have a formal vote."

The chairman bowed his head at once, as if he had received an order. He scribbled a few words on a piece of paper in front of him, then cleared his throat, and his voice acquired a formal tone as he said, "Gentlemen, this is a formal vote. Do you agree to admit the Egyptian student Nagi Abd al-Samad to the histology MS program? Those in favor, please raise your hands."

 At the student dorm at the University of Illinois in Chicago, apartment 303, in front of the elevator on the third floor, Tariq Haseeb leads a life as precise as the hand of a clock: alone, thin, and tense, moving forward in a constant, nonchanging rhythm. From 8:00 A.M. until 3:00 P.M., every day, he moves from lecture hall to lab to library. Then he returns to his apartment to have his lunch in front of the television followed by a full two-hour siesta. At exactly 7:00 P.M., regardless of changing circumstances or events around the world, what Tariq Haseeb does doesn't change one bit: he turns off his cell phone and turns on light music in his room. Then he assumes the position he has throughout his thirty-five years on this earth: he bends over his small desk, studying his lessons, or more precisely, waging a relentless war against the material until he controls it and records it in his mind, never to be erased afterward. He spreads the books and papers in front of him and stares at them with his big, slightly bulging eyes. He knits his brow and purses his thin lips, the muscles of his pale face contracted in a stony expression, as if patiently suffering some kind of pain. When his concentration reaches its peak, he becomes so completely isolated from his surroundings that he doesn't hear the doorbell or forgets the teakettle on the stove until the water in it totally evaporates and it starts burning. He stays like that tirelessly until he suddenly jumps to his feet and shouts loudly or claps his hands and heaps obscene insults on an imaginary person or raises his arms and dances wantonly all over the room. That is the way he expresses joy when he manages to understand a scientific problem that he has had some difficulty comprehending.

With the same determination, Tariq Haseeb continues his holy march every day with the exception of Sunday, which he devotes to chores that might distract him from studying the rest of the week. He does his grocery shopping at the shopping center and his laundry in the apartment building, vacuums his room, and cooks for the week, keeping the food in paper containers that can be easily reheated. It is this military precision that has enabled him to achieve the difficult goal of staying at the top. He placed first in his Cairo primary school, third in preparatory school, and eighth nationally in the general secondary school certificate with a 99.8 percentile. After that Tariq maintained the grade "excellent" throughout his five years in medical school but did not have the right connections, so he was appointed to the histology department rather than the general surgery department as he had dreamed. But it didn't take him long to overcome his sorrow, and he devoted himself to work anew, obtained an MS in histology with distinction, and was nominated for a scholarship to obtain a doctorate from the University of Illinois. In his first two years there he maintained straight As.

Does that mean that Tariq Haseeb does not have any fun?

Not true. He also has his little pleasures, such as the *basbusa* tray whose ingredients he gets from Egypt and which he takes delight in making himself. He places it on the kitchen table, and when he is pleased with the way he studies he decides to reward himself by devouring a piece of *basbusa* commensurate in size to the work done. He also has a recreational hour that he takes pains to observe every night, even during examination periods. It is divided into two parts: watching pro wrestling and fantasizing. He cannot go to sleep before watching on the sports channel a complete match of professional wrestling. From the beginning he roots for the bigger wrestler. When that wrestler rains blows on his rival's face, causing him to bleed profusely, or when he picks him up by the waist and throws him down on the floor of the ring or when he locks his head with his huge arm and slams it on the edge of the ring, as if it were a melon about to explode, Tariq claps and jumps up and down in sheer ecstasy and shouts as if he were an adoring, ecstatic fan at an Umm Kulthum concert in Cairo: "Wonderful, mountain monster! Drink his blood! Break his head! Finish him off tonight." By the end of the match, Tariq collapses on his bed, out of breath, sweat pouring from his pores, as if it were he who'd fought the wrestling match. But he would by then have satisfied something deep inside him (being partial to strength, perhaps, because he is thin and has been in poor health from a young age).

After the delight of wrestling comes the moment of fantasy, the secret pleasure for which he yearns so much that he pants and feels his heartbeat shaking him to his foundations as he takes the CD from its hiding place in the lower desk drawer. He places it in the computer drive, and soon a magical world of utmost beauty reveals itself to him: graceful, voluptuous blond women with soft and delectable legs and extremely splendid breasts of different sizes with aroused erect nipples, the mere sight of which transports him beyond sanity. Then strong muscular men appear with long, swollen, and erect organs, built as if they were giant, well-wrought steel hammers. The women and men soon start making love harmoniously, accompanied by a cacophony of orgiastic screams, with camera close-ups of women crying from sheer pleasure and biting their lower lips. Tariq cannot stand this excitement for more than a few minutes after which he dashes to the bathroom as if in a race or putting out a fire. He stands in front of the sink and gets rid of his pleasure and little by little he calms down and regains his equanimity, then takes a hot bath, performs his ablution and his evening prayers—both mandatory and optional—and finally pulls a woman's nylon stocking that he had brought with him from Egypt over his head so that in the morning his hair would be smooth, thus covering, as much as possible, his bald spot, which, unfortunately, is constantly expanding.

At that point a day in the life of Tariq Haseeb would come to an end. He would turn off the light and lie down on his right side, in emulation of the tradition of the Prophet, peace be upon him. He would whisper in a submissive voice, "O God, I have submitted myself to You and turned my face toward You and left all my affairs up to You. I have entrusted my back to You, out of desire and fear of You. There is no recourse and no succor for me except in You. I believe in Your book that You have revealed and in the Prophet You have sent." Then he'd fall asleep.

THE MORE PRECISE THE MACHINE, the more subject it is to damage. One hard blow to the most sophisticated computer is enough to render it inoperable. Tariq Haseeb received just such a blow last Sunday. In order to understand what happened, we must first examine how Tariq behaves with women.

When a man likes a woman he seeks out her affection with tender talk or gladdens her heart with flirtation and praise, or just makes her laugh and amuses her with interesting stories. This is the nature of humans and animals too; even in the world of insects, if a male wants to have intercourse with a female, he must first fondle her antennae gently and softly until she softens and accepts. This law of nature, unfortunately, does not apply to Tariq Haseeb. He is the opposite of all of that: if he likes a beautiful woman he starts to treat her aggressively and tries to embarrass and harass her in every possible way. And the more he likes the woman the more vicious he is toward her. Why does he do that? No one knows. Perhaps it is to hide his excessive bashfulness before women, or because his attraction to a woman makes him feel weak in comparison to her, so he tries to overcome that by mounting a crushing attack against her. Or because, in the eagle-like loneliness in which he lives and his relentless fight to get to the top, he internally resists any feeling that might distract him from his work. This strange quirk in Tariq's character has ruined several prospective engagements that he had undertaken with the best of intentions but which all ended in regrettable incidents. The most recent had happened two years before his coming to the States on this scholarship, when he went with his mother to ask for the hand of the daughter of a retired army general. The visit started amicably: cold drinks and pastries were served and courtesies exchanged. The young lady, Rasha, was a graduate of the Spanish department in the College of Languages. She was very pretty: she had long, smooth black hair and a captivating smile revealing snow-white, perfectly arranged teeth. She had two enchanting dimples on both sides of her alluring white face. As for her figure it was luscious and curvaceous, filled with vitality and sending off lustful vibrations in the air that made Tariq lose his concentration for a few moments as he imagined himself possessing the bride-to-be's body, and doing such things to it. But his admiration, as usual, turned into an aggressive inclination that he tried to control at first, but he failed and gave in to it and it swept him overboard. The father of the bride, as usually happened on such occasions, was talking about his daughter lovingly and admiringly. Somewhat boastfully he said, "Rasha is our only daughter and we've done all we could to give her the best upbringing and education. Praise God, all her life she was in language schools, from nursery to secondary school."

Tariq looked at him with his bulging eyes for a few moments then asked him with a mocking smile on his flushed face, "Pardon, pasha, what school exactly did Mademoiselle Rasha attend?"

The general fell silent for a moment, taken aback by the question, then answered smiling, still willing to be tolerant, "Amon School."

Thereupon, Tariq found himself in front of the goal, so he kicked the ball hard. With a light laugh on his face that he tried to hide in order to double its impact, he said, "Pardon, General. Amon School was never a language school. Amon is an experimental school, that is, a regular government school but with nominal fees."

The general's face showed signs of distress which soon turned into resentment, and he got into a heated debate with Tariq about the difference between experimental and exclusive language schools. Tariq's mother tried to intervene with pacifying words and secretly gestured to her son several times with her eyebrows and lips to be quiet. But his viciousness was out of his control. He cruelly started to refute the arguments of the father of the bride, having decided to deliver a final, crushing blow. Sighing, as if he had already tired of discussing self-evident platitudes, he said, "With all due respect, sir, what you're saying is absolutely wrong. There's a big difference between Amon School and language schools. Language schools in Egypt are few and well known and one cannot enroll in them easily."

"What do you mean?" asked the general, his face now red with vexation. Tariq took some time before delivering his coup de grâce. "I mean exactly what I said."

Several moments of silence passed during which the general exerted a great effort (almost audible as hyperventilation) to control his anger. Finally he turned to Tariq's mother sitting to his left and said in a tone of voice fraught with meaning as he fidgeted, indicating the end of the visit and the engagement, "We are blessed and honored, dear lady."

The return trip seemed too long. There was heavy silence in the taxicab. Tariq's mother had put on her best outfit for the engagement: a long dark blue suit and a bonnet of the same color adorned with sequins and crystal beads. She wanted her son to be engaged before he traveled on the scholarship, but every time he behaved like this and ruined the engagement. She had given up on giving him any advice; she had told him many times that he was a respectable and highly regarded catch, that many a girl would love to have him as her husband, but that his combative ways left people with the impression that he was aggressive and strange, so they were afraid of him for their daughter.

"Did you see these liars, Mother? They called Amon School a language school!" he said suddenly, as though he sensed what his mother was thinking.

His mother looked at him for a long while then said in a soft voice in which were mixed rebuke and kindness, "It wasn't worth all the fuss, my dear. The man just wanted to brag about his daughter, which is natural."

Tariq interrupted her sharply. "He can brag as much as he likes, but he shouldn't lie to us. When he says that Amon School is a language school, it means that he has little regard for our minds. I cannot let him get away with that."

ON SUNDAY EVENING TARIQ HASEEB woke up from his siesta and said to himself that he'd finish the statistics assignment then go out to do his week's shopping. He applied himself to solving the problems, thinking hard and writing down the numbers then eagerly checking the back of the book, hoping every time that his answer would be correct. Suddenly the alarm sounded throughout the building and a voice came over the public address system warning that there was a fire in the building and demanding that the tenants leave their apartments immediately. Tariq's mind was full of numbers, so it took him a few moments to realize what was happening, and he jumped up and rushed down the stairs in the midst of the panicked students. The firefighters spread throughout the building, making sure that every floor had been evacuated, and then they pushed certain buttons on the walls and immediately nonflammable steel doors were lowered in place. The students gathered in the lobby; they were excited, laughing nervously and whispering anxiously. Most of them had gone out of their apartments in their sleepwear, which gave Tariq (despite the gravity of the situation) a rare chance to check out the girls' bare legs. Three persons appeared, coming from the farther end of the lobby, and little by little their features became recognizable: two Chicago policemen, one white on the short and heavy side, the other a tall, muscular black man. Between them walked Shaymaa Muhammadi in the flannel gallabiya she had had no time to change. They reached the reception desk and the white policeman took out a sheet of paper and said loudly in a formal tone of voice, "Young lady, this is an affidavit that you will sign to be responsible for any damages that might come to light in the future because of the fire you caused. You also have to sign a pledge that this won't happen again in the future."

Shaymaa stared at the white policeman as if she didn't understand, whereupon the black policeman, looking like someone about to tell a biting joke, said, "Listen, my friend, I don't know what kind of food you eat in your country but I advise you to change your favorite dish because it almost burned down the building."

The black policeman laughed unabashedly while his partner tried to decorously hide his smile. Shaymaa bent and signed the paper in silence. Before long the two policemen exchanged a few words and left. A short while later it was announced that the danger was over, and students began to go back up to their apartments. Shaymaa, however, remained standing in front of the reception office. She looked deathly pale and kept shaking and breathing heavily. She was trying to compose herself, as if she had just awakened from a terrifying nightmare. She felt that she was no longer in possession of her soul, that everything that was happening was unreal. She felt particularly humiliated that the firefighter had hugged her, and her back still hurt from the pressure of his hands. Tariq Haseeb stood scrutinizing her slowly, then circled around her twice, exploring, as if he were an animal sniffing another animal of an unknown species. From the first moment he felt attracted toward her, but his admiration, as usual, turned into extreme resentment. He knew her name and had seen her before in the histology department, but he enjoyed pretending that he didn't know her. He approached slowly and when he was right in front of her he fixed her with a scrutinizing, disapproving, suspicious glance that he used to use on Cairo Medical School students as he proctored them during their written exams. Before long he asked her haughtily, "Are you Egyptian?"

She answered with a nod from her tired head. Then his questions, bulletlike, rang out in quick succession: What do you study? Where do you live? How did you cause the fire? She kept answering in a soft voice, avoiding looking at his eyes. Silence fell for a moment, which Tariq thought was appropriate after his lightning attack. He said sharply, "Listen, sister Shaymaa. Here you are in America and not in Tanta. You have to behave in a civilized manner."

She looked at him in silence. What would she tell him? What she's done is proof of her stupidity and backwardness. She was about to answer him when he approached her, ready to pounce on her, to silence and totally crush her.

 Professor Dennis Baker raised his hand in favor of admitting the new Egyptian student, as did Dr. Friedman, who counted the votes with a cursory glance and bent over the paper to record the department's vote to admit Nagi Abd al-Samad. The meeting was adjourned and the professors left. Ra'fat Thabit got in his car to drive home. He felt so vexed at the result of the vote that he tightened his grip on the steering wheel and sighed in exasperation. He thought: Egyptians will ruin the department. That's the truth. Egyptians cannot work in respectable places because they have many negative qualities: cowardice and hypocrisy, lying, evasiveness and laziness, and an inability to think methodically. Worse than that: they are disorganized and tricky. This negative view of the Egyptians is in line with Ra'fat Thabit's own history. He emigrated from Egypt to the States in the early 1960s after Gamal Abdel Nasser nationalized the glass factories owned by his father, Mahmud Pasha Thabit. And despite the iron fist of the regime at that time, he was able to smuggle a large sum of money out of Egypt with which he financed his new life: he went to school and got a doctorate and taught in several American universities in New York and Boston. He then settled in Chicago thirty years ago and married a nurse, Michelle, obtained American citizenship, and became American in every respect: he no longer spoke Arabic at all, thought in English, and spoke it with a cleverly acquired American accent. He even shrugged his shoulders and gestured and made sounds

while speaking exactly like Americans. On Sundays he'd go to baseball games about which he had become such an expert that his American friends often consulted him if they had disagreements about its rules. He would sit in the park, wearing his cap backward, following the game intensely and enthusiastically while sipping beer from the large glass that never left his hand. That was the image that he loved of himself: to be a complete genuine American, pure and without blemish. At receptions and on social occasions, when someone asked him, "Where're you from?" Ra'fat would promptly answer, "I'm from Chicago."

Many people accepted this answer simply, but some of them, sometimes, would look at his Arab features suspiciously then ask, "Where were you before coming to America?"

At that point he would sigh, shrug his shoulders, and repeat his favorite sentence that had become a slogan for him: "I was born in Egypt and I fled the oppression and backwardness to justice and freedom."

This absolute pride in everything American coupled with contempt for everything Egyptian explains everything he does. Because Egyptians are overweight and they lead unhealthy lives, he stays svelte. And even though he is sixty, he still cuts an attractive figure: tall with a graceful, athletic build. He has only a few wrinkles in his smooth complexion and his hair is discreetly dyed in a convincing manner by leaving some gray in the temple area and the front of the head. The truth is, he is handsome with an inherited aristocratic bearing that shows in his clothes and the way he moves. He resembles to a great extent the actor Rushdi Abaza, except for a tentativeness and sluggishness that detract from the magnetism of his face. Because he is proud of his country's accomplishments, Dr. Thabit avidly acquires the latest American technology, starting with his late model Cadillac (the down payment for which he paid with his honorarium for some lectures he gave last winter at Harvard), the latest cell phone, a shaver that sprays aftershave, and a lawn mower that plays music while trimming the grass. In the presence of Egyptians in particular, he loves to show off his modern gadgets and then ask them sarcastically, "When will Egypt be able to produce a machine like this? After how many centuries?" Then he bursts out laughing in the midst of the embarrassed Egyptians. When an Egyptian student in the department excels, Ra'fat must needle him. He goes up to him, shakes his hand, and says, "Congratulations for excelling in spite of the wretched education you've received in Egypt. You must thank America for what you've achieved."

After 9/11 Ra'fat came out publicly against Arabs and Muslims, using language that most fanatical Americans might be reluctant to use. He would say, for instance, "The United States has the right to ban any Arab from coming in until it is certain that such a person is civilized and does not think that killing is a religious duty."

Hence the admission of Nagi Abd al-Samad was a personal defeat for Dr. Thabit. In a short while, however, he decided to forget the whole matter. He lifted his right hand from the steering wheel and pushed the button of the CD player to listen to the songs of Lionel Richie, whom he adored. He thought of spending a quiet evening with his wife, Michelle, and his daughter, Sarah. He remembered the special bottle of Royal Salute scotch that he had bought a few days earlier and decided to open it tonight because he needed a good drink. After a while he arrived at his house, a handsome white two-story building with a beautiful garden and a backyard. He was met by his German shepherd, Metz, who barked loudly for a long time. He went around the house as usual to reach the garage. To his surprise he saw the lights on in the dining room, which meant they had company. He was annoyed, since Michelle had not told him that she was expecting anyone for dinner. He pressed the remote and the car locked automatically, then he closed the garage door and pulled the bolt to make sure it was securely locked. He walked slowly toward the house, trying to guess who the guest might be. He hurriedly patted Metz and got away from him, then entered through the side door and crossed the corridor carefully. Michelle heard his footsteps on the wooden floor and hurried toward him and planted a kiss on his check, saying merrily, "Come quickly. We have a wonderful surprise."

When he went into the dining room Jeff, Sarah's boyfriend, was standing next to her. Jeff is about twenty-five, thin with a pale face. He has beautiful blue eyes, delicate pursed lips, and smooth chestnut-colored hair arranged in a long braid down his back. He had on a white T-shirt, blue jeans stained with colors in many places, and old sandals from which his dirty toes were visible. Jeff came forward to greet Ra'fat as Michelle's voice announced in the background, "Jeff has finished his painting this evening and decided that we'd be the first to see it. Isn't that wonderful?"

"Great. Welcome, Jeff," said Ra'fat, having noticed after a side glance that his wife had had her hair done, preened, and put on her new corduroy pants. Jeff came forward to shake hands with him, laughing as he said, "Let me be frank with you, Ra'fat. Your opinion matters to me, of course, but when I finished my new painting I thought only of one thing: that Sarah be the first to see it."

"Thank you," whispered Sarah as she pressed his hand and looked at his handsome face in admiration. Michelle then asked, as though she were interviewing him on television, "Tell me, Jeff, what does an artist feel when he finishes a new work?"

Jeff raised his head slowly, looked at the ceiling, closed his eyes, and was silent for a moment, then extended his arms in front of him as if embracing the world and said in a dreamy voice, "I don't know how to describe that. The most beautiful moment in my life is when I put the finishing touches on a painting."

His words touched the two women very much and they kept eyeing him fondly and in admiration. Then Michelle said, "Now, what do you think, Ra'fat? Should we have dinner first or see the painting?"

Ra'fat was very hungry, so he said calmly, "Just as you wish."

But Sarah clapped and exclaimed merrily, "I can't wait one more moment to see the painting!"

"Me neither," said Michelle as she led Ra'fat by the hand to a corner of the room. Jeff had placed the painting on an easel and covered it with a shiny white fabric. They all stood in front of it for a moment, then Jeff stepped forward, reached out with his hand, and pulled the edge of the fabric in a quick theatrical flourish. The painting was unveiled and Michelle and Sarah exclaimed at the same time, "Wow! Splendid! Splendid!"

Sarah turned around and stood on tiptoes and kissed Jeff on the cheeks. Ra'fat meanwhile kept looking at the painting, nodding slowly, as if trying to understand it more profoundly. The whole canvas was painted dark blue, in the middle of which were three yellow blotches, and on the top left was one red line almost invisible against the dark background. Sarah and her mother competed in heaping praise on Jeff while Ra'fat remained silent. Michelle asked him softly, but with a touch of rebuke, "Don't you like this magnificent painting?"

"I am trying to understand it. My taste is on the conventional side."

"What do you mean?" asked Jeff, his face clouding over suddenly.

Ra'fat answered apologetically, "Actually, Jeff, I prefer the old way of drawing because I understand it better; the artist, for instance, drawing a portrait or a landscape. As for drawing in the modern art style, I frankly don't understand it."

"I'm sorry that your understanding of art is so archaic. I thought your American education would have taught you more about art. Art is not to be understood by the mind, but appreciated by the feelings. And by the way, Ra'fat, please don't use the word *drawing* in front of me because it upsets me. Drawing is something we learn in grade school. Art is much greater than that."

Jeff was very upset but he breathed deeply and turned his face away disapprovingly, then began looking at the two women, forcing a smile to appear, as an artist who had been harshly insulted but who decided to forget the insult because he was magnanimous by nature. Michelle was moved so she raised her voice, chastising her husband, "If you don't understand art, Ra'fat, it's best you don't talk about it!"

Ra'fat smiled and didn't answer. After a short while the four of them sat down to have dinner: Jeff next to Sarah and Ra'fat next to Michelle, who opened for the dear guest a bottle of good Bolognese wine.

The two lovers engaged in an intimate whispering conversation as Michelle looked on, visibly pleased.

"Michelle, are the problems over in the hospice?" asked Ra'fat loudly.

"Yes," Michelle responded tersely, obviously preferring not to talk about that subject. But Ra'fat went on, addressing the lovers to distract them from loving. "Listen to this interesting story. You know that Michelle works in a hospice in Chicago that helps patients with incurable diseases who are waiting to die."

"Helps them how?" Jeff asked, feigning interest.

Ra'fat replied enthusiastically, "The goal of the hospice is to make the idea of death acceptable and painless for dying patients: they bring clergy and psychologists to talk to them so they'll lose their fear in facing death. Naturally many of the hospice patients are rich. Last week something interesting happened to a wealthy patient whose name is . . ."

"Childs, Stuart Childs," muttered Michelle as she chewed her food.

Ra'fat went on. "He was on the point of dying and the hospice administration sent for his children and they came by plane from California to be at his deathbed and take care of the burial, and so on. As soon as they arrived at the hospice, however, the father's health improved suddenly and he got over the crisis. This happened twice; do you know what his children did? They got a court injunction against the hospice in which it was stated that the hospice prognostication system was woefully deficient, because every time they had to get away from their jobs and businesses and bear the brunt and expenses of travel to attend their father's death, they were surprised to see him alive. They warned the hospice that if it were to happen again, they would demand consider-able damages to compensate them for wasting their time and money. What do you think of that?"

"Very uplifting, Ra'fat," Jeff said sarcastically, then yawned audibly, and Sarah burst out laughing.

Ra'fat ignored the sarcasm and added, "The Eastern mentality would interpret this behavior as ingratitude on the part of the children, but I view it as proof of respect for time in American society."

No one commented on what Ra'fat said; the two lovers got busy whispering anew and Jeff said a few words in Sarah's ear and she smiled and blushed. Michelle was busy cutting her meat. Ra'fat got up, wiping the corner of his mouth with his napkin, saying with a lukewarm smile on his face: "Forgive me, Jeff. I have to go upstairs to my office. I have some work to do. See you this weekend to continue our discussion about art."

Ra'fat waved and climbed the wooden stairs to the second floor. As soon as he closed the door of his office he went directly to the cabinet near the window and took out the new scotch bottle. He fixed himself a drink with soda and ice, sat in his rocking chair, and sipped slowly, feeling that first biting taste that he liked. Soon a feeling of relief came over him. There was no work to be done; he had lied to them because he couldn't stand sitting with that Jeff anymore. Ra'fat smiled bitterly and thought, as he poured his second drink: Oh, God! How did intel-ligent, talented Sarah fall for this insignificant person? And why does Mr. Jeff feel so confident? He deals with people as if he were van Gogh or Picasso—where does he get this sense of importance? He's just a high school dropout and a runaway. Even the gas station where he used to work has fired him. Now he's living in Oakland with vagrants and criminals—an unemployed would-be artist and unbelievably insolent. I tried to start a conversation with him, just trying to be a good host, but he mocked me and yawned in my face. What a jerk! What does Sarah see in him? He is so dirty, he bathes only on special occasions;

how come she's not disgusted when she kisses him? He splashes canvases with his nonsense, and these two foolish women treat him like a genius. He's not content with that; he wants to give me lessons in art? What insolence! Little by little, the drinks eased his irritation and he felt relaxed. He closed his eyes and sipped the drink with great relish. Suddenly the door opened hard and Sarah and Michelle came in and stood in front of him, obviously itching for a confrontation. Michelle asked him, "Where's the work you left us to do?"

"I finished it."

"You're lying."

He looked at his wife in silence then asked her, pretending to be worried, "Where'd Jeff go?"

"He left."

"So soon?"

"He had to leave after what you've done. He has pride, like the rest of us. Do you know he waited for a whole hour to have dinner with you?"

Ra'fat bowed his head and began to shake the glass in his hand to melt the ice. He decided to avoid the confrontation as much as possible. But his silence aggravated Sarah's anger, so she stepped forward until she faced him directly and pounded the table so hard the flower vase shook. Then she screamed in a tone that sounded hysterical and strange to him, "It's not right to treat my boyfriend this way."

"I didn't do anything improper. It's he who descended on us without an appointment."

"Jeff is my boyfriend; I have the right to welcome him any time."

"Enough, Sarah, please. I am tired and I want to go to bed. Good night," said Ra'fat as he got off the chair and headed for the door.

But Sarah kept shouting, "How dare you insult my boyfriend like that. I hate how you treat him. It was so nice of him to come and show us his new painting and you ended up insulting him. But you won't be able to insult him again. I have a fantastic surprise for you. Would you like to know what it is?"

■■■■■■■■■■■

Nagi Abd al-Samad's Journal

The soldier fights his enemies ferociously, wishing to annihilate them all. But if he were destined, just once, to cross to the other side and to walk among them, he would see one of them writing a letter to his wife, another looking at his children's photos, and a third shaving and humming a tune. What would the soldier think then? Perhaps he would think that he was deceived when he was fighting against those good people and now would have to change his attitude toward them. Or he might think that what he saw was just a deceptive appearance, that those peaceful men, as soon as they took their positions and readied their weapons, would turn into criminals who'd kill his family and seek to humiliate his country. How much like this soldier I am!

I am now in America, which I've often attacked, shouted for it to fall and burned its flag in demonstrations; America, which is responsible for the poverty and misery of millions of humans in the world; America, which has supported and armed Israel, enabling it to kill the Palestinians and steal their land; America, which has supported all the corrupt, despotic rulers in the Arab world for its own interests; the evil America I am now seeing from inside. I am gripped by the same dilemma experienced by that soldier. A question persists in my mind: those kind Americans who treat strangers nicely, who smile in your face and like you the moment you meet them, who help you and let you go ahead of them and thank you profusely for the slightest reason? Do they realize the horrendous crimes their governments commit against humanity?

I wrote the section above to start my journal then crossed it out because I didn't like it. I've decided to write simply what I felt. I wouldn't publish this journal and no one else would read it but me. I am writing for myself, in order to record points of change in my life. I am now moving from my old world, the only world

I've known, to a new and exciting world filled with possibilities and probabilities. I arrived this morning in Chicago. I got off the plane and stood in a long line until I got to the passport officer, who examined my papers twice and asked me several questions with a suspicious and hate-filled look on his face before he stamped my passport and let me in. After only a few steps into the terminal I saw my name written in English on a sign carried by a man over sixty. He had Egyptian features and a smooth brown complexion, was totally bald, and wore glasses whose silver frames gave his face a rather formal look. His clothes were elegant and well fitting, indicating a refined taste: dark blue corduroy trousers, a light gray jacket, a white shirt with an open collar and black athletic shoes. I approached him, pulling my suitcase. His face lit up and he asked me, "Are you Nagi Abd al-Samad?"

I nodded. He shook my hand warmly and said, "Welcome to Chicago. I'm Muhammad Salah, professor in the department of histology where you'll be studying."

At the end of the sentence I detected a slight accent in his Arabic. I thanked him profusely, saying I appreciated his generosity for leaving his family on his day off to meet me at the airport. He made a gesture with his hand in the American way, as if he were chasing away a fly, as if to say that thanks were not needed or deserved. He tried to help me carry the suitcase to the car, but I refused, thanking him. He said as he started the car, "We Egyptians like to be welcomed with warm feelings. When we travel, even a short distance, we like to have somebody meet us, right?"

"Thank you very much, Doctor."

"That's the mayor's duty!"

I looked at him quizzically and he laughed loudly then said merrily as he turned the car on the curving road, "Egyptians here call me 'the mayor of Chicago,' and I do my best not to lose the title."

"Sir, have you been here a long time?"

"Thirty years."

"Thirty years?" I repeated in astonishment. We were both silent for a moment, then he said in a different tone of voice, "The president of the Egyptian Student Union in America was supposed to meet you, but he begged to be excused for circumstances. He's your colleague from Cairo University Medical School."

"What's his name?"

"Ahmad Danana."

"Ahmad Abd al-Hafeez Danana?"

"I think this is his full name. Do you know him?"

"All graduates of Qasr al-Ayni know him. He's an agent of the secret police."

Dr. Salah fell silent and looked slightly upset. I felt sorry and said, "Sorry, Doctor, but this Danana got me and many colleagues arrested and detained during the second Gulf war."

He remained silent, his eyes on the road, then said, "Even if that were true, I advise you to forget it; you should start your scientific journey having got rid of all your old quarrels."

I was on the point of answering him, but he quickly asked me, to change the subject, "What do you think of Chicago?"

"It's big and beautiful."

"Chicago is a fantastic city but it is treated unfairly. Its reputation in the world is that it's a city of gangsters. But the truth is, it is one of the most important centers of American culture."

"There are no gangs?"

"In the 1920s and 1930s the Mafia was quite active here, during the days of Al Capone. But now gangs in Chicago are similar to those in any other American city. On the contrary, Chicago is safer than New York, for instance. At least here the dangerous neighborhoods are well known, but in New York, the danger is all over the place; armed men might attack you anywhere in the city. Would you like a little tour?"

He didn't wait for my answer. He left the expressway and for half an hour he showed me around Sears Tower and Water Tower Place, and drove by the Museum of Contemporary Art, slowing down so that I could see the sculpture that Picasso gave as a gift to Chiago. And when he drove on Lake Shore Drive he pointed, saying, "This is Grant Park. Doesn't this spot remind you of the Corniche in Alexandria?"

"You still remember Egypt?"

He smiled and said, "Of course. And by the way, what's happening in Egypt these days? What I read in the newspapers worries me."

"On the contrary, recent events make one optimistic. The Egyptians have awakened and started demanding their rights. The corrupt regime is shaking hard and I believe its days are numbered."

"Don't you think the demonstrations and the strikes will lead the country to anarchy?"

"We cannot obtain freedom without paying a price."

"You think Egyptians are ready for democracy?"

"What do you mean?"

"I mean that half the Egyptians are illiterate. Wouldn't we do better concentrating on teaching them how to read and write?"

"Egypt has the oldest parliament in the East. Besides, illiteracy does not impede the practice of democracy, as witnessed by the success of democracy in India despite the high illiteracy rate. One doesn't need a university diploma to realize that the ruler is oppressive and corrupt. On the other hand, to eradicate illiteracy requires that we elect a fair and efficient political regime."

For the second time I felt that he was upset with what I said. He turned once again onto a highway and said, "You must be quite tired. You've got to rest. We will have time to take a tour of Chicago later on. We're now heading for the university, learn the route."

"I'll try. I'm not good with directions."

"It's impossible to get lost in Chicago because it is organized on regular north-south and east-west lines. It's enough to know the number of a building to reach it easily."

We took a tour of the university shopping center, and he helped me buy groceries. Then he said kindly, "If you like *ful medammis,* there are cans in the back row."

"Do Americans eat *ful* and *taamiya* like us?"

"Of course not, but a Palestinian immigrant produces them here in Chicago. Would you like to try?"

"While in Egypt, I've eaten enough *ful* to last me till Judgment Day."

When he laughs his face looks quite friendly and affectionate. We arrived at the student dormitory. It's a big building surrounded by a large garden. The black receptionist welcomed us, and it was clear that she and Dr. Salah were friends, for he inquired about her family. She typed my name and the information appeared on the monitor. "Apartment 407, fourth floor," she said as she handed me the key with a smile. I said good-bye to Dr. Salah and thanked him anew. I took my suitcase, went up to my apartment, closed the door behind me, and took off my clothes. It was warm, so I stayed in my underwear. As soon as I saw the bed I fell upon it and slept very soundly, waking up in the afternoon. The apartment has one bedroom, a bathroom, and a kitchen opening to a small living room big enough only for a table and two chairs. It's a small but clean place, and because of the patterned wallpaper, the lush carpeting, and the indirect lighting it has the look of handsome Western homes that we see in foreign movies. I took a hot bath, made myself some coffee, then stretched out on the bed and lit a cigarette. At that point something strange happened. I was overcome by vivid sexual fantasies and a violent and persistent desire that was almost painful. I feel embarrassed as I write this down, but I was so greatly aroused for no reason I could think of. Was it my feeling of freedom beginning my new life in America? Was it the clean air I breathed on the shore of Lake Michigan? Or could it be the quiet atmosphere in the apartment and the indirect lighting and the lazy day off? Could all that have reminded me of Friday mornings in the Giza apartment that has witnessed my adventures? I don't know. I tried to resist the desire and think of something else, but I couldn't, so I got off the bed, picked up the telephone, and asked the receptionist whether I could entertain a girlfriend in my apartment. She laughed and said in a merry tone, "Of course you can. This is a free country. But the regulations here do not permit your friend to spend the night with you. She has to leave before ten P.M."

The receptionist's words aroused me even more. I got up and fixed myself a tuna sandwich and opened the bottle of wine I had bought on the plane. I began to drink slowly and leaf through the huge telephone directory. I knew that prostitution was not legal in Chicago but I soon figured out that it existed under another name. I found in the telephone book ads for beautiful women expert in giving "special massage." I said to myself that that was exactly what I wanted. I stayed away from the large ads, which I figured would be exorbitant in price. I chose the smallest ad and dialed the number. I held the receiver to my ear and I heard my heartbeats, strong and fast from sheer excitement. I heard a woman's voice, soft and sleepy, as if she had just awakened.

"How can I help you?"

"I want a beautiful woman to massage me," I blurted out.

"That'll cost you two hundred fifty dollars an hour."

"That's too much. I am a student. I don't have a lot of money."

"What's your name?"

"Nagi. And you?"

"Donna. Where are you from?"

"Egypt."

She cried enthusiastically, "Egypt? I love Egypt. I dream of going one day to the Pyramids, riding a camel, and seeing the crocodiles in the Nile. Listen, Nagi, do you look like Anwar Sadat? He was very handsome."

"Actually I do; so much so that many people think I am his son. How did you know?"

"Just a guess. What are you doing in America?"

"I am studying at the University of Illinois. Listen, I'll invite you next winter to spend your vacation in Egypt. What do you say?"

"It's my life's dream."

"I promise you. But, my dear, I cannot pay two hundred fifty dollars for an hour of love."

She was silent for a moment then said in a soft voice, "I'll help you out, Nagi. Hang up now and call me again in five minutes."

Donna hung up suddenly and the dial tone buzzed in my ear. I was assailed by apprehensions: Why did she end the call in this manner? What's she afraid of? Are the police after her? Did they get my telephone number? Will they arrest me on the charge of getting in touch with a prostitution ring? What an inauspicious beginning for my lucky scholarship. I was gripped with anxiety and began to regret the adventure, but I couldn't go back. I rang up five minutes later. She told me, "Listen, I'll make you an offer outside the company. Instead of two-fifty, I'll come myself for only a hundred fifty an hour."

I hesitated a little as she said, laughing, "This is a special offer from Donna because you're a handsome Egyptian like Sadat. If I were you, I'd accept it at once."

"Will you make me happy?"

"I'll take you to paradise."

"Okay then."

I gave her the address and we agreed that she'd come at seven o'clock. Before she ended the call, she whispered in a frightened voice, "Your number has been recorded by the company. Someone will contact you to ask you why you didn't agree to have a woman come to you. Tell them you've changed your mind because you're tired and that you'll call again tomorrow. Please don't tell them what we've agreed to. I don't think you'd like me to get hurt."

And just as she said, a man called and asked me and I gave him the answer she told me to give. He didn't sound convinced of what I said, but he said good-bye and hung up. Once again I began to worry, but my raging desire, now doubled by the wine, made me forget all other things, to the extent that I ignored the fact that $150 would make a big dent in my budget. There was nothing on my mind except Donna, the beautiful woman I'd make love to. I wondered what she looked like: was she going to be a buxom white woman with full round hips and breasts, like Monica, Clinton's mistress, or one with a graceful Parisian figure and a dreamy, sparrowlike face like Julia Roberts? Even if she were just like Barbra Streisand, with a slightly long nose and an angular body, I'd be happy. I am not going to dwell on such minor shortcomings. Praise the Lord who created beauty in a hundred ways! I began to get ready for the date a whole hour early. I took another bath, during which I went to extra lengths to clean my body. Then I put a silk robe on my naked body like a lady-killer in Egyptian movies. I am now writing this while gulping down wine. There are only a few minutes before the date. I am sitting, waiting for my beloved Donna, on pins and needles. There, the bell is ringing. My beloved is punctual. How beautiful! I'll get up to open the door. Gentlemen, what bliss!

CHAPTER 5

As soon as the train stopped, its doors opened and out came the weekend passengers: young lovers embracing, beggars lugging musical instruments that they would soon play on the platforms, drunkards who have been barhopping since yesterday, European tourists carrying tourist guides and maps, young black men dancing to the music blaring from the huge boom boxes they carry, and traditional American families—a father, a mother, and their kids returning from a day in the park. In the corner of the station stood heavyset policemen in their distinctive uniform, with chests thrust forward bearing the badge CHICAGO POLICE, as though deriving their strength from it, with large trained dogs at their side, noses raised, sniffing for drugs. On some occasions, as soon as one of them barks at a passenger, the policemen rush him, immobilize him, and push him toward the wall, uncovering his chest, especially if black, to look for gang tattoos. Then they search him until they find the drugs and place him under arrest. In the midst of this purely American scene, Dr. Ahmad Danana looked totally out of place, as if he were a genie that had just come out of an enchanted bottle, or had disembarked from a time machine, or as if he were an actor who decided to go for a walk in costume. His features are rural Egyptian with a triangular prayer mark in the middle of his forehead, his kinky hair turning gray. He has a large head and very thick glasses, their bluish lenses reflecting his sly eyes in many intersecting circles

that often disorient his interlocutors. The prayer beads never leave his hand. Summer or winter he wears full suits that he gets from Mahalla, Egypt, together with cartons of super-size Cleopatra cigarettes to save some money. Danana walks the streets of Chicago in the same manner he took walks for exercise in the late afternoon on the rural road in the village of Shuhada in the Minufiya Governorate, his birthplace. He moves slowly, no matter how much in a hurry he is, looking around with a glance in which suspicion is mixed with arrogance, confidently moving his right foot forward followed by his left, straightening his back, causing his huge potbelly, resulting from his fondness for big rich suppers every night, to stick out.

That is how Ahmad Danana, president of the Egyptian Student Union in America, creates an aura of respectability around himself. The union was established during Gamal Abdel Nasser's time; several students became presidents and returned afterward to Egypt to hold important state posts. Danana is the only one who became president three years in a row by acclamation. In addition he enjoys several exceptional privileges: he has been preparing for a PhD in histology for the last seven years, even though the law regulating scholarships limits the maximum time to five years. He had gone around that rule by spending two whole years learning English, then another two years studying industrial security at Loyola before beginning the doctoral program at Illinois. And even though the law prohibited work for Egyptian students in the United States, he was able to get a part-time job for a hefty wage that he receives in dollars and transfers to a special account that no one knows anything about at the National Bank in Egypt. He was able, thanks to his connections and the support of the Egyptian embassy, to organize a concert for the popular Egyptian singer Amr Diab that realized for him a fat profit that he added to his savings, amassing a considerable sum of money that enabled him last year to marry the daughter of a rich merchant who owned a big bathroom fixture store in Ruwai'i, Cairo. All these privileges came on as a result of his close connections with different arms of the Egyptian state. The other students here treat him more like their boss at work than as a fellow student. His older age and his dignified demeanor make him more like a government director general than a student. Besides, he does have control over their affairs, beginning with the Egyptian newspapers and magazines that he distributes among them for free, including his extraordinary ability to help them overcome any obstacle that they confront, and finally his ability to punish and make examples of them. One report from him, confirmed by the Egyptian embassy at once, is enough to get Cairo to cancel the scholarship of the "offending" student.

Danana came out of the station to the street and entered a nearby building. He greeted the old black security guard sitting behind a glass partition, then took the elevator to the fourth floor and opened the door to the apartment. A musty smell resulting from the apartment's being closed all week long greeted his nose. The living room was small; it had a rectangular sofa and several leather chairs. On the wall was a large picture of the president of the Republic, under which the Throne Verse from the Qur'an in gilded letters was hung, then an Arabic poster whose letters were printed in a small blue font with the title written in the cursive *ruq'a* style: EGYPTIAN STUDENT UNION IN AMERICA: THE BYLAWS.

At the end of the corridor were two adjacent rooms, the smaller used by Danana as an office and the other as a meeting room with a rectangular table in the middle with chairs around it. The whole room and the furniture had that old wooden smell of university lecture halls and classrooms in Egyptian schools. Actually, even though the apartment was in Chicago, it had mysteriously acquired an Egyptian bureaucratic character that reminded one of the Mugamma building in Tahrir Square or the old court building in Bab al-Khalq. Danana sat at the head of the table, watching the students as they came into the meeting room. They greeted him with respect and took their places around the table while he took time, in a ponderously royal manner, before he returned their greetings in a hoarse voice and a tone somewhere between standoffish and welcoming, knitting his brow and assuming the pose of a high-ranking state official, busy with grave matters that couldn't be postponed or divulged. Danana looked at the students sitting around the table, then he struck the table with his hand, whereupon all the whispering ended and a profound silence fell. He broke that silence by clearing his throat, an act that usually preceded his speaking and usually ended with a fit of coughing as a result of his excessive smoking. He extended his hand and turned on the tape recorder in front of him. Then his hoarse voice reverberated clearly and strongly in the room: "In the name of God, the Merciful and Compassionate, and prayers and peace on the noblest of creation, our master, the Messenger of God, the one chosen by God, peace be upon him. I welcome you to the Egyptian Student Union in America, Chicago chapter. We are all present today with the exception of Shaymaa Muhammadi and Tariq Haseeb. Shaymaa had a big problem this morning."

The students looked at him inquisitively. He took a drag on his cigarette and said in obvious relish, "Sister Shaymaa was cooking and almost started a big fire had not God intervened, and our brother Tariq, may God recompense him well, is now standing behind her to console her."

He uttered that last part of the sentence in a tone full of insinuation, then laughed loudly. The others felt puzzled and awkward and fell silent.

That was one of Danana's various methods of exercising control over the students: to surprise them by finding out their innermost secrets then making sly comments that could have different interpretations. He extended his large head forward and clasped his arms on the table and said, "I have good news for you, news that will gladden you all, God willing. Yesterday the City of Chicago agreed to designate a four-story building in the fanciest part of town on Michigan Avenue as a mosque and Islamic center, God willing. His Excellency the ambassador has written to Egypt to send over an imam from al-Azhar. In two months at the most we will pray together, God permitting, in the new mosque."

There were murmurs of approval and appreciation and one student cried enthusiastically, "May God recompense you well, Doctor!"

Danana totally ignored him and went on. "Approving the establishment of a mosque in this place was almost impossible, but God Almighty willed us to be successful."

The same student shouted flatteringly, "Thank you, Dr. Danana, for this great effort you're exerting for us!"

Danana fixed him with a disapproving glance and said, feigning anger, "And who told you I am doing that for you? I only expect reward from God Almighty."

"Praise the Lord, sir!"

The other students felt they had to take part in the praise, and murmurs of thanks filled the room, but Danana ignored them and bowed his head in silence, like an actor bowing before his audience and wishing the applause would never stop. Then he said, "Another very important subject: some students are not attending their classes regularly. Yesterday I reviewed rates of absenteeism and found them to be too high. I am not going to mention them by name so as not to embarrass them. They know themselves."

He took a long drag on his cigarette then exhaled hard and said, "Forgive me, folks. I am not going to cover for anyone or intercede for anyone. I've overworked myself a lot for you. If you don't help yourselves, I cannot help you. Anyone exceeding acceptable absence rates I'll report to the educational bureau and they'd take it from there in accordance with the rules."

A tense silence prevailed and Danana kept scrutinizing the students with his fierce stare. Then he announced moving on to the agenda, which, as usual, was filled with various requests from the students: facilitating travel to Egypt, getting discounted tickets or getting free transit cards, and other issues. One student was complaining that his adviser was biased against him; another had exceeded the upper limit for the scholarship; a female student wanted to change her housing arrangement because her American roommate was receiving her lover in the apartment they shared. Danana would listen attentively to each problem, ask for clarification of some details, take a drag on his cigarette and look pensive, then announce the solution simply and confidently. Thereupon the student would look grateful and thank Danana, who would ignore him as if he were not there. He liked, at such moments, to have a rough joke at the student's expense or to insult him, this way tightening his psychological control over him, by saying for instance, "What matters is for you to study and pass, dummy."

Or by wondering sarcastically, "And what would I do with 'thank you'? Which bank can I cash it at? You're such a loser!"

The suddenly humiliated student, weakened by need and silenced by gratitude, would have no choice but to ignore the insult or laugh nervously or fall silent and turn his face away as if he had heard nothing.

"We finished all items on the agenda. Any new business?" Danana asked. No one spoke except a bearded student who said, "Dr. Danana, the Palestinian butcher from whom we bought halal meat has unfortunately closed his store and left Chicago. You know, sir, that meat in ordinary stores is not slaughtered in the Islamic way—"

Danana interrupted him with a gesture of his hand as if saying it wasn't a big deal, then turned around and pulled from the bookcase behind him a sheet of paper that he handed to him, saying, "Here, Ma'mun, is a list of the addresses of all halal butchers in Chicago."

Ma'mun's face lit up and he took the sheet, muttering, "May God recompense you well, sir!"

As usual Danana ignored the thanks and said, "Anything else?"

The students remained silent so Danana turned off the recorder and the meeting was adjourned. Nothing remained, according to the usual routine, except distributing the newspapers among the students. But Danana's cell phone rang suddenly, and as soon as he answered it, the expression on his face changed from ordinary welcome to intense interest. Then he ended the conversation and jumped to his feet, saying, as he gathered his things hastily, "I have to leave at once. A high-ranking official has arrived in Chicago and I've got to welcome him. Take the newspapers and don't forget to close the apartment door and turn off the lights."

CHAPTER

Dr. Muhammad Salah had not expected anyone to visit him at that hour. He had just finished having dinner with his wife, Chris, and together they had finished off a bottle of rosé wine. Then she sat next to him on the sofa; he patted her head affectionately and passed his fingers through her soft blond hair. She let out a soft moan that he understood, so he moved away a little and began to read some of the papers he was holding. She whispered wistfully, "You have work tonight?"

"I have to read this paper because I have to explain it to the students tomorrow."

She fell silent for a moment then sighed and got up, kissed him on the cheek, and whispered affectionately, "Good night."

He listened to her footsteps as they receded on the wooden staircase. When he heard the bedroom door close he put the paper in his briefcase and poured himself a drink. He had no desire to drink but he wanted to while away the time until Chris was fast asleep. Then he came to suddenly when the doorbell rang. At first he didn't believe it was actually ringing until he heard it ring again, clearly and emphatically this time. He got up reluctantly and looked at the wall clock: it was after eleven-thirty. He remembered that the intercom had not been working for a week and that he had asked Chris to get someone to repair it, but she had forgotten as usual. When he was only a few steps from the door, a disturbing idea occurred to him:

had the intercom been deliberately sabotaged? He remembered many similar details that he had read in the crime pages of the newspaper about groups of criminals watching houses and cutting off burglar alarm systems before attacking them. Usually it happened this way: a perfectly innocent-looking girl would knock on the door at a very late hour asking for help. As soon as the owner opened the door the home invaders would attack him. He did his best to dismiss the disquieting thought, but he couldn't. So he stopped in front of the little safe in the wall near the entrance and pushed the secret button. It opened and he took out the old Beretta handgun that he had bought when he first came to Chicago. He'd never used it but took care of it and kept it in good condition. He felt some trepidation when he listened to the click of the bullet chamber. He moved with agility toward the door, his right hand feeling the cold metal with his finger on the trigger. Now, with just one movement of his finger he could shoot the person behind the door if they had evil intentions. He approached with extreme caution and looked through the peephole and at once his hand, still clutching the gun, relaxed. He put the Beretta away and opened the door and shouted enthusiastically while grinning, "Hello, what a surprise!"

Ra'fat Thabit was standing in front of the door, slightly awkward with an apologetic smile on his face. "Sorry to disturb you, Salah. I tried calling but your telephone was turned off and I had to see you tonight."

"You're always disturbing, Ra'fat. So, what's new there?" he said, laughing as he pulled him by the hand. This was their way of joking with each other: sarcastic and somewhat cruel, as if the cruelty masked the affection they felt for each other, their thirty-year friendship as comrades-in-arms. They had been together through sorrows and joys and tempestuous times that had created a rare kind of understanding between them, so much so that one glance from Salah now at Ra'fat's face was sufficient to make him realize that his friend had a serious problem. His smile vanished and he asked him anxiously, "What happened?"

"Make me a drink."

"What would you like?"

"Scotch and soda with lots of ice."

Ra'fat began to drink and speak. He spoke fast and passionately, as if getting rid of a heavy burden. And when he finished, he kept his head bowed for a while. Then Salah asked in a serious and understanding voice, "Did Sarah actually leave?"

"She will, this weekend."

"What did her mother do?"

"I avoid talking with her as much as I can so we won't have to fight. But of course she supports Sarah."

Silence fell again and Ra'fat got up to fix himself another drink, his tired voice mixed with the clinking of the ice cubes. "Don't you find it strange, Salah? That you father a little girl and you grow attached to her and you love her more than any other person on the face of the earth and you do your utmost to provide her with a happy life. And as soon as your little girl grows up, she turns against you and leaves with her boyfriend at the earliest opportunity."

"This is natural."

"I don't find it natural at all."

"Sarah is an American girl, Ra'fat. Girls in America leave their family home to live independently with their boyfriends. You know that better than me. In this country you cannot control your children's personal lives."

"Even you say that? You are talking exactly like my wife. You both really irritate me. What can I do to convince you both that I accept the idea that my daughter has a boyfriend? Please believe, just once and forever, this fact: I am American. I have raised my daughter with American values. I have got rid of, for good, Eastern backwardness. I no longer make a connection between a person and their genitals."

"I didn't mean that."

"But that's what your words meant."

"I am sorry if I've upset you."

"You don't understand me, Salah. That's all. I don't interfere in Sarah's personal life, but I don't trust this creep with her, not for a single moment."

"If Jeff is a bad person, Sarah will discover that one day. She's entitled to have her own experiences, by herself."

"But she's become a different and unfathomable person. It seems to me sometimes that she's another girl, not the Sarah that I carried in my arms as a baby. I really don't understand her. Why is she treating me so cruelly? Why does any word I say provoke her? She will be very calm and nice and suddenly for no reason she'll have these outbursts of rage. Besides, her face is pale and she's in poor health."

"This is the nature of youth: changes in feelings, going from one mood to the opposite mood. Even her cruelty with you is natural. Do you remember how you treated your father when you were a young man? At that age our desire for independence from our parents makes us cruel toward them. Her rudeness toward you does not mean that she no longer loves you. She's just rebelling against the authority that you represent."

They talked for a whole hour in which they repeated what they said in different ways. Then Ra'fat got up and said, "I have to go."

"Do you have classes tomorrow?"

"No."

"Okay then, sleep well, friend, and in the morning you'll discover it's a simple problem."

Ra'fat left and Salah closed the door behind him then went up the stairs leading to the bedroom, trying not to make any noise, so as not to wake up Chris. He took off his silk robe and hung it on the clothes rack and sneaked quietly into bed next to her. There was a faint light from a small side lamp that Chris left on at night because she was afraid of the dark. He stared at the ceiling and saw the shadows as if they were ghosts prancing about. Suddenly he felt pity for Ra'fat. He understood him well. Ra'fat couldn't stand the idea that his daughter was in love with another man. He was in the grips of deathly jealousy toward Jeff. That was the truth. Dostoevsky has written in one of his novels that every father in the world harbored deep-seated hatred for his daughter's husband no matter how much he pretended otherwise. Ra'fat's problem, however, was much more complicated: he couldn't bear the idea of his daughter having a relationship outside marriage, for despite his harangues in defense of Western culture, he still had the mentality of the Eastern man which he attacked and mocked. Salah said to himself: Maybe I'm lucky I didn't have any children. To be barren is better than to be in Ra'fat's shoes right now. But Ra'fat's problem is inherent in his own personality. Many Egyptians have fathered children in America and were able to maintain a balance between the two cultures. But Ra'fat despises his culture and yet carries it within him at the same time, which complicates matters. "Poor Ra'fat," he whispered in English, then caught a glimpse of the alarm clock and was dismayed to find that it was one in the morning. He had only a few hours to sleep. He got under the covers, turned on his side, assumed a fetal position, covered his head with the pillow, closed his eyes, and started gradually to feel that comfortable darkness of sleep. But Chris, lying next to him, suddenly coughed and moved. There was something rigid about her movement that told him she was awake. He ignored her and tried to fall asleep, but she turned toward him and embraced him under the covers, and when she kissed him he could smell alcohol on her breath and whispered in alarm, "Have you had more to drink?"

She clung to him and began to embrace and kiss him, panting. He tried to speak, but she placed her hand gently on his lips, and her face in the soft light for the first time seemed to be burning. He felt her hand sneaking between his thighs as she whispered while bringing her lips close to his mouth, "I miss you."

 Tariq stood on the alert, staring at Shaymaa as if he were a goalkeeper expecting the ball to strike from any direction, ready to catch it or deflect it in an instant. He was waiting for any word from her to refute and to mock. But she did something he did not expect: her features suddenly contracted, then she started to sob like a lost child, her whole body shaking. He looked at her not knowing what to do, and then said in a voice that sounded strange to his ears, "Enough, Doctor. It all ended well, thank God."

"I am tired. I can't take it anymore. Tomorrow I'll withdraw from the scholarship and go back to Egypt."

"Don't be hasty."

"I've made up my mind. It's settled."

"Remember that you'd be getting a doctorate from Illinois. Think how hard you've worked for this scholarship and how many of your colleagues in Tanta wish to be in your place."

Shaymaa bowed her head, and it seemed to him that she'd calmed down a little, so he added, "Don't give in to bad thoughts."

"What should I do?"

"Get accustomed to your new life."

"I tried and I failed."

"Do you have any problems at school?"

"No, thank God."

"What's the problem then?"

She spoke in a soft voice, as if talking to herself, "I am completely alone here, Dr. Tariq. I have no friends or acquaintances. I don't know how to deal with the Americans. I don't understand them. All my life I had a perfect score in my English language classes, but here they speak another kind of English. They speak so fast and they swallow some of the letters so I don't understand what they say."

Tariq interrupted her, "You're feeling homesick, and being out of place here is quite natural. As for the language problem, we've all faced it at the beginning. I advise you to watch television a lot so you'll get used to the American accent."

"Even if my language improves, that won't change anything. I feel I am an outcast in this country. Americans shy away from me because I am Arab and because I am veiled. At the airport they interrogated me as if I were a criminal. At school the students make fun of me when they see me. Did you see how that policeman treated me?"

"That's not your problem alone. We all face unpleasant situations. The image of Muslims here suffered a lot after 9/11."

"What have *I* done wrong?"

"Put yourself in their place. Ordinary Americans know almost nothing about Islam. In their minds Islam is associated with terrorism and killing."

They both were silent for a moment, then she said, "Before coming to America, I complained about how difficult it was to live in Egypt. Now, my dream is to go back."

"We all feel homesick like you. I myself, even though I've spent two years here, miss Egypt a lot and I go through hard times, but I say to myself that the degree I'll get is worth all this hardship. I pray to God to give me patience. Do you perform your prayers regularly?"

"Yes, thank God," she whispered and bowed her head.

He found himself saying, "By the way, Chicago is a beautiful city. Have you been out and about?"

"I only know this campus."

"I am going out to do my shopping for the week. Why don't you come with me?"

Her eyes grew wider; it seemed she was surprised by the offer, and then she looked at her flannel gallabiya and stuck out her foot and jokingly asked him, "In my slippers?"

They both laughed for the first time. Then she asked him, as if she were reluctant, "Are we going to be late? I've a lot of studying to do."

"Me too. I have a long assignment in statistics. We'll be back soon."

He sat waiting for her in the lobby until she changed her clothes. She returned a short while later wearing a loose-fitting blue dress that he thought was elegant. He noticed that she had got over her dejection and seemed almost cheerful. They spent the evening together: they took the L downtown and he showed her the Sears Tower and Water Tower Place and she seemed as happy as a child standing next to him in the glass elevator at the famous Marshall Field's store. Then they went back to the mall and bought what they needed. Finally they took the university bus back to the dorm. They talked the whole time: she told him how she cherished the memory of her father and of her love for her mother and two sisters. She said that despite her missing them she called them only once a week because she had to be careful how she spent every dollar of the meager scholarship. She asked him about himself and he told her that his father was a police officer who was promoted to assistant director of Cairo Security before he died. He told her how his father raised him strictly and beat him hard when he misbehaved. Once, while in preparatory school, his father forced him to eat in the kitchen with the servants for a whole week because he had dared to announce at the table that he didn't like spinach. Tariq laughed as he remembered then added fondly, "My father, God have mercy on his soul, was a school unto himself. He meant this punishment to give me a lesson in manliness. From that day I've learned to eat whatever is placed before me without objection. You know, my father's strictness has done me a world of good. All my life I've excelled in school, and had it not been for nepotism, by now I would have been a great surgeon. Thank God anyway; I've done very well in school. Do you know how high my GPA is? It's three point nine nine out of four."

"Ma sha'Allah!"

"American students often seek me out to help them understand the lessons, which makes me feel proud because I am Egyptian and better than them."

Then he leaned back in his seat and looked in the distance, as if remembering, and went on. "Last year in biology class I had an American classmate named Smith, known throughout the university because he's a genius who has maintained excellence all his years as a student. Smith tried to challenge me academically but I taught him a lesson in manners."

"Really?"

"I floored him. I placed first three times. Now, when he sees me anywhere, he salutes me in deference."

He insisted on carrying her bags and accompanied her to her apartment on the seventh floor. He stood there, saying good-bye; her voice shook as she thanked him. "I don't know what to say, Dr. Tariq. May God recompense you well for what you've done for me."

"Can you call me Tariq, without titles?"

"On condition that you call me Shaymaa."

Her whispering voice almost made him tremble. As he shook her hand he thought how soft it was. He returned to his apartment and found the lights on, the statistics book open, the cup of tea where he had left it, and his pajamas lying on the bed. Everything was as he had left it, but he himself was no longer what he used to be; new feelings were raging inside him. He got so worked up that he took off his clothes and kept pacing the apartment up and down in his underwear, and then he threw himself on the bed and began to stare at the ceiling. What had happened seemed strange to him. Why had he acted that way with her? Where did he get the courage? For the first time in his life he had gone out with a girl. He felt that the person sitting next to her on the L was somebody else, not himself. And even now, he believed that his meeting her was a delusion, that if he looked for her now, he wouldn't find her. O God. Why was he attracted to her like that? She's just a country girl of mediocre beauty like dozens of girls he used to see every day in Cairo. What made her stand out? Did she arouse him sexually? True, she has two full, delicious lips, good for fantastic uses. Besides, her loose-fitting dress sometimes clung to her body, against her will, pronouncing two well-formed breasts, but she could not be compared at all to the American coeds at Illinois or the Egyptian brides-to-be whose hands he had sought in marriage. It was also impossible to mention her in the same breath as the naked beauties who stoked his desire in the porn movies. Why then did she appeal to him? Was it her fragility and vulnerability? Was it her crying that won his sympathy? Or did she make him nostalgic for Egypt? Yes, indeed. Everything about her was Egyptian: the flannel gallabiya with the little flowers, her beautiful snow-white neck and delicate ears with the rustic gold earrings in the shape of bunches of grapes, the *khadduga* slippers that revealed her small, clean feet with their well-trimmed nails left without nail polish (so her ablution would be complete), and that subtle clean smell emanating from her body as he sat next to her. What attracted him to her was something that he felt but couldn't describe, something purely Egyptian like *ful, taamiya, bisara,* the ringing laugh, belly dancing, Sheikh Muhammad Rifaat's voice in Ramadan, and his mother's supplications after dawn prayers. She represented all that he missed after two years away from home. He got lost in thought until the stroke of the living room clock sounded, whereupon he jumped out of bed and remembering his statistics assignment shouted, "What a disaster!" He sat at his desk, placed his head between his palms, concentrated to get out of his dreamy state, and gradually started working. He finished the first problem correctly then the second and the third. When he finished number five, he was entitled, according to his revered tradition, to eat a small piece of *basbusa.*

But, to his surprise and for the first time, he had no appetite for *bas-busa*. The point of the lesson had become quite clear to him, so he finished several other problems in about half an hour. It occurred to him to rest a little but he was afraid he might lose his enthusiasm, so he kept working until he heard the doorbell ring. He got up lazily, his mind still filled with numbers. He opened the door, and there she was in front of him. She was still in her street outfit and her face, in the soft blue light that lit the hallway, seemed more beautiful than ever before. Shyly she said as she extended her hand with a plate covered with aluminum foil, "You're undoubtedly hungry and won't have time to prepare dinner. I made you two sandwiches. Please, enjoy."

■ ■ ■ ■ ■ ■ ■ ■ ■ ■ ■

Not in a million years could I have imagined what happened. I opened the door, ecstatic from the wine and the desire, and I was awakened by the blow. As if I had been soaring among the clouds and I fell suddenly, my head hitting the hard ground. For a few moments I was in shock, unable to think. I saw before me an old woman, over forty, maybe over fifty, black, fat, and clearly cross-eyed in her left eye. She was wearing an old blue dress, worn out at the elbows and quite clearly showing the contours of her fat-laden body. She smiled, showing her crooked, tobacco-stained teeth. She asked merrily, "Are you Nagi?"

"Yes. What can I do for you?" I asked, hanging on to the last thread of hope that there was some mistake, that she was not the woman I was waiting for. But she gently pushed me aside and came in, deliberately jiggling her body to appear seductive.

"I thought your heart would recognize me. I'm Donna, darling. Oh, your apartment is really nice. Where's the bedroom?"

When she sat on the bed her face appeared in the light of the room more ugly than before. It occurred to me that I was dreaming, that it was all unreal. I said to myself that it might be useful to give myself an opportunity to think. I sat on the opposite chair and poured myself a new drink. She said as she looked closely at me, smiling, "You really are handsome but you don't look like Anwar Sadat. You lied to me on the telephone to seduce me, right?"

I swallowed the wine in silence then said, "Would you like some wine?"

"No, thank you. I only have wine with a meal. Do you have any whiskey?"

"No, unfortunately not."

"Okay then, do you have any food? I'm hungry."

"It's in the fridge."

I avoided looking at her. She got up, opened the fridge, then shouted in dismay, "Cheese, eggs, and vegetables? Is that all you have? This is rabbit food. I'd like a hot dinner. You're generous, my love, and you'll invite me to a fancy restaurant, right?"

I didn't say a word. I gulped down my drink, feeling a dejection that made my heart heavy, and poured myself another drink. I kept my head bowed and when I raised it I found that she had taken off her dress and stood in the middle of the room in her slip. Her black body with its many curves and folds appeared in the soft light as if it were a huge sea creature just captured from the ocean. She got so close to me I could feel her chest on my face. She was panting, a result of smoking, no doubt. She placed her hand on my thigh and whispered, "Come on, love. I'll take you to paradise."

She smelled of rotten sweat and cheap, loud perfume. I got up and away from her then gathered up my courage and said, "I am very sorry, Donna. Actually I am not feeling well."

She came close again and whispered, "I know how to make you feel better."

This time I blocked her with my hand to keep her away, saying, as I got bolder and more specific, "I am happy to have met you but actually I am tired and won't be able to . . . "

She looked at me, as if trying to understand, then got down on her knees and placed her hand between my thighs and said in a hissing voice, "How about a blow job? I'm really good at it. You'll like it a lot."

"No, thank you."

"Just as you like."

She got up slowly then said calmly as she looked for her dress, "But you'll pay my fee."

"What?"

"Listen, I am not here to play games with you. We agreed on a hundred fifty dollars that you'll pay, so long as I've come to you, whether you slept with me or not."

"But I—"

"You'll pay me a hundred fifty dollars!" she shouted angrily and began to stare at me with her good eye while her astigmatic eye gave a different impression.

"I won't pay," I said firmly.

"You will."

"I won't pay a single dollar," I shouted, feeling very exasperated. She seemed to have suddenly gone mad. She grabbed the sleeve of my robe and began to shake me hard. "You have to learn how to treat women in America; do you understand what I am saying, darling? Women here are respectable citizens, and not creatures without dignity as you treat them in the desert you came from."

"I respect women but I don't respect whores."

She stared at me for a moment then suddenly tried to slap me on the face. I backed up my head quickly and her hand missed but hit my right ear. I felt dizzy and felt a knot in my stomach and lost control because of the assault, the wine, and the disappointment. So I pushed her shoulder hard, shouting, "Get out!"

She retreated before me and I pushed her even harder. She staggered then lost her balance and fell to the floor.

"Get out now. I am going to call the police to come and get you, whore."

She remained seated in the same position: her legs parted in front of her, her hands lying on the floor, and her head tilted back, as if she were watching something on the ceiling. I began to call her names. I used all the English insults that I knew. She glanced at me resentfully then extended her hand toward me, pointing her finger, as if threatening me. She opened her mouth to say something and suddenly her face convulsed and she broke into tears. I was overcome with a feeling of sorrow that soon turned into regret, so I said in a soft voice, "Donna, I'm sorry. Actually, I'm quite drunk."

She remained silent and I thought she hadn't heard me. Then her voice came hoarsely while her head was still bowed. "You don't know how much I need the money. I'm raising three kids doing this job."

"I'm sorry."

"Their father ran away with a woman twenty years younger and left them to me. I don't have any legal rights because we weren't married. And even if I had any rights, I couldn't get them because I don't know where he is. I can't give the children up. They've done nothing wrong in this drama. I have to pay for everything all on my own: school expenses and food and clothing and the gas and electric bills. I don't like to be a whore but I couldn't find another job. I tried hard but I couldn't."

While she was talking I got up from where I was sitting. I knelt on my knees beside her then got closer and kissed her on the forehead. "Forgive me, Donna."

"It's okay."

"Have you really forgiven me?"

She raised her head slowly toward me and smiled sadly. "I've forgiven you."

We remained silent, totally exhausted, as if we were two boxers who had just finished a grueling match. She looked at me and said tenderly, "Can you pay me half?

I didn't answer. She placed her hand on my shoulder and whispered, "Pay me half the amount, please. I really need the money. The evening is gone and I won't find another customer."

I still didn't answer, so she whispered in a last attempt, "Consider it a loan to a friend. I'll return it when I can."

I went to the closet and came back with a hundred-dollar bill. Donna took it quickly, embraced me, and kissed me on the cheek, saying, "Thank you, Nagi. You really are generous."

After a short while she had put on her clothes and asked me as she regained her gaiety, "I'm going. Do you want anything?"

"No, thank you."

She headed for the door of the apartment, opened it, then turned around, as if she had remembered something and said in an affected, optimistic, enticing tone like that used by publicists, "If you want twenty-year-old women, you can call me. They're really gorgeous, blondes and brunettes, whatever you like. I'll give you the same rate and I'll consider the hundred dollars part of the payment. I have to be generous with you like you were with me."

I observed her in silence until she went out and closed the door.

 When Dr. Ahmad Danana asked for the hand of Miss Marwa Nofal in marriage, he seemed like an excellent prospective bridegroom in all respects. He was pious, as evidenced by the prayer mark on his forehead and the prayer beads in his hand, his constant quoting of the Qur'an and hadith, and his taking pains to perform his prayers at their appointed times no matter what the circumstances. He was ready for marriage: he owned a deluxe two-hundred-square-meter duplex condominium overlooking Faisal Street in the Pyramids area. He had announced that he was ready to pay the requisite dowry and buy the engagement gift selected by the bride (within reason). More important, he was an instructor in the College of Medicine who was studying in America and would get a PhD and come back to Egypt to assume the highest posts. And just as the breeze swayed tree branches, Hagg Nofal (merchant of bathroom fixtures in Ruwai'i) was swayed by the wish that his son-in-law would one day become a minister or even a prime minister. And why not? Dr. Danana was a prominent member of the Youth Secretariat of the ruling party and had important connections. During his vacation in Cairo he met daily with high-ranking officials of the state. What could detract from him as a bridegroom? His being slightly older? That would be an asset and not a liability. A mature man would pamper Marwa and protect her better than a rash young man who might mistreat her. Hagg Nofal was enthusiastic about accepting Danana's proposal, although he calculated (in his merchant's mind) how much the marriage would cost him and came to the conclusion that it would cost him several times what it would cost the bridegroom. But he said to himself that God had given him an immense fortune, so he should spend according to his ability. Besides, no amount of money was too much for his eldest daughter.

As for Marwa herself, she had spent several years after graduating from the English section of business school refusing traditional arranged marriages and making fun of them. She knew she was beautiful and that her beauty was of the kind that aroused men's lust. Ever since she was a teenager she had almost never met a man who did not lust for her soft jet-black hair cascading down her shoulders, her splendid black eyes, her delicious full lips, and her beautiful build: the ample bosom, the narrow waist, then the wide hips resting on beautiful legs, even her little feet with their symmetrical toes and painted nails, which were more like a well-wrought art masterpiece than living body parts. For years Marwa was immersed in her dreams, seeing herself as her highness the princess waiting for her handsome knight to carry her off on his white steed. She turned down many suitors, notables and rich men, because she didn't feel truly attracted to any of them. Then suddenly she discovered that she was over twenty-nine and had yet to find her grand amour. She realized that she had to reconsider matters and take a more practical approach. Her mother told her repeatedly that the love that came after marriage was more solid and steeped in respect than those fickle hot feelings that might disappear suddenly or end in disaster.

Then Marwa read stories to the same effect in answers to readers' problems published in the Friday edition of *Al-Ahram* in the Letters to the Editor section, and she realized that her mother's words spoke to facts of life. Thus she had to give up on her dream of a grand love because she came to believe she could not find it in her lifetime. Life in reality was, after all, different from life in the movies. So maybe she should marry like everybody else. In the end she should have a home, a family, and children. Besides, she was not getting any younger: in a few months she'd be thirty. What mattered more than anything else was for her to get married now; love would come later. She felt nothing against Ahmad Danana but also nothing for him. She had neutral feelings toward him, but rationally, she thought that he would not make a bad husband. If only she could forget his crude features, the wrinkles on his brow, his kinky hair, and his protuberant potbelly, despite the vest that he always wore to appear more slender. If only she were able to dismiss those negatives, she would be able, somehow, to live a love story with him. Was he not kind and gentle with her? Did a single special occasion pass without his giving her a precious gift? Did he not take her to the most expensive restaurants in Cairo? Did he not spend money on her as if there were no tomorrow, so much so that she worried about those exorbitant bills that he gladly paid? How could she forget that wonderful night when they had that two-hour candlelit dinner, with violins playing, on board that giant ship *Atlas* as it made its way up and down the Nile, and how that felt like a beautiful dream? He loved her and spoiled her and was doing his utmost to make her happy. What more could she want? True, sometimes she had bouts of dejection that made her want to shun him, but that was rare. Her mother convinced her that that was the result of an evil eye and convinced her to read the Qur'an a lot, especially at night.

The engagement day passed as well as could be expected. The Grand Sheikh of al-Azhar personally performed the wedding ceremony at the mosque of Sayyidna Hussein (may God be pleased with him). The wedding party was held at the Meridian Hotel and cost Hagg Nofal a quarter of a million Egyptian pounds. Singing sensations Ihab Tawfiq and Hisham Abbas, and Dina, the famous dancer, performed at the fantastic celebration, which was attended, as the newspaper accounts put it, "by an assemblage of society stars and state officials." There were serious religious objections to the presence of an almost naked dancer at a wedding in a family known for its profound religiosity, but Hagg

Nofal confronted the objections with a few decisive words. "Marwa is my eldest daughter and my first joy. A wedding without a dancer would be flavorless and God Almighty knows true intentions and He is forgiving and merciful."

Hagg Nofal had insisted on the dancer Dina (notorious for her revealing outfits and lewdly suggestive moves), then he encouraged her with clapping and loud exclamations while she danced, and had a smiling, whispering conversation with her at the end of the wedding—a conversation that went on so long that his wife, Hagga Insaf, appeared visibly agitated. All of that brought back secretly told stories about Hagg Nofal's hedonistic lifestyle and his pursuit of dancers as a youth before his repentance and going back to the straight and narrow.

At Hagg Nofal's expense the newlyweds went to Turkey on their honeymoon, and from there they flew to Chicago, where Danana rented a new big off-campus apartment. Marwa started her new life enthusiastically and sincerely, hoping wholeheartedly to make her husband happy, to organize his life and support him until he made it to the top. But the sunny picture, from early on, had a few dark spots, and now, after a full year of marriage, Marwa was all alone at home, events running in her mind like a movie that she kept playing time after time, blaming herself harshly for missing signs in her husband's behaviors from the beginning or perhaps noticing but ignoring them to preserve a rosy, unreal outlook. The dreams came crashing down, smashed against the rocks of reality, breaking into smithereens like pieces of glass.

The problems began with the suit incident. Danana had worn a very fancy and handsome white Versace suit for the wedding. Afterward, while organizing her husband's clothes in the closet, Marwa couldn't find the suit. She was extremely alarmed and it occurred to her that it had been stolen or lost on the plane. When he returned from school she asked him, but he remained silent, fixing her with a sly and hesitant glance, then said as if in jest, "The suit is American aid."

She asked him to elaborate, so he said, feigning holding back laughter to hide his embarrassment, "In America you have the right to return any merchandise that you bought, if you also return the receipt, within a month of the purchase."

"I still don't understand. What happened to the wedding suit?"

"Nothing. I thought, I am only going to wear it one night in my life, even though it is prohibitively expensive. So I kept the receipt, returned it, and got my money back."

"Isn't that some kind of fraud? To buy the suit, wear it for your wedding, then return it to the store?"

"Apparel companies in America are colossal and their budgets are in the millions; they would not be affected by the price of a suit. Besides, we are not in a Muslim country. I've consulted several trusted religious scholars and they assured me that according to the canon law, America is considered an abode of infidels and not an abode of Islam. There is also a well-known principle in jurisprudence that says 'necessity makes the forbidden permissible.' Therefore, my need of the price of the suit permits me to return it to the store according to the shari'a."

Marwa thought his line of thinking preposterous and almost asked him, Who told you that Islam commands us to steal from non-Muslims? But she also tried to find an excuse for him. She said to herself, I have to remember that he's not as rich as my father and he does need the price of the suit. That incident passed and she would have forgotten it had not a series of unfortunate events taken place.

Danana began to complain that the scholarship stipend was too low to cover their living expenses. He repeated his complaint several times, but Marwa ignored it (perhaps in response to a mysterious internal warning). But it didn't take Danana long to move from innuendo to a more explicit question. He asked her directly, "Can I borrow from your father a sum of money every month and pay him back when we return to Egypt?"

She looked at him in silence and he continued, laughing insolently, "I can write him an IOU, if he wants me to, so he can be reassured about his money."

Marwa felt shocked and she began to see more clearly what her husband was really like. In spite of that, she called her father and asked him for financial help. Why? Perhaps she was hanging on to a last, flimsy thread to save herself from disappointment. She tried to convince herself that he was going through hard times because he was studying in a foreign country, that it was natural for him to be in financial straits, and that asking her father for help should not be held against him. She was surprised that her father accepted the request calmly, as if he had expected it, and began to send her a thousand dollars on the first of every month, which Danana then took from her without any compunction, even expressing impatience if it was late. Money in itself was not what worried Marwa. She was willing to contribute to the household expenses even more than that because it had been instilled in her while growing up that the model of a good wife was one who stood by her husband to the best of her ability and resources. By sheer coincidence, however, she found in Danana's pocket a bank transfer indicating that he was paid a large sum of money in addition to the amount of the stipend. At that point she could not control herself. She asked him as anger gathered on her face like clouds on an overcast day, "Why did you hide from me your extra salary? And why do you make us ask my father for help when we don't need it?"

Danana was taken aback for a little while, and then he regained his brazenness. "I didn't tell you about the extra salary because no occasion had arisen. Besides, as a wife you are not entitled, by religion, to know your husband's salary. I can provide proof of that from jurisprudence. As for the small sum that your father helps us with, I think it is quite natural because God has given him a lot of money whereas we are beginning our own life and we must save. Saving is a great virtue to which we are enjoined by the noblest of creation, the chosen one, prayers and peace be upon him."

Marwa was naturally not convinced this time. His miserliness revealed itself as clearly as the sun on a hot cloudless day. She began to notice how his face grew ashen if he had to pay anything whatsoever, and he displayed utmost care, to the point of panic, when he counted his money and put it very slowly in his wallet, which he then interred in his inside pocket, as if it were its final resting place. Little by little she was beset by disquieting apprehensions; she was very far from her family, separated from them by the Atlantic Ocean and several thousand miles. She was lonely and a complete stranger in Chicago. No one knew her and no one cared about her. Her poor English made it impossible for her to communicate with people on the street. In this place away from home, she had no one but Danana. Could she really rely on him? What would happen if she were to fall ill or be injured in an accident? This person that she had married would not take care of her at all but would throw her into the street if she were going to cost him ten dollars. That was the truth. He was a selfish miser who thought only of himself. Perhaps now, better than at any other time, she understood why he had chosen to marry her. He had already begun to nibble at her wealth and undoubtedly had plans, after her father's death, to seize her inheritance; perhaps even now he was calculating precisely how much that would be.

The problem, however, was not confined to his miserliness and selfishness. There was another loathsome feeling that was weighing heavily on her and getting worse every day, a very private and embarrassing matter that Marwa could not confide even to those closest to her. She even blamed herself for merely thinking about it, and yet it was painful to her and caused her great discomfort. To put it bluntly, she hated the way her husband had intercourse with her. He would come at her in a strange manner, attacking her without any preliminaries. She would be sitting, watching television in the bedroom or coming out of the bathroom, when he would pounce on her, falling on her suddenly with his erection just as adolescents do with housemaids. His crude ways caused her panic and anxiety in addition to feelings of humiliation. It also led to painful lacerations in her body. One night she hinted to him what she was suffering, avoiding looking at his face for sheer shame. But he laughed sarcastically and said, somewhat boastfully, "Try and get used to that, because my nature is strong and violent. That's how all men are in our family. My maternal uncle in the village got married and had children after the age of eighty."

She felt frustrated because he didn't understand her and she couldn't make this any clearer to him. She wished she could ask him to read the eloquent Qur'anic expression enjoining Muslim husbands to approach their wives gently and gradually so he would understand what she wanted to say but was too shy to say it. She was surprised later to find that he was using an ointment with a pungent smell and she rejected him, pushing him away from her and jumping out of bed, now doubly angry at him. She began to avoid being with him, using all kinds of pretexts, until he attacked her one night. She repelled him hard and jumped away. He shouted angrily, panting with desire and from the effort, "Fear God, Marwa. I'm warning you; God's punishment will be severe. What you are doing is forbidden in the canon law with the consensus of religious scholars. The Messenger of God, peace and prayer be upon him, has been quoted correctly saying that the woman who refuses her husband in bed shall spend the night cursed by the angels."

He was stretched out on the bed in front of her as she stood in her nightclothes. She got very angry and fixed him with a hateful and contemptuous glance. She almost replied that Islam would never force a woman to be intimate with a man as disgusting as he was; that the Prophet, peace be upon him, ordered a woman to be divorced from her husband just because she wasn't pleased with him. Marwa became so incensed that, for the first time, she thought of divorce. Let him divorce her and let her go back to Egypt. A divorce is a much more merciful fate than being violated every night in this disgusting manner. "Divorce me, now." She became so obsessed with the sentence that she saw it written in her mind. But for one reason or another (she tried to figure that out later but was never able to), as soon as she was about to reply, as soon as she opened her lips to utter the fateful sentence, mysterious and contradictory feelings came over her, forcing her to be silent. Then she found herself approaching him slowly, as if hypnotized, and began to take off her clothes, coldly and neutrally, one piece at a time, until she stood in front of him totally naked. When he attacked her she did not resist.

That night a new phase started between them. She started to yield her body to him with the utmost coldness; she would close her eyes and patiently suffer his heavy breaths and the disgusting stickiness of his body. The moments passed, heavy and painful, during which she fought off nausea until he was done and lay down on his back, panting and proud, as if he had won a military battle. She would then rush to the bathroom to throw up and cry from defeat, impotence, and pain. Afterward she felt aches all over her body, as if she had been given a sound beating. Her face changed after every such encounter, turning gloomy, flushed, and swollen.

Despite Marwa's defeat in the sex battle, she persisted in rejecting the idea of having children. He kept after her insistently to have a child in America. He tried to convince her by every means he could muster; he would say to her, "You silly girl."

"Please don't speak to me like that."

She would turn her face and he would get close to her, feigning affection, whispering in a hissing voice, "Listen to me, my love. If we have a child now, he would be a citizen and we will automatically get citizenship later on. People pay tens of thousands of dollars for an American passport and you are turning your back on this bounty?"

"Don't you get tired of saying that? I don't want to have a baby now and I cannot have one just to obtain an American passport."

THAT NIGHT MARWA WAS RELAXING on the sofa in the living room, watching a soap opera on the Egyptian satellite channel, when she heard the doorbell ringing. Because she was not expecting anyone,

she got up reluctantly, somewhat worried, remembering all the warnings she had often heard about opening the door to strangers in Chicago. She looked through the peephole and saw Safwat Shakir standing
there, smiling. It didn't take him long to say loudly, "Is Dr. Danana
home?"

"No, he is not."

"Sorry, madam. I came from Washington especially to meet him.
My telephone, unfortunately, is not working. Can I come in and wait
for him?"

She didn't answer, so he went on persistently, "I want him for an
important matter that cannot wait."

She knew Safwat Shakir; she had seen him more than once at consulate receptions and had never trusted him. He always seemed to
her to be arrogant and suspicious. But she knew that her husband respected him. She had no choice, so she opened the door and let him in.
He was well dressed as usual and wore an expensive cologne. He shook
her hand and sat in the nearest chair in the entryway. She sat in front
of him, leaving the apartment door open. She telephoned Danana and
told him and he assured her he would come right away. She had to
show her guest some hospitality, so she made him a cup of tea and
diplomatically but firmly stopped his repeated attempts to start a conversation with her. As soon as Danana arrived, she withdrew to her
room. Danana did not pay any mind to her but gave his distinguished
guest his undivided attention. He rushed to welcome him, panting
(perhaps exaggerating to some extent to prove that he had run all the
way there). He said with a flattering smile, "Welcome, sir. You've lit up
Chicago."

"I'm sorry I came without an appointment."

"Your Excellency, please, you honor us any time you please."

"Please apologize to the lady for the inconvenience."

"On the contrary, sir. Marwa is happy you are here because she
knows how much respect I have for you."

Safwat sat back in his chair and said, "What I came here for is extremely important."

"May it all be to the good, God willing."

"First I have some questions."

"At your service, sir."

"Do you have any Egyptian Copts in the department?"

"There are no Copts in the histology department. They are in internal medicine, surgery, and physiology. The Medical Center at the University of Illinois in Chicago has only seven Copts, all of whom I know."

Safwat took out of his jacket pocket a folded piece of paper that he slowly opened and handed over to Danana, who took it, read it with interest, then looked angry and said, "Obscene lies!"

"This is one of numerous broadsides that have been distributed last week. Keep it and read it when you have the time. The Copts in Exile are getting more and more active to a worrying degree. They attack Egypt and our revered president with insolence. Unfortunately the American administration listens to them."

"They're all traitors, agents on Israel's payroll."

Safwat Shakir bowed his head for a moment then spoke in a serious tone. "Israel has ties with only one organization. The rest of the Coptic organizations work on their own and raise their own money. They attack the regime to win gains for the Copts in Egypt."

"That's impossible, sir. Egypt does not give in to blackmail. Besides, seeking support from abroad is treason."

Danana recited this quickly, as if it were a lesson he had memorized. Safwat nodded then asked in a serious tone of voice, "What do you know about Karam Doss?"

"He is a heart surgeon, a millionaire who lives in a posh mansion in Oak Park and is one of the leaders of Copts in Exile."

"Write me a detailed report about him."

"At your service."

"I want comprehensive data and a situation assessment."

"By all means."

"As for that boy, Nagi Abd al-Samad, State Security has sent me a complete copy of his dossier. Watch out, he's a troublemaker."

Danana laughed loudly in a derisive tone and said, "That Nagi boy is up to no good. I know him from Egypt and I have prepared for him a program that you'd like, sir."

Silence fell for a few moments, then Safwat sighed and said, "Now to the more important subject."

Danana lit a cigarette and looked through his glasses in utmost attention to Safwat, who continued in a soft voice, "The president, God willing, is coming on a visit to America in two months. It's a very important visit and comes under extremely sensitive circumstances and requires good preparation from us. Time is short, and any mistake on our part would result in a catastrophe."

"Did Your Excellency find out his itinerary?"

"The itinerary is never revealed until the last moment and it is usually changed suddenly for security reasons. But I have found out, in my own way, that the president will visit Washington and New York and come to Chicago. Of course he will meet with his sons and daughters, the Egyptian students here."

"Meeting with our revered president is a national festive occasion for all Egyptian students here."

"You're intelligent, Danana, and you understand that any visit by the revered president could change our lives. After the visit I could leave here to become a minister or be pensioned off."

"To the ministry, sir, God willing. But please don't forget me."

Safwat Shakir laughed and he seemed to be in a good mood. He got up to leave but Danana insisted that he stay for dinner. Almost begging him, he said, "Safwat Bey, please, don't deprive me of this honor, have dinner with us."

"I have an important appointment at the consulate."

"Please, sir, have a quick bite then go in God's peace, to your appointment."

Danana rushed inside, and in about a quarter of an hour Marwa emerged carrying the plates. Safwat received her with a smile and a scrutinizing look.

"Once again, I apologize for disturbing you, madam."

Marwa muttered a few words, as if denying that she had been disturbed, but her face did not reflect that sentiment, which made Danana stare at her more than once to warn her. When he gave up on her face turning toward him, he started on another interlude welcoming Safwat. Marwa turned around to leave and Safwat asked her boldly, "Aren't you going to eat with us?"

"I had dinner a short while ago. Please go ahead, Your Excellency, and enjoy in good health," Marwa answered right away, as if expecting the question. Danana sat at the table opposite Safwat, who opened his briefcase and took out a miniature bottle of scotch. "Would you get me some ice?"

In a few moments Danana brought ice cubes and a large empty glass. Safwat said apologetically as he poured the whiskey, "I acquired this habit living in the West for many years: to have a drink with my meals."

"You, sir, exert a superhuman effort in your work and you are entitled to some recreation."

Safwat answered him with a dignified smile as he sipped his drink. He ate heartily then got up to leave. Danana saw him off to the door, and they had a short, serious conversation about what should be done in the following days. Danana stood bidding his master good-bye with his eyes until he disappeared inside the elevator. Danana sighed and closed the door behind him. And, just as a main character's face changes from good to evil in science fiction movies, Danana's features changed gradually as he crossed the corridor. When he reached the bedroom, his face expressed extreme wrath. He opened the door forcefully and found his wife lying down on the bed. He shouted in a thunderous voice, "Your behavior with the man was in extreme poor taste."

"It's he who doesn't know how to behave properly. How can he come into your house when you are not there?" Marwa responded calmly.

"He wanted me for an important matter."

"He could've left a message."

"It's much more important than that."

"I don't trust him."

"Do you know who Safwat Shakir is?"

"It doesn't matter who he is."

"Safwat Shakir is the intelligence officer in the Egyptian embassy and the most important official there, more important than the ambassador himself. One report from him can raise me sky-high or ruin my future."

Marwa looked at him for a long time, as if seeing him for the first time. "No matter what his post is, he has no right to enter your house when you are not there. Besides, I refuse to turn my house into a tavern."

"I won't allow you to ruin my future. I warn you. If he comes here again and you behave improperly toward him, it will be the end between us."

"How I wish for this end and await it impatiently!" she said, looking at his face, itching for a confrontation.

He shouted at her, "That's my mistake, marrying into an ignorant family."

"I won't allow you to insult my family."

"That's not an insult, it's a fact."

"Don't you dare— "

"Your father, Hagg Nofal: is he educated or ignorant?"

"My father's circumstances did not enable him to get an education, but he did his best and raised us and gave us the best education."

"But he's still ignorant."

"My ignorant father, whom you don't like, is the one spending his money on your house."

Danana raised his hand and slapped her so hard she staggered back. She pounced on him and grabbed his shirt screaming, "You hit me? I won't live with you another single day. Divorce me now, at once."

CHAPTER 9

 Thirty years later he still remembers that night vividly.

He had to abandon his shift at Qasr al-Ayni to go to her. Security forces were cordoning off the Cairo University campus completely, preventing entry or exit. Between University Bridge and the front gate several security checkpoints stopped him. They asked him the same questions and he gave them the same answers. At the last checkpoint there was a colonel who seemed to be the commander in charge. He looked tired and nervous and was smoking voraciously. He exhaled a thick cloud of his cigarette and said after inspecting his doctor's identity card, "What do you want, Doctor?"

"I have a relative in the sit-in. I've come to return her to her family."

"Her name?"

"Zeinab Radwan, College of Economics."

The officer fixed him with an experienced glance and, as if he'd reassured himself that he was telling the truth, said, "I advise you to take her with you as soon as possible. We've given them an ultimatum to end the sit-in, but they seem bent on disobedience. Any moment now we are going to receive instructions to use force. When we do we will beat them without mercy and arrest them all."

"Please, sir, keep in mind that they are young and angry for their country."

"We also are patriotic Egyptians, but we don't demonstrate and wreak havoc."

"I hope Your Excellency would treat them as a father."

"Not father nor mother. I am carrying out orders!" the officer shouted loudly as if resisting an internal sympathy. Then he moved back two steps and gave a signal whereupon the troops moved aside, letting him through. The campus was dark and the January cold was boring into his bones. He buttoned his overcoat tightly and put his hands in his pockets. Posters and wall newspapers covered the buildings. He couldn't make out what was written on them in the dark, with the exception of a large picture of Sadat smoking a waterpipe. He saw hundreds of students sitting on the grass and on the steps. Many were asleep, some were smoking and talking, and some were singing Sheikh Imam songs. He looked for her for a while until he found her. She was standing in front of the large Assembly Hall arguing enthusiastically with several other students. He got close and called out to her. She went toward him and said in that warm way of hers that he couldn't forget, "Hello."

He answered tersely, "You look tired."

"I am fine."

"I'd like you to come with me."

"Where to?"

"To your house and your family."

"You came to take me by the hand to Mama's bosom? You want me to wash my feet and drink my milk so that she will put me in bed, cover me, and tell me a bedtime story?"

He realized from her sarcasm that his task was not going to be easy. He looked at her reproachfully and said in a firm tone of voice, "I am not going to let you hurt yourself."

"That's my business."

"What exactly do you want?"

"I and my colleagues have specific demands, and we will not end the sit-in until they are met."

"You think you'll change the universe?"

"We'll change Egypt."

"Egypt will not be changed by a demonstration."

"We are speaking for all Egyptians."

"Stop these illusions. People outside the university don't know anything about you. Please, Zeinab, come with me. The officer said they will arrest you."

"Let them do what they want."

"Would you like the soldiers to beat you and drag you on the ground?"

"I am not leaving my colleagues, no matter what."

"I am afraid for you," he whispered anxiously. She fixed him with a derisive glance and then turned around, going back to her colleagues. She started talking with them again and ignored him. For a while he stood where he was, looking at her. Then he left angrily and told himself that she was crazy and would never be good for him, and that if he married her their home would turn into a battlefield. He thought that she was conceited and obstinate; she had treated him insolently and scornfully. He had warned her, but she persisted in her foolishness. Let the soldiers beat her or drag her on the ground, let them violate her. From now on he would not feel any sympathy for her. It was she who chose her fate. He went to bed exhausted, but he couldn't sleep. He kept tossing and turning until he heard the call to the dawn prayers. He got up and bathed, put on his clothes, and went back to the university. He found out that the soldiers had stormed it and arrested the students. He made strenuous efforts to contact his acquaintances until he was able, finally, to visit her at the security directorate in the afternoon. She was quite pale, her lower lip swollen, and there were blue bruises around her left brow and on her forehead. He extended his hand and touched her face, saying sadly, "Does it hurt?"

"The whole of Egypt is wounded," she replied.

After all this time he still remembered Zeinab Radwan. In fact, he had never stopped thinking about her for a single day. The old pictures were appearing in his mind with amazing clarity. The floodgates of memory opened, came over and swept him away, as if the past were a gigantic genie let out of the bottle. There she was, standing before him, with her petite figure, her beautiful face, and her long black hair that she gathered in a ponytail. Her eyes were gleaming with enthusiasm as she talked to him in that dreamy voice of hers, as if she were reciting a love poem, "Our country is great, Salah, but it has been oppressed for a long time. Our people have tremendous abilities. If we have democracy, Egypt will become a strong, advanced country in less than ten years."

He would listen to her, hiding his indifference with a neutral smile. How she tried to win him over to her side! But he was in a different world. For his birthday she gave him Abd al-Rahman al-Jabarti's complete history book, saying, "Happy birthday. Read this book to understand me better."

He read a few pages then got bored. So he lied and told her he'd finished it. He didn't like to lie and rarely did, but he didn't want her to get angry with him. He wanted to keep her at her best and most beautiful. When she was in a good mood her smile shone and her face lit up. During their splendid moments of harmony they would sit next to each other in the Orman Garden. She would put her books aside on the round white marble bench. They would sit there oblivious to the passing of hours, talking and dreaming of the future, whispering. As he got closer to her he would smell her perfume, which he was now recalling vividly. He would hold her hand and bend and steal a kiss on her cheek and she would fix him with a glance of reproach and tenderness. But the dreams would soon come to an end. He would recall that final scene a thousand times, pausing and dwelling on every word, every glance, and every moment of silence. They were at their favorite spot in the garden when he told her of his decision to emigrate. He tried to be calm, to have a logical discussion, but she told him right away, "You are running away."

"I am saving myself."

"You are talking about yourself alone."

"I came to invite you to our new life."

"I'll never leave my country."

"Stop these slogans, please."

"They are not slogans, but a sense of duty. And you wouldn't understand."

"Zeinab."

"You've received an education at the expense of the poor Egyptian people and now you are a doctor. There were a thousand young Egyptians who would've loved to take your place in the College of Medicine. Now you want to leave Egypt and go to America, which does not need you; America that has caused all of our catastrophes. What would you call someone who lets his country down at its dire moment of need and places himself at the disposal of its enemies?"

"I've learned medicine and earned my place at the university with my own work and because of my excellence. Besides, learning has no nationality. Learning is neutral."

"The learning that gave Israel napalm bombs to burn the faces of our children in Bahr al-Baqar cannot be neutral."

"I think, Zeinab, that we should see reality as it is rather than as how we wish it to be."

"Speak, philosopher."

"We've been defeated. It is over. They are much stronger than us and can crush us at any moment."

"We will never be victorious if we think like you."

The insult provoked him, and he shouted in a voice that made other visitors to the garden turn toward them. "When will you wake up from your delusions? Our victory is impossible because of backwardness, poverty, and despotism. How can we triumph over them when we are incapable of manufacturing the simplest microscope? We are begging everything from abroad, even the weapons we use to defend ourselves.

The problem is not with the likes of me but with the likes of you. Abdel Nasser, like you, lived in dreams until he ruined us."

They got into a violent argument. Her face turned ashen with anger and she got up and gathered her books, which had fallen accidentally and scattered on the ground. At that moment her soft black hair came cascading down her face and she looked suddenly irresistible. He wished he could pull her to his chest and kiss her. He actually tried to get closer, but she kept him at arm's length with a movement of her hand and said to him in a fateful tone of voice, "You won't see me again."

"Zeinab . . ."

"I regret to say that you are a coward."

WHAT A KILLER HEADACHE! It began at the top of his head then crept like an army of ants devouring him. Was he dreaming or was what was happening real? A flash restored his consciousness: he found himself stretched out on a couch in the psychiatrist's office. There was soft music and soft lighting behind him and the doctor was sitting next to him, carefully writing down everything he said. What was he doing? What brought him here? Was this the doctor who would fix his life? How absurd! He knew this type of youth quite well, children of the upper middle class who got an education compliments of their parents' money, and when they graduated they found their places reserved for them at the top of American society. They were always the worst kind of students that he taught: ignorant, lazy, and arrogant. And here was one of them: athletic build, radiant face, and carefree look. What did this boy know about life? The utmost pain that he had experienced was what he felt after a game of squash. The psychiatrist smiled in an artificial, professional way, saying as he held a pen as if playing a role in the movies, "Tell me more about your beloved Zeinab."

"I don't have any more to tell."

"Please help me so I can help you."

"I am doing all I can."

Looking at the papers in front of him, the doctor said, "How did you meet your American wife, Chris?"

"By chance."

"Where?"

"In a bar."

"What kind of bar?"

"Is that important?"

"Very much so."

"I met her in a singles bar."

"What did she do?"

"She worked in a store."

"Please do not be angry at what I am going to say. Candor is at the basis of your therapy. Did you marry Chris to get citizenship?"

"No, I fell in love with her."

"Was she married?"

"She was divorced."

The psychiatrist fell silent, wrote down a few words, then fixed him with a strange glance and said, "Salah, this is how I read your history: you wanted to get American citizenship, so you went to a singles bar, picked up a poor store clerk, divorced and lonely, preyed on her sexual vulnerability until she married you and gave you citizenship."

"I won't allow this!" Dr. Salah shouted.

But the psychiatrist continued as if he hadn't heard him. "It's a reasonable and fair deal. The colored Arab doctor gives his house and name to the poor white American store clerk in return for an American passport."

Dr. Salah got up and said, panting angrily, "If you are going to use this impudent language with me, I don't want your therapy."

The psychiatrist smiled, as if he had gone back to his nature and said apologetically, "I am sorry. Please forgive me. I just wanted to make sure of something."

He began writing again then asked, "You said you have been impotent with your wife?"

"Yes."

"Since when?"

"Three months; maybe a little longer."

"Did you lose your sexual ability gradually or all at once?"

"All at once."

"Describe to me in detail what you feel before you have sex with your wife."

"Everything proceeds naturally then I lose desire suddenly."

"Why does that happen?"

"If I knew, I wouldn't have come to you."

"Tell me how your feeling changes."

"Desire hides details. Once you see the details you lose the desire."

"I don't understand. Give me examples."

"If you were hungry, you would never notice the little shreds of onion on the edge of the plate. You'd notice them only after you'd become full. If you noticed them before eating, you'd lose your appetite. Do you understand?"

The psychiatrist nodded and made a gesture for him to continue, so he went on. "When you desire a woman, you don't see her minute details. You do that only after you make love to her. You will notice, for instance, that her fingernails are not quite clean or that one of her fingers is too short or that her back is covered with dark spots. If you notice that before you sleep with her, you'll lose the desire. And this is exactly what happens with my wife. When I get close to her, her details show clearly and take hold of my thinking so that I lose desire toward her."

"This will help us a lot," the psychiatrist muttered, then went back to his professional smile and opened a nearby drawer and said confidently, as he handed him a bottle of medication, "One tablet with breakfast for a week."

Then he picked up another drug in front of him and said, "And this pill half an hour before sex."

Salah thought to himself: Do these tablets and pills treat the sorrows of sixty years? How silly it all seems! Why is this boy so self-confident? To hell with you and your pills! What do you know about real life? There he is, getting up to see him off at the door, so affectionately and respectfully. He is applying everything he's learned in medical school under the heading of "How to Deal with Your Patients."

The psychiatrist kept Salah's hand in his for a while and said slowly, "Dr. Salah, in conditions like yours, the patient usually tries to run away from therapy by projecting his hatred on the doctor. I think you are smarter than that. Rest assured that I want to help you and I am sorry if I upset you by what I said. See you in a week, same time."

■ ■ ■ ■ ■ ■ ■ ■ ■ ■

They gave me a small office in the histology department and asked me to print a sign with my name to hang outside my door. I went to the ground floor, where I found the person in charge of signs, an old American man who received me in a friendly way and asked me to write my name on a piece of paper. Then, without taking his eyes off the sign he was working on, he said, "Come after lunch to get your sign."

I was surprised because lunch was only an hour away. I went back to him at the appointed time and he pointed with his hand saying, "You'll find it in there."

I found my name elegantly embossed on the new sign. I picked it up and stood reluctantly then asked him, "What should I do now?"

"Take it."

"Shouldn't I sign a receipt that I have received it?"

"Isn't this your sign?"

"Yes."

"Would anyone else come to take it?"

I shook my head and thanked him. In the elevator I laughed at myself. I must get rid of the Egyptian bureaucratic legacy I was carrying in my blood. This simple American worker has given me a lesson: why should I sign for receiving a sign that bears my name?

The day passed uneventfully. After lunch, I was reading the departmental class schedule when Ahmad Danana appeared. He stormed into the room and said loudly, "Thank God for your safe arrival, Nagi."

I got up and shook his hand. I remembered Dr. Salah's advice and tried to look friendly. We exchanged a few words about nothing in particular when he suddenly nudged me in the shoulder and said in a commanding tone of voice, "Come with me."

He accompanied me through the corridors of the department until we got to a room lined with shelves chock-full of reams of paper and notebooks of different shapes and colors. Then he said to me, "Take all the notebooks, paper, and pens you want."

I took some notebooks and colored pens, and he said, laughing, "These supplies are for the researchers in the department, all free, at the expense of the store owner."

"Thank you. I took what I needed."

We crossed a corridor on our way back, then he said, out of the blue, "All the Egyptians who came to Chicago, I have done all of them all kinds of favors; I have stood by them and helped them but they have rarely been grateful."

I didn't like the way he spoke, but I kept my peace. When we got to the door of my office he shook my hand to say good-bye and said affectionately, "I wish you success, Nagi."

"Thank you."

"Tonight we have a meeting at the Egyptian Student Union. Would you like to come so I can introduce you to our colleagues?"

I looked reluctant but he went on, "I'll wait for you at six. Here's the address."

I went back to my apartment and sat, smoking and thinking: Ahmad Danana was an agent of the State Secret Security. No good would ever come from him. Why was he so friendly with me? There must be something behind it. Why did I get involved with him? I should've avoided him completely. I was about to call him to turn down the invitation, but I said to myself that the union belonged to all Egyptian students in Chicago and I had every right to participate and to get acquainted with them. I wouldn't give up my right because of my fear of Danana. I bathed and put on my clothes and went to the meeting. The address was printed clearly with a detailed map, so I arrived at the union headquarters easily. There were twenty-three students, three of whom were veiled females. I shook hands with them and we introduced ourselves.

When the meeting began I started to look closely at them. They were all hardworking, highly successful young men and women like hundreds of junior faculty members in Egyptian universities. I didn't think any of them cared about anything more than their academic achievement, their future, and improving their income. Most of them were religious and had prayer marks and some were bearded. Most likely they understood religion as nothing more than prayer, fasting, and veiling for the women. I noticed a tape recorder close to Danana, so I asked him, "Do you record what we say?"

"Of course. Do you have any objections?" he said gruffly and fixed me with a hostile stare. I was surprised at the sudden change of his tone with me. I remained silent and watched how he talked with the students. I was surprised by the complete authority he exercised over them. They addressed him in awe and flattered him, as if he were their boss or military commander and not just a colleague. After half an hour of small talk and boring details, Danana announced enthusiastically, "By the way, I have happy news for all of you: I have learned from reliable sources that our revered president will visit the United States soon and will come to Chicago."

There were murmurs and he went on in a louder voice, "You are lucky. One of these days you will be able to tell your children that you have met the great leader face-to-face."

Then, taking a drag on his cigarette he said, "I am asking you for your permission to send, in your names, a telegram to our revered president in which we renew our pledge of allegiance to him and express our happiness for his gracious visit."

"I don't agree," I said quickly. Whispering around me died down, and a heavy silence fell. Danana turned to me slowly and said in a cautionary tone of voice, "What exactly don't you agree with?"

"I object to sending a telegram of allegiance to the president. This hypocrisy does not become us as students."

"We are not hypocrites. We actually love our president. Are you denying his historic leadership? Are you denying that Egypt under him has witnessed gigantic, unprecedented achievements?"

"Do you call corruption, poverty, unemployment, and subservience 'achievements'?"

"Are you still a communist, Nagi? I thought you'd grown up and got wise. Listen, in this union there is no room for communism. We are all, thank God, committed Muslims."

"I am not a communist, and if you understand what it means, it is not a crime to be one."

"Our revered president, whom you don't like, took over a country burdened with chronic problems and, thanks to his wisdom and leadership, was able to steer it to safety."

"These are lies of the ruling party. Actually more than half of all Egyptians live below the poverty line. In Cairo alone about four million people live in unplanned communities and shantytowns—"

He interrupted me loudly. "Even if you think there are negative aspects in the way our revered president rules, your religious duty mandates that you obey him."

"Who said that?"

"Islam, if you are a Muslim. Sunni jurisprudents have unanimously agreed that it is the duty of Muslims to obey their rulers even if they are oppressive, so long as that ruler professes his faith and performs the prayers on time, because sedition arising from opposing the ruler is much more harmful to the Muslim nation than putting up with oppression."

"This has nothing to do with Islam. This was fabricated by the sultan's jurists, who used religion to shore up despotic regimes."

"If you disagree with what I said, you would be contradicting the consensus of religious scholars and, by extension, denying established religion. Do you know what the punishment for that is?"

"Shall I tell him, Doctor?" volunteered a bearded young man sarcastically. Danana, laughing, looked at him gratefully and said, "There's no need for that. Arguing with communists never ends. They are experts in useless debates. We have no time to waste. I am putting the matter to a vote. Everybody, do you agree to send a telegram of allegiance to our revered president? Please do so by show of hands."

They all raised their hands without hesitation. Danana laughed sarcastically as he shot me a disdainful glance. "What do you think now?"

I didn't answer and remained silent until the meeting came to an end. I noticed that my colleagues ignored me. I left hurriedly, saying, "Peace be upon you," but no one returned the greeting. The train was crowded and I had to stand. I said to myself that Danana had invited me to the meeting in order to tarnish my image among my fellow students so that I might not be able to convince them later on to take any patriotic stand. In their view I was an atheist communist: it was an old and hackneyed secret police tactic that still worked to discredit anyone. I felt a hand patting me on the shoulder; I turned around and saw that standing next to me was the bearded young man who had mocked me at the meeting. He smiled and said, "You are at Illinois Medical, right?"

"Yes."

"Your brother Ma'mun Arafa. I am studying for a doctorate in civil engineering at Northwestern University. Do you live at the dorm?"

"Yes."

"I lived in a dorm for some time then moved to a cheaper apartment with a Lebanese roommate."

I remained silent. Something was telling me to avoid talking with him. He suddenly said, "You must be a serious politico. You attack the president of the republic, no less? Don't you know that all the union meetings are recorded?"

I ignored him. I turned my face and began to look out of the nearby window. The train had gone through several stops and I had to get off, so I began to make my way with difficulty through the crowd. Suddenly he grabbed my arm and whispered in my ear, "Listen, don't alienate Ahmad Danana. Everything here is in his hands. If he turns against you he can ruin you."

As soon as I saw Dr. Salah in the morning he said with a smile on his face, "Nagi, your problems don't seem to end."

"Why?"

"Danana told me you had a quarrel with him."

"He's a liar. All that happened was that he wanted to send a hypocritical telegram to the president and I objected."

He looked closely at me and said, "Of course I admire your enthusiasm, but is this an issue worth fighting over?"

"Do you want me to sign a document pledging allegiance like the hypocrites in the National Party?"

"Of course not. But don't waste your energy in these matters. You have a great opportunity for education—don't waste it."

"Learning is worthless if I don't take a stand on what is happening in my country."

"Learn and get your degree then serve your country as much as you like."

"Our colleagues at Cairo University who refused to take part in patriotic marches used the same logic. These are solutions that we resort to in order to deceive ourselves, to replace patriotic duty with professional excellence. No, sir. Egypt now needs direct patriotic action more than teachers and accountants. If we don't demand the people's right to justice and freedom, no learning will do us any good."

I was speaking enthusiastically and it seemed I got carried away, because Dr. Salah suddenly looked angry and shouted at me, "Listen, you are here to learn only. If you want to declare a revolution, go back to Egypt."

I was taken aback by his anger so I kept silent. He took a deep breath then said apologetically, "Please understand me, Nagi. All I want is to help you. You are in one of the biggest and greatest universities in America and this is the opportunity of a lifetime. You were admitted to the department after a battle."

"A battle?"

"They were reluctant to admit you because you are not a university instructor. I was among those who supported your admission enthusiastically."

"Thank you."

"Please don't let me down."

"I won't."

"Promise?"

"Promise."

Dr. Salah sighed in relief then said in a serious tone as he handed me a sheet of paper, "These are my suggestions for the courses you should take."

"And how about research?"

"Do you like math?"

"I used to get a perfect score in math."

"Great. How about doing your research on the way calcium is formed in bones? You'd be working with radioactive calcium. A great portion of your research will be based on statistics."

"Under your supervision?"

"That's not my specialty. There are only two who work in this area: George Roberts and John Graham."

"Would you please tell me which one is more appropriate for me?"

"You won't get along with Dr. Roberts."

"Please don't form a bad opinion of me. I can work with any professor."

"The problem is not you. Dr. Roberts doesn't like to work with Arabs."

"Why?"

"He's just like that. In any case, this should not concern us. Go to Dr. Graham."

"When?"

He looked at the clock on the wall and said, "You can meet with him now."

I got up to leave. He smiled and said, "You'll find him somewhat eccentric, but he is a great professor."

At the end of the corridor I knocked on Dr. Graham's office door. His gruff voice said, "Come in."

I was met by a large cloud of scented pipe tobacco smoke. I looked around to see if there was a window. He said, "Does the smoke bother you?"

"I am a smoker myself."

"This is the first point of agreement between us."

He let out a resounding laugh as he exhaled thick smoke. He was reclining on the chair, propping up his feet on the desk in front of him in the American way. I noticed that there was a constant cynical look in his eyes, as if he were watching something amusing. But as soon as he started talking his face became wholly serious. "How can I help you?"

"I hope you'll supervise my MS thesis," I said, smiling politely, trying to create a good impression.

"I have a question."

"Please go ahead."

"Why bother getting a master's in histology if you don't work in a university?"

"Please don't be surprised at my answer. Actually, I am a poet."

"A poet?"

"Yes. I've published two collections of poetry in Cairo. Poetry is the most important thing in my life, but I have to have a profession to put food on the table. They refused to appoint me at Cairo University because of my political activity. I sued the university, but I don't think it will go anywhere. Even if I won my lawsuit the university administration could pressure me to quit my job, as has happened with some colleagues. I'd like to get a master's from Illinois to work for a few years in an Arab Gulf country and save some money, then go back to Egypt and devote myself to literature."

Graham looked at me then exhaled another cloud of smoke and said, "So, you are studying histology for the sake of literature?"

"Exactly."

"Strange, but interesting. Listen, I don't agree to supervise any student before knowing, to some extent, how he thinks. A student's character for me is more important than what he knows. What are you doing Saturday evening?"

"Nothing in particular."

"How about having dinner with me?"

"I'd be delighted."

 For a whole hour, Ra'fat Thabit kept tossing and turning, trying to fall asleep to no avail. The room was dark and the silence profound, interrupted only by the breathing of his wife, Michelle, sleeping next to him. He pulled his body upward and rested his back on the headboard. The events of the day came back to him: it was no ordinary day, and one that he would never forget. Jeff came in the morning and took from him his only daughter. Just like that. Sarah had deserted him to live with her lover. The two lovers seemed extremely happy as they took the suitcases to the car. They were laughing and exchanging jokes and Jeff seized the opportunity and kissed her. Ra'fat was watching them from the window of his office, and then suddenly he decided to ignore his daughter completely. To hell with her. From now on he won't care; if she didn't love him enough, he also would stop loving her. He would live out the rest of his days as if he never had any children. He moved away from the window and lay down on the sofa. He could hear the sound of their laughter in the garden. His wife, Michelle, was taking part in their merrymaking, as if celebrating. It was then that he felt a deep-seated hatred toward all of them. Moments later, he came to as he heard a light tap on the door. It opened and Sarah appeared. She looked calm and refreshed, her face carefree, with her hair gathered at the back of her head. She fixed him with an innocent look and said in a matter-of-fact voice as if she were going on a school field trip, "I came to say good-bye."

"Where to?"

"I think you know."

"Well, I thought perhaps you'd reconsider."

"I've made up my mind. I'm going."

He went over to her, hugged her tightly, and kissed her forehead and cheeks several times. Her body exuded that pure smell that filled his nostrils when he carried her as a child. He looked at her for a long while and whispered, "Take good care of yourself. If you need anything, get in touch with me."

After Sarah left, he spent an ordinary Sunday with Michelle. They went to the movies then had dinner at an Italian restaurant by the lake. It surprised him that they didn't talk about Sarah all day long, as if they had agreed to ignore the subject. It also surprised him that, as soon as they went back home, he felt an overwhelming desire for her. He had sex with her as he hadn't for years. He fell upon her, his feeling unleashed passionately and hard, as if he were burying his sadness inside her or seeking her protection, or stabbing her in revenge for Sarah's departure. When they were done, she succumbed to a calm sleep but he was lost in his dark thoughts. Suddenly the bedside light was turned on and he saw her still-sleepy face.

"Ra'fat, why aren't you asleep?"

"I can't, because of the coffee I had after dinner."

She smiled compassionately and laid her hand on his head.

"No, Ra'fat. It's not because of the coffee. I know exactly how you feel. I'm also sad that Sarah left, but what can we do? This is life; we must accept it."

He remained silent. She went on, "I'll miss Sarah a lot, but I tell myself that she is living in Chicago and not in a faraway city. In a sense, she's living next door. We'll visit and invite her, from time to time, to spend the weekend with us."

This sadness is not sincere. She's happy for what happened, thought Ra'fat. It was she who encouraged Sarah to leave and was now pretending to be sad.

Michelle got close to him, planted a kiss on his cheek, and embraced him. He felt empty and exhausted and had nothing to say. Suddenly he asked her, "Do you know where Sarah will live with Jeff?"

"At his house."

"Of course at his house. Do you know where that house is? It's in Oakland, the poorest and dirtiest neighborhood in Chicago."

"Jeff explained to me. He cannot pay the rent in a better neighborhood, but when he sells his new painting, his situation will improve."

"Did he convince *you* too of these delusions? Do you think anyone will pay a single dollar to buy this nonsense that he spatters on the canvases?"

"Ra'fat, I don't understand why you hate him so much."

"It's I who don't understand this apathy that's come over you. This creep took your only daughter to the dirtiest neighborhood in Chicago and you're still defending him?"

"I am not defending—"

"You are not only defending, you're actually behind it."

"What are you saying?"

"It was you who encouraged her to leave home."

"Ra'fat!"

"Stop this silly charade."

"Listen."

"*You* listen. I am sick and tired of the role you're playing. You've never loved me. You regret having married me. You've always believed you deserved a better husband. Every day you make me feel inferior to you in everything. You've done everything to prove to me that I was just a backward Egyptian whereas you were created from a superior race."

"Stop this."

"I am not going to stop. We need to face reality. You've hated me and used Sarah as your vengeance. You made me lose her."

Michelle looked at him in alarm. He was standing in the middle of the room. It seemed as if he had lost his mind. He hit the bed with his foot and began to shout, "Speak. Why don't you tell me? Haven't you planned for this day? Congratulations, Michelle. You've succeeded. You've made me lose my only daughter."

He went to the closet, opened it forcefully, took off his pajamas and threw them on the floor, and began putting on his street clothes. Michelle jumped from the bed and tried to restrain him, but he pushed her away. She tried again, standing to block the door with her body. He shouted at her loudly, "Get out of my way."

"Where are you going?"

"It's none of your business."

She tried to say something, but he pulled her forcefully by the hand to push her away. She lost her balance and fell on the edge of the bed. He went out and slammed the door hard. After a little while she heard the sound of his car pulling away.

How Shaymaa has changed!

She followed meticulously all the instructions in the recipes on the program *Sitt al-Husn* (*Lady of Beauty*) broadcast every Wednesday on the Egyptian satellite channel. She got rid of the pimples on her face by using a rub of salt and olive oil. Her complexion became soft and radiant thanks to the yogurt and cucumber mask she used. She started penciling her eyebrows carefully and patiently put up with the sting of Egyptian kohl that burned her eyes and caused her tears to flow copiously before it settled on the eyelids, giving them that captivating look. Even her modest shar'i clothes underwent a transformation: she embroidered the sleeves with sequins and crystal beads and took the dresses in a little, just enough to show the contours of her body (at least her ample bosom, which she consciously and appreciatively put forward). She no longer walked in a straight military-style line: she started to zig and zag and twist her gait ever so slightly, treading a fine line between coquettishness and modesty. Even her glasses, those marks of seriousness and studiousness, she let slide down her nose then suddenly adjusted them with her finger, creating a feeling of gaiety and a hint of naughtiness. All of that was for Tariq. Tariq. She pronounced the name so lovingly, as if kissing it. God be praised! She had waited for her kismet in Tanta and then given up, only to find him here, on the other side of the world. God, may he be praised, sent the scholarship her way and made her persist in trying to get it for her own good. Could she have dreamed of a bridegroom better than Tariq Haseeb? He was a medical school faculty member like her, who would not be jealous of her academic achievements and would not tell her to quit her job and stay home as others had done. He was the right age, and his looks were okay (despite being too thin, having a long nose and bulging eyes); all her life she had not liked excessively handsome men. A beautiful man to her was like too much sugar, which made her queasy.

To attract her, a man had to be rough around the edges, thorny. She loved Tariq, cared for him, and looked after him as if she were his mother. She knew his schedule by heart and lived with him moment by moment. She would look at her watch and smile thinking: now he is out of the lecture hall. She imagined him walking to the lab. She called him on his cell phone several times a day, and when longing got the best of her, she sent him messages to assure herself that he was okay. She cooked for him on Sundays and knew by heart all the dishes he loved: rice pilaf, okra, meat and potato casserole, and baked macaroni. For dessert he liked Umm Ali, *mahalabiya,* and rice pudding. Thank God she had learned to cook from her mother, winning his admiration. Several times as he was enjoying her cooking and devouring the food he told her: "May God bless your hands, Shaymaa."

How this sentence made her happy! She gladly forgot the hours she had spent in the kitchen. She would thank him, blushing, looking at him at length as if saying, That's a drop in the bucket of what I'll do for you when we get married.

At night, when she went to bed, her fantasy would take her far away: she would see herself sitting on the dais in her white wedding gown. What would the wedding be like? A big affair with famous singers and dancers attended by dozens of guests? Or a quiet dinner with relatives only? Where would they spend the honeymoon? Sharm al-Sheikh or Marsa Matruh? People said Turkey was beautiful and inexpensive. Where would they live after the wedding: in Cairo or Tanta? How many children would they have, and would she be allowed to name them Aisha and Muhammadi after her mother and father?

Despite the joy she felt because of Tariq's presence in her life, she couldn't understand the way he behaved sometimes. He cared for her and insisted on seeing her and treated her gently; then suddenly, for no reason or preliminaries, he turned into a gruff person as if possessed by a devil, yelling at her and scolding her for the slightest reasons. When that happened, she would fall silent, never talking back, following her mother's advice: a wise woman does not go into combat with a man like his peer, rather she contains him with her kindness and provides him with rest, as the noble Qur'an put it. That does not detract from her dignity. If she responds to an insult with an insult the argument turns into a fierce battle, but if she holds herself back, his conscience will make him sleepless at night and he will come back to her and apologize.

It was not his fits of anger, however, that worried her the most. She felt somehow that he was not resenting *her*, but rather his feelings toward her. It was as if he were resisting his love for her by quarreling with her. She also took some comfort in the quarrels, for after all, they were rehearsals for married life; since they were happening, then it was possible also for marriage to take place. What really worried her and kept her awake at night was something else: their relationship had lasted for a long time and they had been close in all respects, but to date he had not uttered a single word about love or marriage. And despite her total lack of experience in matters of love (with the exception of her silent, unrequited love for the next-door neighbors' son when she was in her first year of secondary school), she was certain that Tariq's attitude was unnatural. If he loved her, why didn't he tell her? He was serious, brilliant, and religious and couldn't be just after having a good time. He was also respectable and respectful; he hadn't touched her body at all except twice (actually, three times) when they rubbed against each other, accidentally, in the crowded train. Why didn't he say something then? Was he afraid of the responsibility? Or was he an inexperienced boy who didn't know how to deal with women? Did he want to put her to the test before committing to her? Could he have a fiancée in Egypt and he was keeping the engagement secret by taking off the ring? Worse than that: could he be unsure that she was fit to be his children's mother? Like her he came from a conservative religious family. Did he take their spending time together as proof that she was loose?

That would really be a catastrophe! He must understand that she went out with him only because of the exceptional circumstances of her being away from home. Had he met her in Egypt he wouldn't have got from her anything but a casual conversation like any other colleague. Why didn't he say anything? She had hinted and encouraged him several times, but he ignored the hints. O God, all she was hoping for was one sentence: "I love you, Shaymaa, and I want to marry you." Was that too much for him to say? She had been assailed by apprehensions and worries since yesterday, so she woke up this morning having made up her mind. She had to stop at the college lab to check the samples of her research, and then catch up with Tariq in Lincoln Park, where they had lunch together every Saturday. I won't accept any more stalling. Today I bring everything to a definitive resolution, she said to herself as she carried her palm-frond bag. She raised her chin and pursed her lips and quickly went to the L station, where the train took her in a few minutes to the park. Tariq was there, sitting as usual on their favorite marble bench close to the fountain. He welcomed her warmly, but she responded in a reserved manner. She sat next to him and spread a blue tablecloth, and then placed the sandwiches and dessert carefully on paper plates next to the thermos filled with mint tea. Tariq devoured two large pita sandwiches filled to the rim, one with chicken bologna studded with olives and the other with scrambled eggs with *basterma*. Then he took visible delight in sipping a cup of mint tea. Then, looking with interest at the bowl of *mahalabiya* garnished with raisins and coconut, "May God save your hands, Shaymaa. The food is fantastic, as usual."

She immediately began carrying out her plan.

"Have you read Sheikh Shaarawi's commentary on the glorious Qur'an?" she asked.

"I used to follow it on television in Egypt."

"You must read it. I brought it with me and I read it every night."

"Sheikh Shaarawi was a great scholar."

"God have mercy on his soul. God gave him the ability to explain the greatness of Islam."

"God be praised."

"Islam has not neglected any aspect of life, great or small."

"Of course."

"Would you believe that Islam has spoken of love?"

Tariq turned toward the fountain and began to study the water gushing from its openings.

"Islam encourages love so long as it doesn't lead to sin," she went on.

Tariq sighed and looked somewhat worried, but she kept at him. "Sheikh Shaarawi has issued a fatwa that if a young man and a young woman were to feel love for each other it would not be forbidden so long as they intended to get married."

"That stands to reason, of course."

"What do *you* think?"

"By the way, Shaymaa, I've discovered a very inexpensive pizza place on Rush Street."

She fixed him with an angry look and said, "Why are you changing the subject?"

"What subject?"

"Shaarawi."

"What about Shaarawi?"

"He asserts that love is not forbidden so long as it leads to marriage."

"You're repeating what you've said already. I don't understand what this has to do with us," he said sharply. A profound silence ensued, interrupted only by the sound of the water in the fountain and the shouts of the children playing nearby. She got up suddenly and said as she gathered her things in the bag, "I am going back to the dorm."

"Why?"

"I just remembered that I have an exam tomorrow."

"Stay a little. It's early and it's so nice out here."

She looked at him irritably, then adjusted her glasses with her finger and said in exasperation, "Enjoy it all by yourself."

"Wait a minute, Shaymaa," Tariq shouted to stop her, but she moved away quickly. He got up and almost hurried after her, but a few moments later he returned to his seat and followed her with his eyes until she disappeared in the crowd.

CHAPTER

Despite the fearsome aura that surrounded Ahmad Danana, a closer look would uncover an ambiguously feminine side to him. This doesn't mean that he is a hermaphrodite, God forbid, for he was born fully male, but there are various traits that make him look more like a shrewish woman than a stern man: his soft body is chubby with no visible muscles; the way he raises his eyebrows when surprised; the way he purses his lips and places his hands on his hips when angry; his fondness for details and secrets and his passion for gossip and use of expressions that have double meanings; his always kissing those he meets on their cheeks; and his use of womanly terms of endearment such as "darling" and "my heart's love." This feminine side came as a result of the influence his late mother, Hagga Badriya, had on him. For even though she was illiterate, she was a strong-willed and intractable woman who ruled with an iron fist a large household of four boys, two girls, and their father. One glance from her was enough to confound any member of the family, beginning with her husband, who with age had turned into something akin to a private secretary or an obedient underling. Danana had so internalized his mother's personality that, unconsciously, especially when he became tense, he started adopting her mannerisms in expression, emulating the tone of her voice, her glances, and all her gestures.

Thus, after he quarreled with Marwa and slapped her, he began his machinations: he shunned her and whenever he saw her he would pout and glance at her contemptuously or sigh and throw his hands up in the air and ask God's forgiveness in an audible voice. Or, after performing his ablution on his way to the prayer rug, he would pass by her as she watched television and throw a loaded expression at her, such as saying, for instance, "God suffices unto me, He is my best defender. May God enable me to withstand my misfortune." Or he would say, "I hereby recite the Fatiha for my mother's soul, she was a model wife." This was his way of punishing his wife. Someone might ask, why was he punishing her to begin with? Shouldn't he be apologizing to her because he slapped her?

The answer is that Danana belongs to that class of people who never blame themselves. He always thinks he is right while others make all the mistakes. He believes that the only blemish on his character is the excessive goodness of his heart, which the wicked—who were so numerous—exploited to further their own interests at his expense. He was convinced that Marwa had wronged him, that it was she who had behaved insolently toward him, forcing him to hit her. Besides, what was wrong with administering to her, from time to time, one slap of moderate strength to return her to her senses? Didn't the unimpeachable canon law permit a man to beat his wife to discipline her? And what was wrong in his borrowing money from her father? Wasn't it a wife's duty to stand by her husband? Didn't Khadija, may God be pleased with her, help her husband, the noblest of all creation, prayers and peace be upon him, with money? His wife had committed a terrible wrong against him for which she had to apologize. Were he to go easy on her this time, she would continue in her misguided ways until he lost control of her.

As for her complaint about their sexual intercourse, he considered that, with total confidence, a kind of woman's coquettishness, no more and no less. Pleasure and pain for a woman were so intertwined that at the peak of her pleasure she cried, as if someone were beating her up violently. Hence, everything that a woman complained about in sex was, most likely in reality, a source of happiness for her. Danana once heard from one of his friends something that he came to be convinced of: that every woman's deepest desire was to be violently raped. That indeed was what women wanted, even if they pretended otherwise. So that made woman a mysterious, incomprehensible, and contradictory being that said no when she meant yes! Didn't the old poet say, "They show reluctance when [in fact] they desire it"? It is true that women are lacking in reason and religion, and a true man has to subjugate a woman in life as he does in bed; he should control her and lead her and, at the same time, never give her his full trust. The good ancestors handed down to us several sayings to this effect:

"Consult women, then do the opposite."

"Fools are known by three signs: playing with lions, drinking poison to try it, and trusting women with secrets."

And, "Avoid evil women and be cautious with good ones."

That was how Danana viewed women, even though his experience with them before marriage had been confined to the few occasions when he had slept with maids and female farmhands for measly sums, which he had agreed to beforehand but which, once he'd had his way with them, he haggled hard to pay less. Perhaps the fact that his experience was limited to prostitutes could explain his understanding of sex not as a two-way human interaction, but rather as a violent, one-sided male act during which a woman enjoyed being raped.

Danana tightened the siege of his wife and intensified his campaign of innuendo, waiting for the moment when she would cave in and offer him an appropriate apology. But days passed and she still avoided him. In fact, the slap she had received, despite being a horrendous insult, liberated her from any feeling of marital commitment, and the shunning spared her the physical torture she had suffered several times a week. That reprieve gave her a chance to think carefully about her life with him: What did she intend to do? Her hatred of Danana had reached its utmost, but she hadn't told her mother yet that she wanted a divorce. She was waiting until she sorted out her thoughts and knew exactly what she was going to say, like a lawyer giving herself time to study a case so that she could organize her documents and brief in such a way as to guarantee that she would prevail. She was certain of her parents' support if they were convinced of her suffering. Her father, who burst into tears as he saw her off at the airport, and her mother, who couldn't sleep at night if she had a simple common cold, wouldn't leave her in that hell. She was going to call them the following Friday, when Danana would be at the Student Union meeting and her father would be just coming home. She was going to talk to them at length and tell them everything in detail. Even that private matter, she would hint at. She was giving them one option: separation and return to Egypt at once. As soon as she made up her mind she calmed down. She no longer paid any attention to his insinuations, sighs, or provocative comments. Why should she waste her energy on a new quarrel? In a few days she would leave this torment behind.

Something unexpected happened, however. The first of the month came and Marwa didn't give Danana the thousand dollars that her father had sent. She had forgotten the matter in the midst of the problems, but Danana had not. When several days of the new month had passed, his worries increased and he was beset by apprehensions. He even suspected that she had initiated the problem between the two of them deliberately to withhold that monthly sum or to blackmail him with her demands or, more dangerously, to establish the principle that her father's money was negotiable, that she would give it if she was happy and withhold it if she was not. All those considerations made him change his methods; so he stopped his harassment and whenever he saw her would say right away "peace be upon you," then look at her with an understanding, loving glance tinged with a little reproach. Yesterday he took a further step and sat next to her in front of the television. She was watching an Adel Imam movie and he began to laugh out loud as a prelude to speaking with her. But she ignored him completely, as if he were not there. So he gave up and went to bed.

In the morning he got up, washed, and performed his ablution and his prayers, then sat in the living room drinking tea and smoking. After a while Marwa appeared and no sooner did she see him than she turned around to leave, but he said right away, "Please, Marwa. I want to talk to you about an important matter."

"May it be good, God willing," she said with an impassive face. He got up, got close to her, and held her hand. She jerked her hand away and shouted, "Don't touch me."

"Listen, good woman, you've wronged me and behaved insolently toward me. I've given you this time to come back to your senses."

"I don't want to talk about it."

"I am advising you just for God's sake. What you are doing is forbidden by the canon law. True, I hit you. But I used my legitimate right."

"Keep your religious sermons to yourself. What exactly do you want?"

"Nothing but good things."

She smiled derisively and said as she searched in her handbag, "I know what you want."

"What do you mean?"

"You want the money? Here, take it, please, but don't you come near me after that."

The money was several one-hundred-dollar bills folded together. Danana took it with a nimble move of his hand, and then sighed and said as he slipped the bills into his wallet, "May God forgive you, Marwa. I will not hold you accountable for what you've said. Obviously your nerves are strained. I recommend a hot bath, then a two-prostration prayer to end hardship. That will do you a lot of good, God willing."

▪ ▪ ▪ ▪ ▪ ▪ ▪ ▪ ▪ ▪ ▪

At exactly eight o'clock on Saturday evening, I was standing in front of Dr. Graham's house. I had put on my best clothes and carried a bouquet of flowers in my hand. It was a small one-story house surrounded by a narrow garden, with flowerbeds lining both sides of the walkway. A graceful and beautiful young black woman (she looked like Naomi Campbell) opened the door. She had on a simple outfit: a white T-shirt and blue jeans. Behind her stood a black boy, about six years old.

"Hello, I'm Carol McKinley, John's friend, and this is my son, Mark."

I shook hands with them and gave her the flowers. She thanked me warmly as she smelled them. The furniture was all dark wood in the English style, simple and elegant. Dr. Graham was sitting in the living room, relaxing his large body on the sofa. In front of him was a cart table on which were arranged bottles of liquor and glasses. I presented him with a simple gift, a plate inlaid with mother-of-pearl from Khan al-Khalili. He welcomed me and offered me the chair opposite him. The boy approached and whispered something in his ear. Dr. Graham nodded and kissed him on the cheek and the boy ran inside. Dr. Graham turned to me, and smiling, asked, "What would you like to drink?"

"Red wine."

"Isn't wine forbidden in Islam?" Carol asked as she opened the bottle.

"I believe in God in my heart. I am not strict. Besides, religious scholars in Iraq, during the Abbasid caliphate, permitted the drinking of wine."

"I thought the Abbasid caliphate ended a long time ago," commented Dr. Graham.

"It has indeed ended. But I love wine."

We all laughed and Carol said in a gentle voice as she sipped her drink, "John told me you're a poet. Can we hear some of your poetry? That'd be wonderful!"

"I don't know how to translate my poetry."

"Even though your English is so good?"

"Translating poetry is something else."

"Translating poetry is treason," said Dr. Graham, and then added earnestly, "As a poet, your study in America will offer you a good opportunity to understand American society. Perhaps you'll write about it one of these days. New York has inspired the Spanish poet Federico García Lorca to write beautiful poems, and we are waiting for your poems about Chicago."

"I hope so."

"Unfortunately you've come to America at a time when it is swept by a reactionary, conservative current. There was a time, which I personally experienced as a young man, when there was another America, more humane and liberal."

He paused for a moment to pour himself another drink and then went on, his voice acquiring a more profound tone. "I am from the Vietnam generation. We were the ones who unmasked the deception of the American dream and exposed the crimes of the American establishment and fought it ferociously. Thanks to us America in the 1960s witnessed a true ideological revolution when progressive values replaced traditional capitalist ideas. But, unfortunately, all of that is now gone."

"Why?" I asked, and Carol replied, "Because the capitalist system was able to renew itself and co-opt elements opposing it. The young revolutionaries who rejected the system have now become soft, bourgeois middle-aged men, their utmost goal a successful deal or a higher-paying job. Revolutionary ideas are gone. Every American citizen now dreams of a house with a garden, a car, and a vacation in Mexico."

"Does this apply to Dr. Graham?"

Carol laughed and said, "John Graham is an American of a rare kind. He doesn't care at all about money. He might be the only university professor in Chicago who doesn't own a car."

After a short while we had dinner prepared by Carol. They were both very nice to me. I talked to them about Egypt and we discussed various topics. I drank more wine and was in such an ec-static mood that I talked and laughed a lot. Then Carol disappeared suddenly and I realized that she had gone to bed. I took that to be a signal that the evening was over. So I got up to leave, but Graham signaled to me to wait and said as he raised the vodka bottle, "How about one for the road?"

I opened my arms, welcoming the idea, and emboldened by the wine, I said, "I can have a glass of wine."

"You don't like vodka?"

"I only drink wine."

"Following the Abbasid religious scholars?"

"I actually do love the Abbasid era and I have read a lot about it. Maybe my love of wine is an attempt to recapture the golden Arab age now lost. And, by the way, what would you say to doing like Harun al-Rashid?"

"What did he do?"

"One of the paradoxes of history was that Harun al-Rashid, de-spite being able to behead any person with a simple nod to Masrur, the executioner, was at the same time a tender, bashful human being who took care not to slight the feelings of others. He had a cane that he placed next to him when he sat drinking with his friends. When he got tired and wanted them to leave, he placed the cane across his legs, whereupon they would understand that it was the end of the evening. That way he didn't embarrass them and they didn't overstay their welcome."

Graham laughed loudly and got up with childish enthusiasm, fetched a hockey stick that was hanging on the wall, and said, "Let's re-create history then. Here's the stick in an upright position; if I drop it you'll understand that I want to sleep."

We talked about many things, most of which I don't remember now, and we laughed a lot. In my drunken state I felt like talking, so I told John what had happened with the black call girl. Graham guffawed at the beginning, but by the end of the story, he bowed his head pensively and said, "This is a significant experience: millions of citizens in the richest country in the world live in such poverty. But this miserable woman, in my opinion, is more honorable than many American politicians. She's selling her body to feed her children while they control American foreign policy to provoke unnecessary wars to control sources of oil and sell weapons that kill tens of thousands of innocent people so that profits in the millions of dollars continue to pour in for them. There's something else you've got to understand: the American establishment is in control of everything in the life of Americans. Even the relationship between a man and a woman is now heavily regulated."

"What do you mean?"

"In the 1960s our call for sexual freedom was an attempt to have emotional fulfillment away from the control of adults. Now, however, bourgeois conventions have come back with a vengeance. If you want to get to know a woman in America you have to do so through specific steps, as if incorporating a commercial company: first, you have to spend some time talking to her in an entertaining and humorous way; second, you have to buy her a drink; third, you have to ask her for her telephone number; fourth, you have to take her to dinner at a fancy restaurant; and finally, you invite her to visit you at home. Then bourgeois convention gives you the right to sleep with her. At any of these steps a woman can withdraw: if a woman refuses to give you her telephone number or turns down your dinner invitation, that means that she doesn't welcome having a relationship with you. But if she goes through the five steps, that means she wants you."

I looked at him in silence, but his sense of humor soon reasserted itself. He laughed and said, "As you can see, your old professor has information much more important than histology."

It was a wonderful evening. Suddenly I heard a sharp, intermittent buzzing sound. I noticed for the first time the presence of a speaker and a panel with several buttons attached to the wall next to the sofa. Graham brought his head closer to the speaker, pushed a button, and cheerfully exclaimed, "Karam? You're late. I'll impose a fine on you."

Then he turned toward me and said, "This is my surprise for you tonight. An Egyptian friend like you."

The speaker made a noise that I couldn't make out. Graham pushed a button and there was another buzzing sound that I figured was opening the outside door. After a short while there stood in the middle of the room an Egyptian man pushing sixty. He had a tall, slim athletic build, gray hair parted in the middle, and typical Coptic features: dark complexion, a large nose, and big round eyes filled with intelligence and sadness, as if he had just stepped out of one of the paintings of the Fayyum Portraits exhibit. Dr. Graham said, "Let me introduce my friend, Karam Doss, one of the most skilled heart surgeons in Chicago. And this is my friend Nagi Abd al-Samad, a poet who is studying for a master's degree in histology."

"Nice to meet you," said Karam in polished English. From the first impression he seemed strong willed, confident, and extremely well dressed: white shirt with patterned sleeves and the designer's signature on the chest, handsome black trousers, and black patent leather shoes. Around his neck was a thick gold chain bearing a cross, buried in his dense gray chest hair. He looked more like a movie star than a doctor. He sank into the comfortable chair and said, "Sorry I'm late. I was celebrating the retirement of one of our surgery professors with a bunch of colleagues and the celebration just kept going. But I decided to come here if only for a few minutes."

"Thanks for coming," Graham said. Karam went on to say in a soft voice, as if talking to himself, "I work so much that on the weekends I feel like a child in recess at school. I want to enjoy it as much as I can and meet as many of my friends as I am able to. But, as usual, time is not enough."

"What's your drink?" Graham asked, pulling the cart table toward him.

"I drank a lot, John, but I can have a short scotch and soda."

I asked him, smiling affectionately, "Did you learn medicine in America?"

"I am a graduate of Ayn Shams Medical School. But I fled to America to escape persecution."

"Persecution?"

"Yes. In my day the chairman of the general surgery department, Dr. Abd al-Fatah Balbaa, was a fanatic Muslim who didn't make a secret of his hatred for Copts. He believed that teaching surgery to Copts was not permissible in Islam because it enabled infidels to control the lives of Muslims."

"That's very strange!"

"But it happened."

"How can a professor of surgery think in such a backward manner?"

"That's very possible in Egypt," he said as he stared at me in a manner that I thought was somewhat provocative. Graham intervened. "Until when will Copts suffer persecution, even though they're the original Egyptians?"

Silence prevailed for a moment. I looked at Graham and said, "The Arabs mixed with the Egyptians fourteen hundred years ago. We cannot, practically speaking, talk about 'original' Egyptians. Besides, most Egyptian Muslims were Copts who converted to Islam."

"You mean were forced to convert to Islam."

"Dr. Graham, Islam has not forced anyone to convert. The most populous Muslim country in the world, Indonesia, was not conquered by Arabs. Islam spread there at the hands of Muslim merchants."

"Weren't Copts massacred to convert to Islam?"

"That's not true. If Arabs had wanted to exterminate the Copts, no one could've prevented them. But Islam commands its followers to respect the faiths of others. You cannot be a Muslim unless you recognize the other religions."

"Isn't it strange that you're defending Islam so passionately while you're drunk?"

"My being drunk is a personal matter that has nothing to do with the discussion. Islam's tolerance is a historical fact acknowledged by many Western Orientalists."

"But Copts are persecuted in Egypt."

"All Egyptians are persecuted. The regime in Egypt is despotic and corrupt and it persecutes all Egyptians, Muslims and Copts. Of course there are incidents of fanaticism here and there, but they don't constitute a phenomenon in my opinion. Religious persecution is a direct result of political repression. All Egyptians are suffering from discrimination so long as they are not members of the ruling party. I, for instance, am a Muslim, but they refused to appoint me to Cairo University because of my political activity."

Graham played with his beard and said, "Well, let me examine this idea: you mean persecution in Egypt is political and not religious?"

"Exactly."

"It's easy for a Muslim Egyptian like you to assert that everything is hunky-dory," said Karam, itching for a confrontation. It seemed he didn't like what I said.

I responded calmly. "The problem, in my opinion, is not between Muslims and Copts; rather it is between the regime and the Egyptians."

"Do you deny that there is a Coptic problem?"

"There is an Egyptian problem, and the suffering of the Copts is part of it."

"But Copts are passed over in all key posts in the state. Copts are persecuted and they also get killed. Have you heard of what happened in the village of al-Kushh? Twenty Copts were slaughtered right before the eyes of the police and no one lifted a finger to save them."

"This, of course, is a tragedy. But let me remind you also that Egyptians die from torture every day in police stations and state security headquarters. The executioners do not make a distinction between a Muslim and a Copt. All Egyptians are persecuted. I cannot see the problem of Copts as separate from Egypt's problems."

"You are following the well-known Egyptian practice of denying the truth. Until when will Egyptians be like ostriches, burying their heads in the sand so as not to see the sun? You know, John, when I was a new doctor in Egypt, the minister of health came to inspect the hospital where I was working. The director kept warning us not to talk about problems in the hospital. All he cared about was for the minister to think that everything was great, whereas the hospital was suffering from gross neglect. This is a sample of Egyptian thinking."

"This thinking is caused by the corruption of the ruling regime in Egypt and not the Egyptians themselves."

"Egyptians are responsible for the regime."

"So you are blaming the victim?"

"Every people in the world gets the government it deserves. That's what Churchill said, and I agree with him. If the Egyptians were not willing to accept despotism, they wouldn't have lived under it for so many centuries."

"There's no people in the world that was not ruled by despots at one time or another."

"But Egypt was ruled by tyrants more than any other country in history, and the reason for that is that Egyptians by nature are subservient."

"I am surprised that you, an Egyptian, should say that."

"Being Egyptian does not prevent me from stating the faults of Egyptians, whereas *you* consider repeating lies a national duty."

I said in a warning tone of voice, "I do not repeat lies and I hope you'll be more selective in your choice of words."

We were sitting on opposite chairs while Graham was sprawled on the sofa. Suddenly he moved his body forward and stretched his arms, as if separating us, saying, "The last thing I need tonight is for you to fight."

Karam looked toward me, raring to go, as if he was determined to take the matter all the way. He said, "Why are we running away from the truth? Ancient Egypt had a great civilization but right now it's turned into a dead country. The Egyptian people are behind other peoples when it comes to education and thinking. Why do you take this fact as a personal insult?"

"If I have the shortcoming of the Egyptians, I also have their good traits."

"What are these good traits? Name one, please," Karam asked me sarcastically, and I replied, "At least I love my country and haven't fled it."

"What do you mean?"

"I mean *you* fled from Egypt so you don't have the right to speak about it."

"I was forced to leave."

"You left your poor, miserable country for your comfortable life in America. Remember, you got a free education at the expense of those Egyptians you now despise. Egypt gave you this education so that one day you'd be useful to it. But you turned your back on the Egyptian patients who needed you. You left them to die over there and came here to work for the Americans, who don't need you."

Karam stood up suddenly and shouted, "I've never heard anything more stupid in my whole life!"

"You insist on insulting me, but that won't change the facts: those who've fled their country like you should stop criticizing it."

Karam snarled some insults and rushed toward me, raising his fist, so I got up, ready to defend myself. But Graham, despite his considerable heft, sprang up at the right moment and separated us, saying, "Easy, easy. Calm down. You're both drunk."

I was panting in sheer agitation and shouted loudly, "Dr. Graham, I won't allow anyone to insult my country. I am leaving now because if I wait one more minute, I'll beat him up!"

I turned and left hurriedly. As I was crossing the corridor I heard Karam shouting, "It's I who'll break your head, you rude son of a bitch!"

I was so drunk I didn't remember how I got back to the dorm. It seemed I took off my clothes in the living room because I found them later on, piled on the floor next to the table. I woke up at four in the afternoon feeling terrible. I had a horrendous hangover; I threw up more than once and felt very weak. There was an excess of acidity in my stomach and I had a splitting headache, as if hammers were pounding my head. Worst of all, I felt guilty because I had ruined the evening and created a problem for Dr. Graham. I didn't regret one word that I had said to Karam Doss. Whenever I recalled his arrogance and his insults against Egyptians, my resentment toward him was reignited. How can anyone publicly insult his country so easily? And yet I was wrong, because I did not exercise self-control. It wasn't appropriate at all to quarrel. What was Graham's fault? The good man wanted to welcome me and get to know me and I caused him a problem. He had told me that for him a student's character was no less important than his academic standing. What did he think of me after what had happened? I took a hot bath and drank a large cup of coffee. I called Dr. Graham to apologize, but he didn't answer. I remembered that he kept my number in his telephone memory: Did that mean that he was refusing to talk to me? I called several times, but he didn't answer. I drank a second cup of coffee and felt somewhat better. I began to go over what I'd done since arriving in Chicago. It seemed that I indeed, as Dr. Salah said, could not control my negative feelings. There was an essential defect in my character that I had to confront. Why was I so easily provoked? Am I aggressive? Was my viciousness the result of drinking too much or feeling frustrated? Or was it that our feelings became more delicate and sensitive away from home? All these were contributing factors, but I realized what was the true cause of my misery, which I had carried inside me, ignored, and avoided even thinking about. A whole year had passed and I'd been unable to write even one verse of poetry. My real problem was my inability to write. When I wrote I would be more tolerant and accepting of differences. Then I drank less and ate and slept better. Right now, however, I had a short fuse and was prone to quarreling and felt the need to drink nonstop. Poetry was the only thing that restored my balance. I had ideas for poems that sounded excellent from a distance, but no sooner did I sit down to write them on paper than they eluded me, as if I were a thirsty person chasing a mirage in the desert, time after time, endlessly. There was nothing more miserable in the world than a poet who had lost inspiration. Hemingway was the most important novelist of his age, and when he couldn't write, he committed suicide. Wine consoled me but it pushed me to a dark tunnel that had no end. How would I pursue my studies regularly when I was drinking so heavily?

I came to as the doorbell rang. I got up slowly to open the door and when I looked through the peephole, I was taken aback for a moment. I saw the last person I expected a visit from: Dr. Karam Doss.

CHAPTER 13

 Dr. Salah followed the psychiatrist's advice and took his wife to dinner on Saturday at her favorite Mexican restaurant. Chris looked wonderful in her new hairdo, full makeup, and a low-cut red dress and shining brooch in the shape of a rose. The evening went perfectly: they listened to Mexican music and ate delicious spicy food. Chris drank several glasses of tequila while Salah had only one, as the doctor had advised. They whispered affectionately and she laughed happily, saying, "Thank you, darling. It's a wonderful evening."

Before leaving he went to the restroom and swallowed the pill. On their way home, she sat next to him in the car. There was tension in the air between them, as if they were expecting something that they couldn't quite spell out, so they covered it up by engaging in small talk that went on and on, leading nowhere. They got home and he went to the bathroom before her, came out wearing a white cashmere robe, and lay in bed watching television until she was done with her bath. That was their time-honored ritual before lovemaking. He recalled his session with the doctor. Why did he think that what he had said was insolent? The doctor had stated the fact that he had been carrying around deep inside him, even as he tried to avoid it. Yes, indeed. He had used Chris sexually, got her addicted to him while he was implementing his plan of marrying her to get an American passport.

He thought: stop deceiving yourself. Admitting your baseness might help you. You behaved like a gigolo, exactly like those chasing old American tourists in the bars of São Paolo and Madrid. You're exactly like them. The only difference is that you are educated: a gigolo with a PhD. What did you do to Chris? You ignited her physical desire with liquor and fondling, then you played hard to get; you pretended to be preoccupied, and when she persisted you asked her, like a prostitute, "How many proofs of love do you want tonight?" You toyed with her desire until she almost cried; your impudence with her increased your own desire; you kept yourself at arm's length until she almost gave up on you and then suddenly you were all over her, burning her with pleasure until she was fully satiated and dozed off for a long time then came to, looked at you gratefully, and showered your body with kisses. Everything went as planned: you married Chris, got your green card, and afterward, American citizenship.

When he stood up to swear the pledge of allegiance to his new country, he couldn't, even for a moment, keep Zeinab Radwan out of his thoughts. "I regret to say that you're a coward"—that was what Zeinab had said thirty years ago, perhaps a fitting summation of his life. He was roused from his reminiscences by seeing Chris. She had come out of the bathroom wearing a white robe that she had deliberately left open, revealing a snow-white naked body. She sat next to him on the bed and clung to him. He looked at her. Her face was flushed, and she was overcome with desire. He tried to speak but discovered there was nothing more to be said. As soon as he touched her body with his fingers she threw herself at him, embracing him hard and taking his lips into her mouth. He felt the contours of her body, and her beautiful perfume filled his nostrils and he felt his blood rushing. He had an unmistakable full erection. He began to bite her breasts and knead them with his hands. For a moment he felt that he had regained his old vigor, but apprehensions suddenly assailed him and he concentrated on getting rid of them. She felt what he was going through and decided to stand by him until he achieved victory. She began to fondle him patiently and persistently. She did her best, trying several ways to keep him focused, but he wavered and gradually quivered then was out of it completely. Failure loomed like a news flash, or a bolt of lightning. She closed her eyes and moved away a little while he stretched out on his back, as if he had lost his ability to move. He began looking at the shadows cast by the soft light on the ceiling. It occurred to him that they might be depicting something that was tangible: didn't what he was seeing now resemble a big bear and a child next to it? Or two trees next to each other, one taller than the other? He went close to her and kissed her on the head. She looked at him with tearful eyes and he was filled with pity for her. She murmured in a wounded voice, "My problem is not with sex. I'm not young and my needs diminish with age."

He began to pat her on the head silently. She went on, "What pains me is that you no longer love me."

"Chris!"

"You cannot deceive a woman about love."

He sat up and began to speak slowly, as if failure had given them some respite, "In a few weeks I'll be sixty. My life is approaching its end. At best I'll live another ten years. When I look back on the many years that have passed, I become certain that I've made many wrong decisions."

"Was I one of your wrong decisions?"

"You are the most beautiful woman I've known, but I only wish I could live my life over again to make different decisions. This might sound ridiculous, but I now believe that my decision to emigrate was not the right thing to do."

"Nobody can live his life again."

"That's the tragedy."

"Therapy will rid you of these thoughts."

"I'm not going through that again. I am not going to lie on a couch to tell my life's secrets to someone I don't know and accept his reprimands as if I were a child who'd misbehaved. I won't ever do that again."

He said the last sentence loudly as he got off the bed. He turned on the light and picked up a book from the nightstand, then said as he held the doorknob before going out, "You know very well what you mean to me. But I'm going through a crisis that will not be over in the near future. I don't want to cause you any more pain. I suggest that we separate, if only temporarily. Sorry, Chris, but I think it's best for both of us."

"I am not so stupid as to fall for this trap. That's all I need, ending up marrying Shaymaa. I'd be like someone fasting all day, forgoing all kinds of delicacies, and then breaking his fast eating an onion! True, she is an instructor at the College of Medicine, but she is still a peasant. I am the son of General Abd al-Qadir Haseeb, assistant director of Cairo Security; I grew up in Roxy and went to the Heliopolis Club and turned down daughters of notables. Do you expect me to end up marrying a peasant? Let her get as mad as she wants to be! To hell with her!"

That was what Tariq told himself. True, she was quite pleasant and her company delightful. True, she looked after him and cooked for him the dishes he liked. But that did not mean that he should marry her. She had to choose: either their friendship goes on as it was, or she disappears. He would give her some time to come back to her senses. He wouldn't talk to her. Why should he talk to her? It was she who did him wrong. She got angry for no reason and talked to him improperly in a public place. She had to apologize.

He sat down to study, concentrating his thoughts away from her. As usual, before he slept, he watched a wrestling match and enjoyed a pornographic movie (actually he forced himself to have that pleasure, to prove that he had not been affected by Shaymaa). In the morning he went to school and spent the day between lecture hall and lab. He tried strenuously to banish her picture from his mind. At about three o'clock he was walking back to the dorm when he suddenly stopped and dialed her number on his cell phone. He was calling her, not to reconcile with her but to rebuke her. He would explain to her how wrong she had been. He would tell her clearly and decisively that if she wanted to go on like that, then he didn't need her. She could go wherever she wanted. He glued his ear to the cell phone, preparing the harsh words that he would unleash on her. But the ringing went on. She didn't pick up. Maybe she was having her nap as usual. When she woke up she would find his number and call him. Tariq ate lunch (prepared by Shaymaa), had his siesta, and as soon as he awoke he reached for the cell phone and checked the screen: she had not called. He rang her number again, and she didn't answer. When he tried one more time, she hung up. So, it was obvious. She was playing the role of the angry paramour. She wanted him to come running after her, humiliating himself. "Impossible!" he muttered, the angle of his mouth forming a vexed smile, and he began to stare at nothing in exasperation. So long as she hung up on him, she has chosen the end. He wouldn't say good-bye but to hell with her. Who did she think she was? He said to himself: This peasant girl wants to humiliate me? What a farce. So, she doesn't know who Tariq Haseeb is. My dignity is more important than my life. From now on I am going to delete her from my life as if she has never existed. Before I met her what did I lack? I was working, eating, sleeping, enjoying life, and living like a king. On the contrary, ever since I met her I've been anxious and tense.

He sat at his desk as usual, took out his books and notes, and began to study. He wrote down the main points of the lesson and exerted a great effort to stay focused. Half an hour later, however, he suddenly got up and left his apartment. He crossed the corridor quickly, as if someone were chasing him or as if he were afraid to change his mind. He took the elevator to the seventh floor. He looked in the mirror: he was wearing his blue training suit and his face looked tired and in need of a shave. He reached her door and rang the bell several times. Some time passed before she opened the door. She was wearing a house gown. He said with a smile, "Peace upon you."

"Peace upon you, Dr. Tariq."

Her formal tone jarred in his ears. He fixed her with a strong, pensive glance but she ignored it and said, "May it be for the good, God willing."

"Are you still mad at me?" he said in a soft voice.

"Who said that?"

"You left me yesterday and didn't ask about me today, as you usually do."

She looked at him in silence as if saying, You know why.

"Shaymaa, may I come in, please?"

She felt awkward for a moment. She never expected him to ask to come in. Previously, he had never been beyond the threshold of the apartment door. She backed away a few steps and made way for him. He went in quickly, as if he were afraid she would change her mind. He sat on a seat in the living room. She realized for the first time that she was still in her house gown so she took her leave, went inside, and stayed there for what seemed to him like a long time. Then she came back with a cup of tea, having put on an elegant green dress. She sat in the seat far away from him. He started sipping his tea and said, "So, what made you angry?"

"Do you really care to find out?" she said coquettishly, putting out a very tender feminine air.

His heart skipped a beat and he said in a passionate voice, "I missed you very much."

"Me too, but I am not comfortable with our friendship."

"Why?"

"Every day I get more attached to you, but we've never talked about the future."

She was surprised by how forward she was being. Was this the shy Shaymaa, now receiving a man in her home and talking to him like that?

"The future is in God's hands," he said in a soft voice in a final attempt to avoid the subject.

"Please appreciate my position. You are a man and you won't be faulted no matter what you do. I am a girl and my family has strict conventions. Everything we do here in America will reach people in Egypt, thanks to the offices of good people who, as you know, are quite numerous. I don't want to bring shame on my family."

"We are not doing anything wrong."

"Yes we are. Our relationship flies in the face of tradition, in the face of the principles I was raised on. My father, God have mercy on his soul, was an enlightened man who supported women's education and right to work. But that does not mean I should be lax and compromise my reputation."

"Your reputation is beyond reproach, Shaymaa."

She went on as if she hadn't heard him, "Why are we going out together? Why are you here now? Don't tell me it's collegiality because collegiality has its bounds. We have to use our heads and not be driven by emotions. Listen, Tariq, I am going to ask you a question, and I hope you'll answer it frankly."

"Go ahead."

"What am I to you?"

"A friend."

"Just a friend?" she whispered in a soft voice.

His heart shook and he said in a quavering voice, "You are a very dear person to me."

"Only that?"

"I love you," he said quickly, as if it had got away from him, as if he had been resisting for some time then suddenly collapsed. The atmosphere changed in an instant. It was as if he had uttered a magical word that opened all kinds of doors. She smiled and looked at him with the utmost tenderness and whispered, "Say it again."

"I love you."

They kept looking at each other in disbelief, as if they were clinging to that unique moment, knowing it wouldn't last, and not certain what to do once it had passed. She got up, carried the tray and empty cups, and then asked him in a voice that was the sweetest he had heard since he met her, "I've made a dish of Umm Ali, would you like some?"

She didn't wait for his answer but headed for the kitchen, and then came back carrying the plate. She was moving confidently and co-quettishly as if, just now, she was feeling at the peak of her femininity. Tariq stood up to take the plate from her, but suddenly he extended his hand and held her wrist. He pulled her toward him and got so close to her that his hot, panting breath chafed her face. She pushed him away with all her strength and shouted in a choking voice, "Tariq! Are you crazy?"

CHAPTER 15

 Behind the green curtain covering the window, in the room stacked with books and filled over the years with pipe tobacco smoke, John Graham kept a dark brown box covered with old brass ornaments. He would lock it carefully and forget about it for long periods of time. Then it would occur to him suddenly to lock the office door from inside and panting, drag the large box to the middle of the room. He would squat, take out the box's contents, and spread them in front of him, on the floor, his whole life unwrapping itself before his eyes: black and white photographs of himself as a young man; newspaper clippings from the 1960s carrying headlines of important events; angry, antigovernment revolutionary flyers; leaflets showing pictures of children and women killed or maimed during the Vietnam War (some so horrendous he couldn't, even after all these years, look at them for a long time); colorful, hand-painted invitations to demonstrations or open-air rock concerts; the program for Woodstock; buttons bearing the famous love and peace sign; and an Indian musical wood instrument that he used to play well. But the most cherished of the contents was a metal helmet that he took off a policeman during a violent clash in a demonstration. In the old photographs Graham was a slim young man with an unkempt beard and long hair gathered in a ponytail, wearing a loose-fitting Indian shirt, blue jeans, and sandals. Those were the "park days," as he called them. He ate and drank, slept, and made love in Chicago's famous parks: Grant Park and Lincoln Park.

John was one of the angry youth rebelling against the Vietnam War, who rejected everything: the church, the state, marriage, work, and the capitalist system. Most of them left their homes, their families, their jobs, and their studies. They spent the night discussing politics, smoking pot, singing and playing music, and making love. During the day they demonstrated. In August of 1968 the Democratic Party held its convention in Chicago to nominate its candidate for the presidency of the United States. Tens of thousands of young men and women demonstrated, and in a historic spectacle captured by cameras and beamed throughout the world, they lowered the American flag and raised in its place a bloodstained shirt. Then they brought a big fat pig, wrapped it in the American flag, sat it on a raised dais, and declared that they would nominate it as the best candidate for the presidency of the United States. One speaker after the other praised the pig-candidate in the midst of derisive cheers, whistles, and applause. Their message was clear. The government establishment itself was corrupt to the core, no matter which person was at the top: the rulers of America were sending the sons of the poor to Vietnam so that their profits might multiply by millions while their own sons lived a soft life away from danger. They were also saying that the American dream was an illusion, a race with no end in sight in which nobody won. During that race, Americans worked hard and engaged in cutthroat competition that showed no mercy, to get a house, a fancy car, and a second home. They spent their life chasing a mirage only to discover at the end that they had been deceived, that the result of the race had been fixed before it even began: a handful of millionaires controlled everything, and their ratio to the total population hadn't increased at all over fifty years, whereas the number of poor people kept rising at a rapid pace.

The day the pig was nominated was a truly historic day and the message was conveyed to the public. Millions of Americans began to think that those young men and women might be right. There were violent confrontations with the police, and the parks turned into real battlefields. The police struck at the demonstrators with all possible means and with utmost cruelty: with thick nightsticks, water hoses, tear gas bombs, and rubber bullets. The students defended themselves by throwing stones and hair spray canisters that they lit and turned into small bombs. Many were seriously wounded. Ambulances carried hundreds away, and hundreds of others were arrested. That day Graham's head was busted open by a heavy club, and he spent two weeks in the hospital. To this day he still has a scar behind his ear. Those were the days of real struggle. He was arrested several times, put on trial, and imprisoned for various periods of time, one of which was a full six-month sentence on charges of inciting riots, damage to public property, and assaulting the police. But he never regretted what he had done. He was homeless for years, even though he could have, had he wanted, led a comfortable life, for he had a medical degree, with distinction, from the famous University of Chicago and could land a good job any time he wanted. But he believed in the revolution as if it were a religion for which he had to sacrifice. He would come out of prison only to demonstrate again. Without a job or source of income, he lived with his fellow rebels. They were certain that the world would change, that the revolution would triumph in America as it had in many other places, that the capitalist system would collapse and that they, with their hands, would make a new, fair, and humane America; that all Americans would secure the future of their children. They believed that fierce immoral competition would be gone forever, that the signs declaring OUR LOSS IS YOUR GAIN posted by stores going out of business to play on people's greed for cheap bargains, would disappear. Those were the dreams of the revolutionary youth, but they were not realized.

The Vietnam War ended and so did the revolution. Most of the comrades joined the system they had rebelled against only yesterday. They got jobs, had families and children, and some of them made vast fortunes. They all changed their way of thinking, except for John

Graham, who was now over sixty but who remained loyal to the revolution. He didn't marry because he did not believe in the institution of marriage, and he couldn't shoulder the responsibility of bringing children into this rotten world. His faith was never shaken in the possibility of creating a better world if Americans got rid of the capitalist machine that controlled their lives. Despite his advanced age he continued to be active in various leftist organizations: the Friends of Puerto Rico, the American Socialist Union, the Vietnam Generation, the antiglobalization movement, and others. He has paid an exorbitant price for his struggle. He's ended up a lonely old man—no family and no children. He had two relationships that didn't work out and left him with deep emotional wounds. He had two bouts of depression and was institutionalized and tried to commit suicide. But he got over the crises, not because of medication or therapy, but thanks to an internal solid core, which he called on and which didn't fail him. He also got over his problems thanks to his love for his work and his total immersion in it. For despite his controversial political affiliations and his problems, Graham is one of only a few professors in the science of medical statistics, and he has published dozens of important papers throughout the world. He considered statistics to be a creative art depending on inspiration more than just math. He had a favorite sentence with which he began his lectures to graduate students: "Statistics has suffered a historical injustice brought about by mediocre bourgeois minds that consider statistics merely as a means of tallying profit and loss. Keep that in mind: statistics is a truthful means of viewing the world; it is simply logic flying with the two wings of imagination and numbers."

Despite Graham's tremendous popularity at the university as a nice personality, an extraordinary scholar, and a great lecturer, he rarely had genuine friendships: those colleagues sympathetic to him considered him a kind of funny, interesting folkloric personality, eliciting curiosity. But they also kept a distance between him and themselves. As for conservatives, like George Roberts, they shied away from him and attacked him publicly as an atheist, an anarchist, and a communist who espoused evil, subversive ideas. Thus John Graham's life proceeded, approaching its expected end: the old, leftist university professor who would live and die alone, with the most important events in his life behind him. He began to feel, day after day, that his ties to the world were eroding. He tried to imagine what the end would be like: How was he going to die? Perhaps in his office or while giving a lecture, or maybe he would have a heart attack at night and his neighbors would find out that he was dead a few days later.

Two years ago, however, a surprise had changed his life. The antiglobalization movement held a rally in the park and John Graham delivered a scathing speech against neocolonialism hiding behind multinational corporations. He received a loud, long round of applause on account of his advanced age, his enthusiasm, and his reputation as an old warrior who had kept the faith. Graham left the podium carrying his papers, returning the greetings of those present and shaking their hands. It was then that a beautiful young black woman approached him. She introduced herself as Carol McKinley and said she wanted him to clarify some points in his speech. What she asked for required only a few minutes, but John and Carol began talking and soon seemed unaware of anyone around them. They stayed together from midafternoon until midnight. They went to three different bars and drank and talked the whole time. Graham became attracted to her at a phenomenal speed. What was more surprising was that she fell in love with him despite a whole lifetime of difference in age. He appeared irresistibly attractive to her, with his gray hair, his leftist ideas, his unshakable belief in his principles, and his intelligent sarcasm that expressed his disdain for things that ordinary men clamored for. She had just been through a long, failed relationship that had left her with deep sorrow and a five-year-old son. When Graham asked her weeks later to move in with him, she didn't seem surprised. She looked at him with a calm smile and said, "I love you, but I cannot leave my son."

"You won't have to leave him. He'll come and live with us."

"Are you sure you'll accept him?"

"Yes."

"Do you know what it means to live with a child who is not yours?"

"I know."

"I don't want you to regret it later."

"I won't."

"Do you love me that much?"

They were walking along the shore of Lake Michigan. It was bitterly cold and ice covered everything. They were all alone, as if they were the only two people in Chicago. Graham stopped her, held her shoulders, then looked at her for a long time as his hot breath created a constant cloud of steam. He asked her in a serious tone of voice, "You want an answer to your question?"

"Please."

"Now or later?"

"Now. Right away."

He hugged her hard and gave her a long kiss on the mouth, then smiled and said, "That's my answer."

"It's a convincing answer," she said, laughing.

Graham loved little Mark, who grew attached to him, and the two spent a lot of time together. Mark found in him the father he was deprived of, and Graham found that their relationship satisfied his instinctive affection for children. More important, he loved Carol as he hadn't loved a woman before. She was his enchantress, muse, lover, friend, and daughter. He lived with her the most beautiful love experience in his life; so much so that sometimes he imagined that her presence with him was not real, that it was just a dream from which he might wake up suddenly to not find her. The difference in race, however, brought them many problems: when they embraced or engaged in intimate talk or held hands in public, it provoked racist feelings among many people, such as some waiters in certain restaurants and bars who treated them coldly and insolently. They also experienced some prying inquisitive and disapproving glances in public places. This even applied to some of Graham's more conservative neighbors on his street when they met them by chance; the neighbors would address him and totally ignore her, as if she were invisible to them. Many a time did a restaurant owner refuse to seat them with the pretext that the kitchen was closed even though other customers were at the very same moment waiting for the food they had ordered. On weekends, Graham and Carol were used to being on the receiving end of hurtful comments from drunks on the street, like, "Black and White!" (in reference to the famous scotch brand).

"Why don't you go sleep with a black person like you?"

"Do you like making it with Negroes, Grandpa?"

"How much did you pay for this slave girl?"

Even at the University of Illinois where he worked, there was a regrettable incident. One morning, Carol had to drop in on Graham at school. Unfortunately she met George Roberts, whom she didn't know. She greeted him in a normal manner and asked him where John's office was. She was surprised when he asked her, "Why do you want Dr. Graham?"

"I'm his girlfriend."

"His girlfriend?" asked Roberts loudly, clearly expressing his surprise to make the insult complete. Then he fixed her with a scrutinizing glance from head to toe and said, "Dr. Graham's office is at the end of the corridor, room 312. But I don't believe for a moment that you are his girlfriend."

"Why?"

"I think you know why," said Roberts and then turned away and left. When Carol entered Graham's office sobbing and told him what had happened, the histology department witnessed a unique incident. Graham pulled Carol by the hand and rushed through the corridor, dragging her as if she were a child. He stormed Roberts's office and shouted in a thunderous voice, "Listen, you've insulted my girlfriend. Either you apologize to her now or I will break your head. Understand?"

Roberts raised his head slowly. He was busy preparing a lecture he was to deliver in a short while and realized (being intelligent, and from his long experience with Graham, whom he thought capable of any behavior, being an anarchist communist with almost no morals) that Graham would carry out his threat. So he looked calmly at Carol (whose face changed expression from crying to fear of the consequences of a fight) then placed his hands together in front of his chest in the Indian way and bowed his big head, laughing to make it all sound like a joke, "I apologize for what I said to you, madam; please forgive me."

At that point Graham looked like an angry child who was not able to have his revenge, so he sighed and left the room with Carol at his heels.

Racist harassments, however, despite their viciousness, did not affect the lovers. After every racist incident they experienced, they'd go home and take delight in making love passionately. They would rush at the beginning then take their time and enjoy their pleasure leisurely as they used to do in their early days together, as if clinging to each other against that unfair ugly world that persisted in trying to separate them, or as if the person insulting them were watching them making love so they wanted deep down to defy him and prove to him how wrong he was.

One day after mad lovemaking that exhausted them, they lay naked, panting. She lay on his chest and began, as usual, listening to his heartbeat and playing with the gray hair on his chest with her fingers and kissing it. He said to her in a dreamy voice that reverberated in the stillness of the room, "If I could, I'd marry you right away."

"Why can't you?"

"Civil marriage procedures remind me of the articles of incorporating a commercial company. As for standing before a fat, dyspeptic priest to repeat after him prayers that would make us a couple, that's something I couldn't stand."

"Why?"

"If God exists, do you think he needs official papers and seals?"

"These are church rituals."

"The church is one of the biggest lies in history and it has played, in most eras, the role of the commercial, colonialist establishment more than anything else."

"John!"

"I can prove to you, if you wish, with historical evidence that Jesus Christ never existed to begin with. Man has invented religions to get over his fear of the unknown."

She placed her hand on his mouth and said, "Please, I am a believing Christian. Can you respect my feelings a little?"

When she got angry, when she pursed her lips and her face looked like that of a child about to cry, when she stared at him with her beautiful eyes as if he had disappointed her, she became irresistible, and he would take her in his arms and shower her with kisses. That usually led to a new round of lovemaking.

Their love was wonderful, but troubles loomed when Carol lost her job. A new white manager was appointed at the mall where she worked and he fired her and another black colleague for no obvious reason (unless it was their color?). For ten months Carol fought obstinately to find a new job but she couldn't. The two lovers found themselves in unexpected financial straits. Graham had no savings at all. He spent money right away, as if he were getting rid of a burden or shame. Like most people advanced in years, he spent sleepless nights worrying about suffering a debilitating illness, so he chose a very expensive insurance coverage whose monthly premium ate up a considerable portion of his university salary. At the same time, Mark's tuition and his basic expenses were high while Carol's unemployment compensation was negligible. Faced with that, Graham reined in his expenses to overcome the crisis: he stopped taking Carol out to eat and he also did not buy the clothes that he needed for winter. For the first time in many years he stopped buying the expensive Dutch tobacco that he loved very much and replaced it with a cheap local substitute that had an overpowering smell as if it were burning wood. He did all of that gladly, without grumbling or unease. To the contrary, he was more cheerfully playful with Carol and said to her more than once to console her, "I don't have a problem. So long as we can have the young one's tuition and our food, nothing worries me. I've accustomed myself to live on very little. The most beautiful days in my life were those I spent on the street, homeless."

Carol, however, did not accept the crisis so simply. She felt guilty because she had brought him this hardship. She told herself that she had been unfair to him. His salary had been enough for him, and now, together with her son, they had become a burden on him. Why should he suffer when Mark's father didn't want to support his son? She felt very bitter that she had lost her job, not because she was negligent or inefficient, but just because she was black. Graham was surprised one day when he found her hanging a large wooden sign at the entrance to the living room, with the inscription:

You Are White   You Are Right
You Are Black   Stay Back

Graham was disturbed and asked her why she had written the sign. She smiled sadly and said, "Because it's the truth, John. I put it up there so I would never forget."

She became irritable and moody. She would be silent for a long time then suddenly cry, for no reason. Sometimes she was aggressive and combative and fought with John for the most trivial reasons. He met her rage with the understanding and tolerance of someone in love. At the peak of her anger when she yelled at him and waved her hands hysterically, he would resort to silence and smile affectionately. Then he would get close to her, embrace her, and whisper, "I don't want to talk about details. I love you and I apologize for all that angers you, even if I am not responsible for it."

ON SUNDAYS HE USUALLY SLEPT in, but for one reason or another that morning he got up early and didn't find her next to him. He looked for her throughout the house, and when he didn't find her he was worried that she had gone out without telling him. Where had she gone and why hadn't she left him a message? She had left early knowing that, as usual, he wouldn't get up before noon. What was she hiding? Did she go to Mark's father to ask him to support his child? She had told him once that she wanted to do so, but he had objected strenuously. He said she had to maintain her dignity. But he knew that he objected out of jealousy. He was afraid that her love for her old mate might be rekindled. He was a younger man and the two of them had a long history. Had she gone to him? He would never forgive her if she had.

Mark had got up, so Graham prepared breakfast for him, made him a large cup of hot chocolate, and turned on the cartoon channel. Then he went back to his room, closed the door, and lit his pipe, but he couldn't help himself. So he went back and asked Mark, "Did you see your mom going out?"

"I was asleep."

"Do you know where she went?"

"Don't worry about Mom, John. She's a strong woman."

John Graham laughed at his precociousness and hugged Mark and kissed him and sat next to him to play with him. A little while later he heard the door open, squeak, and close slowly. Soon Carol appeared at the door of the room. She was frowning and looked engrossed in distant thoughts despite her elegant appearance, which confirmed his suspicions. Graham led her gently but firmly to their room. He closed the door, doing his best to control his anger. "Where've you been?"

"Is this an official interrogation?"

"I'd like to know."

"You don't have the right."

She was speaking in a hostile tone and at the same time avoiding looking at his face. He threw his stout body into the chair and took a few moments to light his pipe and exhale a thick cloud of smoke. Then he said calmly, "Carol, I am the last person on earth who seeks to possess the woman he loves. But I think, inasmuch as we live together, it is only natural for each of us to know where the other is going."

"I am not going to ask for your written permission to go out," she cried, apparently determined to escalate the disagreement as far as it would go. She was carrying the Sunday *Chicago Tribune* and in sheer anger threw it down and its many pages scattered all over the floor. She shouted, "This is unbearable!"

She started to rush out of the room but just one step away from the door she stopped suddenly, frozen in place. She didn't go out and didn't turn back toward him, as if she had responded to that established mysterious rhythm that grew between people who had been married for a long time. She just stood there, as if waiting for him or summoning him. He got the signal: he rushed toward her and embraced her from the back, then turned her around and hugged her, whispering, "Carol, what's the matter?"

She didn't answer. He started kissing her passionately until he felt her body soften little by little as if opening up before him. He led her gently toward the bed, but he felt her tears wetting his face and he asked her in alarm, "What happened?"

She moved away from him and sat on the edge of the bed. She was exerting an extraordinary effort to control herself but finally collapsed and began to sob uncontrollably. Speaking in a disjointed manner, she said, "I went to a job interview. I told myself I'd tell you only if I get the job. You've had enough disappointment on my account."

He raised her hands and began kissing them. Her mellow voice reverberated, as if coming from the depths of sadness. "I can't take this anymore. With all my experience, what more do I need to prove to get a job."

A profound silence descended upon them. Then she whispered as she buried her head in his chest and succumbed to a new fit of crying, "Oh, John, I feel so humiliated."

 The reverence with which Professor Dennis Baker is regarded could be attributed to various reasons: his strong personality, his integrity, his devotion to science, the way he treats his students and colleagues lovingly and fairly, his simple austere appearance, and his constant silence, which he only breaks to say something necessary and useful. But more important than all of that: his scientific achievements. Baker presents himself as a "photographer of cells," words that encapsulate the hard work and effort that he has exerted over the past forty years to transform the photographing of cells from a mere ancillary method in scientific research into an established independent science that had its own tools and rules. Baker invented methods and techniques in photographing cells that were patented in his name. He published so many papers over the years that including his CV in the program of scientific conferences posed a real problem because it required several times as much space as any other professor's CV. It has become impossible for any book on histology to be published in any university in the world without using Baker's cell photograph collections. Professor Baker approached his work in the spirit of an artist. First, a mysterious thought would come to him; then it would persist and give him sleepless nights; then it would disappear, leaving behind an amazing, but fragile, idea. He would examine that idea and scrutinize it until it took hold in his mind. Then he would spend weeks testing the cells in different light settings and different levels of microscope strength. Finally, inspiration would come, revealing for him what he should do, whereupon he would enthusiastically rush to photograph, record, and print.

In addition to his scientific achievement, Baker is considered one of the greatest lecturers that the University of Illinois has known throughout its history. His lectures about bodily tissues were as simple as they were profound. This led the university administration to market them on CDs that sold thousands of copies. Despite the magnificence of his achievement, Baker, like many great creative minds, was not immune to fears of failure and apprehensions of falling short. There were dark thoughts that sometimes made him wonder about the value of what he did. Those who worked with him were quite familiar with the anxiety that came over him before his lectures, like stage fright. As soon as the lecture ended he would ask one of his assistants, "Don't you think that my explanation was somewhat vague?"

If the assistant did not hurry to refute the accusation enthusiastically, Baker's imagined shortcoming would be confirmed for him and he would shake his head and say sadly, "Next time I'll try to do better."

In Chicago's bitter cold and snowy winter, old Professor Baker often got up at four o'clock in the morning, washed up, put on heavy clothes and gloves, and covered his head and ears well, as if he were a soldier going to the battlefield. He would take the 5:00 A.M. train with cleaning crews and drunkards from the previous night. He would go through this trouble gladly to be able to check the cell samples at the exact time that he had set to the minute. That was how Baker accomplished his glorious achievements day after day, with the perseverance of an ant and the devotion of a monk, until he became a legend. There was a lot of talk at Illinois for years about the likelihood of his getting a Nobel Prize at any moment.

John Graham, during one of his outspoken moments, commented on Baker's achievement by saying, "The great Western civilization was made by unique and devoted scientists like Dennis Baker, but the capitalist system has turned their creative endeavor into production machines and commercial enterprises from which millions of dollars pour in to stupid and corrupt men like George Bush and Dick Cheney."

Baker supervised dozens of MSs and PhDs, and among his students were many Egyptians who achieved dazzling results. He kept in his lab thank-you letters from them, which he always asked them to write in Arabic because he liked the shape of the letters. His positive experience with Egyptians made him curious about their country, so he borrowed several books about Egypt from the university library. One time he was invited with some professors to a reception at De Paul University. There he drank two glasses of whiskey (the limit that he allowed himself). The liquor loosened his tongue and released inside him a torrent of sympathy. He looked at Dr. Salah, who was standing next to him, and asked him in his usual, direct manner, "Dr. Salah, I have a question: all the Egyptians who've worked with me were talented and exceptionally hardworking and yet Egypt, as a country, is still scientifically backward. Do you have an explanation for that?"

Salah answered quickly, as if he had prepared the answer. "Egypt is backward because of the lack of democracy, no more and no less. Talented Egyptians achieve great results when they emigrate to the West; but in Egypt, unfortunately, the despotic regime usually persecutes them and passes them over."

Baker looked at him for a moment then nodded and said, "I get it."

This deep appreciation by the great scientist for Egyptians made him always amenable to being the advisor for their theses and dissertations. It must be mentioned here that Baker, the pious, observant Protestant Christian, did not see any differences among the races and ethnic groups. In his creed humans were all children of God, equally blessed with His sacred spirit. Thus we are able to understand his tolerant, liberal positions in departmental meetings: he evaluated each student according to his or her effort and abilities only, in total disregard for their nationality or the color of their skin (unlike George Roberts). These great ideals in which Dr. Baker believed were recently put to a difficult test. He had welcomed supervising Ahmad Danana for the PhD, but from the first instant, he noticed that Danana was a type of Egyptian that he hadn't seen before: he was older, looked formal, and wore a full suit and a necktie. Baker did not dwell on Danana's appearance, but the problem started with the first course, in which Baker taught his students methods of research. It was an important course because it introduced students to the basic principles they had to follow in their theses. Passing that course depended on class participation rather than on a traditional final examination. So Baker assigned students certain papers that they had to read, summarize, and comment on every week. Then he would listen to them and engage them in discussion and give them grades based on their absorption of the material and the amount of work they had put into it. Since the first class meeting Baker noticed, somewhat anxiously, that Ahmad Danana spoke on matters not germane to the subject at hand. He attributed that, perhaps, to the possibility that he did not understand what was required of him. So he summoned him to his office after class and gave him a new research paper, saying gently, "Read this paper well. Next week, in class, I'll ask you to summarize it and comment on it."

The following class, when it was Danana's turn, he stood up in his full suit, cleared his throat, coughed, and began a long spiel during which he waved his hands, speechifying in his broken English, modulating his voice to influence the listeners as if he were delivering an oration in the National Party. The students followed him in bafflement as he said, "Dear colleagues, believe me. The question is not methods of research. Methods of research, praise the Lord, are copiously abundant. What I'd like for us to discuss today is the idea behind the methods of research. Within each of us there is a certain idea about method. We must, let me repeat here, *must*, come clean to each other, for the sake of the future of science, for our children and our grandchildren."

Baker, as usual, was recording everything said in class so he could accurately evaluate each student. He was so extremely perplexed by what Danana said that for a moment he thought he was an imbecile. But on second thought he deemed that unlikely and had to interrupt him decisively. "Mr. Danana, I'd like to draw your attention to the fact that what you are saying has absolutely nothing to do with the subject of this session."

That sentence would have silenced any student instantly, but Danana, well trained in arguing and polemics in political gatherings, did not bat an eyelash and said loudly, "Professor Baker, please. I am calling upon my colleagues to come clean, to exchange the ideas that each of us has about methods of research."

Baker's face turned red with anger and he shouted: "Listen, you've got to stop talking like that. I won't allow you to confuse your colleagues. You either speak to the subject or stop talking, or get out of here."

Danana fell silent and sighed. His face acquired the features of a great man who has received a cruel insult but, for noble considerations that he alone was aware of, decided to transcend the insult and forget it. The class went on as usual, and when it was over, Baker stared at Danana and asked him in disbelief mixed with exasperation, "Do you have psychological problems?"

"Of course not," answered Danana with a nonchalant smile.

"Then why didn't you read the paper?"

"I read it."

"But you didn't refer to it at all. You wasted class time with meaningless words."

Danana placed his hand on Baker's shoulder as if he were an old friend and said as if counseling him, "I always prefer to present scientific data with a human touch that brings students closer to one another."

Baker looked at him closely then said calmly, "It's I who determines the way this class is taught, not you."

Then he opened a folder he was holding and took out a large stack

of paper that he handed to Danana and said, "I am going to give you
one last chance. Here, read this paper carefully. I want you to present
me with a summary within two days at most."

"I don't have time this week."

"How can you be a student and not find time for your studies?"

"I am not an ordinary student. I am the president of the Egyptian
Student Union in all of America."

"What does this have to do with research?"

"My time is not my own. It belongs to my colleagues who've given
me the responsibility."

Baker fell silent, looking at him in true bewilderment: this was a
type of human being that he hadn't encountered before in his life.

Danana went on to say in an official tone, "Professor Baker, I expect
you to take my political post into consideration."

It was then that Baker burst out, saying angrily, "What you're saying
is nonsense. Do you understand? Here you are a student, no more and
no less. If you don't have time for your studies, quit."

Baker turned and left. Danana ran after him trying to pacify
him, but he dismissed him with a wave of his hand. From that day
on Danana became a heavy psychological burden on Baker, who, despite his long experience, didn't know how to deal with him. He would
attend regularly for a few days and then would miss several classes and
neglect his lessons, coming back every time with a new story about a
problem that one of the students had had that forced him to travel to
Washington, or about a student suddenly falling ill that he had to check
into a hospital. At this point we have to understand that the problem
was much more serious than Danana's preoccupations or his neglect
of his lessons: the academic record that Danana had attained in Egypt
was extremely mediocre, for it was his relationship with the secret State
Security police—which had started when he was an undergraduate—
that had earned him his promotions, and not his work. Every year the
security apparatus exercised tremendous pressure on professors at the

medical school in Cairo University to give Danana high grades that he didn't deserve. Then the pressure continued to appoint him as an instructor, and then he got a master's degree and finally got this scholarship. But his true level of competence was exposed in Illinois and he was not able to keep up with his studies. Professor Baker was shocked at Danana's ignorance of some basics of medicine, so much so that he told him once in disbelief, "I can't understand how you graduated with Tariq Haseeb and Shaymaa Muhammadi. Their academic knowledge is far superior to yours."

Two full years passed and Danana covered only very little in his research. He was supposed to present his results this week but he missed class three days in a row. On the morning of the fourth day, Baker was working in his lab when there was a knock on the door, then it opened and Danana appeared. Baker ignored him and went on with his work. When Danana began the recital of his usual excuses, Baker interrupted him without turning toward him. He said calmly as he looked with one eye inside a glass test tube as if examining the barrel of a gun, "If you do not submit the results of the research this week, I will ask to be relieved of supervising your dissertation."

Danana was about to speak but Baker silenced him with a gesture of his hand. Then he said as he withdrew inside the lab, "I have nothing to say to you. It's your last chance."

■ ■ ■ ■ ■ ■ ■ ■ ■ ■ ■

Karam Doss smiled and said, "Sorry to disturb you, Nagi."

"Welcome."

"Would you allow me to treat you to a cup of coffee somewhere?"

I saw his face in the soft corridor light. He looked tired and pale. It seemed he hadn't slept since yesterday and hadn't changed his clothes, which looked wrinkled and a little dirty. I said to him, "If this has something to do with last night, I've forgotten it."

"No, it's bigger than that."

I was tired and wasn't ready for more arguments and problems. I said, "Can I accept your invitation some other time? I am still hung over."

"Please, I won't keep you long."

"Okay, come on inside. I have to get dressed."

"Take your time. I'll wait for you in the lobby."

After about a quarter of an hour, I was sitting next to him in his red Jaguar. I leaned back in the comfortable seat, feeling as if I were a leading man in a foreign film about car racing. I said, "Your car is wonderful. I imagine it's very expensive."

He smiled and replied calmly, "I make good money, thank God."

The dashboard had so many meters it looked as if it were part of the cockpit of an airplane. The head of the gearshift was in the shape of a big metal fist. Karam grabbed it then moved. The engine roared loudly and the car dashed off at an enormous speed. I asked him, "Do you like car racing?"

"I am crazy about it. As a child I dreamed of becoming a race car driver and here I am, realizing some of my old dreams."

Something deep down in the tone of his voice was different from what it had been yesterday. It was as if he had been performing a role onstage but now he was talking to a friend after the show. He asked me in a friendly voice, "Have you been to Rush Street?"

"No."

"Rush Street is the young people's favorite street in Chicago. It has the most popular bars, restaurants, and dance clubs. On weekends, young men and women come out to the street to dance and drink until dawn, a kind of communal celebration of the end of a week of work. Look."

I looked to where he was pointing and saw several policemen on horseback. They looked strange against the giant skyscrapers in the background. Karam said, laughing, "In the late hours of the night, when drunkenness and revelry reach their peak, Chicago police resort to the mounted detail to disperse the drunks. When I was young, an American friend taught me how to provoke a horse. We would drink and go out on the street, and when the mounted force came to disperse us, I would sneak behind the horse and prod it in such a way that it would neigh and get agitated and gallop away."

He parked the car and locked it. I walked next to him, dazzled by the neon lights glittering on and off endlessly, making the whole street look more like a large nightclub. Suddenly we heard a voice behind us, "Just a moment, sir."

I stopped to look at the source of the sound, but Karam grabbed my arm and whispered in my ear, "Keep walking. Don't look behind and don't talk to anyone."

His tone was stern, so I acquiesced. He moved faster, with me in tow. Before long there appeared beside us a tall, thin young black man, his hair cascading down his shoulders in intersecting braids. He was wearing bracelets on his arms and chains on his chest that jangled as he moved. He said, "Hey, man. You want some pot?"

"No, thank you," Karam answered quickly, but the young man persisted, "I have some excellent stuff that'll make you see the world as it is."

"Thank you. We don't like pot."

Karam stopped and so did I. We remained standing on the side-walk as we were. The young man walked in front of us, jangling until he disappeared down a side street. It was then that Karam started walking again, saying, "You have to be careful with those guys. They're usually under the influence and one of them might fool you with this pot business until you take out the money from your pocket, which he would then snatch and maybe hurt you."

I remained silent and he asked me, "Are you tense because of what happened?"

"Of course."

He laughed loudly and said, "What happened is quite ordinary. People face it here every day. You're in Chicago, my friend. Here we are."

We entered an elegant two-story building with a lighted electric sign saying PIANO BAR. The place had soft lights throughout and there were tall round tables scattered all over. At the end of the room there was a black man wearing a tuxedo and playing the piano. We sat at a nearby table and Karam said, "I hope you like this place. I prefer quiet bars. I can no longer stand noisy dance clubs. It's a sign of old age."

A beautiful blond waitress came over, and when I ordered a glass of wine, he asked me in surprise, "You still want to drink? I haven't recovered from last night's drinking."

"Me too, but one or two glasses will make me okay. This is a well-known way of getting over a hangover—to drink a little the following day. Abu Nuwas said, 'Treat me with that which made me sick.'"

Dr. Karam picked up a piece of paper from the table and took out of his pocket a gold pen and said, "Wasn't Abu Nuwas the poet famous for his poetry on wine during the Abbasid period?"

"Exactly."

"Can you repeat that verse? I'd like to write it down."

He wrote it down quickly then said as he put the pen in his pocket, "I'll have a drink like you to get rid of the headache."

We were avoiding looking at each other, as if we had suddenly remembered the quarrel. He took a large sip of whiskey and sighed, saying, "I am sorry, Nagi."

"It was I who wronged you."

"We were both drunk and we fought and it's over. But I've come tonight for something else."

He was carrying a small valise in his hand. He placed it between us on the round marble table, then put on his gold-framed glasses and took out a sheaf of papers.

"Here, please."

"What's this?"

"Something I want you to read."

The lights were dim and I had a headache, so I said, "With your permission, may I read it later?"

"No, now, please."

I moved a little to the right so I could get closer to the light. The papers were written in Arabic. I began to read, "A proposal submitted by Dr. Karam Doss, professor of open heart surgery at Northwestern University, to the College of Medicine, Ain Shams University."

He didn't let me finish reading. He leaned his elbows on the table and said, "I submitted this proposal last year to Ain Shams University."

He ordered another drink and continued enthusiastically, "I'm now a big name in heart surgery. My fees for each operation are very high. And yet I offered the officials at Ain Shams Medical School Hospital my services, to perform operations for free for a month every year. I wanted to help poor patients and transfer to Egypt advanced surgery techniques."

"That's great."

"More than that. I submitted a proposal to establish a modern surgery unit that would have cost them next to nothing. I was going to secure funding for them through my connections with American universities and research centers."

"Excellent idea!" I exclaimed, my sense of guilt increasing.

"Do you know what their answer was?"

"Of course they welcomed it."

He laughed. "They didn't reply and when I called the dean of Ain Shams Medical School, he said my idea was not feasible at this time."

"Why?"

"I don't know."

He took another sip of his drink, and it seemed to me that he was having a hard time concentrating. I knew that drinking again after a hangover got rid of the headache, but it also made the liquor more potent.

"I haven't told this story to anyone, but you should know it because yesterday you accused me of fleeing from Egypt."

"I apologize again."

He bowed his head and said in a soft voice, as if talking to himself, "Please stop apologizing. I just want you to know me as I really am. For the last thirty years that I've lived in America, I haven't forgotten Egypt for a single day."

"Aren't you happy with your life here?"

He looked at me as if trying to find the right words, and then he smiled and said, "Have you had any American fruits?"

"Not yet."

"Here they use genetic engineering to make the fruit much larger and yet it doesn't taste so good. Life in America, Nagi, is like American fruit: shiny and appetizing on the outside, but tasteless."

"You're saying that after all you've achieved?"

"All success outside one's homeland is deficient."

"Why don't you go back to Egypt?"

"It's difficult to erase thirty years of your life. It's a difficult decision, but I've thought about it. The proposal I submitted was my first step toward going back, but they turned it down."

He said the last few words bitterly, and I said, "It's really sad for Egypt to lose people like you."

"Perhaps you find this hard to understand because you're still young. It's like when a man loves a woman and gets very attached to her and then discovers that she is cheating on him: do you understand this kind of agony? To curse the woman and at the same time to love her and never be able to forget her—that's how I feel toward Egypt. I love her and I wish to offer her all I've got, but she rejects me."

I saw that his eyes were welling up with tears, so I leaned over and put my arm around him and bent over to kiss his head, but he gently pushed me away, saying as he tried to smile, "How about ending this melodrama?"

He began to change the subject and asked me about my studies. We spent about half an hour talking about various subjects, and suddenly we heard a woman's voice close to us: "Hi, sorry to interrupt. I have a question."

"Go ahead," I said quickly. She was a young woman in her twenties, blond and shapely. I had noticed her while we were talking, coming in from the bar and sitting at the table next to us.

"What language are you speaking?"

"Arabic."

"Are you Arabs?"

"We're from Egypt. Dr. Karam is a heart surgeon and I am studying medicine at the University of Illinois at Chicago."

"I'm Wendy Shore. I work at the Chicago Stock Exchange."

"You're lucky, then. You have lots of money."

She laughed. "I only handle the money. I don't own it, unfortunately."

A jovial atmosphere filled the place. Suddenly Dr. Karam got up and patted me on the shoulder, saying, "I have to go now. I haven't slept since yesterday and I have surgery at seven in the morning."

Then he turned to Wendy, shook hands with her, and said, "Glad to meet you, Ms. Shore. I hope to see you again."

I kept following him with my eyes until he disappeared through the bar door. I felt that I loved him and said to myself that I should take my time before judging people so as not to jump to the wrong conclusions as I had done. I came to when I heard Wendy's merry voice saying, "Okay, tell me about Egypt."

I carried my glass and moved to her table. She was beautiful; she had gathered her blond hair up and her gorgeous neck showed. There were light freckles on her cheeks that gave her a childlike appearance made all the more pronounced by her big blue eyes, which made her look as if she were in a state of constant astonishment. I remembered Graham's advice, so I said, "I won't tell you about Egypt until you let me buy you a drink."

"That's nice of you."

"What would you like?"

"A gin and tonic, please."

CHAPTER 17

 Since Chicago was settled, black migration to it has not stopped. Hundreds of thousands escaped slavery in the southern states and came to Chicago driven by the dream of becoming free citizens with dignity. The men worked in factories and their wives worked as domestics in homes or as nannies. They soon discovered that they had replaced slaves' iron chains with other invisible but no less cruel shackles. In the early 1900s black people were allowed to live only on the South Side of the city, where the authorities built affordable housing for the poor. Many black people were unable to move to better neighborhoods because they were poor and were not able to leave the ghetto. For over a hundred years white people had an aversion, as deeply held as if it were a creed, to living together with black people. That aversion was sometimes referred to in American psychological literature as "Negrophobia." All attempts, spontaneous and deliberate, to break the barrier failed. On July 27, 1919, it got very hot in Chicago and this made a seventeen-year-old black man, Eugene Williams, seek relief on the beach at Twenty-ninth Street. The beach, like everything else in the city, had its white and its black sections. Eugene felt wonderfully refreshed as he jumped into the cool water and kept swimming for about an hour. Then it occurred to him, unfortunately, to test his ability to stay underwater. So he held his breath and dived under the surface. And because a diver cannot precisely fix his location, Eugene bobbed up and opened his eyes only to discover that he had crossed the barrier and found himself in the white swimming area. He heard angry shouts and before he could hurry back to where he had come from, white swimmers grabbed him, blinded by anger at his sullying their territorial waters. They started calling him names and beating him; they punched him in the stomach and face as hard as they could. Some used wooden oars to beat him repeatedly on the head until he died. Then they discarded his body on the beach. What made matters worse was the fact that white policemen persistently refused to arrest the killers or interrogate them. During the six days that followed Chicago witnessed horrific racial clashes between white and black people, which left thirty-eight people dead and hundreds of others injured or homeless. The memory of Eugene Williams remained for a long time as a strong lesson for anyone who thought of breaking the barrier. In the year 1966, at the height of the civil rights movement against racism and the Vietnam War, the famous black American leader Martin Luther King Jr. arrived in Chicago and led a procession of tens of thousands of predominantly black marchers through white neighborhoods. King wanted to send a Christian message of love and brotherhood and to declare, at the same time, that the race situation was no longer tolerable. But the result was violent and frustrating. White people attacked the march viciously, throwing stones and rotten eggs and tomatoes on the marchers. They attacked them with clubs and gunfire, and many black people were injured. It wasn't long afterward that King himself was shot by a white racist fanatic. In 1984, a black couple made a fortune and bought a house in a rich white neighborhood. The answer came right away: their white neighbors harassed them and threw stones at them, which resulted in serious injuries. Then the angry neighbors went further, burning first the garage and then the whole house. The couple fled. A similar thing happened to another black couple the same year, and the result was even more tragic.

And thus, throughout Chicago's history, the racial barrier remained as solid as a rock that could not be ignored or transcended: the north of the city and its suburbs were made up of upscale communities inhabited by a white elite in the highest income brackets in the country, while in the black South Side poverty reached levels hard to imagine in America. Unemployment there was rampant, as were drugs, murders, rapes, and robberies. Education and health services were substandard, and everything was distorted, even the concept of family. Many black children were raised by their mothers alone because the fathers left, were killed, or were in jail. It was this glaring contrast between those two worlds that made the famous sociologist Gregory Squires resort to the language of literature when he prefaced his research on Chicago with the following: "It's not the many contradictions that Chicago embodies that distinguish it. What makes it a unique city is that it always takes its contradictions to the utmost."

AS SOON AS RA'FAT THABIT drove into Oakland, he was horrified: many of the redbrick homes were in ruins; backyards were filled with old junk and garbage; gang slogans were sprayed in black and red on the walls; groups of young black people were standing on street corners smoking marijuana; loud music and noise came from some open bars. Ra'fat's anguish increased as he asked himself: How does my daughter live in such a dump? He was determined to see her by any means. He had not thought about what he would tell her when he knocked on her door and awakened her at two o'clock in the morning. He was going to see her now and let come what may. That was what he told himself as he slowed down and looked at the house numbers. He knew Jeff's address by heart. When he got close to the house he went into the parking lot across the street. He locked the car using his remote and hurried to get to the street. It was pitch-dark, and he was suddenly overcome by an uncomfortable feeling. As soon as he passed the first row of cars, he sensed that someone was following him. He tried to dispel the thought but heard, clearly this time, something moving in the dark next to him. He stopped and turned around and little by little was able to make out a large body approaching.

"Why hasn't the old man gone to bed yet?"

The surprise paralyzed Ra'fat, so he fell silent. The man laughed loudly and it seemed from his soft, languorous voice that he was stoned.

"Why'd you come to Oakland, old man? Are you looking for a woman or do you want a fix?"

"I came to visit my daughter."

"What's your daughter doing in Oakland?"

"She's living with her boyfriend."

"Her boyfriend must be a real man. Only men are born in Oakland. What do you want from your daughter, pops?"

"I just came to check in on her."

"What a loving father! Listen, pops. I'm Max, a man from Oakland, and I need a fix now, pops."

There was silence for a moment, then Max's voice changed into a deeper and more serious tone, "I want fifty bucks, pops, to buy some herb and get high."

Ra'fat did not reply; Max extended his big hand and placed it on his shoulders, saying, "Give me fifty bucks. Don't be a coldhearted miser. Come on, come on."

With lightning speed, Max took out of his pocket a switchblade and snapped it open, revealing its long blade that shone in the dark.

"Come on, pops. I don't have time to waste. Are you going to pay or would you like me to save you from the cruelty of this world?"

Ra'fat slowly reached into his pocket and took out his wallet then realized that he wouldn't be able to see anything in the pitch-dark. It seemed Max had realized that too, so he shone a small flashlight.

"There, see? I'm helping you see the money you have. I only want fifty bucks, pops. You're lucky, man. You met good ol' Max. If I was evil I would've took the whole wallet. But I ain't no thief, pops. I'm an honest man who can't find a job in all of goddamn Chicago, a penniless honest man who needs to get high, that's all."

Ra'fat took out a fifty-dollar bill. Max snatched it and backed off a step, still brandishing the switchblade, and said, "Okay, you can go to your daughter now. But a piece of advice, pops: don't hang out in Oakland at night. Not everybody here is as good-hearted as Max."

Ra'fat, during his long residence in Chicago, had been through and told about similar incidents and knew the right way to deal with them: don't ignore your assailant or resist him. The person mugging you most likely is not sober: he's either drunk or high. He might kill you at any moment. Give him what he wants. Don't argue. Don't carry a lot of money with you because he will take it all and don't walk without money, because if you disappoint him he might kill you.

Ra'fat hurried away and heard Max behind him talking to someone else whom he guessed was hiding in the dark. Jeff's house was about a hundred yards away from the parking lot. Ra'fat walked quickly, getting angrier and thinking: Why did Sarah leave the upscale neighborhood where she grew up and come to live among criminals? Her life is in real danger because of her attachment to this bum. My duty as a father is to save her as fast as I can. And this is what I'm going to do right now. He kicked the gate in the iron fence and it made a dull squeaking sound. He crossed the small garden in the pitch-dark quickly and went up three stairs and stood in front of the door of the house. He was panting from effort and agitation. He reached out to ring the bell but let his arm drop to his side right away: What was he going to say to her? Would he wake her up at two o'clock in the morning to ask her to go back home with him? Would she agree so simply?

He stood for a few moments reluctantly in front of the door then decided to give himself a chance to think. So he turned around and began to walk slowly around the house. The side walkway was narrow, and he saw at the end of it a small window through which some light came. So, they're still awake, he said to himself. He was gripped by a strange desire, so he sneaked carefully until he reached the window. There was a faded curtain blocking the view inside, but he found a small gap between the edge of the curtain and the windowpane that made it possible for him to look in from a narrow side angle. He glued his face to the glass of the window, feeling its cold on his ear. He looked and saw a sofa on which Jeff was sitting in his jeans, his chest bare. He looked emaciated and pale, and there were black rings around his beautiful eyes. He was laughing and waving his hand, speaking to someone whom Ra'fat couldn't see but guessed to be Sarah. The conversation lasted for several minutes and Ra'fat gave in to his voyeuristic desire, so he stuck to his place. Soon Sarah appeared. She was wearing a very short blue nightgown that completely revealed her breasts and thighs. She threw herself next to Jeff, who suddenly bent down and was out of sight. Ra'fat stood on tiptoe to follow the scene.

He saw before the lovers a small table on which was a white plate filled with something resembling soft white sand. Jeff rolled a piece of paper into the shape of a straw, raised it, and inserted it into his nostril and took several successive hits on it. He raised his eyes slowly and looked at the ceiling, and then closed his eyes, his features contracting, as if he were overcome with sudden pain. Then he gave the funnel to Sarah and she took one hit and sank back into the sofa, seemingly relaxed. They snorted once again and suddenly Jeff turned to Sarah and hugged her hard. They began to kiss slowly and lustfully. He began to lick her ear then moved down to her neck, kissing it voraciously. She opened her mouth, as if moaning. He put his hand inside her gown, in exciting, pleasurable slow motion, and then took out her breasts and began to squeeze them with his hands. Then he began to speak to them while smiling, as if he were rocking a child while she screamed from sheer pleasure. The two seemed to be in an acute condition of arousal, as if they wanted to enjoy sex before the effect of the drug wore off or as if, somehow, inexplicably, they felt as if they were being observed and so they deliberately showed off their passion to the hilt. Jeff kept biting her breasts and licking them and sucking her nipples until she pushed him gently and he lay on his back. At that moment they seemed to be moving according to a well-established, mutually agreeable rhythm. She bent over him and reached out, undid his zipper, took out his organ and stared at it lustfully. She licked it several times then began to suck it delightedly. Ra'fat found himself rushing unaware toward the door. He rang the bell hard and nonstop. He pounded on the door and kicked it as hard as he could. A long interval passed, then he heard footsteps approaching. The outside light was turned on, then the door opened and Sarah appeared, having put on a silk robe over the nightgown. She looked at him with frightened eyes, as if in disbelief. She opened her mouth to say something, but he didn't give her a chance: he slapped her hard on the face then kicked her in the belly. She screamed at the top of her voice as his own thundered while he stormed into the house, "You junkie whore! I'm going to kill you!"

18

 Shaymaa banged the tray down hard on the table. Some bits of Umm Ali scattered out of the plate. She looked at Tariq combatively and said, agitated, "How dare you permit yourself to touch me?"

His face turned completely pale and he mumbled in a soft voice, "I'm sorry."

"Listen, Tariq, if you think I'm an easy girl, you are mistaken. If you misbehave again you will never see me again. Do you understand?"

He remained silent and bowed his head, as if he were a naughty child who had broken a very expensive vase. He took his leave and she followed him with a reprimanding look until he closed the door behind him. Her body kept shaking as she still felt his hand touching hers and his hot breath on her face. His sudden move had shocked her, so it had taken her a moment to figure out what had happened and to quickly move away from him, but that moment also sent her into new territory in which she had never been before, a secret area filled with delicious and titillating sensations that she had known only stealthily in her forbidden dreams. That immediately brought to her mind her mother's warnings as if they were air raid sirens. She recalled the stern words she had heard a thousand times since her first monthly period took her by surprise during geography class in her first year in preparatory school: "Men, Shaymaa, only want a woman's body. They would do anything to get it. They seduce girls with sweet talk, selling them the illusion of love until they have their way with them. Your body is your honor, Shaymaa, and your father's honor. Your body is the whole family's dignity. If you are lax with it we will spend the rest of our lives humiliated, in shame. Your body is a trust that God Almighty has placed in your hands to preserve, sound and pure, until you hand it over to the man who marries you in accordance with God's commandments and the Prophet's way. Know, Shaymaa, that a man never marries a woman who yields any part of her body to him. A man has no respect for an easy woman and he can never trust her with his honor and his children."

After Shaymaa recalled these principles she had grown up with, she felt content that she had stopped Tariq in his tracks. After a while she thought more calmly: even though he had made a monstrous mistake by trying to embrace her, he, on the other hand, has declared his love for her, which meant that he respected her and wanted to marry her.

She sat down to study, determined to give it her all. She said to herself, Our love should give us an added impetus to work hard and get the degree, so we can go back to Egypt and marry. When she finished studying, she went to the bathroom, where she performed her ablution. She performed the obligatory night prayer and the recommended extra prayers. Then she turned off the light and went to bed in the dark. She kept staring at the dark and then something happened that surprised her: she recalled what Tariq had done and did not disapprove of it and was not angry with him for it. To the contrary, she was swept by an overpowering affection for him. He was in love with her and wanted to embrace her as all lovers did. That was all. Could she have exaggerated her anger? Once again her mother's harsh warnings came back to her mind, but for the first time in her life, she found herself rethinking them.

If what her mother was saying was true, then a girl who was lax with her body, even just a little bit, could never marry. But she knew many stories proving the opposite of that. She knew girls who had given men liberally of their bodies and yet ended up with excellent marriages. Her friend Radwa, instructor in the pathology department in Tanta Medical School, became her professor's mistress, and their illicit relationship was the talk of the whole school for a long time. In the end the professor divorced his wife, the mother of his children, and married Radwa and had children with her. What about her neighbor in Tanta, Lubna? Did she not go out with several young men and tell her in person about physical relations with them? Kisses and hugs and more, things that Shaymaa could not even imagine. What had happened in the end? Was Lubna's reputation sullied and her life ruined? Was she cursed and despised forever? On the contrary, she married Tamir, son of the millionaire Farag al-Bahtimi, owner of the famous candy factories. And Tamir was now madly in love with her and wouldn't refuse her anything. That same Lubna whose body was handled freely by young men was now living like a princess in a palace-like villa on the outskirts of Tanta, a happy wife and mother of two children. And why should she go far for examples? How about she herself? Hadn't she lived chastely? Hadn't she reached her thirties untouched by a man? All her life she had acted properly and had not permitted anyone at school to go beyond the bounds of collegiality; even her professors she had treated with much reserve. Her reputation at school and in the neighborhood was unblemished. So why wasn't she married yet? Why hadn't suitors beaten a path to her door for the sake of her superior morals?

All these instances disproved what her mother said. Was her mother exaggerating or was she talking about the morals of a bygone era? Couldn't a girl's permissiveness (within limits) with the man she loved be a clever way to entice him to marry her? Wasn't it possible that if he kissed and hugged her that he would get more attached to her? Despite her medical study she knew nothing about men's feelings. Wasn't it possible that a man's love for a woman made him, against his own will, think about her body? Besides, if every relationship outside marriage was a horribly shameful and forbidden sin and those committing it were unequivocally cursed, then why didn't God damn those Americans, most of whom lived in sin? Those young men and women that she saw on weekends at train stops and parks, exchanging passionate kisses publicly and sometimes going even further, doing openly what she would be ashamed to do with the husband she had lawfully married in a closed room. Why didn't God's wrath befall such wanton sinners?

The months that Shaymaa had spent in Chicago made her think about her life differently. She began to have doubts about the established principles that she grew up holding to be sacred. Was God going to judge us Muslims one way and judge Americans another way? Those Americans were committing all the great sins: they fornicate, gamble, drink liquor, and engage in all kinds of deviant acts, but God Almighty didn't seem to be angry with them; instead of punishing them for their sins, he was giving them so much wealth, knowledge, and power that they had become the greatest and strongest country in the world. Why does God punish us Muslims when we commit sins, while going easy on the Americans?

"I take refuge in God away from Satan who deserves to be stoned. I ask God for forgiveness and I repent," she repeated, being frightened at where her thoughts had gone. She turned on her side and pressed the pillow against her head to stop the flow of thoughts, but when she closed her eyes, a final, deep-rooted fact revealed itself to her: Tariq loved her and respected her and he meant her no harm. He wanted to embrace her to express his feelings, no more and no less. The whole episode did not justify her behavior toward him. She had been cruel to him. She was now remembering his beloved pale face as he mumbled his apology in shame. She fell asleep feeling profound sympathy for him. The first thing she did when she got up in the morning was to call him. He sounded awkward, as if he expected her to chide him again, but she started talking lightheartedly to prove to him that she had forgotten the matter. They planned their day as usual and the week passed uneventfully, except that their relationship became more intimate, as if what had happened had brought them closer. A new feeling came into play in their relationship: whenever their bodies got close to each other, even for a moment, unintentionally, a great tension arose between them, whereupon they got confused and stammered and her face turned red, as if he had suddenly opened the door while she was naked. When Saturday came around they started to plan to spend it together as usual. Tariq said, "Let's go to the movies and then I'll treat you to dinner at the pizza place I discovered. What do you think?"

She didn't seem thrilled and said, "Frankly, it's cold outside and I am tired of taking the L. Listen, we'll have dinner in my apartment. I'll make a pizza that's a hundred times better than the restaurant's. What do you say?"

He seemed at a loss to understand what was happening. He stared at her face, which turned red suddenly as she laughed nervously. What exactly did she want? He tried to embrace her and she made a scene. So why was she inviting him to her place again? Tariq was so totally confused and unable to concentrate that he could not understand the new biochemistry lesson. And, strangely enough, that did not disturb him much. He said to himself as he closed the book: I'll try to understand it later on. He threw himself onto the bed and crossed his legs (his favorite posture for thinking) and then asked himself what he was going to do with Shaymaa. The answer came right away: I'll go to her place and come what may!

At the appointed time exactly he stood before her door. He was wearing his sharpest outfit: dark blue jeans, a white woolen turtleneck, and a black leather jacket. As soon as he stepped inside, the smell of the dough baking in the oven greeted him. He sat watching television until Shaymaa finished cooking. She set the table and called out to him in a voice that rang soft and affectionate in his ear. She was wearing a blue brocade Moroccan gown. His heart skipped several beats when he noticed that it was closed by a long zipper from top to bottom. Her body was completely covered, but the thought that one pull of the zipper would render her totally naked began to peck at his mind, just as a bird did to a leaf until it finished it off. He was so overcome by wild sexual fantasies (all beginning with the undoing of the zipper) that he became a nervous wreck. The pizza was delicious. They sat eating and talking about different topics and her voice was melodious and deep. There were warm and mysterious signals in it that so charged the atmosphere that his ability to concentrate was diminished to the extent that he didn't hear most of what she said. After dinner he insisted on carrying the dishes to the kitchen himself. He washed them well, dried them, and returned them to the shelves. He rinsed the kettle, filled it with water, and placed it on the stove to make tea. He was surprised when she came into the kitchen. She came close to him and said in a soft, hoarse voice that sounded strange to him, "Would you like some help?"

He didn't answer. He felt his heart beating as if it were a drum. She came closer and stood next to him. He felt the soft fabric of the gown on his hand and his nostrils were filled with her strong perfume. He found it hard to breathe and lost his ability to focus. He felt his stomach contracting, and it occurred to him that he might be about to faint.

■■■■■■■■■■

We drank and talked. Wendy told me about her family. Her mother was a social worker and her father a dentist. She lived with them in New York until she got the job at the Chicago Stock Exchange. She was living by herself in a studio near Rush Street. She said that she loved Chicago but that sometimes she felt lonely and depressed. She thought sometimes that her life had no meaning. She asked me, "Do you think I should see a psychiatrist?"

"I don't think so. These are normal sad moods that all people have at one time or another, especially since you're living by yourself. Don't you have a boyfriend?"

"I found true love once, and it was wonderful, but unfortunately it ended last summer."

I took comfort in her answer and began to tell her about myself and about my love of poetry. She said, somewhat diffidently, "Unfortunately I don't read literature; I don't have the time."

"You yourself are a beautiful poem."

"Thank you."

She picked up her purse and said, "I must go. I have work in the morning."

"Would it bother you if I called you?"

"Not at all."

I called her twice during the week and then I invited her on Friday to coffee at the school cafeteria (to minimize expenses). On the subsequent Saturday, following the instructions of the sage Graham, I invited her to dinner. This time she seemed to have paid more attention to her appearance. She wore black silk pants, a sleeveless white blouse, and a red jacket with a red flower pin on the lapel. Her simple attempt at dressing elegantly was touching and sincere. We had dinner in an Italian restaurant downtown. We talked and laughed as if we were old intimate friends. I actually felt very comfortable in her company. I told her everything, about my mother and my sister, my problem at Cairo University and my love of poetry. She asked me, "Do you dream of becoming a famous poet one day?"

"Fame is not a measure of a poet's success. There are famous poets whose work has no value and great poets that people don't know about."

"So, why do you write?"

"I write because I have something to say. What matters to me is not fame but appreciation, that what I write reaches a number of people, no matter how few, and changes their thoughts and feelings."

"Ever since I was a child, I've dreamed of meeting a real poet."

"You are sitting with one."

I held her hands across the table. I raised them slowly to my lips and kissed them. She looked at me with a captivating smile. We went out to the street, tipsy from the wine. The sound of her footfalls next to me gave me joy. She asked me suddenly, "Where are we going now?"

My heart raced and I said, "I have a great documentary about Egypt. Would you like to watch it with me?"

"Of course. Where is it?"

"In my apartment."

"Okay."

We walked to the L station. I hurried my steps, as if I were afraid she might change her mind. We took the Blue Line. I sat in the seat opposite her. I studied her features slowly. She seemed extremely tender and sweet. I thought that my strong attraction to her was probably due to the problems I had encountered since arriving in Chicago. I definitely needed a woman's affection. When we arrived at my apartment we sat next to each other on the sofa in the living room. We drank wine and talked. I was worried, afraid I might be too precipitous and ruin the occasion. I put my arms around her as she spoke. Her face tensed for a moment and I felt her body warm and vivacious. I was one step away from happiness and I knew from experience that it was a decisive moment, that if it slipped out of my hand, everything would be lost. We stopped talking suddenly and I felt her hot breaths warming me. She seemed to be breathing heavily and I thought she was about to cry. I took her in my arms and began to kiss her passionately on the face and neck. I felt her body contract, then relax little by little. I extended my hand spontaneously to her back to undo her bra. She pulled away gently and planted a quick kiss on my cheek, then whispered tenderly as she got up, "I'll go to the bathroom and I'll be back in a moment."

As soon as she appeared, naked, I eagerly embraced her. We made love a first time, strong and hard, as if getting rid of our pent-up feelings, or as if we had suddenly discovered the possibilities of pleasure and started devouring them in disbelief. Afterward I lay down breathing heavily next to her on the bed and strangely enough I felt desire looming in the distance. That was quite rare, for my chronic problem with women was that weariness that came over me after lovemaking. As soon as I reached orgasm, the fog of lust would be dispelled and I'd lose my awareness of beauty. With Wendy it was different. I looked at her naked body and it looked capable of seducing me endlessly. I felt blood rushing through my veins as if I hadn't satisfied my desire only a few moments ago. She rested her head on my chest and said in a melodious, content voice, "You know something, the first time I saw you, I was sure we'd end up in bed."

"That's because I'm lucky."

"I had made up my mind not to come to your apartment until we went out one more time, but I lost my resistance suddenly."

I planted a kiss on her forehead and said, "You're my wonderful princess!"

"You're obviously experienced in bed even though you're not married. In Egypt, are you permitted to have sex outside marriage?"

"We permit ourselves."

It was a lame answer, but I wasn't ready for any serious discussion at that moment. Wendy laid her chin on my chest and looked at me. She extended her finger and stroked my lips as if I were a child and then exclaimed playfully, "Come on, tell me all about your romantic liaisons with Egyptian women!"

I felt her breasts on my chest emitting unbearably soft warmth. I pulled her gently by the arm and she moved in such a way that she was on top of me. This time I kissed her gently and slowly and then we made love again. I had got to know the contours of her body, so I conducted the second time around in an unhurried and focused manner until we peaked together in a blaze of passion. She savored her ecstasy for a long time and then came to and jumped gleefully out of bed. She took a small camera out of her handbag and said as she readied it, "I'm going to take a picture of you."

"Wait 'til I'm ready."

"I'd like to take your picture in the buff."

I was about to object but she was quicker. The flash lit several times as she took pictures from different angles. Then she laughed and said, "One of these days I'll blackmail you with these photos."

"That'll be the most beautiful blackmail in my life!"

"I hope you'll still think like that always. I've got to go now."

"Can't you stay a little longer?"

"Unfortunately I can't. Next time I'll plan to spend a longer time with you."

She went to the bathroom and soon came back, having put on her clothes. Her face was rosy, radiant with a smile of gratitude. I was waiting for her, having also put on my clothes. She said, "Please don't worry about escorting me."

"I'd like to."

"It's best if I go alone," she said in a calm, decisive tone. I was somewhat surprised but I respected her wish. I embraced her affectionately and said, "Wendy, I'm happy I met you."

"Me too," she whispered as she looked at my face and ran her fingers through my hair, then said, "Where's that documentary movie you promised me?"

I was embarrassed, but she laughed loudly and said as she winked, "I was on to you from the beginning but I pretended to believe you."

"When will I see you again?"

"That depends on you."

"I don't understand."

"There's something I have to tell you. I don't know how you'll take it."

She had opened the door and left it ajar as she got ready to leave. Then she said simply, "I'm Jewish."

"Jewish?"

"Are you shocked?"

"No, not at all."

"Perhaps I was wrong. I should have told you from the beginning. But you'd have found out anyway. No one can hide their religion."

I remained silent. She pulled the door to close it behind her and said with a mysterious smile on her face, "Take your time thinking about our relationship. You can call me anytime. If you don't, I'll still thank you for the wonderful time we had together."

CHAPTER 19

 When instructor Karam Abd al-Malak Doss found out that he'd failed his MS exams for the second time, he went straight to see Dr. Abd al-Fatah Balbaa, chairman of the department of surgery at Ain Shams Medical School. It was a hot day in the summer of 1975. Karam went into the office drenched in sweat from the heat and agitation. When the secretary asked him why he wanted to see the chairman he said, "It's a personal matter."

"Dr. Abd al-Fatah Bey went to perform the midafternoon prayers at the mosque."

"I'll wait for him," said Karam defiantly and sat in the chair facing the secretary, who ignored him and went back to reading some papers in front of him. A whole half hour passed before the door opened and Dr. Balbaa's hulking figure, balding head, crude, stern features, thin beard, and the amber prayer beads that never left his hand appeared. Karam stood up right away and approached his professor, who scrutinized him with a suspicious glance then asked him as if in alarm, "Yes, *khawaga*?"

Dr. Balbaa used the *khawaga* as a term of address when speaking to all Copts, be they professors or messengers. He used this seemingly jocular term to disguise his profound contempt for them. Karam gathered his courage and said, "I hope you have a few minutes, sir, for a subject that concerns me."

"Come on in."

The professor went ahead and sat at his desk and motioned him to sit down.

"What can I do for you?"

"I'd like to know why I failed the exam."

"Your grades were bad, *khawaga*," answered Dr. Balbaa right away, as if he had expected the question.

"All my answers were correct."

"How do you know?"

"I verified them myself. Can we review the answer sheets? Please, sir."

Dr. Balbaa played with his beard, then smiled and said, "Even if all your answers were correct, it wouldn't change your result."

"I don't understand."

"My words are clear. Passing the exam alone is not enough for success."

"But this is against the university rules."

"The university rules are not binding on us, *khawaga*. Not everyone who answers a couple of questions is allowed to become a surgeon with control over people's lives. We select those who deserve the degree."

"On what basis?"

"On important bases which I am not going to share with you. Listen, Karam. Don't waste my time. I'll tell you frankly: you were admitted in the department before I became chairman. Had it been in my hands, I wouldn't have approved your appointment. Think carefully of what I am saying and don't get angry. You will never be a surgeon. I advise you to save your time and effort. Try another department. I'll personally intervene on your behalf."

A heavy silence fell on the room and suddenly Karam cried bitterly, "You are being unfair to me, sir, because I am a Copt."

Dr. Balbaa fixed him with a stern glance, as if warning him not to go any further. Then he got up and said calmly, "The meeting is over, *khawaga*."

———————

THAT NIGHT KARAM COULDN'T SLEEP at all. He locked himself in his room and opened a bottle of whiskey he had bought from a store in Zamalek. He drank nonstop and whenever he finished one glass he got more tense and stood up and started pacing up and down his room, thinking. How could he abandon surgery? He had enrolled in medical school and worked hard for years to fulfill one dream that consumed his life: to be a surgeon. He couldn't change to another specialty. He would never give up surgery come what may. He knew that Dr. Balbaa's authority was absolute, that his word was like irreversible fate. He had told him explicitly: Save your time and effort. You'll never be a surgeon.

If he persisted in trying he would fail him repeatedly until he got expelled from the university, and Balbaa had done that more than once to other doctors. Jesus Christ, how can Balbaa permit himself to destroy the futures of others so easily? Didn't he feel any pangs of conscience whatsoever when he did such injustice? How can he stand before God and pray afterward?

The following morning Karam took a warm bath and drank several cups of coffee to overcome fatigue and the hangover, and then he headed for the American embassy, where he applied for immigration. In a few months he was leaving O'Hare Airport to tread on Chicago's soil for the first time. From the earliest days he came to grasp several truths. First, being a Christian was not a plus for him in American society, for to Americans he was, first and foremost, a colored Arab. Second: America was the land of opportunity, but it was also the land of cutthroat competition. Therefore, if he wanted to be a great surgeon he had to exert a tremendous effort to be at least twice as good as any American colleague. Karam fought valiantly for many critical years: he passed many exams and studied very hard. He would start in the early morning and go on until midnight without complaining or grumbling. He got used to contenting himself with four or five hours of sleep, after which he got up, alert and energetic. He spent days on end at the hospital, working all the time until he earned from his colleagues and professors the nickname "Dr. Ready" because he immediately accepted any task to which he was assigned. Every day he would be present at operations, attend lectures, and study his lessons. His great capacity for work surprised his professors and earned their admiration. When he got tired, the moment he felt he couldn't go on anymore, Karam Doss would close the door and kneel before the cross he kept above his bed. He would close his eyes and repeat in supplication "Our Father who art in Heaven," then pray to God to give him strength and patience. He spoke to the Lord as if he saw him in front of him: "You know how much I love You and believe in You. I've been wronged and you will give me back my rights. Bless me and don't forsake me."

The Lord answered his prayers, and he moved from one success to another. He completed his MS and MD with flying colors then got a position as a surgeon. He got the most important break in his life when he worked, for a full five years, as an assistant to one of the greatest legends of heart surgery in the world, Professor Albert Linz. That was the last step before the top for Karam Doss, and after this he became, as he had dreamed, a capable and famous surgeon who performed operations three days a week at the renowned Northwestern Memorial Hospital. Dr. Karam would arrive at the hospital at exactly 6:30 A.M., greet the workers busy cleaning the floor and exchange lighthearted words with the old black woman receptionist. He would put on his face that reassuring smile he'd acquired during his training as he answered the patient's family's anxious questions. Then he would take off his clothes and put on surgeon's scrubs, and rub his arms, fingers, and fingernails with the brush and sterilizing solution. After that he would stand erect as the nurse wrapped the operating gown around him and tied it in the back, and then he would extend his hands, which she would fit into the gloves. It was only then that Karam Doss got rid of his ordinary day-to-day existence and acquired a mythical dimension, as if he were an imaginary person or a hero in an epic. He would become unique, lofty, invincible, using his will to control everything around him. He would become the embodiment of the famous saying "A true surgeon has the heart of a lion, the eyes of a hawk, and the fingers of a piano player."

It's cold in the operating room; floodlights are trained on the chest of the patient lying there awaiting his fate. The sound of his breathing in the machine and his heartbeats, which are amplified dozens of times, compound the awe of the situation. The surgical team comprises the nurses, the anesthesiologists, and the assistants. Dr. Karam greets them then tells them a joke or something funny at which they laugh in an exaggerated manner to disguise their tension. He follows them as they work, with a scrutinizing look, not without affection, as if he is a maestro watching his musicians playing and awaiting, in accordance with a mysterious internal rhythm, the moment he joins in. When that moment comes, Dr. Karam extends his hand forward with the scalpel, as if inaugurating the show. He turns the scalpel in the air to the right and the left, and then brings it down to the patient's skin, touching it gently several times as though testing it out. Then suddenly he pounces on it, plunging the blade into the tissues with one deep cut, almost lustful and unbelievable. The blood bursts profusely and the assistants' hands hurry with suction tubes and dressings. Dr. Karam works slowly, confidently, and calmly with an amazing concentration that makes him the first to warn the anesthesiologist about an almost invisible blueness on the patient's face, or to notice the eruption of a microscopic drop of blood a full ten seconds before his assistants notice it. During the surgery, everything is done with strict precision: the patient's heart is taken out and the patient is connected to the artificial heart machine. Then Dr. Karam replaces the patient's clogged arteries with other ones taken from the leg and tested well outside the body. Then he attaches the new arteries and ultimately he resumes pumping the blood to the heart that he has fixed with his own hands. The operation lasts many hours, during which his hands don't stop working while the eyes of the assistants are hanging on to the slightest gesture from him, to act upon it immediately. They often understand what he wants before he opens his mouth. With long experience they are able to read his face behind the mask, and so long as he is working in silence it means that everything is all right. If his hands stop working, it means something is wrong. His hoarse voice soon reverberates around the room in a warning dramatic tone as if he were the captain of a ship about to go down—"Operate auxiliary suction," "Give him something to raise the pressure," or "I'll need another hour." They all obey him at once; he is the professor, the surgeon, and the experienced skillful leader who shoulders the responsibility for bringing this sleeping patient back to life. The fate of a whole family is now hanging on his ever-moving fingers.

Karam Doss was a truly great surgeon, and like many greats, he was eccentric. For instance, he would always take off his underwear and wear his scrubs directly on top of his naked body, giving him a sense of freedom that also gave his mind clarity and focus. Ever since he headed the surgical team ten years ago he started performing his surgeries listening to Umm Kulthum's songs, whose voice reverberated in the operating room from speakers that Dr. Karam ordered to be installed in the wall, connected to a stereo in the adjacent room. The scene, though strange, became familiar: the listeners on the tape applauding and shouting so that Umm Kulthum would repeat a phrase of "Inta Umri" ("You Are My Life") or "Ba'id 'Annak" ("Away from You"), saying how great the Sitt was, or screaming in ecstasy when Muhammad Abdu played one of his incomparable solos on the *qanun*. Dr. Karam would hum softly with the music while busy suturing an artery or cutting more skin and muscle with the scalpel to give himself more room to finish the surgery. He would say that Umm Kulthum's voice helped calm his nerves while he worked. Amazingly, the American members of his team began to enjoy Umm Kulthum's voice, or perhaps pretended to in order to please him.

One time, two years ago, an assistant surgeon named Jack joined the team. As soon as Dr. Karam saw him he realized from his long experience in America that he was a bigot. Not long after Jack joined the team, silent skirmishes, intangible, wordless quarrels began to take place between him and Dr. Karam. Jack never laughed at Karam's jokes and fixed him with long, cold, scrutinizing stares. He also followed his instructions reluctantly, carrying them out in a deliberately slow manner as if telling him, "Yes, I work under you; I'm just an assistant and you're a big-time surgeon, but don't you forget that I'm a white American, master of this country, and you're just a colored Arab who has come from Africa and we have taught you and trained you and made a civilized person out of you."

Dr. Karam ignored Jack's provocative gestures and took pains to deal with him in a formal and neutral manner. One day, however, he was surprised to see him come in a few minutes before the operation while he was sterilizing his hands and arms. Jack stood next to him and greeted him curtly then said in a voice choked with confusion and hatred, "Professor Karam, please stop playing those depressing Egyptian songs during surgery, because they prevent me from focusing on my work."

Karam Doss remained silent, finished the sterilization carefully, and turned toward Jack with his hands raised and his frowning face flushed with anger, looking more like a wise Coptic priest about to dumbfound the wicked with the truth, and said calmly, "Listen, son, I've worked very hard for thirty years so that I can have the right to listen to whatever I like in the operating room."

He advanced a few steps in a manner fraught with meaning, then pushed the door leading to the operating room with his foot and said before disappearing behind it, "You can find a place in another surgery team if you like."

———————

THERE IS NOTHING IN KARAM Doss's life except surgery; it is his job and his great pleasure at the same time. Very simply, he is a workaholic. He has a few friends that he rarely has the time to see. His only pleasure, next to surgery, is a few glasses of whiskey and a good book. He is over sixty and is still unmarried because he doesn't have the time for all that.

He told his students (when they complained about working long hours) his story about the beautiful Italian woman he met twenty years earlier. They had gone out more than once and they had a good relationship, but it so happened that whenever he was about to sleep with her, he would be called for an emergency. Then there was that one night when things were proceeding as well as could be hoped for: he went with her to her apartment, where they had dinner, had a few drinks, took off their clothes, and actually started to make love. Suddenly his pager emitted that abominable buzz. Karam jumped up, getting off her, then started putting on his clothes in no particular order and began to apologize to her, using moving language about it being his duty to save the life of a person who needed him right away. But he was surprised that she hurled a whole dictionary of Italian insults at him and his parents. Then she got so angry that she started chasing him like a furious, ferocious tigress, which made him run for his life as she threw everything in the room she could lay hands on at him. Dr. Karam would laugh heartily whenever he related the story, but his face would turn serious again as he advised young surgeons, "If you fall in love with surgery, you won't be able to love anything else."

Karam Doss's life, however, despite his loneliness, was not without exciting events, the strangest of which had happened a few years earlier. One evening, as he was about to leave his office after a hard day, he heard the fax machine turn on. He extended his hand to close the office door, intending to read the fax in the morning, but he changed his mind, turned on the light, and took the sheet from the fax machine and read the following:

From: The office of the minister of higher education in
Egypt
To: Professor Karam Doss, Northwestern Memorial
Hospital, Chicago
Re: We have a sick university professor who is in
urgent need of an operation to change several
arteries. Please indicate whether you can take
him at the earliest opportunity. Please respond
promptly so we can take necessary measures.
Name of patient: Dr. Abd al-Fatah Balbaa

Karam stared at the fax for about a minute then put it in his pocket
and left. He drove home, exerting great effort to stay focused. On the
balcony overlooking his large garden he poured himself a drink, then
opened the fax and reread it slowly. What was happening? What an
extraordinary coincidence! It was as if he were watching an Egyptian
soap opera. Dr. Abd al-Fatah Balbaa himself had succumbed to heart
disease and was asking him in particular to save his life? He smiled
sarcastically and little by little found himself laughing out loud. Then
he started thinking again: Who said that was a coincidence? The Lord
didn't do things by chance. What was happening was quite fair and
logical. Was he not wronged? Was he not persecuted? Didn't he feel
he had no worth and no dignity? Didn't he cry and kneel before Jesus,
the savior? The Lord was now righting the wrong. The man who one
day told him he couldn't be a surgeon, the one who ruined his future
in Egypt and doomed him to a life of total exile, was now sick and
begging him to save his life. He thought: Well, Mr. Balbaa, if you want
me to perform the surgery, first we have to settle our old score. How
many times do you have to apologize? A hundred times? A thousand
times? What good will that do now? When he finished his third glass
he had made up his mind. He was not going to perform the operation
on Balbaa. Let him find another surgeon. Let him die. We all are going
to in the end. He was going to decline the operation and his response

should be cold and extremely overbearing. He formulated this reply:

> Professor Karam Doss cannot perform the operation on
> patient Balbaa because his schedule is overbooked with urgent
> cases for months and he has no room for a new patient.

He started typing the letter on the computer but suddenly got up, as if he had remembered something. He stood reluctantly in the middle of the room, and then walked over slowly toward the cross. He knelt down and began to recite the Lord's Prayer in sincere humility. He whispered in a trembling voice, "O, Father, not my will, but thine. For thine is the kingdom, and the power, and the glory, forever. Amen."

He remained kneeling, his eyes closed for some time, then he got up and opened his eyes, as if he had awakened from sleep. He sat in front of the computer and found himself deleting what he had written and starting a new reply:

> From: Karam Doss
>   To: The Office of the Minister of Higher Education in
>   Egypt
>
> Professor Abd al-Fatah Balbaa was my professor at Ain Shams
> Medical School. I will do my best to save his life. Please take
> necessary measures so that he may come as soon as possible.
> The cost will be just the hospital expenses, as I am waiving my
> fee in appreciation of my professor.

He printed the letter then sent it by fax, and when the machine printed the transmission-completed report, Karam put his head between his hands and sobbed like a child. All his assistants said that he had never performed an operation the way he had on Dr. Balbaa, as if everything he had learned in surgery had been concentrated in his hands that morning. He was glowing, on top of the world; moving from one step to the next gracefully, skillfully, and in utmost control, so much so that he went several times around the operating table to reassure himself of certain details. Catherine, the most senior nurse on his team, said as she congratulated him after the operation, "You were not just successful, sir. You were inspired. It seemed like you were operating in a most affectionate manner, as if you were treating your father's injured foot or adjusting his head as he slept."

The days after the operation, Dr. Karam followed up with his former professor as he did with all his patients. And when he examined the X-ray one week after the operation, he laughed happily and said his favorite sentence, the one he always used to reassure the patients: "In a few months, you will be able to play soccer if you want to."

He got up to leave, but Dr. Balbaa grabbed his hand suddenly and said in a weak voice, "I don't know how to thank you, Dr. Karam. Please forgive me."

That was the first reference to their past. Karam felt a little awkward, then held his professor's hand gently and was about to say something, but he just smiled awkwardly and hurried out of the room.

Marwa called her parents on Friday. As soon as her mother asked her how she was, she burst out crying. Her mother was quite moved and began to calm her down and ask her what the matter was. Marwa told her everything: Danana's miserliness, his selfishness, and his coveting her fortune. She also hinted at their intimacy problem. When she said that he slapped her on the face her mother got extremely angry and shouted, "May his hand be cut off! He should learn how to respect the daughters of good families."

Marwa was reassured by her mother's angry reaction in solidarity with her, and after a lengthy interlude of complaining and consoling, Marwa said she insisted on getting a divorce from Danana. Thereupon, much to her surprise, the mother's position went to the other extreme. She rejected talk of divorce "because it is not a game." She said that if every marital problem ended in divorce, not one woman would stay married. She assured her daughter that all houses had problems and that the first year was the most difficult in any marriage. A wise wife, she reminded her daughter, would patiently put up with the shortcomings of her husband and strive to rectify them so that life might go on. She gave herself as an example: early on in her own marriage she had to put up with Hagg Nofal's extremely short fuse (and other bad traits to which she alluded without giving any details) until God finally guided him to the right path and he became such a model husband that all women envied her on his account. But Marwa said, "You cannot compare Danana to my father at all."

"Listen, what do you want?"

"Divorce."

Her mother burst into a violent, typical Egyptian woman's reaction. "I don't want to hear this word, understand?"

"But I hate him. I can no longer stand him touching me."

"I don't like beating around the bush. I am going to ask you one question. Is your husband a man?"

Marwa made no reply.

"Answer me: is he a man?"

"Yes."

"Okay then, time will take care of all problems."

"But he—"

"For shame, Marwa, stop. Girls of good families don't talk about these subjects, ever. Have you gone crazy or has life in America made you forget the way you were brought up? This thing in particular most women do out of a sense of duty and tomorrow God will bless you with children and you'll forget it completely."

Marwa saw no use in continuing the conversation so she ended the call with a few ambiguous words. Then she sat down to think about what her mother had said, but the telephone rang again and she was surprised to hear her father's voice. He spoke to her more calmly and in a more affectionate way and yet he repeated what her mother had said. At the end he said, begging her, "You've always been a dutiful girl. Don't do anything rash. There's nothing worse than a wrecked home."

That night she didn't go to bed. She tossed and turned on the sofa until she came to when she heard Danana performing ablution for the morning prayer. She recalled what had happened and reflected on it: her father and mother were the ones who loved her most in this world and yet they were both strongly against the idea of divorce. Could she be mistaken? Could she be rushing to conclusions and ruining her home, something she would possibly regret when it was too late? She recalled the word *divorce*, and for the first time it sounded strange to her and frightening. For the first time divorce seemed to be something mysterious and tragic, like death or suicide. Images of divorced women she had crossed paths with came rushing to her mind. A divorced woman was one who had failed to keep her husband, who was suffering loss and distress, who was a burden on her family and friends, who was chased by all kinds of men because, not being a virgin, she had nothing to lose. She was a woman whom people pitied and accused in many unstated ways. She did not want that image for herself and she had to respect the advice of her parents because they had more experience than she and because they wanted nothing for her except happiness and a good life. Besides, she had never married before and had no experience with men (except light, casual attraction to some college classmates that never went beyond lengthy telephone conversations). What did she know? Couldn't it be that most women suffered like her and just stuck it out to keep the family together? Didn't her mother say explicitly: "This intimate relationship we women consider just a matter of duty, and after having children we might forget it completely"? Couldn't it be that her mother, like her, had suffered in bed and yet was able to love her father and have children with him and go on living with him for many years? Wouldn't it be better for her to reconsider her relationship with Danana?

True he was greedy, a miser, and only cared about himself, but didn't he also have some good qualities? Was all he did just evil? To be fair, she had to admit that he was pious, had a sense of humor, and often, during those rare moments of peace and contentment, made her laugh with his sarcastic similes and comments. Her husband had his good and bad points like everyone else in the world and she had to remember the good as she did the bad. Marwa spent the night thinking, and in the morning she got up, took a bath, performed her ablutions and her prayers, and when she looked at her face in the mirror, she felt she had changed, that her features were showing signs of determination. She felt she was beginning a new, different chapter in her life. She heard her husband's footsteps and deliberately stood close by and said with a smile, "Good morning."

"Good morning," Danana replied in a lukewarm tone of voice, realizing that his wife had rejoined the fold. He decided to take his time before taking her back, in order to teach her a lesson so she wouldn't deviate again. She went on in an apologetic, placating tone, "Would you like me to fix you breakfast?"

"I'll eat at school."

"I'll make you some eggs with *basterma*, quick."

"Thanks."

Danana played hard to get for a whole day, and then he showed signs of relenting after delivering a short speech. "Your father called me yesterday. Thank God he is a good and pious man, and I am saying that just for the sake of the truth. I told him what you have done and I said that I used my shari'a-sanctioned right to discipline you within the minimum boundaries. Anyway, Marwa, for the sake of Hagg Nofal, I have forgiven you this time, but I am warning you, good woman, not to listen to Satan's evil temptations. Take refuge in God away from Satan, who deserves to be stoned, perform your prayers regularly and fear God as you tend your husband and your home."

Life between the two of them went back to what it used to be. In fact, it was much better. Marwa started to show interest in her husband and was sweet to him. She cooked his favorite dishes and waited to eat with him and had long conversations with him. The change in her was so great it astonished Danana himself and confirmed his idea that women were mysterious beings full of contradictions and that it was impossible to fathom their reactions or deep desires. Marwa did all she could to get along with her husband and seemed to be playing the role of the contented wife quite well. Even their encounters in bed, which had often tormented her, she was able to cope with in a creative way. As soon as Danana fell upon her with his erection, the moment she felt his feverish panting on her face as he tried to kiss her and as his saliva mixed with the bitter taste of tobacco reached her mouth, and as she felt his heavy paunch pressed against her belly causing her to feel almost nauseated—at that moment that had often tormented her, Marwa learned to close her eyes and forget Danana. She would concentrate first on banishing his picture from her mind, then she imagined that she was embracing another man: handsome, attractive, and exciting.

In time, Marwa was able to assemble a group of secret lovers, all of whom she slept with in her imagination: Rushdi Abaza, Kadhim al-Sahir, and Mahmud Abd al-Aziz. Even Dr. Said al-Daqqaq, professor of general finance at Cairo University Business School, who was universally admired by all the female students; Marwa had him in bed more than once. Thus imagination provided her with a novel and effective way of overcoming her physical problem. The whole thing even turned into a delightful secret game. As soon as she sensed Danana's impending attack, she would wonder: with whom am I going to sleep tonight? Rushdi Abaza already had his turn, twice. That's enough for him. Oh, how I miss Kadhim! As she kept doing that she got so thoroughly caught up in the act that she feared her tongue might let slip the name of her imagined lover in front of her husband, resulting in a major scandal. As soon as she felt Danana letting go of his disgusting warm pleasure inside her she would run to the bathroom, her eyes almost closed so that she wouldn't lose the fantasy, and then continue to arouse herself to orgasm. Those were Marwa's attempts to adapt, endure, and live. She began to accept life with Danana as it was and not as she wished it to be. And here a question might arise: Wasn't it strange that Marwa should go from one extreme to the other so quickly? Was the advice of her parents enough to push her to the bosom of Danana, whom, only a few days earlier, she couldn't stand to see? To answer yes would not be a complete answer. There was a deep, hidden feeling that impelled her to win Danana over with all her might: not out of love, of course, nor out of fear of the fate of divorced women, but because her parents' warning had caused her great confusion. So she wanted to give her marriage the best possible chance. If she succeeded she would be happy, but if she failed she would not blame herself and her parents would not be able to blame her. Hence her attempts to win her husband over, despite their strong persistence, had a phony celebratory aspect to them, like two lawyers on opposite sides, or two tennis players who had just finished a very close match, shaking hands. Marwa treated her husband in an excessively nice way as if making her parents her witnesses so that in the future they wouldn't rush to judgment and accuse her of wrecking her home. Her new behavior, despite its affectionate tenderness, also had the smoothness of a trap. Danana felt that instinctively and realized that the battle between them was still raging, even if it had taken another form. So he was reserved in what he said to her or did with her.

Danana, however, did not have any surplus energy because the final warning that Dr. Dennis Baker had given him had caused great turmoil in his life. The old man did not leave him any choice: he had to submit the results of his research within a few days, otherwise he would ask to be relieved of supervising him. Were that catastrophe to happen, it would put an end to both his academic and political future. He had to act fast or else everything would be lost. How his enemies would gloat if his research were terminated! Those who hated him would rejoice at the news: Did you hear? They took away Ahmad Danana's scholarship because he didn't finish his research on time. Haven't I told you? He's always been a loser!

Danana spent several days in his office at school. He locked himself in from the morning until the evening. He didn't open his door to anybody and didn't attend lectures or classes of any kind. Three days passed that way until last Wednesday when a unique incident in the history of the department of histology occurred, which people recounted in different ways, some of which were exaggerated. What was certain was that at about one o'clock, after lunch break, Dr. Baker was busy conducting some experiments while humming softly on account of the small bottle of white wine that he had had with lunch. He was preoccupied, with the utmost concentration, with testing a new photograph of some nerve cells that he had taken with the electron microscope. He came to at a sudden knock on the door. In his hoarse voice, without raising his head, he said, "Come in."

The door opened and Danana appeared, carefully carrying some papers. Baker looked at him and, remembering what had happened between them, frowned and said in a not-too-friendly tone, "How can I help you?"

Danana laughed, as if he had just heard a friend tell a joke, and said, "Dr. Baker, why are you treating me so harshly?"

"Tell me what you want. I don't have time to waste with you."

Danana sighed then moved two steps forward and extended his hand with the papers toward Baker, his face looking like someone about to give a surprise. "Please."

"What's this?"

"The results you asked of me."

"Really? Did you get it done?" Baker exclaimed in disbelief as he looked at the results with great interest. He soon looked pleased and said to Danana, who sat in front of him, "Well, my friend. You are finally taking your work seriously."

"I had to work hard after you kicked me out of your office last week," said Danana in a tone of feminine reproach bordering on the coquettish.

Baker seemed at a loss and said apologetically, "Please appreciate the fact that I am responsible for the research I supervise. Any negligence there impinges on me personally."

"Dr. Baker, was it really necessary to kick me out? I too have dignity."

"I am sorry if I hurt your feelings."

Danana didn't look as if he had forgiven but made a gesture with his hand, as if he would forget what had happened for the time being. Then he assumed the pose of a generous man turning a new page, saying, "Let's talk about work. That's more important to me."

Baker pulled a piece of paper and a pen and said enthusiastically, "After obtaining these results, we have to start the statistics phase. We are going to feed all these figures to the computer to see if they are statistically significant."

Danana asked in annoyance, "After all the effort I exerted and the long hours I spent working, could the results be without statistical significance?"

"I don't think so."

"But it is possible that my hard work will be wasted and the results be statistically insignificant!"

"In that case I'd be responsible because I laid out the research plan. But let's think positively. The results will be significant, I am sure."

Danana stood up and it occurred to him, before leaving, to say something pithy. He said, "Professor Baker, despite everything, I am happy and proud to work with you."

"Me too, Danana, and, once again, I am sorry," said Baker and gave him a strong handshake. Then he sat down and laid out the results and started studying them. After half an hour, Danana was sitting in his office when Baker came in, rubbing his bald head with the finger of his right hand as he usually did when he was engaged in deep thought. Then he said slowly, his eyes gleaming, "Once again, congratulations, Danana. The results are logical and strong."

"Thanks."

"An idea has occurred to me that would support your results. Show me one of your slides."

Danana got up slowly and opened the cabinet next to the desk and gave Baker a slide. Baker held it carefully, put on his glasses, and examined it under the microscope. He soon raised his head and said, "The number of black spots on this slide is a hundred sixty-seven."

Danana nodded and remained silent. Baker examined the results and said in surprise, "That's strange. The number you recorded is greater than that."

He looked at Danana as if he didn't understand then went over to the cabinet himself and took two other slides that he put through a similar examination, and then looked at Danana, who bowed his head slowly. For a few moments, a silence, charged with an unknown energy, prevailed so quietly that the soft hum made by the lab's fridge sounded like destiny. Suddenly Dr. Baker threw the slides on the floor and they broke into shiny shards. Then he roared with an angry resounding voice that no one had heard from him before. "What a scumbag! The results you submitted are fabricated. Where is your honor? I will revoke your dissertation and expel you from the department at once."

CHAPTER 21

"Good morning. I'm calling about the job you advertised."

"It's taken," the man replied tersely then hung up. The dial tone rang in Carol's ear and she felt bitter. Nothing new there. It was her daily routine: every morning after Graham went to the university and little Mark to school, she made herself a large cup of black coffee and sat in the living room, spreading the help wanted pages in the *Chicago Tribune,* the *Sun-Times,* and the *Reader.* Then she prepared for her calls. She concentrated on controlling the tone of her voice in such a way as if she were inquiring about the job with dignified interest. She was not an unemployed black woman on welfare; she was not starving or begging and didn't need anyone's pity.

She was just inquiring about a job that she liked, no more and no less, as if she were asking about tickets for a concert or the closing time of her favorite restaurant. If she found what she wanted she'd be happy, but if she didn't, that would not be the end of the world. That was what she came up with to combat humiliation. Every time, she asked the same questions and received the same answers. By the end of the day she would have accumulated all kinds of lists, addresses, and numbers. Over the last few months she had been all over Chicago and had had interviews for various jobs: secretary, receptionist, babysitter, day-care supervisor. But she never got the job. The head of human resources at the Hyatt told her with an embarrassed smile, "You'll find a job somewhere else. But be patient, unemployment is at its highest rate. Dozens, sometimes hundreds of people apply for one job. The competition is horrendous."

Two months ago she applied for a job as a telephone operator for an elevator company. She passed the first interview and had to pass a voice test. The company executive told her, "You'll get this job if you know how to make your voice smooth, feminine, and seductive but at the same time not vulgar. Your voice must carry a sense of humor and superiority. It should sound as if you were making ten times your salary. It's your voice that introduces our company to the customers."

Carol trained seriously. She recorded her voice dozens of times saying the same thing: "Hendrix Elevator Company. Good morning. How may I help you?" Every time she listened to the recording she discovered a new flaw: the voice was too soft, a little shaky, faltering, too fast, letters elided, she had to pronounce the name of the company better, and so on.

After days of training she settled on a good delivery and went to take the test. There were five other applicants. They all sat in the same room in front of the company executive, who was a fat white man, over fifty, completely bald with wide sideburns that made him look unpleasant. It seemed from his swollen eyelids, bloodshot eyes, and foul mood that he had drunk too much the night before and hadn't had enough sleep. He began to signal to one applicant after another to deliver the sentence, looked at the ceiling as if evaluating the performance in his mind, and then bent over a sheet of paper and wrote something down. At the end of the day the result was announced. Carol didn't get the job. She received the news coldly; she had got so used to being disappointed nothing shocked her anymore. What pained her the most was the way some white employers treated her. None of them came out and said they didn't hire black people. That would be against the law. But as soon as one of them saw her, his face would have a cold, arrogant expression, and he would end the interview promising to give her a call that she knew very well would not come. These successive humiliating situations felt like slaps on her face. She sometimes cried on her way back home and some nights stayed awake imagining that she was taking revenge against the racist employer, teaching him a lesson, and assuring him that it was she who refused to work with a despicable racist like him. The drama reached its peak when she had an interview for a job as a dog walker for twelve dollars an hour. The job was so menial that it took her three days just to convince herself to go. She needed the money badly. She couldn't stand the suffering she was putting Graham through. What had he done to deserve living through this hardship to support her and her son? What pained her most was that he was bearing the hardship without grumbling. If he complained or treated her in an unfriendly way she would have been somewhat relieved. But on the contrary he was treating her very nicely, amusing her, and always laughing merrily. He was unbearably tender. She was going to get that job for his sake. Wasn't dog walking a job like any other in the final analysis? Even if she didn't like it, did she have any other choice? She would tend dogs for the time being until she found something better.

The interview was at a luxurious mansion in a northern suburb of Chicago. It was so elegant and extravagant that she imagined it to be part of a movie set. She was met by a dignified butler in a formal black suit and led to a large room. She sat on a comfortable Louis Seize-style chair and began to look at the large oil paintings on the wall. After a little while an old lady came in and welcomed her tepidly. She sat in front of her and began a disconnected conversation about the weather and public transit in Chicago. This vacuous dialogue went on until Carol interrupted it by asking in an affected, miserable merriment, "Where's the dog I'll walk? I looove dogs."

The old lady fell silent. She had been taken aback a little and avoided looking at her face. "Well, I am going to be frank with you. I don't think the job suits you. Leave your telephone number and I'll find another job for you as soon as possible."

Carol's sad days continued. She became so frustrated that she totally lost her enthusiasm. She no longer read the newspapers looking for jobs. She spent the morning sprawled on the bed, drinking several cups of coffee and looking at the ceiling, thinking about her life. She was thirty-six years old, but she had never lived life as she had wanted to. No one treated her fairly. She recalled the faces that had shaped her destiny: her kind, peaceful mother; her drunken stepfather, who beat her up cruelly, and when she grew up, wanted to sleep with her (she sought her mother's help several times, but her mother was so sexually dependent on him that she was not much help); her boyfriend Thomas, with whom she lived for ten years and with whom she had little Mark and who ran off, leaving her to shoulder everything alone. She also recalled the face of good old Graham, whom she loved, but instead of making him happy, she'd brought him hardship. She had always been treated harshly, that was a fact. She had always been hardworking, organized, and ambitious, and what had been the result? Total misery. She had lost her job at the mall because she was black and now she couldn't find another job. The old lady even thought dog walking was too good for her; maybe she didn't want her beloved dog to be exposed to a black face.

That morning Carol was lying in bed drowned in her sorrows when the telephone rang. She was surprised that anyone would call at such an hour. She turned over and decided to ignore the call, but the ringing continued. She finally got up to answer and it was the voice of her friend Emily, a black friend from her high school days who finished college because her father, a lawyer, could afford to pay the tuition. Carol had not seen her friend in months, so she was happy she called and welcomed her invitation to grab a bite at the French restaurant Lafayette in downtown Chicago. From her high school days Emily loved fancy restaurants and had taken Carol along. Carol was always happy to go because she couldn't afford to go on her own. The Lafayette was truly magnificent, with elegant tables and Vivaldi playing in the background, adding to the luxurious ambience. Carol ordered a spinach croissant and pâté and café au lait. She looked at her friend's face for a while then teased her, "I can tell from your rosy complexion that your love life is going very well."

They laughed from the heart and Emily told her about her new love. Carol tried to keep up with her in her happiness but something heavy was weighing on her. Emily noticed that, and as soon as she asked her, Carol started sobbing and told her everything. She needed to vent with an old friend like Emily. Looking far into the distance, Emily said, "If there were any jobs available in Dad's office I could've got you one. But I'll try somewhere else."

It was a beautiful outing and Carol came back ready to resume the struggle. The following morning she started looking for a job again. For a week it was the same old story: the telephone calls, interviews, apologies, and a few brazen racist remarks. It was getting close to one in the afternoon when she received an unexpected call from Emily. As soon as she said hello, Emily asked her in an earnest voice, "What are you doing now?"

"I'm cooking."

"Leave everything and come right away."

"I can't. John and Mark will come and find nothing to eat."

"Leave them a message."

"Can I come later on?"

"It can't wait."

She asked persistently, but Emily would not tell her why. Carol guessed it had to do with a job. She wrote a few words and posted them on the refrigerator door, put on her clothes in a hurry, and went out. Emily lived half an hour away by train. She opened the door immediately as though she had been waiting behind it. She permitted Carol to say hello to her mother, then pulled her by the hand to her room and locked the door from the inside.

"Emily, what's come over you?" Carol asked, still panting. Emily smiled mysteriously then gave her a strange, scrutinizing look and said, "Show me your chest."

"What?"

"Take off your shirt so I can see your chest."

"Are you crazy?"

"Do what I tell you."

"I don't understand."

"I'll explain to you after you take this off."

She reached for the buttons on Carol's blouse, but Carol restrained her hand and said somewhat angrily, "No, you won't."

Emily sighed hard, as if her patience had run out. Then she looked at her for a long time and said, "Listen. I didn't ask you to come here to play. I have to see your chest."

 After Dr. Salah told his wife that he wanted a separation, he felt relief and said to himself that it was a step that he should have taken a long time ago. From now on he wouldn't have to face her chasing him, her physical demands, the humiliating, exhausting moments of his impotence, the expectations and disappointments. He was done with that fierce tension, which was always lying in wait just beneath their quiet conversations and their living together under the same roof while avoiding looking at each other. After today he wouldn't have to pretend or lie. Their relationship was over. That was the truth. There was no doubt that he had loved her at a certain time in his life. She had helped him a lot. He was grateful to her and felt toward her that deep, calm appreciation that one has for a colleague that one has worked with for years. They would separate quietly and he was willing to meet all her demands. He would pay her any sum she wanted. She could have the furniture and the car, even the house if she wanted it. He would rent a small place for himself. All he wanted was to be alone, to enjoy a calm, comfortable old age, to be able to relive his life over and over, nonstop. Oh God, how did he get to be sixty? How quickly the years had passed! His whole life had passed before he realized it, before he began. He hadn't lived. What had he done in his life? What had he achieved? Could he measure his happy times? How much? How many? Several days, a few months at best? It was not fair to advance in years without realizing the value of time, not fair that no one drew our attention to the time that was slipping through our fingers by the moment. It was a clever trick: to realize the value of life only just before it ended.

Salah went out, leaving his wife alone in the bedroom. He closed the door gently and thought that, from now on, he would live in the living room until the separation was complete. He had no desire to sleep. He said to himself that he was going to have a quiet drink and read a little of Isabelle Allende's new novel. He strode to the door as he did every night, but as soon as he crossed the hallway, exactly before he entered the short corridor leading to the living room, he stopped suddenly, bent over, and looked at the floor as if looking for one thing or another. He was overcome by a strange sensation, quick and sharp like a blade: a distant, mysterious vision as if it were a dream that had been revealed to him. No one would believe him if he were to relate it, but it was quite real. He was possessed by a feeling such as that which overcomes us when we enter a place or see a person for the first time and know, in no uncertain terms, that we have been there before, that what we are living now is something that we had lived before in an earlier time. He found himself turning to the left and going toward the door to the basement. He descended the stairs as if hypnotized, as if he were being carried, as if it were someone else moving his feet while he contented himself with looking at them as they carried him forward. He opened the door and entered the basement and was immediately greeted by the dampness. The air was heavy and stagnant and he had difficulty breathing. He felt for the light switch and turned on the light. The basement was empty except for a few things that Chris had stored to dispose of later: an old television set, a dishwasher that didn't work, and a few chairs that had been used in the garden for years before she bought a new set that previous summer. Salah stood examining the place with a distant look. What brought him here? What did he want? What were those vague feelings raging inside him? The questions kept droning in his ears without an answer until he found himself moving again. He was now certain that he was being driven by an overpowering force that he couldn't resist. He headed directly for the corner and opened the closet and with both hands pulled out the old blue suitcase. He found it to be heavier than he had expected, so he paused for a moment to catch his breath, then pulled it again and placed it under the light. He bent down and began to undo the straps surrounding it. As soon as he opened it, his nostrils were filled with the overpowering smell of mothballs. He felt nauseated for about a minute, then he got a hold of himself and began to take out the contents of the suitcase: there were the clothes he had brought with him from Egypt, thirty years ago. He thought at the time they were elegant but discovered immediately that they were not suitable for America; wearing them he looked as if he had come from another planet or as if he were a character who had stepped out of a period play. He'd bought American clothes but he couldn't bring himself to get rid of his Egyptian clothes. He packed them into this suitcase and hid them in the basement, as if he knew that one day he'd go back to them. He emptied the suitcase on the floor in front of him: elevator black patent leather shoes with pointed tips in the style of the 1960s, a gray English woolen suit that he used to wear at Qasr al-Aini hospital, a number of narrow neckties of the same time period. These were the clothes he was wearing the last time he met Zeinab: the white shirt with red pinstripes, the dark blue pants, and the black leather jacket he bought with her at the La Boursa Nova store on Suleiman Pasha Street in Cairo. Oh, God, why was he remembering everything so clearly? He extended his hand and felt the clothes. He was overcome by an overpowering, burning desire that made him pant and sweat profusely. He tried to resist that desire, but it swept over him like a hurricane. He stood where he was, took off his house robe then his pajamas, and stood in the middle of the basement in his underwear. It occurred to him that he had actually gone crazy. What was he doing? It was madness itself. Couldn't he control that perverse desire? What would Chris say if she opened the door and saw him?

He said to himself: let her say what she wants to. There's nothing for me to fear anymore. She'll say I've gone crazy? So be it. Even if what I am doing is crazy, I'll do it. It is time for me to do all I want to do. He began to put on his old clothes, one piece at a time. His body had filled out and they no longer fit him. He couldn't fasten the belt on his belly; the shirt stuck to his body in a way that almost hurt. As for the jacket, he was able to insert his arms into the sleeves with difficulty but he couldn't move them. Despite the strangeness of the situation a comfortable feeling came over him. He was filled with wonderful serenity and felt contained in dark, moist security, as if he were once again at his mother's bosom. He looked at his reflection in the mirror in the corner of the basement and burst out laughing. He remembered the concave mirrors before which he had played in amusement parks as a child. Then a thought occurred to him and he went back quickly to the open suitcase, whose innards had spilled on the floor. He was moving with difficulty, limping as if his feet were injured due to the tight clothes. He squatted before the suitcase and reached for the inner pocket, and then he found it, exactly where he expected to, exactly as he had put it there thirty years ago. He brought it slowly out into the light—a broad green address book that he used to carry in his medical bag and which Zeinab often made fun of because of its large size. She would shout in childlike mirth, "This, dear, is not an address book. It is the Cairo telephone directory. When I have the time, I'll explain to you the difference."

He smiled when he remembered and opened the book gently. The pages had yellowed and the letters were slightly faded with age, but the names and numbers were still clear.

▮▮▮▮▮▮▮▮▮▮

I saw a strange sight, as though in a dream: the sky grew dark in the middle of the day. A strong wind blew which I imagined would uproot the trees. Then thousands of soft white particles like pieces of cotton flew into the air and fell down softly until they covered everything: houses, roads, and cars.

I stood dazzled, watching what was happening outside the

closed window, wearing my robe on my naked body. The central heating was so high I felt hot. There were ice drops accumulating like beads of sweat on the window glass on the inside as a result of the difference between the cold outside and the warmth inside. I sipped my drink slowly and put my arms around Wendy, who was naked. We had just finished a spell of fantastic lovemaking that, together with the heat and the wine, made her face even more like a rose in full bloom. She whispered in my ear, "Do you like to watch the snow?"

"It's fantastic."

"Unfortunately it no longer excites me because I've seen it since I was a child."

After a short while, Wendy prepared dinner. She turned off the lights then lit two candles in a candelabra she had brought with her. We began to eat in an enchanting atmosphere.

"This is Jewish chicken soup. Do you like it?" she said.

"It's delicious."

She looked at me, her eyes gleaming in the candlelight. Her beautiful face changed expression sometimes in a mysterious way: it would cloud over and its muscles would contract, as if she had remembered something that gave her pain, as if she had inherited an ancient sorrow that remained hidden inside her then appeared suddenly, crossing her face then disappearing.

"Nagi, you're an exceptional event in my life. I expected our relationship to be casual, just having a good time. I never imagined loving you."

"Why?"

"Because you're an Arab."

"What's the problem there?"

"You're the only Arab who doesn't dream of exterminating the Jews," she said, laughing.

"That's not true. The Arabs hate Israel not because it is a state for the Jews but because it stole Palestine and committed dozens of massacres against the Palestinians. If the Israelis were Hindus or Buddhists, it wouldn't have changed anything for us. Our conflict with Israel is political and not religious."

"Are you sure of that?"

"Read the history. Jews lived under Arab rule for many centuries without problems or persecution. They even enjoyed the trust of the Arabs, as evidenced by the fact that, for a period of a thousand years, an Arab sultan's personal physician was most likely to be a Jew. In the midst of the endless conspiracies and schemes surrounding the throne, the sultan trusted his Jewish private physician perhaps more than he did his wife and children. In Muslim Spain, Jews lived as citizens with full rights, and when Andalusia fell into the hands of the Christian Spaniards, they persecuted both Muslims and Jews. They gave them the choice between Christianity and death. Then they went as far as coming up with the Inquisition for the first time in history, to get rid of Jews and Muslims who had recently converted to Christianity. The priests would ask them theological questions, and when they failed to answer, they gave them the choice between being burned or drowned."

Wendy closed her eyes in pain, so I said in an attempt to reintroduce some gaiety, "And thus, my dear, your ancestors and mine were persecuted together. It is quite possible that you and I are the descendants of a Muslim man and a Jewish woman who fell in love with each other in Andalusia."

"You have a very fertile imagination."

"It is the truth. I feel I have known you in another life, otherwise how would you explain our mutual attraction from the first moment?"

I bent over and kissed her hands, then a thought occurred to me. I got up quickly and looked for the Andalusian song tape until I found it. Before long Fairouz's voice was all over the place. "Return,

O thousand nights, the mist of perfume/Love slakes its thirst on the dew of dawn."

I said, "This is Andalusian music."

"I don't understand the words but the music speaks to my heart."

I started translating for her as much as I could of the meaning. Everything around me was captivating: the snow, the warmth, the love, the candles, the wine, and the music, and my beloved Wendy. I was so transported with happiness I got up, held Wendy by her shoulders, and pulled her gently. I stood her in the middle of the room and said as I returned to my place, "This bed on which I am sitting is the throne of Andalusia. I am the prince. I am now sitting to run the affairs of the principality. When I clap once, you start dancing. You are the most talented and most beautiful dancer in Andalusia, therefore the prince has chosen you to dance for him alone."

Wendy let out a shout of joy and stood ready with a mirthful expression on her face, as if she were a child yearning to start playing. Fairouz was singing to a dancing tune:

> *O luscious branch crowned with gold*
> *I ransom you from death with my mother and my father.*
> *If I have overstepped the bounds in my love for you,*
> *Only prophets are infallible.*

I clapped and Wendy began to dance. She moved according to her notions of belly dancing. She kept shaking her arms and chest nervously as if trembling. She looked like a child mimicking adults, eliciting laughter and affection. She looked at me as she was dancing and sent me an air kiss that made her charm irresistible. I got up, embraced her, and showered her with kisses. We made love while Fairouz's voice filled the whole place with ecstasy as if blessing us. When we were done, we lay down, naked in each other's arms. I kissed her nose and whispered, "I'll always be in your debt."

"If you don't go easy on the tenderness I'll cry from compassion."

"I'm really grateful. You've brought poetry back to me after a whole year of loss. This morning I started a new poem."

"Wonderful. What's your new poem about?"

"You."

She hugged me hard and I whispered in her ear, "Wendy, you've saved me from feeling miserable. You made a beautiful dream for me."

We remained embraced and I felt her breath warming my face. Then she backed off gently and said as she got up, "Even beautiful dreams come to an end. I must go."

She planted a quick kiss on my forehead as if in apology, then went to the bathroom and came out fully dressed. I had got lost in contemplation so I jumped up, saying, "Wait. I'll accompany you to the L station."

"You don't have to."

"Why do you always refuse to let me walk with you?"

She looked ill at ease and hesitated for a while then said, "Do you remember Henry, my old boyfriend I told you about? He is a receptionist here at the dorm. I don't like him to see us together."

"Why do you care, if your relationship is over?"

"Please don't get angry. If I still loved him, I couldn't love you."

"So why are you afraid that he would see us together?"

"I'll tell you frankly. Henry is Jewish and the fact that you're an Arab will give him an opportunity to cause us problems."

"What's he got to do with us?"

"I know him well. He won't tolerate that at all."

"I can't believe that in America we have to keep love hidden."

She walked over to me, kissed me, and said, "All I want you to be sure of is that I love you."

I didn't insist on escorting her so as not to cause her any trouble. I knew her ex-boyfriend and had had dealings with him more than once in the receptionist's office. He used to treat me in a normal, one could say affable, way. But since Wendy started visiting me in my apartment, I noticed that he looked at me in a hostile manner. I asked him once if there was any mail for me, but he didn't answer. When I repeated the question he said rudely without lifting his head from the papers he was reading, "When mail comes we will send it to you. There is no need to ask me a hundred times every day."

I left in silence. I did not wish to get into a fight nor was I ready for one. I asked myself: How did Henry find out about my relationship with Wendy? I remembered that in his office there was a monitor showing the whole building from inside. That was it then. Wendy was his ex-girlfriend and it was natural for him to keep her under surveillance to find out which apartment she was going to. I made a point of avoiding him and confined my dealings to the kind black woman receptionist who had the morning shift.

Matters, however, did not stop at Henry's door. It seemed he spread news of my relationship with Wendy in Jewish circles at the university. Some second-year students began harassing me. I was attending the general course on histology with them. I was the oldest student, and in the past they had treated me with respect, but they suddenly turned. Whenever I passed by them they would whisper and laugh. I ignored them at the beginning, telling myself that perhaps they were laughing for reasons of their own and that I should resist negative thinking so that my relationship with Wendy might not give me a persecution complex. But their harassment grew worse: whenever they saw me, they followed me and repeated provocative words. The most insolent among them was a tall, skinny young man with red hair and slightly protruding upper teeth who wore a small black skullcap on his head. He played the clown for the benefit of his friends. Whenever he saw me he would shout loudly "*Assalamu alaikum*," then they would all burst out laughing. I kept ignoring them until he surprised me after class on Friday, surrounded by his friends, stopping me with his hand, acting in an unbelievable childish manner. He asked me derisively, "Where are you from?"

"I am Egyptian."

"Why are you studying histology? You think it is useful in breeding camels?"

They all burst out laughing. That time I couldn't control myself. I held him by his collar and shouted, "Speak politely or I'll break your head."

I was holding him with my left hand while my right hand was free. That was to my good fortune because he punched me in the stomach, but I jumped backward, which softened the blow. I pulled him toward me then aimed a punch at his face with my right hand. My fist was fast and the punch was strong; it made a muffled thudding sound and his nose began to bleed profusely. His defeat was now certain, so he started wailing, "You're a barbarian. I'll get you kicked out of the university for this."

His friends split into two groups; some spoke with him and others looked askance at me. I don't know how the university police appeared on the scene. They took us all to the security office. In front of the old, completely white-haired policeman, my adversary said that I had been following him and harassing him for some time and that he insisted on his right before the law because I had assaulted him. I kept silent until the officer questioned me. I told him what had happened and said calmly, "Yes, I actually hit him because he insulted my country and made fun of it."

"What did he say about your country? Try to remember the exact words."

He bent and wrote down everything I said. Then he looked

pensive and said in a calm voice, "Listen, both of you, according to university regulations you have committed two violations: you (and he pointed at him) used racist language to denigrate your colleagues, and you assaulted one of your colleagues. If I finish the report against you, both of you would have a disciplinary hearing."

A profound silence prevailed. I started imagining myself going back on the plane after being expelled from the university. I came to as the officer, who smiled and looked kind for the first time, was saying, "It's possible, of course, if you both wanted, for the matter to end amicably, if you both exchanged apologies now. In that case it would be enough if you both pledge not to do it again."

The other did not give me an opportunity to think. He came over to me and said in a loud voice, "I'm sorry."

His apology was devoid of any remorse. He just uttered the words, as if playing a role in a play, as if he wanted me to understand that in reality he was not sorry for what he had done, but that he had to apologize for fear of the disciplinary board. I looked at him for a moment and said, "I'm sorry too."

The harassment bothered me, but I didn't let it take up too much of my time. I had gotten used to my new life and my morale improved. I took up my studies regularly and seriously and almost finished my new poem. My dates with Wendy washed away my sorrows. More important, I found a great friend. I will always be indebted to Dr. Karam Doss for the wonderful times we spent together. We met on weekends at Graham's house, and during the week he would often call me to have a drink together in Rush Street. I discovered that he was a wonderful human being, extremely modest and sensitive, a true artist. We listened together to Umm Kulthum, about whom he was quite an expert: he knew the story of every song and when it was broadcast for the first time. He loved Egypt so much that he followed everything going on there with the utmost interest. We spent long hours discussing conditions in Egypt. He spoke enthusiastically, which made me share ideas with him as soon as they occurred to me. On Sunday evening we were, as usual, drinking at Dr. Graham's house. I waited until we had a few drinks to get us going, then asked Karam, "Have you heard about the demonstrations in Cairo?"

"I saw them yesterday on al-Jazeera."

"What do you think?"

"You think a few hundred demonstrators can change the regime?"

"Had it not been for the central security cordon around the demonstrators, all Egyptians would have joined them."

"It seems you're an optimist."

"Of course. The fact that Egyptians go out on the street to demand that the president of the republic step down is a sure sign that something has changed and will never be the same again."

"Those who demonstrate are members of the elite. The masses are not concerned with the issue of democracy."

"All revolutions in the history of Egypt have started with the elite."

"We'll see."

"We can't just wait and see."

"What can we do?"

"We can do a lot. But much depends on you."

"Me?"

"Are you willing to take a stand on what's happening in Egypt?"

"Are you planning for a coup d'état?"

"I am not kidding."

"What do you have in mind?"

"Listen, the president will visit Chicago in a few weeks. That's an opportunity we should not waste."

Graham was following the conversation. Laughing as he poured himself a new drink, he shouted, "Uh-oh, anything but that! I won't be a witness to a criminal conspiracy. Are you planning to kill the Egyptian president? How about if we start by killing George W. Bush instead?"

I waited until the laughter died down and continued seriously. "The president will meet with the Egyptian students in Chicago. I've thought of preparing a statement that we would deliver in front of him."

"A statement?"

"Yes, we'll demand that he step down, abrogate the emergency laws, and adopt democracy."

"You think he'll listen?"

"I am not that naive. It's just a step but it will be effective. There are demonstrations all over Egypt for freedom. Demonstrators are being beaten and arrested; women demonstrators are being violated by the police. Isn't it our duty to do something for those demonstrators? If we wrote the statement and Egyptians in Chicago signed it then delivered it in the presence of the president before journalists and television cameras, we'd be aiming a hard blow to the face of the Egyptian regime."

"You think Egyptians here will sign the statement with you?"

"I don't know, of course, but I'll try."

He stayed silent. I said, "I see that you're reluctant."

"Not at all."

"Haven't you always tried to do something for your country?"

"In the field of surgery, not politics."

"The corrupt regime is the main reason for our backwardness. The dean of Ain Shams Medical School who turned down your proposal was appointed to his post because he's loyal to the regime, regardless of his administrative or medical efficiency. Most likely he's a corrupt and hypocritical person who spies on his colleagues for state security. If deans were elected, a better and more qualified person would have been chosen. Such a person would undoubtedly have been happy to cooperate with you. If we love Egypt, we have to do our utmost to change this regime. Anything else is a waste of time."

Karam looked at me then drank the rest of his drink in one gulp and said, "Let me think about it."

CHAPTER 23

Everything that happened to Tariq Haseeb that evening was out of his control. He was not in a position to accept or reject it. If what happened had taken place a hundred times, he would've done exactly what he had done. He had found himself glued to Shaymaa, who raised her hand to pick up a tin from the shelf. He felt her whole breast brushing against him. He spontaneously reached out and embraced her. She didn't object. He felt her luscious body filling his whole being; he plunged his hands around her back and showered her with kisses all over: her lips, her face, her hair, then her neck and chin. Her fresh skin was so soft it aroused him even more. He kept kissing her neck and began licking her ear then took it between his lips (as he had seen in pornographic movies). It was then that she let out a soft passionate moan and murmured a few indistinct words in a low voice, as if making a weak, formal objection that she was the first to know would not change anything, or as if she were proclaiming her innocence one last time before being swept away by the flood of pleasurable lust.

After a few moments of passionate embracing, Tariq extended his hand and undid the zipper in the middle of the dress, making a light whizzing sound. Shaymaa did not object and kept watching his hands as if she were hypnotized. Her chest was revealed behind a rose-colored cotton bra. He pressed the breasts out of the bra as if they were two ripe fruits hanging on a branch. Tariq inhaled strongly then exhaled and

pressed his whole face between her breasts, rubbing it against their unbelievable softness. He was suddenly overcome by an urgent desire to
cry, as if he were sad that he hadn't done it before, as if he were a child
who had been lost for such a long time that he'd given up hope then
suddenly found his mother, as if the warmth coming from her breasts
was his original abode, which he had known at an earlier time then lost
and was now coming back to. He kissed her breasts all over and gently
bit them and she let out a soft, pained, and coquettish scream, whereupon he became certain that her body was now at his disposal, obedient and responding and clamoring for him to go forward. He undid his
fly and clung to her tightly. He didn't dare take off her dress but they
embraced closely and their muscles contracted in instinctive successive
thrusts until they both crossed the gate of pleasure together. His body
shook with great ecstasy, real flesh-and-blood ecstasy, not that artificial
one that he experienced in the bathroom every night. It occurred to
him that he was being born at that moment, brought back from the
dead, leaving behind forever that old colorless life for another, a real
and wonderful life. He closed his eyes and hugged her hard, as if cleav-
ing to her, seeking shelter with her so that she wouldn't leave him. He
began once again savoring her fresh smell voraciously and kissing her
anew. He was ready to make love to her time after time, forever. But he
came to when he felt her tears wetting his face. He opened his eyes and
withdrew his head as if waking up. He patted her on the cheek and she
burst out sobbing and speaking in a disjointed voice:

"How I despise myself!"

"I love you," he whispered, kissing her hands.

"I am now an immoral woman!"

"Who said that?"

"I've fallen!"

"You are the most beautiful woman in the world!"

She looked at him from behind her tears and said, "You couldn't
respect me now after what I've done with you."

"You're my wife: how could I not respect you?"

"I am not your wife."

"Aren't we going to get married?"

"Yes, but right now I am forbidden to you."

"We haven't committed fornication, Shaymaa. And there are noble hadiths, all authentic, all unanimous, in stating that God Almighty forgives the trespasses that do not amount to fornication of those He wills. We love each other and intend to be lawfully wedded, God willing. And God the Merciful forgives us."

She looked at him for a long time, as if to see whether he was telling the truth, and then whispered, "Won't your opinion of me change after what I've done with you?"

"It won't change."

"Swear that you will continue to respect me."

"I swear by God Almighty that I will go on respecting you."

"And I swear to you by God's mercy to my father, Tariq, that I haven't done this with anyone before you and that I've done it with you only because I love you."

"Of course."

"Are you going to leave me?"

"I'll never leave you."

As they went out of the kitchen, her steps looked confident and graceful, as if she had found fulfillment or got rid of a burden. He sat her next to him on the sofa and they exchanged a few whispered words interspersed with tender and heartfelt kisses from him on her hair and hands. Little by little the troubled look left her face, replaced by a warm softness. In a moment, as if he had just received a sign from her, he extended his arm and pulled her toward him, slowly and confidently this time. He felt her neck and lips with his fingers, then lifted her face, and they lost themselves in a long kiss.

24

 When Sarah opened the door, Jeff was standing behind her, high, staring at what was happening with unfocused looks. Dr. Ra'fat rained blows on her, and strangely enough, she didn't resist him. She cried only once after the first slap then succumbed after that, as if she were receiving a legal punishment. When he kicked her hard and she fell to the floor, Jeff came to and rushed at Ra'fat to grab him, but he pushed Jeff with his hand and Jeff staggered under the influence of the drug. Ra'fat roared at him, "As for you, dirty junkie, I'm going to put you in jail tonight."

Ra'fat stood in the middle of the hallway as if he didn't know what to do next. Then he turned around and hurried outside, and soon the sound of his car could be heard pulling away. The outside door remained open and the entryway lights on. Jeff began to pace back and forth, muttering angry curses. Then he stopped suddenly and for a moment seemed out of it, as if just waking from a dream. He walked slowly, closed the door, and turned off the lights, then extended his hand to help Sarah get up. He accompanied her inside and they sat next to each other on the sofa that had witnessed the climax of their pleasure a little earlier. He looked at her face in the light, and for the first time, he noticed a bruise around her left eye and a thin line of blood trickling from the side of her mouth. He extended his hand and felt her face gently then said in a hoarse voice, "We've been assaulted."

She remained silent, as if she hadn't heard him. He went on, "Your father has shown his true colors. He wants to control the life of his adult daughter as if he were still living in the desert."

She started crying in silence. He extended his hand with the dish that contained the dope, whispering in a confused tone of voice, "Wash the dish well. We've got to move fast. I'll hide the dope at a friend's on a nearby street. Then we'll call the police."

"I am not going to call the police."

He looked at her for a long time and said, "Sarah, this is serious. We've got to turn your father in before he turns us in."

"He won't turn us in."

"You're beginning to worry me. How can you be so sure?"

"Because he's my father."

"How can you trust him after what he's done?"

"Listen, Jeff. I know my father well and he's not going to call the police. Okay? Isn't that all you're worried about? Now, back off."

"What do you mean?"

"Leave me alone. I want to sit quietly for a little while, please."

She leaned her head to the wall. She really needed some quiet. Despite her fatigue and pain her mind was seething with successive images that were astonishingly strong and clear. Her father's angry face appeared as his hand rose in the air and slapped her, time after time. She kept recalling what had happened in full detail, as if she had not absorbed it or as if she wanted to inflict more pain on herself. Old scenes kept coming to her mind, shining and disappearing like flashes from the dark past. She saw herself as a child in her father's arms, and her mother's face came to her. She remembered how, for years, whenever she went to her little bed every night, she would close her eyes and put her head under the pillow, praying to God passionately that her father and mother not fight during the night so she wouldn't be awakened in fright, as often happened. She recalled her first night with Jeff, the first tremor of pleasure and her alarm at the drops of blood that had stained the bed and Jeff's voice whispering, "Now you're a real woman."

The first time she saw Jeff snorting, she chided him harshly, reciting all she had learned at school about the danger of drugs. But he laughed and said simply, "If you haven't tried it you don't have the right to talk about it. It's a fantastic medium. Without it I wouldn't have seen the world as I depict it in my paintings."

He kept insisting that she snort with him, but she adamantly refused. One night she was in bed with him and he persisted again more strongly. He said, as if pleading with her, "Listen to me. I want what's good for you. Dope doesn't take away your consciousness; it gives you additional consciousness. Try it just once, and if you don't like it, don't ever touch it again."

She will never forget the first ecstasy. As soon as she snorted the powder she felt as if she were flying, soaring among the clouds: no sorrows, no worries, no fear about the future; a pure burning and raging happiness. Then she had sex with him and climaxed. Next time he offered her the dope she didn't mind. When she asked him for it the third time he laughed out loud for a long time and said as he handed her the rolled-up paper, "Welcome to Club Happiness!"

Making love came to be associated with snorting, which took her to the highest levels of orgasm. It made her shake strongly several times, scream loudly, and then her body would subside, dying and being reborn from sheer love. Now Jeff was trying to resume what had been interrupted. He got closer until he clung to her then whispered, "Goddamn your foolish father; he ruined our trip."

He was talking in a matter-of-fact tone of voice, as if commenting on bad weather conditions or a traffic jam. His voice was neutral and his regret light and passing. He didn't wait for her reply, as if he took it for granted. He reached out for the bottle that originally had vitamins in it, raised it against the light, looked at it and shook it carefully, then emptied a little of the powder onto the dish, using a small razor to separate a thin line. When he started snorting through the tube, Sarah got up suddenly. She moved away and went toward the window quickly, as if she were running away. She was making a feeble, low-key attempt that she knew deep down was doomed to fail before it even began. She turned her face away and began to look out of the window. Jeff, as usual, seemed confident of her response. He looked at her with a smile, as if making fun of her childlike attempt to play hard to get. He extended his hand with the funnel. His blue eyes were exuding total control and when he sensed her reluctance, he said in a confident voice, as if concluding a pending matter, "Come on, little girl. Enough playing outside. Come back to the garden!"

She lowered her gaze and moved toward him, her head bowed, her will bent, burdened with all the hopelessness that in a few moments would turn into overpowering, boisterous pleasure. She threw herself next to him on the sofa, picked up the tube, raised it slowly to her nostril, closed her eyes, and snorted hard.

CHAPTER 25

 Ever since General Safwat Shakir was a student at the police academy, his instructors predicted that he would have a brilliant future because of the strength of his personality, his precision, and his mental and physical capabilities. After graduation he worked as an assistant in the Azbakiya secret detective division and was able, despite his young age, to greatly optimize the way the system there worked. Back then, the work of a detective simply consisted of arresting suspects and torturing them until they confessed. Methods of torture were conventional: suspects were beaten, bastinadoed, or flogged with oversize whips. If a suspect insisted on denying the charges, he would be violated by the insertion of a thick stick up his anus, the putting out of cigarettes on his penis, or the administering of electric shocks to his naked body. Torture continued until the suspect gave in and confessed to what he was accused of. Those conventional methods were useful, of course, but they resulted in the death of many suspects, which led to some embarrassing situations. A detective would then have one of two options: either to obtain a medical report indicating that the suspect had died as a result of a sudden drop in blood circulation, then order him to be buried secretly after threatening his family with detention and torture if they opened their mouths, or to order the plainclothesmen to throw the suspect's body from the police station balcony, then write a report afterward indicating that he had committed suicide.

The young officer Safwat Shakir, after obtaining his supervisor's permission, introduced a new protocol: instead of beatings and electric shocks, he would arrest the suspect's wife (his mother or sister if he was a bachelor); then he would order his men to take off the woman's clothes, one item at a time until she was naked, then they would begin to fondle her body in front of her husband, who would soon collapse and confess to whatever he was asked to confess. The new protocol led to brilliant results, and bringing cases to closure took half the customary time, so much so that the head of the Azbakiya precinct, for several years in a row, received letters of thanks from the minister of the interior, commending the precinct for its productivity and precision. Only one time was there a problem: one of the suspects couldn't stand seeing his old mother naked, with the policemen fondling her private parts. He let loose a loud, rasping scream, as if he were on fire. Then he lost consciousness and later it turned out he had become a hemiplegic as a result. Safwat Shakir, as usual, did not lose his composure and dealt with the situation wisely. He ordered the suspect moved to the hospital and obtained a medical report stating that the detainee had hypertension and had suffered a clot in the brain. Apart from that fleeting incident, the new protocol achieved such brilliant success that other precincts adopted it. News of Safwat Shakir's genius reverberated so strongly throughout the halls of the ministry that he was transferred to the State Secret Security detective division. There he used his method with political dissidents, achieving the same rate of success, which made his supervisors rotate him to different governorates. With repetition and experience Safwat Shakir finessed his method and added to it a theatrical dimension that made it more effective. So when a suspect's wife or mother was stripped naked, he would scrutinize her in a leisurely fashion and tell the suspect in a neutral tone, "Look at that! Your wife is very beautiful. Isn't it a shame that you leave her starved for sex, while you worry about politics?" Or he would say, "True, your mother is old, but when we took off her clothes and saw her naked, we discovered that she'd still be good in bed!"

The detainee might then cry or scream, cursing or begging for mercy. Safwat, like veteran stage actors, had learned how to remain silent until the suspect was through with his reaction. He would wait a moment then say in a soft voice that would reverberate in the detainee's ears like evil suggestions hissed by Satan, "That's my last offer. You either agree to talk or I'll let the policemen violate your wife before your eyes. You should thank me—I'll be offering you the chance to watch a pornographic movie for free."

For many years, not a single detainee stood his ground vis-à-vis Safwat Shakir. Many detainees confessed to belonging to several organizations at the same time or signed blank sheets of paper that Safwat Bey later filled in to his heart's content with any confession he wanted.

In addition to his rare efficiency, Safwat Shakir was also well known for encouraging younger officers. He taught them patiently, and he sincerely tried to make them benefit from his experience. He would pick up a pen and a sheet of paper and draw a sloping graph that began from a high point and stayed in a straight horizontal line for some distance then plummeted fast to zero. He would explain to his students, the young officers, "This graph represents the resistance of the detainees: you'll notice from the drawing that the resistance always starts at a high point and remains constant for a while then suddenly collapses at a certain point. The efficient officer will bring about that point of collapse quickly. Don't rely on beating only: after a certain point of physical pain, the detainee might lose sensation. As for electric shocks, they might kill the detainee, creating an unnecessary problem. Try my way and you'll appreciate it. The most hardened and most vicious detainee cannot bear to see his wife or mother violated in front of his own eyes."

Safwat Shakir stayed in State Security until he made the rank of colonel, and then the state wanted to utilize his genius in a new field. So he was transferred to General Intelligence, where the modus operandi was different, of course. His new job consisted of keeping spy rings under surveillance, following and documenting public opinions, and controlling and coordinating agents of the service—university professors, media personalities and executives, party and government officials—and assigning them specific tasks.

General Intelligence in its long and eventful history would, however, remember one of Safwat Shakir's greatest feats. Back at the time of strong opposition to the Egyptian regime by Egyptian intellectuals living in Paris, led by a well-known writer who enjoyed respect in French circles, Safwat Shakir asked the head of General Intelligence to give him a free hand in the operation to deal with the situation. Permission was granted and Shakir went to Paris. After getting permission from French intelligence, he hired a prostitute for a quarter million francs. He trained her and she started a relationship with the Egyptian author. She slipped him a sleeping pill in his whiskey then called Safwat and his men, who injected him with a strong drug and shipped him in a box that they had carefully prepared. The author regained consciousness a few hours later and found himself in intelligence headquarters in Heliopolis. It was a brilliant coup; French investigations led nowhere, so the incident was attributed to person or persons unknown. As for Egyptian dissidents, their voices were muffled for a long time afterward for fear of a similar fate.

In fact, recording all of General Safwat Shakir's professional achievements would require another lengthy book. He kept going from one success to the next until he was appointed counselor (the official and publicly announced title of the head intelligence officer in Egyptian embassies) in Accra, Tokyo, and finally in the most important capital for the Egyptian regime: Washington. He knew quite well that that post was the last stepping-stone to glory, and he worked extraordinarily hard and proved quite successful at it. He saw the forthcoming visit by the president as the chance of a lifetime: if the president saw him and liked him he would appoint him in the next cabinet as minister of the interior or foreign minister or even minister of international cooperation. But if he made a single mistake in preparing for the visit, he would be pensioned off in the next round of appointments and promotions.

Have we learned everything about Safwat Shakir? There are still two aspects of his life that we have not touched upon: power and women. After many years in which he had absolute power over and control of the destiny of thousands upon thousands of detainees, he acquired a mysterious, well-established, instinctive power that would be hard to explain fully. The nature of his job enabled him to see people at their weakest, made it possible for him to penetrate the most private secrets between a man and his wife, and taught him to crush the manhood of the strongest fighters, to make them prostrate themselves in tears, begging him, kissing his feet so he wouldn't order their wives to be violated before their very eyes. That deep-rooted, perverse human experience gave him an extraordinary power over those around him. It was as if he had broken the bounds of that invisible domain where all humans moved, acquiring a superhuman authority that no one could withstand. He no longer needed to speak much, and there was nothing that surprised him or made him hesitate anymore. To that should be added his stonelike features, hard chiseled as if they represent implacable fate; his strong, terrifying look that penetrates the heart; his dignified, always unhurried movements that are controlled by a rhythm all their own and which make light of any tension around him; his few words, which he delivers slowly and distinctly; and his very presence, which in itself creates a state of impenetrable anxiety around him. All of those elements magnify his power to the utmost, to godlike dimensions. When he makes a decision, it is irreversible, carrying out the dictates of fate without being subject to them. He decides, with one word or gesture, the destiny of a whole family for several generations to come. The stupendous power that he has would impel one to wonder: Can our wishes change the course of events? If we really and strongly wish for something, can we make it happen somehow? If that were true, then Safwat Shakir's power is caused primarily by his very strong awareness of it, as evidenced by the fact that he instantly imposes his will on those who do not know his position.

That power took a different mode with women, the love of whom Shakir inherited from his grandfathers. (Most men in his family had two or more women at the same time as either wives or mistresses.) He remembered from his childhood many quarrels between his mother and father because of his relations with other women. He even remembered that, as a student at the police academy, he had had a relationship with a servant in their house. When he slept with her every Thursday upon his return from spending the evening with his friends, he felt that her body was already fulfilled and content, which created in his mind a strong suspicion, supported by other indications, that she was sleeping with both him and his father. The wild sexual vigor, in both desire and performance, that Safwat Shakir maintained despite being fifty-five, was not due only to heredity but also to the nature of his work. For those who live on the edge of danger—such as soldiers in combat, bullfighters, and gangsters on the run—have burning, insatiable sexual desires, as if they voraciously partake of that pleasure because they might lose it (together with their lives) at any moment, or as if by sexual activity they intensify their awareness of every moment of their threatened lives.

One of Safwat Shakir's major peculiarities was the way he went about pursuing and having his way with women. After years of detention without trial, the wife of a detained man would lose hope that her husband would be freed and would devote all her efforts to improving his conditions as much as possible, or getting him transferred to a nearby detention center, or getting medications to him regularly. Under such circumstances, a detainee's wife would have no choice but to beg the State Security officers, who alone would be able to make the lives of their husbands less miserable. Thus one of the familiar scenes in front of State Security headquarters would be that of a crowd of women, clad in black, standing since the early morning in front of the gate, waiting for hours in silence or chatting in low voices or crying, until finally they would be let in. When that happened, they'd begin passionate supplications accompanied by crying and begging the officers to agree to their modest requests for their husbands' well-being. The officers usually looked upon these requests coldly and in a bored, almost exasperated manner. Most of the time they rejected them and threatened the women with being detained and tortured themselves if they didn't leave. Only if the detainee's wife was beautiful would the treatment be different: they would tell her to meet Safwat Bey Shakir. When they said that, their eyes would gleam with a hidden sarcastic meaning. They knew that their boss loved women and they made jokes about it secretly among themselves, but they still sent him the beautiful ones to curry favor with him. Thus a detainee's beautiful wife would enter Safwat Shakir's office, stumbling over her fear and misery. From the first glance he would be able to tell what kind of woman she was and whether she would accept or refuse. He would evaluate her response with one long, unhurried look, scrutinizing her body with obvious lust and at the same time measuring her reaction. The woman would stand in front of him in anguish, complaining, crying, and begging him to grant her requests. If Safwat Shakir realized from his experience that she would say no, he would send her papers back to his underlings to take the necessary measures. But if he felt she was available, he would grant her requests immediately. In the midst of the thanks and prayers on the woman's part, Safwat Shakir would once again feast his eyes on her charms and say slowly, "You're a gorgeous girl. How can you do without?"

That sudden and open transition would be necessary to rule out the last possibility of a wrong inference. If the woman smiled or resorted to embarrassed silence without anger or even whispered in a soft but animated voice, he would be sure that the coast was clear, so he would talk explicitly about sex. At the end of the conversation he would take a piece of paper and write the address of his apartment on Shawarbi Street, then mutter in a businesslike manner, "Tomorrow, at five o'clock, I'll wait for you at this address."

It never happened that the woman didn't keep the appointment. There were numerous reasons for that: a detainee's wife, ultimately, was a human being with her desires preying on her nerves with no hope of satisfying them in the near future. It might satisfy her to know, deep down, that a high-ranking officer like Safwat Shakir would want her, which meant that he had preferred her, the poor woman, to women of high society available to him. Besides, by accepting the relationship with Safwat Shakir she would be securing for her husband better conditions in detention. The acquiescence of detainees' wives, however, could be attributed to a more profound cause, related to the graph that Shakir drew to teach his young officer students. A woman, broken by poverty and different ordeals, exhausted by fighting on more than one front, one who had given up on resuming a normal life, one who was ganged up on by deprivation, men's lust, and her miserable daily struggle to feed her children, would be like a besieged, exhausted soldier just a few moments before surrender. Such a woman would be driven by a deep desire to fall. Yes, falling would almost bring her relief because it would suppress forever the inner conflict that had often tormented her. Now she would be indeed a fallen woman; there was no longer any room for hesitation, thinking, or resistance. As soon as she entered the apartment, Safwat Shakir would take her to bed, and every time he would discover that, from the way she had taken care of her intimate details, she had expected and prepared for it. Strangely enough, he never kissed them and often had intercourse with them without a single word. He would fondle their bodies, already burning with desire to begin with, igniting them further to insane degrees, then at a moment that he knew by intuition, like a bullfighter brandishing his sword to finish off his animal opponent, Safwat Shakir would penetrate the women with extreme violence, devoid of any tenderness or kindness, mercilessly. He would penetrate her over and over again as if he were whipping her, as he had done to her husband earlier. She would scream as if crying for help, and in her screams her pleasure would be mixed with pain, or maybe the pleasure resulted from the pain. Roughing her up like that brought her a profound pleasure arising not from the sex but from her being liberated for good from her dignity. Humiliating her by sleeping with her, while despising her, took his contempt to the lowest depths because she deserved it: she was now a fallen woman who did not deserve to be treated tenderly or with respect; he took her as fallen women were usually taken. Once such a woman climaxed, she would cling to Shakir; she never dared to kiss him (for a kiss implied parity), but she would embrace him, cleave to his body, feeling it, smelling and sometimes licking it with her tongue. She'd often bend and kiss his hand as he remained stretched out, relaxed, smoking, his mind far away as if he were a god indifferently receiving offerings from his worshippers.

GENERAL SAFWAT SHAKIR WAS NOW sitting in his office in the Egyptian embassy in Washington, busily reading security reports that he had just received from Cairo. The office was quiet until the silence was broken by the voice of his secretary, Hasan, over the intercom. "Sorry to disturb you, sir."

"I said I didn't want any calls."

"It's Dr. Ahmad Danana, who came from Chicago to see you, sir. He assures me it's urgent and important."

Safwat Shakir was silent for a moment then said in a gruff voice, "Let him in."

After a moment, Danana rushed into the room, panting and sweating profusely, as if he had run all the way from Chicago. He threw himself onto the sofa facing the desk and said in a hoarse voice, as if crying for help, "Sorry to bother Your Excellency, but there's a catastrophe, sir. A catastrophe."

Safwat Shakir kept watching him in silence as Danana continued in a shaking voice, "Dr. Dennis Baker, my doctoral dissertation advisor, has accused me of forging the results of my research and has sent me up for investigation."

Safwat Shakir remained silent. He took out a cigarette from the golden cigarette case open in front of him, lit it slowly, then took a drag and kept staring at Danana, who pleaded in a prayerful voice, "If the investigation finds me guilty, they will expel me."

Safwat answered slowly, piercing him with a glance like a bullet, "And what do you want me to do?"

"My future will be ruined, sir. They'll kick me out of the university."

"And who told you to make up the results of the research?"

"I didn't make them up, sir. I had been late doing my research as a result of the assignments Your Excellency gave me. Dr. Baker kept pressuring me to give him results. So I told myself I'd give him the results and then I'd take my time doing the experiments."

"You fool! Didn't it occur to you that he would review the results?"

"In other dissertations he frequently just reviewed the numbers. And he was satisfied with the numbers I submitted to him," Danana mumbled. He then went on talking in a soft voice as if to himself, "It almost passed, but, unfortunately for me, he wanted to apply a new idea to the research, so he examined my slides and discovered what I had done."

Safwat Shakir remained silent and Danana began to beg again, "I beseech you, Safwat Bey, I've been serving the state since I was a college student. I have never been lazy and I've never hesitated to carry out what you've ordered me to do. Don't I deserve that you stand by me during this ordeal?"

"We don't stand by forgers."

"I implore you, sir."

"If the university doesn't expel you, we will. You cannot keep your position when you're a forger."

Danana opened his mouth to say something, but his face trembled and he started to weep. "All this hard work for nothing! All those nights I burned the midnight oil, for what? For a scandal and expulsion?"

"Shut up," Safwat, visibly annoyed, shouted at him. Danana took that as a slight glimmer of hope, so he persisted anew. "I beseech you for the memory of your parents, may God have mercy on their souls. Please, Safwat Bey, you are my boss and my professor and I am your disciple. You have every right to punish me when I make a mistake. Do anything you want to me, Your Excellency, but don't abandon me."

Perhaps that was what Safwat had been waiting for. He sat back in his comfortable chair, raised his head, and kept staring at the ceiling in silence until he said, "I'll help you. Not for your own sake, but for the sake of your unfortunate wife."

"May God give you long life, sir."

"When is the investigation?"

"Tomorrow."

"Go to them."

"I could get a letter from a doctor and postpone it for a week."

"No. Go tomorrow as they want you to."

"Sir, Dr. Baker is well respected in the department and they will definitely expel me."

"Let them expel you. They have to send us your expulsion decision. We can bury the decision here and the educational bureau will not know about it."

"May God give you long life, sir, but I'd no longer be enrolled."

"Once things calm down, I'll try to get you enrolled in another university."

That was more than Danana had hoped for. He kept staring at his master's face then said in a hesitant voice, "I'll consider that a promise from you, sir."

Safwat shot him a disapproving look that almost transfixed him in his place, and then said in a bored tone of voice, "Go back now to Chicago and finish the tasks I assigned to you. Our revered president's visit is drawing near and we don't have much time."

Danana tried to start a spiel, however short, of thanks and gratitude, but Safwat Shakir once again started reading the reports scattered on the desk in front of him and said, "Don't take up my time. I have a lot of work to do."

Danana sighed and his features relaxed. He turned to leave, but before he reached the door, Safwat's voice, in a different tone, stopped him. "By the way, I have a request for you."

"I am at your disposal, sir, upon my life."

CHAPTER 26

Carol was so terrified she looked pale. Her heart raced, her breathing became irregular, and she almost fainted as she, with her friend Emily, entered the crowded elevator in a skyscraper overlooking Michigan Avenue. Emily whispered something to the elevator operator and he pressed the button for the thirtieth floor. The elevator made a musical sound before it started up. Carol and Emily remained silent; they had talked so much that nothing was left to be said. Carol posed many questions. She hesitated for a long time and almost changed her mind more than once, but Emily reassured her. She looked at her with a mother's smile and said, "This is the opportunity of a lifetime. If I were in your place, I wouldn't hesitate."

"I can't help feeling ashamed."

"There's nothing to be ashamed of if you look at it from a purely aesthetic point of view."

They left the elevator. Emily proceeded with Carol, following her to the end of the corridor to the right. She stopped in front of a tinted glass door on top of which was an elegant sign: FERNANDO ADVERTISING AGENCY. Emily pushed the button and said her name into the intercom. The door soon opened and out came a forty-something man with his hair in long thin intersecting braids. It seemed from his soft movements and the light makeup on his face that he was gay. He was smoking a fat cigarette from which came a strong smell of marijuana. He exchanged cries of welcome with Emily, who hugged him warmly and kissed him on the cheeks, and then said cheerfully, "My friend Carol. My friend Fernando."

"Happy to meet you." Carol shook his hand and struggled to feign a smile.

The apartment was big and furnished in a modern, luxurious style. On the walls Carol now saw enlarged snapshots of faces and landscapes that she guessed had been taken by Fernando, who led them through a long corridor, on one side of which was the open door of a bedroom bathed in a soft red light. At the end of the corridor they entered the studio: a small round room with a very high ceiling in the four corners of which cameras of different sizes were placed. In the middle there was a chair, a small table, and a sofa. From the ceiling hung floodlights casting yellow, blue, and red light. Fernando invited them to sit on the sofa while he sat on the chair in front of them. Then he said in a friendly tone, "Sorry for this mess. I'm a disorganized person."

"Like all artists."

"Would you like an excellent joint?"

"No, thank you," Emily mumbled while Carol remained speechless.

"What would you like to drink?"

"Anything cold."

He opened the fridge and brought out two cans of Pepsi, and then he said in a practical tone, "Okay, Carol, I don't want to waste your time. I think Emily has told you."

Carol nodded. Fernando went on, "I must see your breasts first, so we can have a constructive basis for discussion."

He let out a loud laugh, then shook his head and gathered his braids in his hands and got up, almost dancing. He stood in front of the camera and hit the remote control turning on a floodlight, which made a round spot of shining light on the wooden floor. He signaled for Carol to approach. She got up slowly, and it actually occurred to her at that moment to run away, to open the door of the apartment and run as fast as she could, leaving everything behind and going home to Mark and Graham. But, in spite of everything, she moved toward him as if her feet were moving on their own. Fernando smiled at her gently as if he realized what she was going through. In a calm voice he said, "Take off this shirt, please?"

That was too much for her. She stood there, her head bowed, totally still. He said simply, "I'll help you."

He went over to her and began to undo the buttons slowly, as if he enjoyed it. She trembled and felt queasy and thought her soul was ebbing away from her, and yet she succumbed to his hands. He undid the bra from the back and dropped it on the table. Her breasts came down as if freed from a shackle. He turned around, his face having acquired a neutral professional expression. He stood behind the camera and peered carefully through the lens, then he went back to her and adjusted the way she stood in order to examine the image of her breasts in the camera from different angles. Before long he sighed and exclaimed, as if resolving a pending matter, "Not bad. Let's talk a little bit."

She extended her hand and covered her chest with the shirt, but to her own surprise, she left it unbuttoned. He sat in front of her and lit a new marijuana cigarette whose end glowed intensely before it produced thick smoke. He coughed hard and said, "This is the story, dear friend. There are two adult lingerie companies in Chicago, the Double X Company and Rocky Company. I think you've heard of them. Competition between them is fierce, cutthroat, as they say. They compete in promoting bras in particular because they sell the most. Performance levels in the two companies are close to each other, which makes advertising more important. A few months ago, Rocky started a new advertising campaign on cable television using real women rather than professional models. A woman would appear on television next to her real name and profession. The audience would watch her taking off her clothes and putting on a Rocky brand bra, then she would talk about its advantages. Have you seen these commercials on late-night television?"

"Yes."

"We must admit that it was an ingenious advertising campaign by Rocky, leading to a twenty percent decline in Double X brand bra sales, which meant a loss in the millions of dollars. Double X has asked me to organize an advertising countercampaign. This is a major professional opportunity for me. If it succeeds, my little advertising agency will make it to the top. I've given the matter a lot of thought and I've come up with a totally original concept for an ad."

"Emily has assured me that my face won't appear in the commercials," said Carol, looking at her friend as if seeking her help.

Fernando said, "Calm down, baby. We can't imitate Rocky's commercials. Our look will be totally different. I will shoot you only taking off a Rocky bra and putting on a Double X one. The camera will not show your face. I will show the viewers by your body language how much more comfortable you feel wearing Double X. That's the real challenge. We've got a lot of work ahead of us. We will run a lot of rehearsals in order to teach you how to express yourself using your body."

"Why did you pick me in particular?" Carol asked, her confusion turning into a profound sense of disbelief, as if she were part of a surreal scene that would come to an end at any moment, after which she would come back to reality.

Fernando took a long drag on the marijuana cigarette, closed his lips, swallowed and coughed, then said as his eyes turned red, "In this commercial, the body should not be splendidly beautiful because it would place the merchandise out of the grasp of the potential customer. I was looking for an ordinary chest, a chest like that of most women viewers, an average black American chest that is neither an artistic masterpiece nor very ugly. Did Emily tell you about the fee?"

"One thousand dollars for every hour of shooting."

"You have an excellent memory for numbers." He laughed loudly then got up, left the studio, and came back soon thereafter holding a small glass, saying:

"We'll do the first dry run. Please leave yourself totally to me. Drink this."

"What is it?"

"It's a small glass of cognac that will give you courage before the camera."

She felt the liquid burning her throat. As soon as she put the glass on the table, Fernando took her by the hand and said, "Come on. We've got work to do."

■■■■■■■■■■

We, the undersigned, Egyptians residing in the city of Chicago, United States of America, feel extremely worried about current conditions in Egypt: the poverty, unemployment, corruption, and domestic and foreign debts. We believe that our country deserves a democratic political system. We believe that all Egyptians have a right to justice and freedom. On the occasion of the president's visit to the United States, we demand the following of him:

First: abrogation of the emergency law;

Second: implementation of democratic reform and guarantee of public freedoms;

Third: election of a national assembly to draft a new constitution guaranteeing true democracy for Egyptians;

Fourth: abdication of the president and a promise not to bequeath the presidency to his son, thus opening up an opportunity for a real contest for the presidency based on elections subject to international supervision.

We sat drafting the statement, Karam Doss and I, at Dr. Graham's house. John participated with the enthusiasm of an old revolutionary. We translated the text for him and he gave us some important ideas. He said, "The language of the statement has to be precise and definitive. If it is rhetorical or emotional, it will not be taken seriously. If it is too militant, as if it were a declaration of war, it will look like a caricature."

We added some demands: to release detainees, to do away with special tribunals, and to ban torture. We finished the statement in its final form late on Friday night. I got up early in the morning, printed the statement, and made twenty copies, then began my mission: I had to meet Egyptian students and convince them to sign. During the day, I met five students who responded with useless debate, then refused to sign. The strangest reaction came from Tariq Haseeb and Shaymaa Muhammadi, two colleagues from the histology department who are inseparable (I think they are romantically involved). This Tariq is a strange man, very brilliant, but introspective and aggressive, and he always seems to be in a bad mood, as if someone has just awakened him. He, with Shaymaa by his side, listened to me in silence. I described conditions in Egypt and said it was our duty to do something for change. I noticed a sarcastic expression on his face, and as soon as I mentioned the statement, he interrupted me derisively. "Are you kidding? You want me to sign a statement against the president of the republic?"

"Yes, for the sake of your country."

"I am not interested in politics."

"When you go back to Egypt, aren't you going to get married and have children?" I asked him as I looked at Shaymaa.

"God willing."

"Don't you care about the future of your children?"

"My children will have a better future if I concentrate on my studies and go back to Egypt with a PhD."

"Why do you accept that they will live in the midst of injustice and corruption?"

"Would their conditions be better after I am detained?"

"Who'd detain you?"

"Of course everyone who'll sign this statement will be harmed," said Shaymaa, her very first sentence. I tried to be patient and to explain, but Tariq got up and said, "Don't waste your time, Nagi. We are not going to sign any statements, nor, I think, will a single Egyptian in Chicago. Let me give you some advice for God's sake, don't go down that road—it doesn't end well. Concentrate on your studies. Mind your own business and don't try to change the universe," he said again derisively and grabbed Shaymaa's arm and the two left me alone. When I met Karam in the evening, I was frustrated. I told him, "I am close to giving up on the idea."

"Why?"

"All the students I met refused to sign."

"Did you expect to convince them easily?"

"They treated me like a madman."

"That's natural."

"Why?"

"All the students are at the government's mercy. If they sign this statement, they'll actually be penalized."

"But I'm a student like them."

"You're an exception. Besides, you don't work at the university, hence there's nothing for you to lose."

"If everyone thought of it this way, we wouldn't get anything done."

"What a dreamer!"

"I am not a dreamer, but I find their position to be selfish and despicable. People like that are the reason we're where we are. It is from them that the regime chooses its ministers and experts, who turn a blind eye to the truth and who lie and curry favor with the president to keep their posts."

"Don't give up," Dr. Doss said.

"I no longer see the point in what we are doing."

He smiled and patted me on the shoulder, then took out of his pocket a folded paper. When I looked at it, I recognized it as a copy of the statement with several signatures. He laughed loudly and said, "You have to admit I beat you!"

I began to read the names; they were both Coptic and Muslim names. He went on, not trying to hide how happy he was, "At the beginning I was not enthusiastic about the idea of the statement but afterward I found it to be an excellent idea. And most of those I met have responded well. We will succeed, Nagi, but we have to look in the right places. Don't waste your time with the students. I've brought you a list of Egyptian immigrants in Chicago, with their addresses and telephone numbers. Let's split the list and contact them."

During the following days, as soon as I came back from school, I'd work the phone, ringing up Egyptians. I introduced myself as a student who wanted to start a new association of Egyptians, and then I'd ask the person for an appointment to see them. The reactions differed from one person to the next: some told me frankly that they had severed their ties to Egypt and couldn't care less what happened there. But many of them were quite enthusiastic. I visited several neighborhoods in Chicago. Most Egyptians I met were upset at the conditions in Egypt. At the end of my presentation, I'd ask each of them a direct question, "Do you want to do something for your country?"

I could guess the answer from the way they looked at me: an indifferent or awkward look meant no signature; a friendly look meant that they would sign. By 4:00 P.M. on the following Sunday, when I took the Blue Line going back to the dorm, I had obtained ten signatures in addition to the twenty-nine that Karam got, a total of thirty-nine signatures, in addition to five persons who had asked for time to think about it. That was an achievement beyond our expectations in the short period since we started. We still had a whole month to go. If we continued at this rate, we would get hundreds of signatures. I remembered an article I had read a few years ago about something mysterious in the makeup of Egyptians that made it difficult to predict their reactions. The article asserted that revolution in Egypt always began unexpectedly, that a ferment went on beneath the Egyptians' calm surface, which made them, at the very moment they seemed to give in to oppression, erupt suddenly in revolution. That theory seemed to be valid. I was overcome with a sense of pride and joy. There I was, doing something for my compatriots who were being beaten up, dragged, and violated on the streets of Cairo, who were detained and tortured in horrific ways just because they expressed their opinions. Soon we were going to embarrass the Egyptian regime before the whole world. In front of the cameras and the international press corps, a person, speaking for the Egyptians in Chicago, would stand up and demand that the president abdicate and that democracy be adopted. There wouldn't be a more important news item in all the media.

As I walked through the entrance to the dorm, I caught a glimpse of Henry, Wendy's former boyfriend, sitting at his desk. He shot a disdainful look at me, but I ignored him. I walked slowly so he'd know I couldn't care less about him. All of a sudden I felt I was strong; I no longer feared him. He could go to hell. From now on, if he oversteps the bounds or utters an insulting word, I'll teach him a lesson he will not forget.

I got out of the elevator and turned the key in the door of the apartment and as soon as I stepped inside, I noticed something strange; the lights were on, even though I remembered well that I had turned them off before leaving. I went in slowly and cautiously. Suddenly I saw a man sitting in the chair in the living room. I froze, shocked, then shouted at the top of my voice, "Who are you? And how did you get in here?"

He got up steadily and advanced toward me. He smiled and extended his hand to shake mine, saying, "Good evening, Nagi. I am sorry I came this way, but it is very important that I speak to you. My name is Safwat Shakir, counselor at the Egyptian embassy in Washington."

CHAPTER

That morning, Chris gave in to an inner call that she did not understand. She put on conservative clothes: a long-sleeved dark green suit and dark sunglasses. She looked like an undercover officer in a police drama. She found the store a few steps from the entrance to the train station, exactly as she had read in the paper. The glass facade was covered with a black curtain and there was a neon sign that read MAXIM'S FOR TOOLS OF DELIGHT. She stopped hesitantly before the door for a few moments, then the door opened and a twenty-something woman appeared. She greeted her with a friendly smile and invited her in. Chris said to herself that it was only natural at a place like that to monitor the entrance with secret cameras. She looked around and immediately felt disoriented and somewhat queasy. She saw dozens of sex toys for all purposes: for heterosexual men and women, gays, and lesbians. In the back was a screen showing an X-rated movie. The saleswoman looked strange, smiling politely and speaking calmly while moans of pleasure came loudly from the movie playing behind her.

"How can I help you?"

"I'd like to buy a vibrator," Chris blurted out in a tone she tried to make sound neutral and nonchalant. But her voice came out loud, which increased her embarrassment. The saleswoman asked her simply, "What kind of vibrator do you want?"

Chris went closer to the saleswoman and whispered in a shaking voice, "Actually, I'd be using a vibrator for the first time and I don't know what kind to choose."

The saleswoman's smile broadened and she said, "If you want counseling from our sex expert, that will cost you fifty dollars a session."

Chris grew more confused; the woman went on, "If you want basic information on vibrators, one session would be enough. But if you have sexual problems, or if you want to improve your performance in bed, you'd need several sessions. The expert will be able to tell you how many sessions you'll need after you meet with her."

"I am only interested in the vibrator."

"One session then: fifty dollars."

She took out a fifty-dollar bill, which the saleswoman took and put in the drawer, then motioned to Chris to follow her. She led her through a long corridor until they got to a door with the sign JANE DEHAN, LICENSED SEX EXPERT. The saleswoman entered, disappeared for a few moments, then said as she extended her hand in welcome, "This way, please."

The expert, who was over fifty years old, with glasses, a white coat, and gray hair gathered in a bun at the back of her head, looked more like a dietitian employed by a television channel. After introductions and reserved pleasantries, the expert exhaled and said like someone who wanted to get to work, "Okay, Chris, what do you know about vibrators?"

"All I know is that it's a tool that enables a woman to achieve orgasm without a man."

"And how does a vibrator work?"

"It tickles the vagina in a certain way that takes a woman to orgasm."

The expert smiled and said cheerfully, "That's a good beginning. But actually, a vibrator is much more than a tool for masturbation. The vibrator represents the culmination of scientific progress and society's changing view of women."

Chris looked at her in silence. The expert went on, "Throughout human history, information about women's sexuality was sparse and insufficient. This was due to old societies' view of woman as Satan's means of seducing man. This taboo led to our almost total ignorance of how a woman achieves orgasm. The idea that gained currency and which prevailed for many centuries was that a woman achieved orgasm by stimulation of the clitoris. This belief persisted until 1950, when a great German scientist named Ernst Gräfenburg was able to discover the G-spot. Then the discovery was confirmed by the research of the two scientists, Perry and Whipple, in 1978. We've come to know that every woman has a G-spot, which is a very sensitive area on the front wall of the vagina whose arousal brings about a strong orgasm, different from that of the clitoris. This begins with a feeling like the desire to urinate then turns into strong successive waves of pleasure leading, in the case of some women, to the discharge of a thick liquid without a smell, similar to milk. Have you experienced that before?"

"No. Actually, I don't know. Until recently I enjoyed a satisfactory sex life."

The expert laughed and said, "Of course you don't know. Most likely you've only experienced clitoral orgasm. That's our fate as women: our ignorance of our own bodies leads to our not enjoying them. Take this brochure; you'll find everything about the G-spot and there are also some useful exercises that will teach you how to discover it for yourself."

Chris took the brochure and put it in her bag. The expert went on, "The discovery of the G-spot, women's equality with men, and their emancipation from their control forever have led to thinking about a way that enables a woman to enjoy her body on her own. A woman is no longer a tool for man's pleasure or his physical subordinate; she is now his equal and has the same rights, most important of which is sexual fulfillment. A woman's satisfaction is no longer dependent upon a man's desire or the strength of his performance. And this is where the vibrator comes in. It is not just a gadget for masturbation but in reality is a scientific apparatus that guarantees a woman her sexual fulfillment regardless of the efficacy of her sexual partner or even his being there. Many of my clients use the vibrator with their husbands to achieve additional pleasure. There are husbands who buy vibrators for their wives to use with them or while they are away or for those nights when the husband has had too much to drink and cannot achieve an erection. Vibrators have so changed sexual behavior that now there is what we can call a vibrator culture. Please feel free to ask me any questions you may have."

Chris hesitated a little, then, encouraged by the expert's presentation, she asked, "What's the difference between a clitoral orgasm and that of the G-spot?"

The expert smiled and said, "An orgasm achieved by the G-spot is much stronger and takes place over long, successive waves. Most women who try it regret that they hadn't known about it earlier."

Silence fell again; she asked if Chris had any other questions and Chris said she didn't, so the expert sighed and said as she got up, "Great. Come and choose your new friend."

The expert, followed by Chris, went through a small door to a side room and stood in front of a glass display case filled with different models of vibrators. The expert put her hand on Chris's shoulder and asked in a friendly tone of voice, "May I ask how much you're willing to spend on a vibrator? We have models ranging from ten dollars to two hundred dollars."

"I can pay. It should be a good model though."

"This makes my job easier."

The expert bent and took out a gadget in the shape of a long, large penis with a bent part that looked like a tree branch jutting out on the side. On the bottom was a white round part that, Chris figured out, was the housing for the battery. Pointing to it proudly, the expert said, "This model is called the new and improved Impulse Jackrabbit; in my opinion, it is the best in the world. You'll see how it takes you to heaven. It will cost you a hundred and fifty dollars plus twenty dollars for a box of cleaner. Is the price okay?"

Chris nodded. The expert explained the component parts of the vibrator and the way to use it, and then she took out a DVD and said, "Before using it, I advise that you watch this DVD. Is it going to be cash or charge?"

The expert swiped Chris's card then gave her the receipt to sign. Then she wrapped the vibrator, the box, and the DVD carefully and put them in an elegant bag bearing the store's logo. She handed it to her and said, "I wish you happiness with the Impulse Jackrabbit. You can call me any time if you have any questions. Consultation is free for a month. I'll think I've done a successful job not only when you use the device, but also when you've got rid of the slightest embarrassment when you do it. Always remember that you're exercising your right to sexual fulfillment. Please consider the vibrator like a shaver or hair dryer, just a device that makes our life easier and more beautiful."

BUT CHRIS DIDN'T GET OVER her embarrassment easily. It wasn't exactly embarrassment, but a sort of strange feeling. She took the train with the Impulse Jackrabbit resting in its elegant bag. At the beginning, she felt that the hand holding the bag was somehow separate from her body. Then she fell prey to the fear that the bag would fall to the floor or tear suddenly, revealing the vibrator, and all the passengers on the train would discover that the dignified lady in the dark green suit and dark glasses had bought a gizmo so that she could have fun with her vagina. Chris resisted the worries, assuring herself that the bag was sturdy and impossible to tear. She recalled what the expert had said and told herself: I am not doing anything shameful. My body belongs to me and I have a right to enjoy it in the manner that pleases me. It's not fair that I should suffer deprivation just because Salah is unhappy with his life. I am not going to deny my desires or bury myself because after thirty years, he discovered that he did the wrong thing by immigrating to America. I have a right to enjoy sex as much as I want.

The logic of her thoughts was convincing but it did not reflect the whole truth. There was something missing that she knew but ignored. Her sexual problem was only the scab on her wound. There were profound sorrows burdening her heart. Salah was asking for a divorce? After all the years they'd lived together, he wanted to leave her? Just like that? Shake her hand and go? He wanted to turn into a person from the past, from memory, a picture in an album that she'd look at sometimes and return to the drawer? Why had he stopped loving her? Had he fallen in love with another woman? Had he lost interest in her because she was getting older? Had she, without knowing it, turned into a boring, talkative old woman? Had she neglected her appearance? Did Arab men always need younger women and was that why they had more than one wife? Had Salah kept an Oriental man's mentality in spite of the years he'd spent in America? Or was the truth that he had never loved her? Had he deceived her all those years? Had he married her to get an American passport? To enhance his social status? To be the successful immigrant university professor married to an American woman? If that was true, why had he stayed with her all those years? Had he left her after getting his American citizenship, it would have been easier. She would've been able to forget, even forgive him. She was young then and could've started all over again. But now it was as if he had used her all those years then decided to throw her in the garbage. How could he bring himself to hurt her so much? Even if he didn't love her. They had lived together a whole lifetime and he couldn't undo that in just one moment. He had no right to do that. Those thoughts kept boring into her like bouts of chronic pain; her feelings of misery doubled her need for pleasure. She was instinctively driven to confine her consciousness to her body to escape the heavy burden of her sorrow.

Chris took a hot bath then went back to her room, where she had been sleeping alone ever since Salah left her. She turned on the laptop, inserted the DVD, and followed the operating instructions attentively. Then she lay on the bed, took out the vibrator, and felt it with her fingers. Its head was extremely smooth; the stem was studded with protuberances like pointed beads. Why was it called "rabbit"? Was it because it looked like a rabbit or because it was obedient and amicable? She slipped under the covers and rubbed the vibrator with the moisturizing liquid according to the instructions then gently inserted it. For the first time she felt how large and hard it was. As soon as she pushed the operating button, she felt an urgent desire to urinate. That feeling left her little by little, leading to strong, exciting, and escalating sensations: waves of devilish tremors that shook her whole body relentlessly. She bit the pillow in order to prevent herself from screaming. The pleasure was fierce and brutal, without fantasy, affection, or a partner. It was pure, wicked, burning pleasure that kept hitting her hard, as if it were a whip or a bolt of lightning, delivering her in the end into the throes of a mighty orgasm that shook her in successive waves then left her exhausted with delight.

In the morning, under the stream of a hot shower, she felt her body invigorated, as if born anew. Her head was clear and her muscles were rid of tension, as if she had slept soundly for a whole day. The Impulse Jackrabbit had catapulted her into soaring orbits of pleasure that she had not known even in her wildest nights with Salah. Day after day she celebrated nightfall, taking care of her body then bringing the rabbit to it as if it were a real lover, as if she were in love with it. She was going to love anything that gave her all that happiness, even if it was a battery-operated device. She treated it kindly, cleaned it carefully, rubbed it with the liquid with extreme care, and wrapped her fingers around it softly, as if afraid of hurting it or causing it pain.

After spending several nights with the rabbit, she began to introduce new variations. She would begin with watching a pornographic movie, fondling herself, then inserting the rabbit; that way she could have two, sometimes three orgasms. She also let herself go totally un-constrained: she screamed loudly with pleasure until she got hoarse. She no longer worried that Salah might hear her. She was sure their life together was over. He had breakfast alone and lunch out and closed his office door to avoid seeing her. So what if he heard her nightly screams? Or even saw her sleeping with the Impulse Jackrabbit? She no longer cared about him. Actually, she overdid the screaming bit, motivated by a deep inner desire that he hear her. She wanted to tell him, "Here I am getting the pleasure you've deprived me of! Here is my body, which you have abandoned and tormented with your impotence, enjoying plea-sure and being liberated time after time!"

Dr. Salah, however, did not hear her. Not only because the basement was isolated and far off, but also because *he* was no longer there, because he had crossed over to the other side. He had discovered an enchanted world hidden deep in an Arabian Nights vault to which he stole at night to enjoy beauty before being assailed by the hostile, ugly daylight. He no longer cared about day-to-day life. He stopped thinking about Chris, divorce, his sexual impotence, or even his job. He spent his days half there, in a casual and nonchalant manner, waiting for the moment of release. At midnight he would begin his trip: he would take a bath and wear cologne as if going on a date. Then he would go downstairs to the basement and put on his 1970s clothes. He had found a good tailor who restored his old clothes to a new life by taking them out to his new measurements for a fee that would have been enough for a brand-new wardrobe. Before starting his nightly journey, he locked himself in, per-haps to feel completely isolated from the outside world or perhaps for fear that Chris might open the door; if she did, she would be certain that he had gone crazy. He wouldn't be able to explain what he was doing. He himself did not understand it. His overpowering desire was stronger than understanding or resistance. The clothes carried within their folds his history, the scent of his real days. Every piece of clothing brought back a different memory: those were the light cotton Shurbagi shirts that he used to buy from the Swailam store in downtown Cairo; the white sharkskin suit that he wore during summer evening special occasions; the blue suit for Thursday outings; and that was the striped black suit that he had bought especially to celebrate Zeinab's birthday. They had dinner at Le Restaurant Union in front of the High Court building then went to the Cinema Rivoli, where they watched the movie *My Father Is up the Tree*. In the inner jacket pocket he found a folded piece of paper that had been in the same place for thirty years: the stub of a ticket for an Umm Kulthum concert that he had attended in 1969. An idea occurred to him, so he left the basement and came back carrying a tape recorder. He put on the song "al-Atlal" and sat listening to it wearing the same suit that he was wearing when he heard it for the first time.

There, he was finally going back to his true self, riding the time machine described by H. G. Wells in the famous novel. He began to hum with Umm Kulthum and shout in ecstasy and cheer at the cadences exactly as he had done at the concert. Now he was listening to Umm Kulthum every night, and when it got close to 2 A.M. Chicago time, 9 A.M. Cairo time, Dr. Muhammad Salah turned off the recorder, put on his reading glasses, opened his telephone book, and began to call his old friends and acquaintances. All Cairo's telephone numbers had changed: all the five-digit numbers were changed to seven-digit numbers. The numbers beginning with 3 now became 35 or 79. Every time he dialed, there were surprises. It was as if he were one of those cave sleepers at Ephesus, as if he had been asleep for thirty years then woke up and went back to his city. He dialed many wrong numbers, probably because the people he knew had moved. Sometimes he found the right number and then discovered that the person had died. Sometimes he reached those he was calling, whereupon he would say enthusiastically right away, "Don't you remember me? I am Muhammad Salah, your colleague at Cairo University College of Medicine 1970."

They all remembered him, some immediately and the others after a little thought. There would be shouts of greeting and laughter, and then he would go on, "I'm now a professor in a medical school in Chicago."

"That's great."

After the surprise and the shouting and the remembering of bygone days, there was bound to come a moment when the warmth of the conversation wore off. As if the person on the other end were asking, "What reminded you of me now? Why are you calling me?" He had to offer an answer. He would lie by talking of a fictitious reunion of the Class of 1970 of the College of Medicine at Cairo University, or claim that there was a cooperative project between doctors in Illinois and Egypt. He talked fast and lied with an enthusiasm that surprised even him, aiming to distract the other person so that he wouldn't think how bizarre the conversation was and so that he wouldn't pity him. They should not find out that nostalgia had crushed him, that he had discovered, after turning sixty, that he had made a mistake leaving his country, that he regretted emigration to death. He should not show them his weakness and sorrows. All that he wanted was for them to talk to him a little about the past, to remember with them his real life.

Salah spent the late hours of the night making calls until the morning. Then he would take a bath and drink several cups of coffee and go to the university. Every two or three days his nervous system collapsed and he slept like a log until the following morning then once again resumed his journey to the past. He stumbled upon a true treasure when he discovered, on the Internet, a complete Cairo telephone directory. He gave up the old telephone book and started using the directory. Now he was able to make direct hits: he would remember the full name, then look it up in the Internet directory until he found the number and call. He was able to reconnect with a group of old acquaintances until he got to his target, his destination, the name that had persistently pressed itself on him from the beginning but which he had avoided, the name that he had exerted strenuous effort to dismiss from his mind, but finally gave into. He sat at the computer, opened the directory then tapped: "Zeinab Abd al-Rahim Muhammad Radwan." He looked at the screen, panting with anticipation. A few seconds later the answer came: "Sorry, name not found."

. He looked at the letters on the screen, crushed by disappointment. He thought: Zeinab was five years younger; she must have been married for quite some time. The telephone must be in her husband's name, if she were still alive. He felt a lump in his throat: Was she dead? Suppose she had died, how could that concern him? Wasn't it ironic that he should grieve for her death thirty years after he had left her? He remembered that there was a professional directory that gave work numbers. He found it and typed her full name then clicked on "search." A few moments later his heart almost jumped for joy. Her name appeared with "Planning Controller, Ministry of Economy" next to it, then her office numbers. Has Zeinab now become a high-ranking government official? Has she kept her revolutionary ideas or had she turned into an ordinary woman, a government employee who punches the clock, curries favor with her bosses, engages in office intrigues against her colleagues, then rushes home to cook before husband and children return? What did Zeinab look like now? Has time been kind to her and left her some of the old charm? Or has she turned into a fat, veiled woman like the tens of thousands crowding Cairo streets that he saw on television? How sad that would make him. "I still cherish you in my memory, Zeinab, as you sat next to me in the Orman garden! How beautiful you were! Can we go back as we were, Zeinab? There must be a way of going back."

It was now ten in the morning Cairo time, a good time to call. Perhaps she went to the office a little late, like big shots. He waited another half hour to make sure she would be there, and then he called. He exerted an extraordinary effort to control his emotions. The secretary answered in a soft voice. He asked her about Ustaza Zeinab. She asked for his name. His voice was choking with emotions as he said, "I am an old colleague of hers and I am calling from America."

"Just a moment," she said and left him with a musical tune that kept playing endlessly. Finally the music stopped and her voice came on. "Good morning."

"Good morning. It is Muhammad Salah, Zeinab."

CHAPTER 28

 Not a day passed without Tariq Haseeb dipping into the spring of happiness. He would finish his studying, take a hot bath, and as soon as he looked at his naked body in the mirror and imagined what he would do in a few moments, his desire would blaze. He would comb his hair from right to left to hide his baldness then spray some expensive Pino Silvestre cologne on his neck and upper chest. Then he would bolt out of his apartment, take the elevator to Shaymaa's apartment, ring the bell, and she would open the door so quickly he would think she had been waiting for him behind it. He would rush to her, embrace her, and shower her with kisses. She would whisper in a soft, chiding voice, "Enough, Tariq."

"No."

"Do we have to meet every day?"

"Of course."

"Isn't what we do on Saturday enough?"

"I want you every minute."

"We have to watch it. Finals are approaching."

"This time we will do better on the tests than before."

"God willing."

The daily love encounter didn't last more than half an hour. Tariq called it "the quick salute to love," after which he would return to his apartment, take another bath, and sleep like a baby. On Saturdays, the "salute" was not quick; they lived like a real couple. They did their shopping for the week, then went to the movies, then went back to Shaymaa's apartment, where he would put on the pajamas that he had left there especially. He would get to the bed before her and watch television until she finished her bath. He would feel breathless with desire when he saw her approaching slowly, her face rosy from the hot water. In bed she would take off all her clothes except her panties (which they agreed to consider a red line that should never be crossed under any circumstances). She would cleave to him as a wife anxious to please her husband. When they were done with their peculiar way of lovemaking, they would have an affectionate, pleasant, comfortable conversation during which they didn't feel the passage of time. Sometimes they spent the whole day in bed, sleeping naked, with her panties on—the red line, of course—in each other's arms, and then they would wake up, eat, and drink tea and make love more than once.

At the beginning Shaymaa was assailed several times by heavy pangs of conscience. Her prayers became irregular, then she stopped performing them entirely. She had frightening nightmares. Her father appeared to her more than once yelling at her then giving her sound beatings while her mother, in the background, cried in agony but could do nothing to protect her from the beating. Gradually she reached a comforting logical resolution. She went to the Arabic section at the Chicago Public Library and verified the noble hadiths that Tariq spoke of. She found them in al-Bukhari. The canonical punishment was for *zina* only: what did *zina* mean? "The flesh entering the flesh like the kohl applicator entering the kohl jar." There was an authenticated story about a man who had committed *zina* and he went to the Prophet, peace be upon him, to apply the penalty of the canon law on him. The Prophet, out of mercy on him, pretended not to pay attention; perhaps the man would think it through or run away, but the man insisted that the Prophet punish him. The Prophet then asked him: "Have you actually committed *zina*? Perhaps you just kissed, touched, or your thighs touched." So all of those were degrees of sexual contact that fell short of *zina* and there were no canonical punishments for them, but God forgave whomever he willed.

So she was not committing *zina* with Tariq, and they both had great hopes for God's forgiveness because he knew their sincere intention to get married. If they could get married right now they wouldn't hesitate for a moment. But what could they do? They couldn't marry in Chicago without the families' approval, and at the same time they couldn't interrupt their scholarships. They would get married on the first trip that the scholarships' conditions allow, in two years. Tariq would have his PhD and she would be entitled to a midscholarship furlough. She made him swear on the Holy Qur'an that they would write the marriage contract as soon as they arrived in Egypt. She even made him repeat after her a formula that she improvised: "I marry you, Shaymaa, before God and in the manner sanctioned by the Prophet's practice and I will conclude the contract with you as soon as we arrive in Egypt and God is my witness." Thus she was reassured; nightmares no longer oppressed her and she resumed performing her prayers. Now she was a full-fledged legally married wife (except for the red line). The only thing lacking was registering the marriage. And, by the way, registration procedures were not prescribed by the principal legal edicts of Islam; rather, they were a necessity imposed by governments only recently. During the days of the Prophet, peace be upon him, marriage vows were oral: the man and woman said a few words whereupon they were married before God Almighty. And this was exactly what she had done with Tariq. She convinced herself that she was his wife before God and in the manner sanctioned by the Prophet's practice, and began to read about the duties of a Muslim wife toward her husband in religious books and tried to fulfill them: to protect his honor and property, to cherish him in his presence and absence, and to provide him with comfort and safe refuge.

As for Tariq, his life was turned upside down. It was as if he had discovered a treasure. All this pleasure? All this happiness? Now he could understand the crimes he read about in the newspapers: a man stealing or killing to keep the woman he loved. At one point that pleasure became more important than life itself. How much he regretted not knowing of it earlier. For thirty-five years he'd lived a harsh, hermetic existence, like a hungry man trying to fill himself by imagining food. Now he was a new person; he was different. He no longer resented the world. He no longer treated others provocatively, ready to fight at any moment. He'd become so calm and contented that his face looked different. "I swear by God Almighty that it now looks different," he would say as he examined his face in the mirror. His complexion looked fresh and clean, his bulging eyes became less so, and his muscles no longer contracted and his mouth did not become crooked when he spoke. More surprising, he was no longer fond of pornographic movies. Even wrestling matches, which he had loved watching ever since he was a child, he rarely desired to watch anymore. The well-being that he felt as he surrendered his body to the hot shower after lovemaking could not be described in words. But did he really intend to marry Shaymaa? That was a difficult question that no one, not even Tariq himself, could definitively answer. He was passionately in love with her. He had once read that a man could test his real feelings for a woman after he had slept with her: if he got bored and wanted to leave her company soon after achieving his pleasure, that meant that he didn't love her and vice versa. And Tariq could never get his fill of Shaymaa. He clung to her in bed. In her bosom he felt so serene, as if she were his mother. Sometimes he became so full of longing that he kissed every part of her body, licked it, wished he could devour it. His relationship with her then was not one of mere lust that he satisfied. He loved her and missed her very much all day long. But did that mean that he would marry her? The answer was an incomprehensible mumbling. He had promised to marry her and had repeated her vow to that intent. He had assured her a thousand times that he still respected her and that he was sure he was to be her first and last man. Had he done that out of conviction or pity, or (oh what an evil thought!) had he gone with her as far as he had from the beginning knowing that by so doing he was excluding her for good from any possibility of marriage? Could it be that, when he felt he was getting attached to her, he had deliberately had sex with her to undermine the thought of marrying her? He didn't know the answer and did not dwell on it long. Why should he ruin his happiness with unsettling thoughts? Why was he in a hurry to worry? He had two years to face up to the decision. So let him dip into the spring of happiness, then let come what may. That was what he told himself, thereby achieving peace of mind and several months, the sweetest of his life, in heaven.

When did happiness last, and for whom? Yesterday, at about 3:00 P.M., Tariq finished reviewing samples of his research as usual, closed his office, and got ready to leave. But he was surprised to see Dr. Bill Friedman, chairman of the department, standing in front of him. He greeted him with a nod and said in a serious tone of voice, "I've come to see you, Tariq. Do you have a few minutes?"

"Yes."

"Okay, come with me then."

 It was an elegant three-story building surrounded by a beautiful garden. Dr. Thabit crossed the entryway in a hurry. The office of the counselor was to the right. He knocked on the door and went in. Then he smiled and said, "My name is Ra'fat Thabit. Sorry for being late. I had a hard time finding parking."

"Don't worry about it. Please have a seat."

The counselor looked like a kindhearted grandmother. Her short gray hair covered the sides of her small head. Her smiling face conveyed a sense of familiarity and kindness. By way of introduction she said, "My name is Catherine. I am here to help you."

"Have you been working here a long time?"

"Actually I don't work. I am a volunteer, helping addicts and their families."

"I salute you for your noble sentiment."

Ra'fat was trying to steer the conversation away from the subject for which he came, perhaps until he decided how he should begin.

"Thank you, but what made me volunteer was not exactly a noble sentiment. My only son, Teddy, died of addiction," Catherine said calmly, her smile disappearing. "I felt I was primarily responsible for his death. After separating from his father, I gave myself over completely to my work for twenty years. I wanted to prove to myself that I was a successful person. I owned a detergent sales company, to which I gave all my time until it became one of the most important companies in Chicago. Then I woke up when it was too late to save my son."

Ra'fat listened in silence. She took a sip of water from a glass in front of her and added, "I think you, as a father, can fully feel my shock at his death. I was in therapy for a full year after he died. The first thing I did after coming out of the hospital was to liquidate my company. I began to hate it, as if it were the reason he died. Right now I am living off my bank savings and I spend my time helping addicts and their families. Whenever I help an addict with their recovery, I feel I am doing something for Teddy."

The room was plunged into profound silence. Ra'fat stared at the wall to escape the gloom. There were many certificates of appreciation for Catherine from various organizations and pictures of her with young men and women whom he supposed were addicts that she had helped. Catherine sighed and smiled gently, as if turning over that page of sorrow, and said, "I'm sorry. I'm here to listen to you, not to talk about myself. Please go ahead. Tell me the story. I'm all ears."

Ra'fat told her everything about Sarah, as if he were making a confession behind a curtain to a benevolent priest. He told her what he had seen and how he felt then, exerting extraordinary effort to control his features, and finished the story with the words "My life has stopped completely. I can hardly work. I want to do something for her."

The counselor held a pen between her fingers and began to examine it closely, as if weighing what to say.

"The way you describe it, your daughter is most likely doing cocaine. Treating this kind of addiction is not easy. Young people are enticed to try it because early on it increases the levels of dopamine in the brain, which produces a heightened feeling of delight and comfort."

"Have you treated such addicts before?" The words *addicts* sounded strange to his ears.

"I don't treat. I am a counselor. I've taken courses on helping addicts. When we start the treatment we will have psychiatrists on our team. But I have taken part in helping cocaine addicts before."

"What's the success rate?"

"Fifty-fifty, it depends."

"That's a low rate."

"I consider it high because half the addicts are in recovery. Remember, treating addiction is not easy. We have to lower our expectations so as not to be disappointed."

Ra'fat bowed his head in silence. Catherine added, "Now to work. Listen, from my experience, in the case of your daughter Sarah, the love team might be an effective way to begin."

He looked at her quizzically. She went on, "The love team is a method to motivate the addict to accept treatment. We bring together a group of people they love: relatives, neighbors, and colleagues at work or school. They begin to visit him or her regularly and help him admit he's an addict and in need of help. If the love team is successful, the addict will be ready to begin a twelve-step treatment program. Allow me to ask you a question I don't like to ask but I have to."

"Please go ahead."

"Concerning the costs of the program?"

"The insurance company will take care of that. I have requested that addiction be added in the policy."

"Well, then. Please take this form and fill it in, and before you leave, drop it at the receptionist's office."

Ra'fat took the form, and for a few moments he didn't know what to do with it as he continued to look at her. She said, "Your task now is to convince two or three of Sarah's friends to come with us to visit her. This brochure explains the role of the love team in treating addiction."

Ra'fat left her office carrying many brochures and flyers about addiction and the work of the society. At home he carefully started to read. Turning the situation into tasks, procedures, and data helped him run away from the tragedy that began to present itself to him gradually as a huge mountain. Sarah has turned into an addict. It wasn't fair to blame her. She assured him that what had happened to Sarah could happen to anyone: to try once, and then try once more to recapture the pleasure. Eventually that person could become an addict. How could he blame her? She was not in full control of her faculties and was not responsible for her actions. It was not her fault. It was that criminal Jeff who had led her to addiction. What a poor girl! How he blamed himself for hitting her! He was so upset about it that he felt that his right hand was separate from his body. It was the hand that had hit Sarah. Why had he hit her? Why couldn't he control himself? How cruel he was to her! He spent several days grappling with his thoughts before he was able to cope with his sorrow. He said to himself: there are two ways to deal with this tragedy. One is to be a backward Oriental father and disown and curse her; the other is to act like a civilized person and help her get over her ordeal.

He and Michelle went over the list of Sarah's friends who could join the love team. When he contacted them he discovered that they all knew she had a problem. Her friend Sylvia told him, "Jeff is the reason she's an addict. I've often warned her about him, but she loved him too much to listen to me."

Sylvia agreed to join the love team and so did a young man named Jesse who used to sit next to her in class. The two of them started developing a plan: Sylvia said she'd buy Sarah an apple and banana pie, which she knew she just loved. Jesse, on the other hand, decided to get her a kitten or a puppy because she loved animals. Catherine, the counselor, got very enthusiastic and said, "These are very positive ideas; reminding her of her favorite dishes and raising a little animal would put her in a mood to help her combat addiction."

Everything was ready, and the following Sunday, at about ten in the morning, the love team headed for Sarah's house in Oakland. Michelle sat next to Ra'fat while Sylvia and Jesse sat in the Cadillac's backseat. They talked about various things in short, disconnected spurts and laughed nervously for no reason in order to escape the gravity of the situation. Ra'fat was driving at an incredibly high speed, which prompted Michelle to ask him, "Are you trying to get a speeding ticket?"

But he was driven by a mysterious, resentful energy, so he didn't reduce his speed until he got to Oakland, where he slowed down to remember the way. The neighborhood looked different during the day: the streets were empty, as if they had been abandoned. Graffiti in black and red was sprayed on the walls. Ra'fat parked the car in the parking lot where he had been robbed. As soon as they got out of the car they stood in front of Catherine, the counselor, as if they were players receiving the coach's instructions before the game. Catherine, maintaining her calm smile, said, "Please, Ra'fat, wait in the car. Last time you saw Sarah, you had a fight. We don't want to provoke her negative feelings. Unfortunately addicts tend to be irascible. Stay here, and after we talk with her for a little bit, we'll ask her if she would like to see you."

Ra'fat acquiesced. He bowed his head and moved one step away as Catherine resumed her instructions to the team. "The most important thing we should convey to Sarah is that we love her: no pity and no sermons. Remember that well. It's quite possible that we'll find her in a condition that we don't like. She might receive us badly or be hostile. She might even kick us out. Prepare yourselves for the worst possibility. The young lady we will see in a few moments is not the Sarah that we know. Now she is an addict. This is the truth we should not forget."

They listened to her in silence, but Sylvia suddenly cried in a hoarse voice that sounded strange, "Oh, Jesus, save poor Sarah," then started to sob. Michelle hugged her. The counselor's voice came calm and firm this time. "Sylvia, get a grip on yourself. We have to convey to her our positive feelings. If you cannot stop crying, it'd be best if you stayed in the car with Ra'fat."

Ra'fat backed off slowly, opened the car, and sat behind the steering wheel while the rest of the team proceeded toward the house: Jesse holding the little puppy and Sylvia carrying the apple and banana pie. They walked slowly toward the house as if in a funeral procession. They found the garden gate open and the outside lights on even though it was daylight. They climbed the front stairs and Michelle rang the bell. A whole minute passed and no one opened. She rang again. After another minute the door opened and a large black man, wearing a blue work-man's suit, appeared. Michelle said, "Good morning. Is Sarah here?"

"Who?"

"Pardon me. Isn't this Jeff Anderson and Sarah Thabit's house?"

"I believe those are the names of the tenants who moved."

"Did they move?"

"Yes, a few days ago. The landlord sent me over to paint the house. I think he's renting it to a new tenant."

They remained silent for a moment, then Michelle said, "I'm Sarah's mom. I've come to check on her with these friends of hers. Do you have her new address?"

"Sorry, ma'am, I don't know it."

▪ ▪ ▪ ▪ ▪ ▪ ▪ ▪ ▪ ▪ ▪

"Even if you are an official at the Egyptian embassy, that doesn't give you the right to break into my house," I shouted. He looked at me defiantly and moved one step to the center of the living room, taking his time as if affirming his control of the situation.

"I've invited myself to a cup of coffee with you. Listen, Nagi, you have a superior academic record, you're intelligent, and you have a great future ahead of you."

"What exactly do you want?"

"I want to help you."

"What makes you want to do that?"

"My fear for you."

"Fear of what?"

"Your stupidity."

"Watch your words."

"You've come to America to get an education, and instead of looking after your future, you've brought a catastrophe upon yourself."

"What do you mean?"

"You're collecting signatures on a statement against our revered president. Aren't you ashamed of yourself?"

"I'm proud of what I'm doing."

"The problem with intellectuals like you is that you are prisoners of books and theories. You don't know anything about what really happens in your country. I've worked as a police officer for ten years in different governorates, in villages, hamlets, and alleys. I've come to know the lower depths of Egyptian society. I can assure you that Egyptians are not concerned with democracy at all. Besides, they are not cut out for it. Egyptians are concerned about three things only: their religion, their livelihood, and their children. And religion is the most important; the only thing that pushes Egyptians to revolt is when someone attacks their religion. When Napoleon came to Egypt and pretended to respect Islam, Egyptians supported him and forgot that he was an occupier."

"It seems you haven't read your history. Egyptians revolted against the French expedition twice within a three-year period and they killed the commander."

He looked at me angrily. I felt some comfort in having insulted him. He went on in an arrogant tone of voice, "I don't have time to waste with you. I wanted to help you but you insist on your stupidity. One thing you can be sure of is: that statement for which you are gathering signatures is just child's play."

"If it was just child's play, then why did you take the trouble of coming here?"

"You're playing with fire."

"Are you threatening me?"

"I am just warning you. If you don't give up on this statement, you cannot imagine what I'll do to you."

"Do your worst," I shouted, having got over the surprise. For the first time, it occurred to me to kick him out. He moved, backing off a few steps toward the door, saying, "You are plowing the sea. Do you think you'll embarrass the regime in front of the Americans? I assure you the regime is as solid as a mountain and organically connected to the American establishment. Everything you've written in the statement is well known to the Americans and they couldn't care less, so long as the Egyptian regime is looking after their interests."

"So, you admit that the Egyptian regime is just a servant of the Americans."

"I warn you for the last time. You're mistaken to think that being in America will protect you from punishment. Come back to your senses, Nagi, if not for your own future then for the sake of your mother, who has toiled for years for you, and for your sister Noha, the student in the College of Economics and Political Science. She is a tender girl and would not withstand one night of detention at State Security. The officers there are lowlifes and they love women."

"Get out of here."

"You will pay dearly. You'll discover how we can teach you manners, but it will be too late." He said the last few words as he opened the door, then he suddenly turned toward me and said, "By the way, greetings to your Jewish beloved, Wendy. I've received videos of the two of you having sex. Thank you. They are very enjoyable."

He let out a loud laugh then closed the door and disappeared. I collapsed on the nearest chair. I couldn't describe how I felt at that moment. It was a mixture of shock, anger, and humiliation. I opened a bottle of wine and lit a cigarette and began to smoke and drink. How did Safwat get a copy of the statement? How did he come to know everything about me? More seriously: How did he enter the apartment? I got up and opened the door and examined it carefully. I found no sign of forced entry. He had used a copy of the key. Where did he get it from? There must be some kind of cooperation between Egyptian intelligence and the university administration. I should change residence at the earliest opportunity. I could cut down on my expenses to afford off-campus housing. I was possessed by a strange desire, so I got up and went to the bedroom, turned on the lights, and began to examine the walls, as if I were going to find the secret camera that had filmed Wendy and me. In a short while I laughed at myself, turned off the lights, and went back to the living room. I soon heard the sound of a key turning in the door. I got up, ready for a confrontation, but I saw Wendy, who said, smiling as soon as she saw me, "Hello. How are you?"

I kissed her as usual. I tried to seem natural. She exclaimed cheerfully, "Listen, Nagi. I'm going to the bathroom. Please close your eyes and don't open them until I tell you."

"Can we do this some other time?"

"No, we can't," she said good-naturedly and planted a quick kiss on my cheek then dashed off to the bathroom. I gulped down my glass of wine and poured myself another and began to chide myself anew. How did I allow Safwat Shakir to break into my house and threaten me? Why didn't I call the police? What he had done was a crime in American law; even if he had diplomatic immunity, I would have caused a major scandal for him. Why didn't I do that?

"Are your eyes closed?" Wendy's voice came from the bathroom. I closed my eyes as I lost myself in thought then I came to when I heard her voice nearby: "Now open your eyes."

It was a strange sight: Wendy was wearing a belly dancing outfit; her breasts bulging out of a tight, low bra, revealing most of her chest, her belly fully exposed with a star covering her belly button, and her waist tied by a scarf that accentuated her hips. From that girdle long tassels descended, barely covering her bare legs. She was excited and happy. She turned around several times and cried, "What do you think? I am now a dancer from Andalusia. Do I look like the picture in your imagination?"

"Of course."

"I had a very hard time finding the store that sold belly dancing outfits. Do you know what I did?"

"What?"

"I went to a costume party last year and I saw a girl wearing an outfit like this one. I kept looking for her telephone number until I found it and she told me where the store was."

My ability to keep up with her was limited and fragile. I kept following her with my eyes while my mind was wandering off. She soon realized that, and her face clouded over. She sat next to me and asked me in alarm, "What's wrong?"

Her appearance as she sat next to me in the dance outfit was bizarre. It was as if she were an actress sitting in the wings in her costume. It occurred to me to conceal what had happened, to ask her to leave, or to leave myself, using any excuse. Suddenly, however, I found myself telling her everything. She looked lost in deep thought and then said in a soft voice, "I had no idea you lived in such a police state."

"Without American support the Egyptian regime wouldn't last a single day."

She put her arms around me and got so close I could feel her breath. She whispered, "What are you going to do?"

"I'll go on collecting signatures."

"Aren't you afraid to?"

"Yes, naturally, but I'll overcome it."

"But it is no longer just you. They'll harm your mother and sister."

The faces of Noha and my mother materialized in my mind. I could see the scene with the officers and plainclothesmen storming the house and arresting them. I said in a loud voice, "Let them do what they want to do. I am not backing off."

"You are free to take a stand. But what have your mother and sister done to deserve this?"

"They are no better than the mothers and sisters of tens of thousands of detainees."

"Nagi, I truly don't understand you. Why do you go looking for trouble?"

"What do you mean?"

"Why do you still care about Egypt's problems now that you're out of it?"

"It's my country."

"Egypt, like so many countries in the third world, is suffering from many deep-rooted problems that have accumulated over centuries. Your lifetime and my lifetime would not be enough to fix these problems."

What she said was unexpected to me. I downed my drink, staring at her in disbelief. She got up and stood in front of me. Then she pulled my face toward her bare belly and whispered, "Our relationship is wonderful. With you I have feelings I've never known before. Please, think of our future."

"I am not going to give up on my duty."

"Why don't you think in a different way? America was built on the shoulders of talented, ambitious young people like you. They came from all over the world looking for a better future. America is the land of opportunity. If you stay here, you'll do great things."

"You're talking like Safwat Shakir."

"What?"

"Yes. You even use his very words."

My voice sounded strange to me and it occurred to me that I

was drunk. I knew that alcohol had a greater influence on me when I was tense. I responded to a fateful, persistent, mysterious feeling and asked her, "Isn't it strange that Safwat Shakir knew about our relationship? Even more strange, where did he get a copy of the apartment key? Wendy, who fed him all this information?"

She stared at me, her eyes growing wider in disbelief. She said in a voice shaking with uncontrollable agitation, "What do you mean?"

"I don't mean anything specific. I am just wondering: How did he know the details of our relationship? And if he had videotapes of us, there must be a camera in the bedroom. Who put it here?"

She looked at me for a moment then turned and rushed to the bathroom. I stayed put. I had no ability or desire to do anything. I was hurtling down the abyss at breakneck speed and I couldn't stop. I poured another drink and took a big gulp. After a short while Wendy appeared. She'd put on her clothes and put the dance outfit back in the bag she had brought. Her face was different. She avoided looking at me and hurried toward the door. I hurried after her.

"Wendy."

She didn't turn around. I held on to her, but she struggled loose and pushed me with her hand. I saw her face at that moment, wet with tears. I said in a pleading voice, "Please, listen to me."

But she left and slammed the door.

 "Dr. Baker is known for his fanaticism against Muslims, and I, thank God, am a Muslim proud of my religion. He tried more than once to make fun of Islam in front of me but I dumbfounded and scolded him, so he decided to take his revenge on me and fabricated this issue," Danana said to Marwa, who was sitting in front of him on the sofa. Then he bowed his head, his face looking like that of someone stoically and patiently withstanding excruciating pain. Marwa, of course, had noticed several gaping holes in his account, so she said, trying to maintain a neutral smile, "This is a strange story."

"Strange? Why? Your enemy is the enemy of your religion and God Almighty has said in the Noble Book: 'Never will the Jews be satisfied with thee, neither the Christians, not till thou followest their religion.'"

"But you told me before that Dr. Baker likes Egyptians."

"That's what I thought until the dirty reality revealed itself. You know that I am kindhearted and am easily deceived by people."

"Couldn't it just be a misunderstanding?"

"I tell you he is going to expel me from the department, you tell me it's a misunderstanding?" Danana shouted angrily.

Marwa kept silent for a moment then asked him, "What are you going to do?"

"I don't know."

"Why don't you go to the investigation hearing and tell them the truth?"

"You think Baker's American colleagues will disbelieve him and believe me?"

He bowed his head then said in a subdued voice, "An injustice has been done to me. But God is great. He sent me Safwat Bey Shakir to help me."

Marwa felt that the conversation was drifting into unknown territory filled with hidden possibilities, so she maintained her silence. Danana went on, as if talking to himself. "Safwat Bey promised me that he would settle the matter with the educational bureau, and after that, he'll enroll me in another university."

"Thank God."

"Have you seen in your life a kinder and more generous man?"

"Of course not!"

"So, I ask you, for God's sake, can I turn down any request by this man?"

Marwa looked at him in silence, but he persisted sharply, "Answer me."

"What exactly do you want?"

"I want nothing but what's good. We, Marwa, are a couple. We are partners, in good times and bad. Right now I am going through an ordeal. Safwat Bey has done me a big favor."

"What's that got to do with me?"

"Safwat Bey wants you to work with him."

"Me?"

"Yes. He'll appoint you as a secretary in his office."

"But I've never worked as a secretary before."

"It's not that difficult. You're intelligent and you'll catch on quickly. If Safwat Bey wanted he could appoint ten American secretaries. But work in his office is subject to special considerations."

"I don't understand."

278   *Alaa Al Aswany*

"Whoever works with him will get to see highly classified documents. He wants you because he trusts you. American and Israeli intelligence will seek to recruit any secretary working with him to have access to our country's secrets. Your work with Safwat Bey is a small return of his great favor, but it is also a patriotic act."

Marwa fell silent again, as if the rush of events had discombobulated her and made her unable to think.

"What do you think?" Danana asked quickly and looked at her like someone who had thrown the dice in a backgammon game and was waiting for the result. He had prepared himself to convince her by any means. She must work with Safwat Shakir. He would urge her, beg her, quarrel with her, use her father to convince her if need be. He sat before her, ready for any reaction. Several moments passed, and then she raised her head toward him and said calmly with a mysterious smile on her face, "I accept."

CHAPTER 31

 How does winter turn into spring?

First the ice melts, and then life comes back to the dry branches and the flowers begin to come alive. That was how Carol's life changed after she started working in commercials. She stopped her miserable search for a job and repaid, in installments, the money she had borrowed from her friend Emily. She bought new clothes for little Mark and got him a pass for the nearby bowling club. She gave Graham three elegant summer outfits and persisted until he started to buy his favorite Dutch pipe tobacco (about which he couldn't hide his happiness). Then she bought a used Buick and painted the whole house, and she planted beautiful trees in the garden. One morning, she was having breakfast with Graham on the porch and wearing an elegant white cotton kimono (that she had bought from the popular Tigoro store). While he was smoking his pipe, drinking coffee, and reading the *Chicago Tribune,* she asked him, "What do you think, John? Our house has appreciated after renovation; if we put it up for sale now it can fetch a reasonable price. I can add to that from my savings and we can buy another house."

Graham looked stunned. He kept playing with his beard for a few moments then said slowly, "That's a good idea, but I'm attached to this house, Carol. I've lived here for twenty years. Everything in it reminds me of parts of my life."

"We'll move to a bigger and more beautiful house."

"My feelings might be foolishly romantic, but I actually can't imagine myself in another house."

She looked disappointed. He held her hand and whispered, "In any case, I promise you I'll think about it."

"Don't do anything against your will."

"I'll do whatever makes you happy."

She looked at him, overflowing with feeling toward him. She rushed to him, put her arms around him, and showered him with kisses. She loved him more than she ever had.

Carol had finally come to terms with her new job and was at peace with herself. The first time she took off her clothes in front of Fernando, when she felt his cold hand touching her bare body as he prepared her for the shoot, she was crushed by humiliation; she felt dizzy, as if she were going to faint. With time, however, her aversion diminished and she began to get used to it. She said to herself: Fernando is gay; he is not aroused by a woman's body; actually he might be disgusted by it. Why do I feel awkward when I bare myself before him? Isn't this my job and his job? Would I have felt ashamed if he were shooting my hands or feet? Isn't this a paradox? Aren't my breasts part of my body, like other parts? My feeling of shame is a result of remnants of ancient, inherited ideas that consider a woman's body private property that can only be used after permission is granted by her father or her husband. These are just cock-and-bull stories. I have nothing to be ashamed of. I am an actress, using my body to express myself before the camera, no more and no less. What's so shameful about that? Besides, did I have any other choice? I couldn't have turned down this job. I couldn't stand causing more troubles for Graham, who loves me and loves my son and has endured endless hardship for us, and in return, I gave him nothing but misery. A person might endure poverty when young, but to have to bear it after sixty is really a tragedy. Moreover, what has little Mark done? His father refuses to support him. *I* have to provide him with a life of dignity. I won't forget how happy he

was with the new clothes and how overjoyed he was rolling that bowling ball, aiming it at the pins. If offered this job again I would accept
it a hundred times for Mark and Graham, the two people I love the
most in this world.

Thus she convinced herself and calmed her doubts. She hid the
truth from Graham. She told him that she'd found a job in radio commercials, that they liked her voice and the way she delivered, so they
gave her a high salary. When Graham asked her when the commercials were broadcast, she had prepared the answer. She sighed and said,
"The commercials I record are bought by a small station in Boston that
you can't get in Chicago." Then she feigned a smile and whispered in a
dreamy tone, "If I am successful, maybe I'll sign a contract with a major
station in Chicago."

Graham planted a quick kiss on her lips and said, "Well, we have to
protect your larynx, since it is our national treasure."

Amazingly she actually did become successful. Executives at Double
X liked her and asked Fernando to shoot another commercial in which
she did even better because she had gained experience expressing herself with her body before the camera. Two weeks later, Fernando called
her and asked to meet. He welcomed her warmly and said as he lit a
joint as usual, "Carol dear, we are going from success to success. They
called me this morning and said they wanted you for a third commercial."

"Great."

"This time we will shoot your legs as you put on lingerie made by
the company."

"I am not going to bare myself completely before the camera, even
if they paid a million dollars."

Fernando laughed loudly and said mockingly, "If they offered you a
million dollars you'd do anything."

She looked at him in silence, feeling insulted. It seemed he realized
it, so he bowed his head, placed it between his hands, and murmured in

a tired voice, "What did I just say? It seems I've smoked too much pot. Sorry, Carol."

She nodded and affected a smile as he went on in a matter-of-fact voice: "In any case no one will ask you to bare yourself completely."

They had several rehearsals until she understood her role and did it well. He would shoot the lower part of her body as she put on the Double X lingerie and, over the following thirty seconds, she had to relax totally before the camera, feel her underwear with her hands, extend her legs, wrapping one on top of the other slowly to give the impression of total comfort, then the caption "Double X underwear . . . for your comfort" would be superimposed.

The commercial was a great success and her fee was raised to $1,200 per hour of shooting. Soon afterward, Fernando offered her another commercial. "This time we will work on a more modest part of your body: your feet. The next commercial is about Double X socks."

For a whole week Carol gave herself over to a pedicurist, who worked diligently for two hours every morning on her toenails and heels, and on scrubbing and softening her feet to make them look delicate and smooth. The result was so dazzling that Fernando shouted as he was doing the camera test, "What splendid feet worthy of a Roman emperor's concubine!"

This time she had to raise her leg gracefully in front of the camera, point her toes like a ballet dancer, then coquettishly pause for a moment and put the socks on in a suggestive manner. After the commercial was broadcast, Fernando said to her, his face beaming with happiness, "Our success has become legendary! You're quite an inspiration, Carol. You bring out the best in me."

As usual he offered her something new. "The new commercial is different from all the previous ones."

"What's its idea?"

"Your fee will be raised to fifteen hundred dollars an hour."

"Thanks. The idea?"

"It's not conventional, but I won't give it up. If you refuse to do it, I'll have another model do it."

"Talk, Fernando."

"Okay. Double X has produced a brand-new bra model that's totally see-through."

He paused for a moment then continued gruffly, to hide his embarrassment, "The idea of the commercial is as follows: I will shoot your bare breasts, and you will be sexually aroused so I can shoot your nipples erect."

"You're such a bastard!" she shouted and got up angrily. She picked up her purse from the chair and hurried to the door. Fernando hurried after her and grabbed her by the arm, trying to calm her down.

"Carol, it's much simpler than you imagine. Think about it for a bit. We've shot your bare breasts dozens of times. How would it hurt to shoot them erect?"

"I'll never do that."

He looked at her in vexation and said, "Listen, this is my last offer. I'll pay you a special fee, two thousand dollars per hour. You'll get this fee only for the commercials involving sexual arousal. In ordinary commercials, your fee will remain as it was."

Carol looked at him in silence. It seemed that events were moving too fast for her to absorb. Fernando, sounding as if he wanted to end the meeting, said, "You have until the morning to think about it. The company is in a hurry to get the commercial and you have to give me a chance to get somebody else if you refuse."

The following day Carol came, stood before him, and before he asked her, she mumbled without looking at his face, "Okay. When do we begin?"

Fernando laughed loudly and hugged her tightly, lifting her off the floor. "What a magnificent woman. If I were interested in women, I'd have done my best to seduce you. Come on, let's get to work."

She went with him to the studio and took off her clothes as usual.

He spent a long time adjusting the lights and cameras. After several attempts he shot the part where she appeared bare chested. The harder part remained. He asked her to put on the bra, and he himself snapped it closed at the back, and then he stood her in the middle of the frame that he had prepared and said, "Carol, I'm going to help you get aroused. Don't be embarrassed; I'll touch you in a perfectly professional manner."

He got close to her, put his hands through the bra, cupped her breasts with his hands, and began to knead them slowly. Then he took the nipples between his fingers and began to rub them gently. A whole minute passed without any response. He said, "It seems I'm not arousing you sufficiently. Should I go on?"

She didn't answer. She stood where she was, looking at his hands stuck between the bra and her chest. He took out his hands and jumped behind the camera to make sure it was adjusted, and then went back and whispered to her, "I've prepared something to help you. Look at the screen."

She noticed for the first time that he had placed a laptop on a nearby table. He pushed a button and she could see scenes from a pornographic movie: a white woman was sleeping with a black man and screaming with pleasure. Carol shouted, "Please turn it off."

"What?"

"I can't stand those movies."

"Why?"

"Because they are phony and naive."

"Do you have a problem with this?"

"I'm perfectly normal."

He looked at her almost angrily and said, "Listen, I've got to do one or two shoots today. Don't ruin my work."

"Give me a chance. Let me be natural and I'll do it."

He glanced at her uneasily. She whispered as she pushed him to stand behind the camera, "Go on, please."

He dragged his feet like an unruly student kicked out by the teacher. Carol closed her eyes and began to recall her intimate moments with Graham, that burning pleasure that engulfed her when she was with him. Little by little she forgot her surroundings and got totally absorbed in the wonderful feeling that she was reliving. When she realized, somewhat vaguely and from a distance, that the lighting was getting more intense in front of her closed eyes, she ignored it and continued in her reverie until she came to as Fernando exclaimed while putting his hand on her bare shoulder, "Brava. A wonderful shot."

Shooting took several sessions. Carol used the same method to arouse herself. The commercial was a great success. A few days later, Fernando invited her to dinner, and after two glasses of red wine added to the ever-present effect of marijuana, he started humming the old song "Oh, Carol," then he said to her as his eyes gleamed with enthusiasm, "Where've you been all this time?"

"It's all thanks to your talent."

Fernando looked at her for a little while, as if reluctant to speak. Then he said with a childlike spontaneity that she liked, "The owner of the company would like to meet you."

"Really?"

"Your guardian angel is working with extraordinary efficiency. This meeting might change your life. It's Henry Davis, owner of Double X, one of the wealthiest people in America. Do you know that I've never met him? I've asked to meet him more than once, but they've always had all kinds of excuses."

"In my case it's different. You want to meet him but he refuses; he wants to meet me but I don't know if I'll say yes or no," she said in jest, but he didn't laugh.

He looked her in the eye and said in a serious tone, "I hope you appreciate my honesty. Someone else in my place would never have let you meet the company owner before signing an exclusive contract with you."

"I appreciate all you've done for me."

"You have to prove that. I'll give you Henry Davis's office number to schedule an appointment with him. In return, you will not sign a contract with him before getting back to me."

"I'll do that."

"Promise?"

"Promise."

CHAPTER 32

 "It's Salah, Zeinab."

His breathing was painful. His voice sounded strange to his own ears, as if it were someone else's. It was as though, after a thirty-year separation, he had suddenly seen her in the street and kept running after her until he caught up with her. How strange it all was. He could not believe that he was talking to her, as if he had not been absent for a whole lifetime, as if he had not longed for her a thousand times and cursed her a thousand times. His voice meant much more than his actual words: "It's Salah, Zeinab." His voice was really saying: Do you remember me? It's Salah who loved you as no one has loved you. When I lost you, Zeinab, I lost my life. Thirty years I've lived, lost, away from you. I've tried and failed, Zeinab, and here I am coming back to you.

"Salah? I don't believe it!"

Despite age, her voice had kept its old passion.

"Did I call you at a convenient time? I don't want to take you from work."

"I work for the Egyptian government, Salah. Working here just means showing up. We always have extra time."

Oh, my God. Her wonderful laugh was still there. She said she couldn't describe how happy she was to hear from him. She told him about her life: she was living alone after the death of her husband and the marriage of her only daughter. He avoided talking about her husband. He asked her about Egypt and she said in sorrow, "Egypt is living its worst days, Salah. As if everything we've struggled for, my colleagues and I, was just a mirage. We don't have democracy; we have not been liberated from backwardness, ignorance, and corruption. Everything has changed for the worse. Reactionary ideas are spreading like the plague. Can you imagine that I am the only female Muslim in the department of planning, out of fifty employees, who is not wearing the veil?"

"How did Egypt change like that?"

"Repression, poverty, oppression, having no hope in the future, the absence of any national goal: Egyptians have given up on justice in this world, so they are waiting for it in the next. What's widespread in Egypt right now is not true religiosity but a collective depression accompanied by religious symptoms. What makes matters worse is that millions of Egyptians have worked in Saudi Arabia for years and have come back with Wahhabi ideas. The regime has helped spread these ideas because they support it."

"How?"

"Wahhabi Islam forbids rising against a Muslim ruler even if he oppresses the people. The thing that preoccupies Wahhabis most is covering a woman's body."

"Can Egyptians' thinking fall so low?"

"Even lower. There are in Egypt now women who wear gloves so they won't feel lust shaking men's hands."

"Isn't Abdel Nasser responsible for all that?"

She let out a laugh that touched a soft spot in his heart and said, "You want us to resume our quarrels about Abdel Nasser? I still believe that he is the greatest man who ruled Egypt. His worst mistake, however, was his failure to bring about democracy and the fact that he left us with military rule inherited by those less sincere and less efficient."

She paused for a moment then sighed and said, "Thank God, despite my failure in the national sphere, God granted me success on the family front. My daughter is an engineer who is successful in her work and marriage and has given me two wonderful grandchildren. How about you?"

"I got a PhD and became a university professor."

"Did you get married?"

"Yes, married and divorced."

"And children?"

"No children."

He felt that his answer gave her some comfort. They talked for about two hours, and from that night on his life changed. His nocturnal life was complete. His enchanted city that he kept secret because no one would believe him if he spoke about it came into being. He kept it to himself because people would think he was crazy. During the day he lived halfheartedly, but at nightfall he turned into another creature as if he were a mythical hero, his wings soaring back into the past: he put on his old clothes, watched a 1960s black-and-white movie and listened to songs of Umm Kulthum and Abd al-Halim Hafiz until it was morning in Cairo. He would call Zeinab and tell her truthfully and sincerely everything that he did, as if he were a child who had come back from school and run to the bosom of his mother, who kissed him, took off his clothes, and washed the dust of the road off his face and hands. One night they reminisced about the old days, and the memories brought about pure sweetness to both of them. He suddenly told her, "How about me inviting you to come to America?"

"Why?"

"Perhaps to begin a new life."

She laughed and said, "You think like Americans, Salah. What new life? At our age we ask God for a good ending."

"Sometimes I get angry at you."

"Why?"

"Because you brought about our separation."

"That's ancient history."

"I can't help thinking about it."

"What good would that do now?"

"Why did you leave me, Zeinab?"

"It was you who decided to emigrate."

"You could've convinced me to stay."

"I tried but you were determined."

"Why didn't you come with me?"

"I can't leave Egypt."

"If you'd really loved me, you would've come with me."

"It's absurd to disagree now about what happened thirty years ago."

"Do you still think I am a coward?"

"Why do you insist on bringing back bad memories?"

"Don't be evasive: am I a coward in your opinion?"

"If I considered you a coward, I wouldn't have had a relationship with you."

"The last time we met you said: 'I regret to tell you that you're a coward.'"

"We were quarreling so I had a slip of the tongue."

"That sentence gave me pain for years."

"I'm sorry."

"I don't think it was a slip of the tongue."

"What exactly do you want?"

"Your real opinion: am I a coward in your view?"

"Duty dictated that you stay in Egypt."

"You've stayed; what was the result?"

"I wasn't waiting for any results."

"Not one goal that you struggled for has been accomplished."

"But I did my duty."

"To no avail."

"At least I didn't run away."

Her words had a heavy impact. They both fell silent until she whispered in an apologetic tone, "Sorry, Salah. Please don't be angry with me. It was you who insisted on talking about this."

It was as though a muscle in Dr. Ra'fat Thabit's face had contracted forever, giving his features a look of indelible bitterness, as if he were carrying a heavy burden that slowed his steps and crooked his back, replacing his former sprightly athletic gait. He lost his ability to concentrate and seemed most of the time to be staring at nothing. Only one question weighed down on him: Where had Sarah disappeared to? He looked for her everywhere to no avail. Had she escaped with Jeff to another city? Has she been attacked by a gang in Oakland? There were crimes in Chicago's poor black neighborhoods that were discovered only by chance; some might never be discovered. He asked himself: What has happened to you, Sarah? I will never forgive myself if anything bad happened to you. How cruel I was with you! How could I have insulted you like that?

After a few days of strenuous searching he decided to inform the police. He was met by a polite black officer who listened to his story with interest, then sighed and said, "Sorry, sir. I'm a father like you and I appreciate your feelings, but your daughter is now an adult and, under the law, is a free citizen who has the right to go wherever she wants. So there's no legal justification at this point to look for her if she's missing."

Ra'fat went back home, despondent, and found Michelle lying on the sofa in the living room. She looked at him blankly and asked him, "What did you do?"

He told her in a soft voice, then sat next to her and held her hand. They looked at that moment like an old couple whose long life together enabled them to communicate without words. The ordeal had brought them closer, and they had stopped fighting. They were brought together by an instinctive solidarity, like that uniting people facing a fire or a natural disaster. She removed his hand gently and said as she got up, "Is there anything we can do?"

"I'll publish an ad."

"You think she'd read it?"

"I remember that sometimes she read ads in newspapers."

She looked at him for a long time then hugged him. He felt her body shaking, so he tried to console her and calm her down. He walked her to bed then returned and threw himself on the sofa. He had a splitting headache, and a heavy sense of dejection was choking him. Since Sarah's disappearance he couldn't sleep without a sleeping pill and was unable to do anything, night or day. He repeatedly missed his classes, and the chairman, Dr. Friedman, called him to a meeting and said to him with a smile, "Ra'fat, all of us in the department understand the situation. Please let us do something to help a little. If you feel you're not up to giving a class, all you have to do is let me know beforehand and we'll manage."

It was a magnanimous gesture from colleagues that he had worked with for twenty years, but he knew that such magnanimity was not going to last forever. His contract with the university would end in April, and if he went on like that they wouldn't renew it no matter how sympathetic they were. Work was work, and many professors with degrees and experience like his, and maybe better, would love to get their hands on his position. He got up slowly and took the sleeping pill. He had forty minutes to fall asleep. What was he going to do? Deep down he knew that he would do what he did every night: he was going to pour himself a double drink (in defiance of his doctor's warning against combining liquor and sleeping pills). He would take out the large photo album that Michelle kept in the living room next to the piano. He would drink and look at the old pictures. The happy days were all there: days of love and youth, a picture of him and Michelle embracing in Lincoln Park, another on New Year's Eve at Davie's Club. What year was that? He'd find the date stamped on the back of the photo. Soon Sarah would begin to make an appearance in the pictures: first as a baby, then in the blue navy suit he had bought her for her fifth birthday, then an entrancing picture of her playing with her bike in the garden. He looked at her laughing face: how beautiful she was! Where was she now?

A strange idea occurred to him as he studied her picture: Did a human being have his fate etched on his features from childhood? Could we, with some concentration or strong foresight, read children's futures on their faces? To know from the beginning that this little girl would die an untimely death or be unhappy in her life? Or that little boy who looked ordinary and lazy would achieve illustrious professional eminence or make a huge fortune? In the pictures Sarah was laughing and had a sunny face filled with joy. But he could somehow see what was happening to her now, imprinted on her little face; there was a darkish cloud hovering between her smile and her innocent, astonished look. There was an almost imperceptible look of defeat in her glance, a premonition of a sad destiny that she couldn't avoid. He put the album aside and got up, as he did every night when sorrows ganged up on him so much that he couldn't look at any more pictures. He would have another drink in front of the window until the sleeping pill worked in conjunction with the whiskey, plunging him in a dark, heavy, deathlike sleep.

Ra'fat suddenly imagined that he was hearing sounds coming from another part of the house, a door opening and closing, steps squeaking on the wooden floor. He listened carefully. Oh, God, was the doctor's warning coming true? Was the mixture of alcohol and sleeping pill making him hallucinate? There, he was hearing the sound again. It wasn't hallucination. He was certain this time. Someone was moving around. Had Michelle woken up and come downstairs to do something? He put the drink on the table and hurried to the bedroom. He opened the door as gently as he was able and in the dark could make out that Michelle was still asleep. He was now fully alert. His sense of danger brought back his concentration. The sound persisted; it was defying him. The person who had broken in did not even try to conceal his movements. He was not moving stealthily like a thief; perhaps he was drunk or high or perhaps he was carrying a weapon that made him sure that he could handle the situation at any moment. Who said it was one person? Most likely it was a group of armed men. What did they want with him? Unfortunately he didn't have a gun like Salah. He had always refused to own a gun. The idea of shooting somebody, no matter what the circumstances, seemed strange and frightening to him. He opened his cell phone and readied it to dial the police emergency number. He was going to go to the first floor, confront the intruders, and at the right moment call the police. He held on to the wooden banister very carefully, and then stopped. It took him a few moments to absorb what he saw. The door of the room was wide open. In the soft light of the corridor he saw a person from the back. He knew that figure very well.

"Sarah?" he shouted as he rushed toward her. He turned on the light and he could see the details of the scene. She turned around for a moment, stared vacantly at him, then turned around again as if she did not see him. She was looking for something, anxiously opening the desk drawers and slamming them closed, one after the other. Ra'fat moved toward her and looked at her. She looked strange: she had lost a lot of weight and her face was extremely pale. There were black rings around her eyes and sweat was pouring from her. Her hair was disheveled and dusty and her clothes dirty, as though she had spent the night on the sidewalk.

"Sarah? Where've you been?" he exclaimed, but she didn't answer. She didn't even turn, as if she were not aware of his presence. She went on opening the drawers then slamming them shut. Then she turned to the closet, pulling the door hard, and began to throw the contents on the bed: folded shirts, underwear, and towels of several colors. Ra'fat held her by the arm and asked her, "What are you looking for?"

She pushed him away and said in a raspy voice, "Let me go."

"What's wrong, Sarah?"

"That's none of your business."

She kept looking at the closet, which was now empty. Then she threw herself onto the bed and put her hands on her head and said, as if talking to herself, "Goddammit! Where'd the money go? I'm sure I left it here."

"Sarah."

"Leave me alone."

"I know you're mad at me. Forgive me. I've treated you cruelly. Believe me, I'm the one who loves you the most in this world."

"Stop this emotional blackmail. You've ruined my life."

Her voice was hoarse and her glances strange. Her face began to contract and sweat poured from it and she began to gasp, as if she were having difficulty breathing. He came closer to her and extended his arms to embrace her, but she got up, moved two steps away, then turned around and confronted him with a hostile glare. He said in a soft voice, "I want to talk with you for a little bit."

"I don't have time."

"I want to help you."

"I don't want your help."

"Where do you live now?"

"In a place a thousand times better than your house."

"Why are you treating me this way? You have a big problem. You must quit doing drugs."

She looked at him in anger and shouted, "What do *you* know about drugs? You don't know anything in the world except your damn slides."

"Please, Sarah. I'll take you to a counselor."

"This is stupid. I don't need a counselor. If I have problems in my life, you're responsible for them."

"Me?"

"As usual you don't see the horrible things you're doing."

"Sarah!"

"Enough with the lies. You've made me miserable. There's not a single thing that's genuine in this house: my mother doesn't love you, she never has. And you don't love her. Yet you go on pretending to be such a wonderful couple. It's about time you heard what I think of you: you're phony. You're a bad actor playing a silly role that doesn't convince anyone. Who are you? Are you Egyptian or American? You've lived all your life wanting to be an American. And you failed."

"All these catastrophes are because of that lowlife Jeff!" Ra'fat shouted suddenly, but she screamed, "Don't call him names. He's better than you. He's poor and unemployed but he's genuine. He loves me and I love him. We're not phony like you."

She turned around suddenly and headed for the door, but he followed her to keep her from leaving. She pushed him away from her, but he stepped forward quickly and embraced her from behind, saying in a loud voice, "I won't allow you to destroy yourself."

"Let me go," she shouted as she pushed him with all her strength, but he clung to her, putting up with her blows on his body. She exerted a strenuous effort to struggle free, and suddenly her muscles convulsed violently and she began to cry. He held her tightly. She calmed down in his embrace. They clung to each other in total silence. After a few moments she said in a different voice, calm and deep, as if she had awakened from a dream or come back to consciousness after an attack of nerves, "I have to go now."

"Do you want some money?"

She looked hesitant then said in a soft voice, "Give me a hundred dollars and I'll repay it in a week."

He took out his wallet and gave her a bill that she took quickly and put nonchalantly in her pants pocket. He smiled and said, "Do you want more money?"

"We're doing okay. In a few days Jeff will start his new work. He's found an excellent job at a brokerage firm."

He was sure she was lying. He looked at her affectionately and said, "Can you tell me your new address?"

"I can't."

"I just want to know that you're all right. I won't bother you. I won't visit you unless you ask me."

"*I* will get in touch with you. I promise."

She seemed as if she had regained her old tenderness suddenly. He hugged her again and kept showering her with kisses on her face and hair until she gently pushed him away. She looked at him with a faint smile then planted a quick kiss on his cheek and hurried out.

CHAPTER 34

Dr. Friedman sat behind his desk and asked Tariq to sit down. He bowed his head and looked at his hands, which he had clasped in front of him, then blushed a little as he usually did when he started to speak and said, "Ever since I've become chairman, I've always been enthusiastic to admit Egyptian students because they're intelligent and hardworking. Of course from time to time there might be a bad student, but that's the exception, not the rule. You, for instance, are an excellent student: you've obtained early and good results in your research and you got straight As in all your courses."

"Thank you," Tariq murmured gratefully. Dr. Friedman cleared his throat, opened his desk drawer, and took out some papers, which he spread in front of him then went on, still avoiding looking at Tariq. "Your outstanding practical work makes it my duty to talk to you frankly: your standards have suffered greatly over the last few months. This is the fourth test in which you got a poor grade after previously always having a perfect score."

Turning pale and seeming to have lost his powers of speech, Tariq kept looking at him. Friedman held the answer sheets and said in an angry tone, "I was shocked when I saw your recent performance. You're making elementary mistakes that don't seem to have come from a student of your diligence. Doesn't that make you wonder why your grades are suffering?"

Tariq remained silent, his face growing paler. Friedman smiled and said in a sympathetic voice, "Listen, Tariq. You have a great opportunity to make your future. Life in America has drawbacks, but its big advantage is that it gives everyone a chance: if you work hard, you'll achieve your goals. This is what makes this country so great. What you can accomplish here you cannot accomplish anywhere else in the world. My advice to you is to not let your private life distract you from your work."

"But . . ."

"I don't want to pry; I just want to convey to you my own experience. I think you understand me well. I used to be a young man like you, and during my academic career I've suffered emotional jolts: happy and unhappy relationships that often affected my performance. But I learned how to keep my emotions in check and go back to work. Nothing is harder than work, but it is the only value that remains."

Friedman got up and shook Tariq's hand warmly. "Take care of your work, Tariq, and think of me like a father. If you need any help, don't hesitate to ask. Even if you just need to talk about your problems, I'll always have time for you."

"Thank you, Doctor," Tariq said gratefully.

Friedman placed his hand on Tariq's shoulder and said as he saw him to the door, "Unfortunately the decline in your grades makes it mandatory for the department to give you a warning. That's spelled out in the rules. You'll receive the warning within two days. That's bad, of course, but it is not the end of the world. If you work hard and regain your standing we can annul the warning as if it were never issued."

Tariq looked in silence at Dr. Friedman. He couldn't speak and was unable to concentrate on his surroundings. Distraught, he walked down the corridor with heavy steps, staggering as if he had received a violent blow to the head. Dark and misty pictures kept appearing and vanishing in his mind. He kept walking, so lost in thought that he passed the dorm without realizing it. He knew that his performance had suffered recently, but he hadn't made much of it. Whenever he got a bad grade he'd say, "I didn't do well in this test, but I'll do better next time."

Dr. Friedman had made him look in the mirror and see reality. He was falling to the bottom. His academic future was threatened. Today they had issued him a warning; tomorrow they'd expel him like Danana. The difference was: Danana was supported by the Egyptian government. As for him, if they dismissed him he would be lost forever. What had happened to him? How did Tariq Haseeb, the genius, the legend of academic superiority, come to fear failure and expect expulsion?

Tariq closed the apartment door calmly then threw himself onto the bed with all his clothes on; he didn't even take off his shoes. He stared at the ceiling in silence for about half an hour then got up, left his apartment, and took the elevator to the seventh floor. He stood in front of Shaymaa's apartment hesitantly, and then rang the bell two consecutive times: that was the code that Shaymaa knew, and she would hurry to him, opening the door as if she had been waiting behind it. This time she didn't open up. He thought she had gone out for one reason or another. He called her and found the telephone turned off. He rang the bell again. A long time passed, and he thought of leaving. Finally she opened the door. She was wearing her house clothes and had a scarf on her hair. She had not preened herself as usual for their meeting. She didn't say a word but turned and made room for him, so he could enter, and then she sat in front of him on the sofa in the living room. In the light he saw that her eyes were bloodshot and her face wet from tears.

"What has happened?"

She remained silent, avoiding looking at him, which added to his apprehension. He went over and placed his hand on her shoulder. She pushed it harshly.

"What's wrong, Shaymaa?"

She bowed her head for a while then started sobbing, saying in a breaking voice, "A catastrophe, Tariq."

"What happened?"

"I'm pregnant."

He stood there looking at her as if he didn't understand, as if frozen in place. He was no longer able to think. His consciousness was scattered, broken into thousands of little pieces. He began to notice things around him as separate sights unconnected by anything: the lamp on the side table, the fridge with its humming sound, the floor covered with thick dark brown carpeting. Shaymaa suddenly got up and began to slap her face with her hands and scream, "Now do you know the catastrophe, Tariq? I am pregnant in sin, Tariq. In sin!"

He rushed to her and held her hands and after some effort was able to stop her from slapping herself, but she threw herself on the chair and began to sob with such despair that she broke his heart. He spoke for the first time and his voice came out deep, as if coming from a well, "You're mistaken."

"What do you mean?"

"You couldn't be pregnant."

"I did the test twice."

"I assure you it is impossible."

She looked at him shrewishly and said, "You are a doctor and you know very well that what happened is possible." It seemed the red line had been compromised.

A deep silence fell and she began to cry again, then she said in a shaking voice, "This morning I thought of committing suicide, but I fear God Almighty."

She got up suddenly, got close to him, held his hand, and whispered in a hoarse voice: "Please protect me, Tariq. I implore you."

He kept staring at her in silence. She said in a supplicating voice, "I've asked about the procedures. We can get married here in the consulate."

"Marry here?"

"Our families will be upset because we didn't ask them, but we have no choice. I've asked at the consulate. It's a simple procedure that would take less than half an hour. After that a copy of the marriage document would be sent to the civil registry in Cairo."

She said the last sentence in a matter-of-fact tone, as if he had agreed to the marriage and only the procedure remained. A heavy silence settled between them. He turned his face away so as not to look at her and said in a soft voice, as if talking to himself, "I also have a big problem. I've received an official warning from the university: my GPA has plunged."

"We have to resolve our situation first. When do we go to the consulate?"

"Why?"

"To get married."

"My circumstances would not permit marriage now."

Silence prevailed again. She began to breathe unsteadily. He went on in a pleading voice, "Please, Shaymaa. Understand me. I will never let you down. I will do all I can to help you, but I cannot marry this way."

She stared at his face. She tried to say something but finally she half sighed, half sobbed, then pushed him with her hands as she shouted, "Get out of here! Go. I don't want to see your face."

■ ■ ■ ■ ■ ■ ■ ■ ■ ■ ■

I spent one of the worst nights in my life. I didn't sleep at all. I called Wendy several times, but she didn't answer then turned off her telephone. Early in the morning I put on my clothes and took the train to the Chicago Stock Exchange, where I had accompanied her several times. I stood waiting for her at the intersection. The snow that had fallen overnight had covered everything. I tightened the heavy coat around my body and covered my head and wrapped the scarf around my face. I remembered how Wendy had chosen these clothes for me. I had, due to my lack of experience with Chicago winters, bought a raincoat thinking it could ward off the cold of winter. When Wendy saw it she had laughed and then controlled herself and said in a low voice as if apologizing, "This coat is too light. Winter in Chicago requires heavy coats lined with fur."

She took me to the Marshall Field's department store and told me as the glass elevator took us upstairs, "Here they sell fancy fashions from the biggest names in design all over the world, but thank God they haven't forgotten poor people like us, so on the last floor they sell slightly irregular or older-model merchandise at affordable prices."

How she had loved me and has taken care of me! And I had treated her as harshly as she had treated me nicely. Yesterday she came to celebrate with me, bringing the dancing outfit that she had bought especially for me; she wanted to look like the Andalusian dancer that I had imagined. All this love I met with incredible cruelty. I accused her of spying, of treachery. I will apologize to her as soon as I see her. I'll kiss her hands and beg her to forgive me. How could I have been so cruel? I was not myself. I was tense and miserable, so I took all my frustrations out on her: Safwat Shakir's breaking into my apartment, his knowing all the details of my life, and his attempt to frighten me by threatening my mother and sister. All that made me a nervous wreck. My sister Noha, I can't imagine that they'd actually arrest her. If they harm her I'll kill this Safwat Shakir. Can they be humans like us? Were they at one time innocent children? How could a person's job be simply to beat and torture people? How can a man who tortures another eat and sleep and make love to his wife and play with his children? Strangely enough, all State Security officers have the same features. The officer who tortured me when I was arrested at the university looked like Safwat Shakir: the same cold, sticky shine in his complexion, the same dead cruel eyes, and the same wooden, ashen face filled with bitterness.

A gust of icy wind blew, so I closed my eyes and started walking on the sidewalk in brisk steps so that blood would rush to my limbs. This method of coping with the cold I had also learned from Wendy. There are dozens of details and situations that we had shared that I couldn't forget. I looked at my watch. It was seven-thirty. Why hadn't she come? This is the route she took every day. Has she changed it to avoid me? I felt sadness weighing heavily on my heart. With the cold and exhaustion, I began to separate myself from my surroundings, as if I had suddenly moved to another, far-away realm, as if what I was seeing was happening to other people I was watching from behind glass. It was a trick that my mind involuntarily played to reduce my feeling of pain. Little by little mist covered the field of visibility before me, as if I were seeing the street and passersby through cloudy glasses. I don't know how long I stayed in that condition but suddenly I saw her coming. There she was, walking with the measured, even gait that I like. She moved in accordance with a graceful, steady rhythm as if she were dancing. (I asked her once, "Why don't you walk fast like other Americans?" She answered me, laughing, "Because I'm carrying the blood of my Andalusian grandmother who was in love with your grandfather.") I rushed toward her as fast as I could. She stopped and looked at me. It seemed that, like me, she hadn't had any sleep.

"Wendy."

"I have to go to work."

"Please. Just one minute."

A bitter wind blew and showered our faces with drifting snow. I motioned to her and she hesitated for a while then followed me to the entryway of a nearby building. We were warmer there. I was breathing heavily with emotion. I held her by the shoulders and said, "Please forgive me. I don't know why I said that. I was frus-trated and drunk. I wasn't myself."

She bowed her head to avoid looking at me and said, "Our fight brought the truth out in the open."

"I'll do anything for you to forget what I said yesterday."

"I can't forget it. I can't deceive myself."

"What do you mean?"

"Our relationship is wonderful, but it has no future."

"Why?"

"Because we belong to two different worlds."

"Wendy, I made a mistake and I came to apologize."

"There's no mistake: ultimately I belong to the enemies of your country. No matter how much you love me, you'll never forget that I'm Jewish. No matter how faithful I remain to you, your trust in me will always be fragile. I'll be the first suspect in your view."

"This isn't true. I trust you and respect you."

"We're finished, Nagi."

I was about to register one last desperate objection, but she smiled mysteriously and there came to her face that old sadness that would come over her. She moved toward me and hugged me and kissed me quickly on the cheek then said in a soft voice as she gave me my apartment key, "Please don't call me. I'd like for our relationship to end as beautifully as it began. Thank you for the wonderful feelings I've shared with you."

She turned around and left quietly. I kept watching her as she crossed the threshold of the glass door to the street then disappeared in the crowd.

Karam Doss looked worried. He sighed and said, "So, the war has started."

"I don't understand how Safwat Shakir found everything out about us."

"Spying on people is his profession. Remember that we've met with many Egyptians to convince them to sign the statement. It's only natural that one of them has informed on us."

"How did he get the key to my apartment?"

"Collaboration between American and Egyptian intelligence services is tight and long-standing. They send suspects to Egypt, where State Security agents torture them and force them to confess then return them to America."

"I thought human rights were protected here."

"After 9/11 the American administration gave security agencies the right to do whatever they saw as necessary, beginning with spying on people up to arresting them for mere suspicion."

"And what do we do now?"

"You still insist on the statement?"

"What are you saying?"

"I know that you are courageous and patriotic. But I also appreciate that your fear for your family might make you reconsider."

I threw him a look that must have seemed decisive, for he raised his hand and said, "Don't get angry. I had to ask you."

We were sitting in the piano bar where I had met Wendy for the first time. I was struggling to stop the onslaught of memories. Wendy's picture had not left my mind. There I was, losing one of the most beautiful experiences in my life. I recalled our last meeting. Was she right? Do we really belong to two different worlds? Our hostility, as Arabs, should be directed at the Zionist movement, not at Judaism. We should not be hostile to adherents of a certain religion. Such a fascist attitude is alien to Islam's tolerance; besides, it gives others the right to treat us in a similarly racist manner. This is the opinion that I have stated and written dozens of times, but it seems I failed to apply it. If Wendy were not Jewish would I have accused her of treachery? Why was I so easily suspicious of her? But, on the other hand, wasn't Wendy an exception? Don't most Jews in the world support Israel with all their might? Doesn't Israel commit all its massacres of the Arabs as the state of the Jews? Didn't my relationship with Wendy anger the Jews in the university? Didn't they harass me and insult me? How many Jews are like Wendy and how many like the student who made fun of me?

I gulped down the rest of the wine and ordered another drink. I looked at Karam's face. He knit his brows and said seriously, "We have to analyze the situation correctly. So long as Safwat Shakir has found everything out, he will most definitely bar those who signed the statement from meeting with the president."

"Does he have that right?"

"Of course. The president's visit is supervised by Egyptian and American security. They have the right to prevent anyone from entering the hall."

"Even if they prevented us from entering, we will demonstrate outside and read the statement to the media."

"Demonstrations are important, of course, but what makes this a strong plan is for one Egyptian to surprise the president and deliver the statement to his face."

"You are right. But how?"

"We still have two weeks. We have to find an Egyptian who hasn't signed the statement and convince him to deliver it. We have to choose someone that Safwat Shakir doesn't expect at all."

"Do you know anyone who can do that?"

"I have some names we can review together."

Why did Marwa agree to work with Safwat Shakir?

The answer could be gleaned from a few small details such as: her quizzical, suspicious look at her husband when he broached the subject; her tense, somewhat defiant smile as she preened in front of the mirror before going to the consulate; the tight blue dress that she chose in order to show the contours of her body; the strong perfume she applied behind her ears and between her breasts; the quick, surreptitious movement of her hand as she undid the top button of her dress before entering the office; and her slow movements, her sighs, and her melodious voice. She was driven by an overpowering inner desire to encourage Safwat Shakir, to give him a chance to show his true intentions. Marwa did that, not because she liked the man or because she was deviant or given to fooling around, but because she wanted to bring matters to a head, to push the story to an ending. She needed to find some certainty in her tumultuous life, which was draining her incessantly. She was tired of her hesitations and apprehensions, of her fear of divorce and her aversion to Danana. She couldn't bear to go on living in that gray area. Her fears had either to materialize or be dispelled. No matter how cruel reality was, it was still more merciful than illusions. She realized from the first day that there was no real work for her in Safwat Shakir's office, and that his secretary, Hasan, was handling the major tasks. It was clear that Safwat Shakir was burning with desire for her. More than once, during the day, he would call her to his office and ask her to close the door, inviting her to sit in front of him and then talking to her in an effort to win her affection, piercing her the whole time with his eyes, his voice blazing with passion that almost scorched her. At times his lust would overflow, filling the air between them, forcing him into a reluctant silence.

He wasn't going to withstand it much longer, Marwa thought. Before long now, he was going to show his face. What was he going to do? Grab her hand? Cling to her and try to kiss her forcibly? The first and second days passed. At the end of the third, Safwat asked her to stay after hours. He went up to the small bar behind the folding screen, poured himself a drink and an orange juice for her, then went back to his chair and sat back, his eyes getting a little misty.

"I want to talk to you about myself."

"That's an honor."

"I am now at the peak of my professional life. I might be asked to join the cabinet as a minister at any time."

"Congratulations," she said in a cheerful voice, and then her inner plan sprang into action; she moved a little, then crossed her legs, and her dress revealed a few more details of her body. He went on in a serious tone. "I have gone as far as any security man can go. Perhaps you don't know what security means in our country. It is security and no other entity that is ruling Egypt. With one word I can move the president of the Republic any way I want. I can make him change his route from one place to another or leave his palace and sleep in some other palace that I designate. One report from me can destroy the future of any official in the state."

"I am beginning to feel afraid of you."

"On the contrary. I want you to depend on me."

"Thank you."

"Your husband came to me in Washington and cried and begged me to save his future."

"I know."

"I am going to save him for your sake."

"Thank you very much."

"I want you to thank me in another way."

"What is it?"

"I am older and I have more experience than you. Life has taught me that an opportunity comes only once. We either seize it or lose it forever."

"I don't understand."

"You understand quite well."

"What do you want?"

"I want *you*."

He got up from behind the desk, walked slowly over to her, held her hand, and pulled her. She got up. He extended his arm and put it around her waist. She fidgeted but did not move away. As his cologne filled her nose he whispered, "You're beautiful."

She moved slightly, as if objecting, which aroused him even more. He tightened his grip on her arm and said in a hoarse voice, "I'll make you the happiest woman in the world."

"And if I refuse?"

"You won't refuse."

"How do you know?"

"Because you're intelligent."

"I need to think."

Safwat looked at her, frowning and beginning to breathe heavily with desire for her. But he pulled himself together and said as he moved away: "You have until tomorrow."

MARWA WAS NOT SHOCKED OR confused. She felt neither resentment nor anger. On the contrary, she felt some relief, as if she were an investigator who had finally found uncontestable evidence to get a conviction. There she was: absolutely certain of the truth; no more doubts and no hesitation from now on. Safwat Shakir wanted her to be his mistress: he had said it explicitly. She went home and sat in the living room waiting for Danana, who as soon as he saw her realized that something had happened. He greeted her and then said with an exaggerated yawn in preparation for an escape, "I spent the whole day working very hard."

"I want to talk to you."

"Let's postpone it until tomorrow."

"It cannot be postponed."

She told him what had happened, taking her time, clearly enunciating Safwat Shakir's words. She fixed him with a strong glance as she said, "Can you imagine how low! The one you considered your friend wants to sully your honor."

Danana was sitting in front of her, still in his street clothes. He kept staring at her through his glasses then threw his hands up in the air and said, "There is no power or strength save in God. What an indecorous man!"

Marwa was not convinced by what she understood to be a feigned expression of disgust, so she asked Danana in a loud voice, "So what are you going to do?"

"I will hold him to account, of course, and I'll be tough on him."

Moments of silence passed. He suddenly got up and sat next to her, placed his hand on her shoulder, and said, "I'll make him pay the price for his ignominy. I will get word of what happened to his superiors. But we have to be a little patient because the president's visit is taking place in a few days and Safwat promised to get me enrolled at DePaul."

"What do you mean?"

"We don't want him to create difficulties."

"He said to me explicitly that he wanted to have a relationship with me. Do you understand?"

"Of course I understand. I will teach him a lesson that he won't forget. You'll see for yourself. All I am asking is that we wait just one month, no more. If I anger him now, he can destroy me with the stroke of a pen. I'll just give him time until the president's visit is over and he enrolls me in the other university. Then we settle the account."

She fixed him with a slow, probing look, as if recording what was happening, etching it deep into her consciousness once and for all. She didn't say anything but got up slowly, went into the bedroom, and closed the door.

CHAPTER 36

That morning the Egyptian consulate building looked different, as if it had acquired a mythical dimension, as if a magician's wand had changed it from a merely elegant building overlooking Lake Michigan into a stage for major events that would be recorded by history. Security preparations started early: the building was examined by high-tech equipment that X-rayed the walls to make sure no foreign substances were embedded within them. Shortly after that ten large police dogs toured the building sniffing everywhere for any hidden explosives. In the meantime, a group of Egyptian sharpshooters, carrying their long-barreled rifles fitted with telescopes, climbed onto the roof, accompanied by another group of Republican Guard officers armed with automatic rifles. They took their positions in different places, covering the area surrounding the consulate from all directions. After a short while, four metal detector gates were set up, two in front of each of the entrances in such a way that every person coming in would be checked twice. About ten meters before these gates, checkpoints manned by FBI agents together with Egyptian intelligence and State Security were also set up.

As invitees began to arrive, they were checked very thoroughly: Americans' invitations were checked by a laser machine to make sure they were not forged. Egyptians, of course, were subjected to additional measures: their passports were scanned on a special laptop to make sure they did not have security files. After that the Egyptian security officer would ask them, with a formal smile and a scrutinizing gaze, about details of their lives. If he noticed the slightest confusion or contradiction in their answers they would be escorted to an office for more elaborate cross-examination. The security procedures were strict and, like justice, blind, and were imposed on everyone regardless of profession or social standing, so much so that the man in charge of the cafeteria at the consulate, an old black American named Jack Mahoney, was not allowed to enter because he had forgotten his special pass. For a whole half hour the officers turned a deaf ear to his pleas to prove his identity despite his colleagues vouching for him. In the end he had to go back home—quite a distance away—to collect his pass.

Egyptian security men were profoundly aware of the serious and lofty nature of their task: ensuring the personal safety of the revered president. They loved him with all their hearts and pronounced his name reverently and prayerfully. Had it not been for their closeness to him, they wouldn't have enjoyed their cushy lives and tremendous influence on all departments of the state. They were so linked to him that what happened to him determined their future. If something bad, God forbid, were to happen to him, if he were assassinated like his predecessor, they'd be lost. They'd be pensioned off or cashiered. They might be put on trial and sent to jail if power passed on to the president's enemies, who were quite numerous. All these apprehensions would prick them like needles if they felt any relaxation or boredom, so they would immediately regain their enthusiasm. Absolute loyalty to the president was embodied in the person of General Mahmud al-Manawi, commander of the Republican Guard, who had spent a whole quarter century close to him and which made him one of the few who enjoyed the president's full trust. It also made him entitled to be on the receiving end of the president's sometimes obscene jokes. Sometimes when the president was in a good mood, he would pat the general's protruding paunch and say in a loud, laughing voice, "Stop eating, Manawi boy! You look like Apis, the bull!"

Or he would shout derisively, "It seems you've given up on the plow, Manawi boy!" (In a reference to dwindling sexual prowess with age.)

When that happened, General Manawi would blush at the great honor he received. Many would envy him that humor, because it was a mark of trust and love from the president. He would bow and mumble in a prayerful voice, "At your service, sir. May God give you long life for the sake of Egypt, sir."

While security procedures were in full swing, a few hundred Egyptians led by Nagi Abd al-Samad and Karam Doss together with John Graham gathered in front of the consulate in the green space close to the lake. The appearance of Graham in the middle of the group, with his natural charisma, being an old American who came to fight for the rights of Egyptians, galvanized the demonstrators, who kept shouting slogans and waving signs in English and Arabic: FREE THE DETAINEES, STOP THE TORTURE, STOP PERSECUTING THE COPTS, DOWN WITH THE TYRANT, and DEMOCRACY FOR EGYPTIANS.

Demonstrations against the president during his visits in the West were familiar to the Republican Guard officers. This time, however, they noticed that there were large numbers of demonstrators and that they were making a lot of noise. That caused General Manawi some concern, so he went to the head of the American security detail and asked him for permission to disperse the demonstration. The latter told him, "American law prohibits dispersing them."

General Manawi smiled and said, "We can do it without taking the least responsibility. Some of my men in civilian clothes will slip among the demonstrators and discipline them. It would all appear to the media like an ordinary brawl."

The American officer threw him a disapproving glance and a dismissive smile, then signaled his refusal with his hand and moved away. General Manawi was very angry at the arrogant American officer's behavior but of course wouldn't cause any problems with him. He had learned from experience that nothing worried the president more than having

316 Alaa Al Aswany

a problem with any American, no matter how lowly his position. There was a saying that he often repeated: "A ruler who challenges the American administration is like a fool who puts his head in a lion's mouth."

The story of the president's information secretary, Dr. Na'il al-Tukhi, was still fresh in people's minds. He had had a quarrel with an employee of the American embassy about the right of way on one of the streets in Maadi. This was an ordinary quarrel that took place dozens of times every day in Cairo, but it had developed into name-calling in English, which so enraged Dr. al-Tukhi that he pushed the other man in the chest. The American employee had complained to the American ambassador, who had called the president's office to report the incident. The following day the American embassy received an official reply to the effect that the president was very disturbed by what happened, and that he had ordered an immediate investigation. He then decided to terminate the employment of his information secretary as punishment for his irresponsible action.

The demonstrators grew more enthusiastic and in Arabic and English shouted in unison in a thunderous voice, "Down with the president." General Manawi kept observing them in exasperation from the other side of the wide street then ordered an officer in civilian clothes to film them with a video camera bearing the logo of a fictitious television news service, intending to send the footage to State Security to identify and pursue them.

The crescendo of the shouts coincided with the impending arrival of the president. Soon the procession appeared in the distance, approaching gradually until it came fully into view: the president's huge bulletproof black Mercedes guarded by two armored cars to the front and rear. General Manawi let loose a shout that wailed like a cheerless warning siren. "Aaaatention!" All the officers tensed up and took up their positions, brandishing their weapons in every direction to guard against any eventuality. The procession slowed down then stopped in front of the entrance, and instantly, the bodyguards jumped and formed a full circle several meters in diameter around the car, observing the road from all directions without appearing in the photographs. They were huge men with shaved heads and tiny earpieces, pointing their guns at an enemy whose appearance was anticipated at any moment. The chief of protocol rushed toward the presidential car, bent toward it, and opened the door. Soon thereafter the president appeared slowly and haughtily, as if he were a crowned king, his face displaying that famous cheerless smile that, a quarter century earlier, he had deemed photogenic and so never changed it. He was wearing a very elegant light gray suit, a blue-and-white-striped necktie, and shiny Italian shoes with an eye-catching golden buckle on the side. Anyone seeing the president face-to-face, however, despite the awe surrounding him, would inevitably feel that his presence was somehow contrived. His hair, dyed jet-black, was rumored to be (in whole or in part) one of the best hairpieces available in the world. His complexion was exhausted by all the scraping, sanding, and daily ointments he used to give it a youthful appearance. His face was covered with layers of fine makeup so he would appear younger in photographs. That glasslike, cold, detached, and distant presence, devoid of any traces of dust or sweat, as if it were sterile, left in those who saw the president an uncomfortable, raw feeling like that experienced by viewing babies immediately after their birth, featureless lumps of flesh still displaying the stickiness of the womb.

The president, slowed down by his seventy-five years, had a diminished level of concentration and was noticing things around him a little late. So he looked at the other side of the road and waved to the demonstrators, and when their shouts grew louder he realized what was going on and turned toward the consulate's entrance. He swaggered along and reached for his jacket buttons, feeling them. (This gesture has stayed with him since he replaced his military uniform with civilian clothes and discovered that his buttons came undone without his being aware of them.)

The president began to shake hands with those receiving him in a predetermined order: the Egyptian ambassador to the United States, Egypt's consul in Chicago, Safwat Shakir, whose face looked calm because everything was going according to plan, and then members of the embassy staff according to seniority. At the end of the line Ahmad Danana looked as though he was attending a fancy dress party. He was wearing a blue Christian Dior suit that he had bought especially for the occasion and which cost him (together with the shirt, the socks, and necktie) fifteen hundred dollars that he paid for gladly with his credit card, keeping the receipts as usual, hoping that he could return them afterward and get his money back (as he had done with his wedding suit). He realized that meeting the president might change his life. He had heard of many prominent personages in the state whose careers were made under similar circumstances. They met the president, he liked them, and their faces made an impression on his magnanimous memory, and so he gave them important posts at the earliest change in cabinets. It would indeed be a turning point in which the smallest details acquired maximum importance: a missing button or one that was loose, or a crooked necktie or shoes that were dusty or not sufficiently shiny—any insignificant detail might give the president a bad impression and negatively affect Danana's future. Another reason he took such care of his appearance was his attempt to prove to himself that he had completely recovered from what his wife Marwa had done. When he got up last Tuesday, he couldn't find her. He went through the apartment in a daze, still sleepy, until he finally noticed a piece of paper on the refrigerator door in the kitchen, written hastily in large, uneven letters: "I left for Egypt. My father will contact you for divorce proceedings."

Danana exerted a great effort to absorb the shock. He said to himself that he had never been happy with her. He could, undoubtedly, find dozens of women better than she. Yes, he would divorce her as she requested, but she should pay the price of the misery she cost him (and his expenses as well). A few days after she ran away, Hagg Nofal called him and started talking about kismet and how the most loathsome permitted thing in God's view was divorce. Danana replied that Marwa had run away from their home and caused him a scandal, and that he needed time to get over the crisis emotionally. Then he promised to meet Hagg Nofal next time he was in Cairo, and to sit with him man to man to discuss their respective demands. He deliberately used the word "demands" to prepare him for the idea that he was going to demand money. Of course he would demand money: his life, his name, and his reputation were not little toys in the hands of Madam Marwa to play with at will. He made up his mind (motivated by greed disguised as anger) to demand from Hagg Nofal one million Egyptian pounds in return for divorcing his daughter. A million pounds for Nofal was nothing. Danana would purchase a certificate of deposit in the National Bank, and that should fetch him a respectable annual return. He rehearsed in his head: you'll pay, Nofal, against your will. If you refuse or if your daughter sues me for *khul'*, then I'll show you my other face. I will sully her reputation, you dog, Nofal, everywhere, in such a way that she will never marry ever after. I'll say that I didn't find her to be a virgin.

He made up his mind and reassured himself, focusing on preparing for the president's visit. He thought for a long time about the moment of the meeting. What should he do when he saw His Excellency? How would he stand in front of him? What should he say to him? The president shook the hands of all of those standing in line. When it was Danana's turn, he rushed and hugged the president and kissed him on both cheeks then shouted loudly in a rural accent, "May God give you long life and victory for the sake of Egypt. I am your son, sir, Ahmad Abd al-Hafeez Danana from Shuhada, Minufiya Governorate."

Thus he chose to present a comic folkloric act to prove his love for his leader and his authentic Egyptianness. The plan worked. The president looked pleased and the pleasure was immediately transferred to the faces of those around him and they began looking at Danana sweetly and affectionately. The president placed his hand on Danana's shoulder and said, "So, you're from Minufiya? That means we come from the same place."

"That's an honor for me, sir."

"It seems you are a peasant to the core!" said the president and let out a loud laugh. The camera flashes captured the moment and Danana got the honor of appearing in a presidential snapshot that would be published in government papers with the caption "Our revered president jests with one of his student sons during his successful historic visit to the United States."

The president crossed the entrance, followed, two respectful steps behind, by the ambassador, then the others in the receiving line in a semicircle to maintain a respectful distance. The large hall was designed in Oriental fashion, its walls decorated with Islamic motifs and inscriptions, while glittering crystal chandeliers hanging from the ceiling provided lighting. The hall was originally meant for lectures and showing movies. Today a stately dais for the distinguished guest was installed, surrounded with bouquets of roses. In the back, a life-size photograph of the president was hung. Under the photograph was a huge sign in Arabic reading: EGYPTIANS IN AMERICA WELCOME THE REVERED LEADER. WE PLEDGE ALLEGIANCE TO YOU FOR MORE PROSPERITY AND DEMOCRACY.

Everything taking place in the hall was carried by video cameras to a huge screen outside, next to the consulate's main entrance. Guests sat on the auditorium seats, exchanging small talk and laughter, perhaps to mask their tension. As soon as the president appeared they all jumped to their feet and the whole auditorium was filled with continuous applause. Danana gave an agreed-upon signal to a group of students that he had sat in a section of the auditorium to the right: they started a rhythmic chant accompanied by two successive hand claps, as he had trained them. The din kept getting louder until the president extended his hands and waved them in front of him as if to say "enough, thank you."

Everything proceeded as planned except for a strange incident that took place moments later. A number of guests rushed forward, asking to have their picture taken with the president. He agreed and signaled to the guards to let them approach. They shook hands with him and stood around him proudly. The presidential photographer got closer, carrying his high-tech cameras. He was a fat, bald man in his fifties (it was ascertained definitively later on that he was a new employee with the presidency and was allowed to travel with the president for the first time after the original photographer fell ill). The president and those around him fixed a photogenic smile on their faces, but moments passed while the photographer fixed his eye on the camera without taking any pictures. Suddenly he extended his hand and said, "Please, Mr. President, move a little to the right."

A profound silence prevailed, heavily and ominously. The president did not move as the photographer had asked. He remained standing where he was, looking upward, as if watching something moving on the ceiling. That was a well-known sign of his anger: to look upward when something happened that he didn't like. Those around him had to correct the mistake immediately. It seemed the photographer was not intelligent enough to notice what had happened or he imagined that the president had not heard him. He pushed the camera away from his eyes and said, loudly this time, "Mr. President, you're outside the frame; please move to the right." Before he uttered that last word, a hard slap had landed on his face. The chief of protocol grabbed the camera and threw it up in the air, whereupon it fell a distance away, breaking into smithereens and making a loud smashing sound. Then he held the photographer by the shirt collar and roared in anger, "Did you tell our revered president to move, you donkey son of a bitch? The whole of Egypt would move while our revered president remains standing where he is. Get out of here, animal!"

The chief of protocol pushed him hard with his hands in the back and kicked him so violently that the man almost fell on his face. The photographer rushed outside in shock, dazed by the surprise and the abuse, while the chief of protocol kept hurling insults and curses at him. Those who had wanted the picture moved away when the hitting began and then returned to their seats slowly and cautiously, trying to forget the whole thing.

As for the president, he seemed pleased with the punishment that the impudent photographer had received. He looked around slowly and deliberately, as if to reassure everyone that his pride was unaffected. Then he continued walking in the midst of tense silence, which was broken as soon as he arrived at the dais, greeted by another roaring round of applause. The ceremony began with a recitation from the Qur'an by the bearded student Ma'mun, who chose the chapter of al-Fath: "Surely We have given thee a manifest victory." After that, there was more shouting of slogans and applause, then, from the podium, the president began to read his speech from the piece of paper in front of him covered in large print (because he never used reading glasses in front of cameras). He spoke of his achievements, which he could not have accomplished without God's help and the greatness of the true and genuine Egyptian people. Then he concluded the speech by addressing the students, reminding them that each of them was an ambassador for Egypt, which he had to keep in his heart, mind, and soul. The speech was conventional, rhetorical, and boring like all the speeches written for him by Mahmud Kamil, editor in chief of the newspaper *Biladi*, published by the ruling party. As soon as he was finished, applause and melodic slogan shouting was resumed, led by Danana, whose enthusiasm had reached its peak. He began to wave his hand as the veins in his neck swelled while he shouted at the top of his voice, "Long live the Commander President!" "Long live the hero of war and peace!" "Long live the founder of modern Egypt!"

Words of welcome from the ambassador and the consul followed.

Then came the resounding words of Ahmad Danana, president of the Egyptian Student Union. "We pledge to you, our revered president, that we will love the fatherland as you have taught us; to follow your example, Mr. President, to work as wholeheartedly as you have, to be graced with integrity and honesty as you have been graced. May God preserve you as Egypt's treasure and for her might."

Shouting and applause were resumed, then the ambassador began to introduce speakers according to a schedule. All the comments had been prepared ahead of time and screened very carefully, and they all constituted various forms of praise of the president. Even the questions tended to glorify him rather than demand an answer. One person asked, "How were you so able, sir, to overcome all the major challenges facing Egypt?" Another asked, "How did you benefit, sir, from your military experience in running the affairs of the state so successfully?" During his answers the president repeated the usual words that those present had read dozens of times in the newspapers. From time to time he would tell a joke at which they laughed with great alacrity. Danana, of course, laughed the loudest (he would start laughing after everybody had stopped, to gain the president's attention). Finally, the ambassador said in his dignified voice: "Now, a word from Dr. Muhammad Salah, professor of medicine at the University of Illinois."

THE DISTANCE BETWEEN THE SECOND row, where Dr. Salah was sitting, and the podium at which he was going to deliver his speech was no more than ten steps, but it formed the separating line between two lives: between his sixty-year history and his future, which was being shaped at that very moment. There he was, carrying out the plan, exactly as he had agreed with Karam Doss and Nagi Abd al-Samad. Security asked to preview the speech he was going to give. He gave them a two-line speech in which he glorified the president, which they approved immediately. In the meantime, he had kept in his inside pocket the text of the statement that he was going to deliver in the name of Egyptians. His worst fear was that they might search him as he entered the hall, find the statement, and ruin everything. But it seemed his dignified appearance had reassured the officer, so he did not subject him to any additional procedures. Dr. Salah stood up and slowly approached the podium, his head bowed so that he wouldn't look at anyone. He first had to make sure that he was fully within the range of the cameras so that he could aim his blow precisely. He was going to read the statement in a strong and clear voice, quickly, so that he could finish it before they prevented him. It was naive to imagine that they'd let him finish. They would be overcome with shock for a few moments, but they would soon come to and move. What were they going to do to him? It was unlikely that they'd shoot him. They would arrest him, beat him up, even muzzle him by force to prevent him from finishing the statement. All of that would expose them even further. Only two steps to go. He was hearing a subdued droning sound in the hall. If he raised his head now, he would see the head of the state face-to-face. What a life-changing moment! He would leave this hall a different human being. He was unafraid. All he feared was not being able to finish delivering the statement. What happened after didn't worry him. Where had this spirit been? If he had had it thirty years earlier, his life would have changed. Zeinab would not have told him, "I regret to tell you that you're a coward." There he was, going the final step, standing in front of the president of the republic, delivering a statement defending Egyptians' right to democracy and freedom. He was going to do that before the whole world. Cameras were going to beam his picture everywhere. When Nagi offered him the opportunity to read the statement, he felt that fate was providing him with a way out of his suffering. His instantaneous acceptance surprised Nagi himself.

Last night he had said to Zeinab on the telephone, "I'll prove to you that I am not a coward." She asked him how and he answered with a proud laugh, "Tomorrow you'll know. The whole world will know."

He reached the podium and brought his head close to the microphone. He thought to himself: I am not a coward, Zeinab. You'll see for yourself. I've never been a coward. I left Egypt because it closed her doors in my face. I didn't run away. I'll show you now what courage is like. What I am going to do is considered by the jurists as the highest form of jihad: telling the truth to an oppressive ruler's face. Now he was going to be rid of his ordinary life; he would take it off and discard it as if it were an old, worn-out coat. His name would be written in history and would be passed on from generation to generation: the hero who confronted the tyrant.

He stood erect, adjusted his glasses with his finger, then nervously reached into his shirt pocket and took several folded sheets of paper. He opened them and began to read, his voice coming out tentative and a little raspy, "A statement from Egyptians living in Chicago." He stopped suddenly, looked at the president sitting on the dais, and saw on his face a sort of welcoming smile. A profound silence fell on the whole place. He seemed somewhat confused as he dried with his handkerchief the copious sweat that had gathered on his forehead. The longer his silence continued, the more pronounced an uneasy hum from the crowd grew. He opened his mouth to go on reading, but suddenly his face changed and he looked upward, as if he had suddenly remembered something he had forgotten. In a very quick movement, he put the papers he had taken out into his jacket and took out of the other pocket a small piece of paper that he spread in front of him and started to read in a shaking voice. "Speaking for myself and on behalf of all Egyptians in Chicago, we welcome you, Mr. President, and thank you from the bottom of our hearts for all the historic achievements you have offered the fatherland. We pledge to you that we will follow your example—that we will continue to love our country and offer her our best, as you have taught us. Long live Egypt and may you live long for Egypt." When he was finished, there was enthusiastic applause. Then he turned around, going back to his seat in slow, heavy steps.

The receptionist was a beautiful young woman with a smiling, sunny face. As soon as she heard the name Ra'fat Thabit, however, her smile vanished and she bowed her head slowly. She tried to say something appropriate, but she got confused and let out some incomprehensible murmur. She came out from behind the reception desk's marble counter and, followed by Ra'fat, crossed the hallway then the long corridor. Then she went left and entered another corridor. Her pace was heavy and hesitant at the beginning, and then it became regular and acquired a dignified rhythm fraught with meaning. Finally they reached a room. The receptionist held the doorknob and brought her head closer, as if pricking up her ears. Then she tapped with her fingers and a gruff voice came from inside. She opened the door slowly and motioned to Dr. Ra'fat, and he went in with her. The room was of a medium size, quiet and clean. To the right, there was a window that let in the daylight. The doctor was in his forties, bald, and wearing a white coat and glasses with silver frames. He stood in silence next to the bed. Ra'fat saw Sarah stretched out in the same clothes she had on the last time he saw her: the worn-out blue jeans and the yellow T-shirt with a dirty collar. Her face was totally calm, her eyes closed, and her lips relaxed but not open. The doctor said in a deep voice, whose reverberations echoed in the silence, "Last night at about three A.M. a car dropped her at the door of the hospital and sped away. We did all we could to save her, but the overdose caused a sharp drop in brain function. Please accept my sincere condolences."

■ ■ ■ ■ ■ ■ ■ ■ ■ ■

The demonstration was over. We walked to the car: Karam Doss, John Graham, and me. I left the front seat for Graham and rode in the back. We remained silent for a while. We were dejected. Karam suggested we have a drink. Graham murmured in agreement. I remained silent. We went to our favorite place on Rush Street. With drinks we warmed up. Karam Doss said, "I don't understand Dr. Salah. Why did he do that? He could've refused to read the statement from the beginning. He ruined everything."

I was bitter over what had happened, so I said, "You have no idea how angry I am with this man. I don't know how I'll have any dealings with him in the department after this." We fell silent again, then Karam said, "I think what Salah has done was totally deliberate. He conspired with Safwat Shakir to sabotage the whole thing."

I didn't comment. My disappointment was mixed with a feeling of guilt. It was I who agreed with Salah that he would deliver the statement. I remembered how he showed an enthusiasm that surprised me when I offered him the task. I asked Karam, still unable to think clearly, "You think he works for Security?"

"Of course."

"No," said Graham. He took a sip from his drink and added, "I think the man really wanted to deliver the statement but was frightened at the last moment."

"Why did he accept, and why was he so enthusiastic at the beginning?"

"A man may sometimes try to overcome his fear then fail."

———————————

I went home at about midnight. I took off my clothes and threw myself on the bed and was soon fast asleep. I still remember what happened in an uncertain way, as if recalling a dream. I opened my eyes and saw shadows moving in the dark of the room. I was frightened and stayed in that state between being awake and being in a dream until the light was turned on and I saw them clearly. They were three large American men, two in military uniform and the third in civilian clothes. It was very clear that he was in charge. He came over to me and said, as he showed a card from his inside pocket, "FBI. We have a search warrant and another for your arrest."

It took me a while to collect my thoughts, and then I asked him why. He said, "We'll show you the information we have later on."

He was talking to me as the other two were carefully searching the house. Finally he allowed me to put on my clothes. He came over to me and put the handcuffs on. Strangely enough, I gave in, as if I were hypnotized and had no will. We rode in a large car driven by a black driver with whom the man in charge rode in front. The two military men sat on either side of me in the backseat. I said as I tried to concentrate again, "I want to see your badge again."

He was taken aback for a moment then reached in his pocket in slow, suppressed anger and showed the badge. We remained silent. After about half an hour, we arrived at an isolated building in north Chicago, surrounded by a garden and a winding driveway that we ascended in the car until we stopped at the entrance. There were some guards who gave military salutes. We entered an office on the left side of the hallway. As soon as the door was closed, the features of the man in charge changed. The muscles of his face contracted, as if he were grinding his teeth. He fixed me with a stern look and said, "We have definitive information that you are part of a cell planning a terrorist attack in the United States. What do you say to that?"

I remained silent. Events were moving too fast for me to think. He got so close to me I could smell a light aftershave scent. He shouted angrily, "Speak! Are you deaf?"

Then suddenly he slapped me in the face. I felt a sharp stinging heat and a dark spot began to form on my left eye. I shouted in a raspy voice, "You have no right to hit me. What you're doing is illegal."

He slapped me again several times then punched me hard in the belly. I felt nauseated and was about to lose consciousness.

"Egyptian intelligence has given us everything about the organization you belong to. It's no use denying it."

"All of this is made up."

He hit me again. I began to feel sticky blood trickling down from my nose onto my lips. He shouted in an angry voice, "Speak, you son of a bitch. Why do you want to destroy our country? We've opened America's doors to you. We welcomed you to get an education and become a respectable human being. In return you are conspiring to kill innocent Americans. If you don't confess, I'll do to you what they do in your country: whip you, give you electric shocks, and rape you."

 Dr. Bill Friedman bowed his head and placed it between his hands. Chris was sitting before him. The silence was so profound that the soft music from the PA system sounded melancholy. He looked at her and asked, "When did Salah's problem begin?"

"A year ago."

"Did he see a doctor?"

"He went once and refused to continue."

"I thought the change I noticed was because of work exhaustion."

"He's sick, Bill. Since he came back from the Egyptian president's meeting his condition has deteriorated rapidly. He hasn't eaten or slept in three days. The doctor says that under such conditions he has to be involuntarily institutionalized."

"Involuntarily?"

"Yes. The usual practice is to forcibly inject him with a tranquilizer, then move him to the hospital."

"If that's the only way to help him, I guess we have no choice."

Silence fell again. Chris began to sob then said, "It's hard for me to see him like this."

Bill Friedman held her hand and said in a consoling tone, "Don't worry. He'll be all right."

"You're a dear friend. I came to you to help me."

"I'll do whatever I can."

"I hope he won't lose his job."

Dr. Friedman looked pensive then said, "Administratively speaking, we have to indicate why he has stopped coming to work. I won't mention that he's undergoing psychiatric care because that would be a negative in his professional record. I will consider his absence part of his annual vacation and I'll ask one of his colleagues to take up his classes."

"Thank you, Bill."

"It's the least I can do."

"I have to go now."

Bill Friedman got up, shook her hand warmly, and kissed her cheek, saying, "If you need anything, don't hesitate to get in touch with me."

Chris left the building and as she drove she thought that her lesser task had been accomplished: now, at least, Salah won't lose his job. The greater task remained—to move him to the hospital to receive treatment. Unfortunately, she was going to have to be tough with him, so that he could be cured and return to normal. It was for his own good. She no longer remembered their disagreement. She forgot their problems and their agreeing to divorce. All she could think of now was that he was sick and needed her. She couldn't just let him collapse without doing something for him. Even if he no longer loved her. Even if he wanted to divorce her. Even if he was in love with another woman. Even if he had been deceiving her all those years. She couldn't give up on him. He was all alone. If she left him, he wouldn't find anyone by his side. Her tears flowed again; she dabbed her eyes and then parked in front of the hospital. She waited for a few moments until she got a grip on herself then hurried into the building. Half an hour later, she came out accompanied by a young doctor. He sat next to her in her car as she drove and an ambulance followed. They agreed that she would go alone to Salah and try to convince him to go to the hospital. If he refused, the doctor would join her. Ultimately, if he persisted in refusing, the two paramedics would be called upon to give him the injection. The two cars stopped in front of the house. Chris went ahead, opened the door, and looked inside. She sighed and said, "Well, he's in his study. This should make our task easier."

She went up the stairs quickly, followed by the doctor. Once in front of the door outside his room, Chris stopped him with her hand and whispered, "Please sit here."

The doctor nodded and turned, going slowly toward the nearby chair. Chris entered quietly, and as soon as she opened the door she saw the scene that would never leave her mind. Dr. Muhammad Salah, professor of histology at the University of Illinois medical school, was wearing his blue silk pajamas, stretched out on the floor, staring at nothing in particular, as if he had been surprised by something once and forever. There was blood trickling from a deep wound on the side of his head, creating a stain that was getting bigger and bigger on the carpet. Next to his relaxed, outstretched right hand was his old Beretta.

CHAPTER 39

It was a wonderful night to celebrate the victory. Graham and Carol went to the movies then had dinner at the revolving restaurant on top of that famous Chicago tower. As the view through the glass windows changed, Carol clapped and exclaimed in childlike joy. She looked very elegant in an evening gown that revealed her shoulders and décolletage. She had gathered her hair on top of her head, highlighting her beautiful neck, and wore pearl earrings and a necklace. She insisted on ordering an expensive bottle of French wine, and as soon as the waiter turned to leave, Graham asked her, laughing, "Are you sure you can afford to pay for this dinner?"

"Don't worry, my dear," she said, adding enthusiastically, "the contract I signed this week comes only once in a lifetime. Many broadcasters have worked many years for a contract like this but couldn't get one. I've made it to the top, John."

"Congratulations," said John as he looked at her lovingly. She tasted the wine and he suggested a toast to love and success. As usual, the wine had a quick effect on her, so her eyes glistened as she said with emotion, "Because I've suffered so much in my life, God wanted to make it up to me for all my previous pain."

"Why does God single you out for special treatment while not caring about millions of wretched people?"

"Would you hold back the heretical views for tonight, at least?"

Carol looked at him with a mix of reproach and fun. They talked and laughed a lot, and when they drove back in Carol's new car, everything promised a night of love. As soon as they got home, she paid the babysitter and hurried to look in on Mark and found him sleeping peacefully as she had left him. She extended her hand and adjusted the covers around him. Then she returned to Graham, who received her with burning passionate desire. He embraced her so hard that she felt his strong arms hurting her, so she moaned lightly, which heightened his desire, and he showered her with passionate kisses on her face and neck. She backed off lightly and said in a mellow, dreamy voice, "I'll be back in just a second."

He sat waiting for her on the bed. She came back from the bathroom in a little while, wearing a white robe over her naked body. She stood preening and putting on perfume in front of the mirror. John put out his pipe quickly and said in a hasty voice, hoarse with desire, "I'll take a shower too."

In a few minutes they were rolling in bed, naked in the soft light coming from the lamp on the bedside table. He started kissing her all over her face, hands, shoulders, and breasts. When he finally entered her, she whispered his name, which aroused him so much more that he thrust at her so hard she moaned with pleasure. She felt her whole being melting in his embrace, as if she was shedding her body and soaring high. From behind her closed eyes she caught a glimpse of colored lights shining in the dark and felt that she was close to coming. Suddenly, a vague, worrying feeling came over her. She tried to remove it from her consciousness, but her pleasure continued to seep away. John slowed down his thrusting movements little by little, and then stopped. It took her a moment to come to. She felt his big body moving away. He leaned on his knees and got off her. She extended her arms and clung to his shoulders and begged, "Stay with me."

Hearing her own voice in the dark told her that what was happening was real. Graham withdrew more, always slowly, breathing heavily, not from pleasure this time but in agitation. He lowered his feet to the floor, sat on the edge of the bed, and turned his back to her. It took her another minute to collect herself. She got up and turned on the light and said in alarm, "What happened?"

He kept his head bowed. She moved toward him and her naked body appeared graceful and beautiful. She sat next to him and again spoke tentatively. "What's wrong?"

Graham pushed her arm aside. He raised his head and looked at the ceiling. He opened his mouth to say something then bowed his head again. His voice came out hoarse. "Who is he?"

"Who are you talking about?" she asked as her eyes blazed with consternation. It took Graham some time to get up. She followed him and stood in front of him. He said in a louder voice, "Who did you sleep with?"

"John, are you crazy?"

He looked strange. He lit his pipe while still naked, then said with a resigned smile, "You and I are too intelligent to waste our time on accusations and denials. You've slept with someone. Who is he?"

"John!"

"I want to know his name."

She fell silent until she got over the surprise then said in a pitifully fragile tone of voice, "You've got no right to accuse me."

With lightning speed he slapped her on the face. She let out a loud cry. He moved away and said, "I may be old; I may be hanging on to old, worn-out ideas, but I'm not a fool. I have enough human experience not to be deceived by anyone. You've cheated on me, Carol. My feeling about your body doesn't lie. I don't understand why you'd do it. We're not married. We don't have to act stupidly. Why didn't you leave me when you fell in love with somebody else?"

He was speaking in disconnected sentences while putting on his clothes and buckling his belt and placing his feet in his shoes. Once again he stood in front of her. She was still naked, her hand on her cheek. He said in a calmer voice, "I am sorry I slapped you. I'm leaving. I'll stay in a hotel until you find another place. You're rich now, you'll easily find a place."

"John!"

He ignored her and took two steps toward the door. She jumped behind him. "I didn't cheat on you."

"Lying won't do you any good."

"John," she cried one last time and tried to embrace him, but he removed her arms forcibly. She cried, "I didn't cheat on you. The head of the company used my body. That's the truth. That was his condition: one time in return for the new contract. I couldn't say no. I just couldn't. I needed to think of my son. I assure you I haven't betrayed you. All my feelings are with you. What I did with the man was disgusting and I almost throw up whenever I remember it. Our bodies hit each other, that was all. I didn't betray you, John. I love you. Please stay with me."

He had placed his hand on the doorknob. He kept looking at her as she confessed, then bowed his head forward, looking at that moment like an old, wretched man, helpless and weighed down with sorrow. As he closed the door he said, "When Mark wakes up in the morning, tell him I had to travel and that I love him very much."

CHAPTER 40

The clock in the dorm lobby said it was 5:30 A.M. Ever since Shaymaa first arrived in Chicago, she had never left the building so early, but her errand this time was far away. She pushed the glass door with her hand and was immediately assailed by cold wind, laden with flakes of snow. She backed off and tightened the heavy woolen scarf around her face and put her hands, already protected with fur-lined gloves, in her coat pockets to preserve as much heat as she could. She moved fast, as if to prevent herself from hesitating. The street was dark and totally empty and snow covered everything. She dashed at top speed toward the train station, deliberately not looking around. She felt her heart pounding hard, and terrifying apprehension assailed her: What if someone attacked me now or abducted me under the threat of armed violence? She began to recite the last two chapters of the Qur'an as she increased her speed until she finally made it to the train station. She had to go ten stations, then change trains and go another ten stations to get to the address she had memorized by heart.

The train passengers at that hour were a mix of black, Latino, and Asian cleaning crews who cleaned offices before employees arrived, and vagrants who had spent the night drinking. Shaymaa sat in a far-away seat next to the window, deliberately not looking around. She was frightened of the drunks, who didn't stop shouting and laughing while they filled the whole car with the smell of stale alcohol. Her mind was foggy, like the surface of a mirror covered with steam, as if what she saw were unreal, as if she were dreaming. She opened her handbag and took out the small Qur'an and began to read in a soft voice, "'I take refuge in God from Satan who deserves to be stoned. In the name of God, the Compassionate, the Merciful. Ya Sin. By the Wise Koran, thou art truly among the Envoys on a straight path; the sending down of the All-mighty, the All-wise, that thou mayest warn a people whose fathers were never warned, so they are heedless. The Word has never been realized against most of them, yet they do not believe. Surely We have put on their necks fetters up to the chin, so their heads are raised; and We have put before them a barrier and behind them a barrier; and We have covered them, so they do not see.'"

The effect of the Qur'anic verses on her was so strong she cried and her tears flowed, wetting the Qur'an. She turned her face away, got close to the window until she could feel the cold glass and began to whisper, "Please, God. There is no God but You, may You be exalted. I have been among the sinners, so please forgive me. I seek Your mercy, so please do not leave me to my own devices for the blink of an eye. Alive! Eternal!"

She changed trains and finished the second leg of her journey. When she left the station she had to walk a short distance to reach the center. It was daylight already. She hurried up until she saw the large sign still lit from last night: CHICAGO AID CENTER. She noticed on the opposite sidewalk a group of blacks and whites of various ages and some clergymen. They were demonstrating, carrying signs saying STOP THE MASSACRE and SHAME ON THE MURDERERS.

They began to wave the signs and shout more enthusiastically, as if performing a religious ritual. Shaymaa got more worried and hastened her steps toward the door of the center, but her appearance and the veil and Islamic garb apparently heightened the enthusiasm of the demonstrators. They got more noisy, then began shouting from the opposite sidewalk, "Ruthless murderer!"

"Are you Muslim?"

"Does your God allow the killing of children?"

Shaymaa avoided looking toward them, but she was trembling with fright and raced to cover the few steps remaining before the entrance. They began to throw tomatoes and raw eggs at her. An egg passed right next to her head then exploded on the wall. Several policemen standing in front of the center hurried toward the crowd to contain the situation. Shaymaa crossed the entryway quickly and was met by a black receptionist with an encouraging smile. "Don't pay any attention to those crazies."

Shaymaa looked at her and asked, panting, "What do they want?"

"They are antiabortion groups. They know we operate in the early morning, so they come to make trouble."

"Why don't the police arrest them?"

"The law permits abortion, but it also permits peaceful demonstration. Don't worry about it. They are a bunch of fascist fanatics, no more and no less. I think you have an appointment with Dr. Karen?"

"Yes."

"Come with me."

Dr. Karen was a slim young woman in her late twenties. She had long chestnut-colored hair coming down on her elegant white coat. She received Shaymaa very warmly; she shook her hand, embraced and kissed her, then smiled at her and whispered, like a mother coddling her little daughter, "How are you? Don't worry. Everything will be all right."

This sudden display of kindness was too much for Shaymaa, who started crying as Dr. Karen kept calming her down. She asked her to wash her face. Shaymaa went to the bathroom and came back, and sat before the doctor, who gave her some papers, saying, "This is some necessary paperwork. This is some information about you that we need you to fill out; this is a statement that you agree to the operation that we need you to sign. This is a cost list. Do you have a credit card?"

Shaymaa shook her head. The doctor asked in a matter-of-fact voice, "Can you pay cash?"

The paperwork took about half an hour. She spent the following half hour undergoing medical tests: a urine test, a blood pressure test, and a sonogram. In the end, Shaymaa took off her clothes with the help of the nurses, and put the blue hospital gown on her naked body.

When Dr. Karen held her hand, she noticed that she was shaking. "Don't be afraid. It's not a dangerous operation."

"I'm not afraid of death."

"What're you afraid of then?"

Shaymaa fell silent then said in a shaking voice, "Of God's punishment. What I've done is a big sin in our religion."

"I don't know much about Islam but I believe that God must be fair. Right?"

"Yes."

"Is it fair for a woman to be deprived of the right to respond to her feelings with the one she loves? Is it fair for the woman, alone, to bear the responsibility of an unwanted pregnancy? Is it fair to bring into this world a baby that nobody wants? To doom it to a miserable life before it even begins?"

Shaymaa looked at her in silence. She could no longer speak. She had nothing to say. The moment was much bigger than anything that could be said about it. She was now in an abortion clinic because she'd become pregnant out of wedlock. Shaymaa Muhammadi was bearing a baby in sin and was going to have an abortion. She didn't really have a way to describe all that. Was she anxious to find out what fate was hiding from her? If she was going to die during the operation, if these were the last moments in her life, she would accept the punishment as just. All she cared about was not to create a scandal for her family that would haunt them forever. The woman in charge at the clinic had reassured her that the operation was confidential. Even if she died, the official papers would not mention that she was having an abortion.

Shaymaa stood in her hospital gown, looking blankly at Dr. Karen, who put her arms around her and said, "We'll have time later on to talk about many things. We've become friends, right?"

Shaymaa nodded and walked with her across the short corridor leading to the operating room. They went through the double doors, and then Dr. Karen left her with a nurse who helped her get onto a gurney. A gray-haired white man appeared. He smiled and said, "Good morning. My name is Adam. I'm the anesthesiologist."

He held her arm and asked her what her name was. Then he stung her lightly in the arm and soon she felt her body loosen up. Little by little her mind changed, as if it were a large screen to which transmission had stopped, so it remained dark for a while, then colored pictures fraught with strange and wild feelings came onto it. She saw everything: her father, mother, sisters, their house in Tanta, Tariq Haseeb, and the histology department. Persons and things appeared different from what they ordinarily looked like. She had a hard time making them out and felt unhappy seeing their distorted gray images. She opened her mouth more than once to object to the way they were made to look, but she discovered that she had no voice, as if her larynx had been removed. She was terrified and kept screaming but had no voice. She remained a prisoner of that strange, frightening condition for a while. Then she finally saw a thread of light looming in the distance. It was as if the dark had resulted from heavy black curtains that now began to be opened slowly. As the light increased, new shapes appeared, blended at first; then they soon separated and appeared more clearly, little by little. Finally, with difficulty, she was able to make out Dr. Karen's face. She saw her smile and heard her say, "Congratulations, Shaymaa. Everything went fine. In a short while you'll be home."

She smiled as much as she could. Dr. Karen went on in a voice that was now quite clear, "In addition to the success of the operation, I have another surprise for you."

Shaymaa looked at her with exhausted and unfocused eyes. Karen winked and laughed, saying, "Of course you can't wait to know what the surprise is. Well, we have a visitor who cares about you and who has been begging us to see you."

Shaymaa extended her arm to object, but Karen hurried toward the door. She opened it and made a gesture with her hand. Soon Tariq Haseeb appeared. He was unshaven and looked pale and exhausted, as if he hadn't slept in a while. He moved forward a few steps until he stood next to the bed. He looked at Shaymaa, staring with his bulging eyes, and a wide smile appeared on his face.